STRONG ENOUGH TO WALK AWAY, YET TOO WEAK TO STAY

STRONG ENOUGH TO WALK AWAY,
YET TOO WEAK TO STAY

"A PIECE OF A MAN"

KAMRYN MOSLEY

To order additional copies of this book, contact:
Xlibris Corporation
1-888-795-4274
www.Xlibris.com
Orders@Xlibris.com
53917

CONTENTS

THIS BOOK IS ALSO DEDICATED TO, KAMRYN
MY SWEET BABY. I FAILED YOU ONCE THIS
IS FOR YOU BABY! I KNOW YOU'RE UP THERE
SMILING DOWN . . . I'LL MOURN YOU TO I
JOIN YOU! MOMMY LOVES YOU!

First off, I want to thank God, without him then I wouldn't've had the willpower or sanity to finish, wow! Thanks for always being on time.

Then my cousin Kayla, for coming long and far to help me. You'll never know how much that really meant to me, I guess I'll forever be indebted to you. I'll never forget it, Lucy I love you girl!

My cousin Kiley, for never doubting me and pushing me to do this. She was the one of few that said I had potential and really meant it. No one else I told really even cared. She also said she's ready to get the first copy. Wow! I love you cousin!

My cousins, Shon, Shanna, Jackie, Lanaya, I love you guys!

My aunties Sandra, Teresa, Kimbala I Love you all!

My auntie Jennifer Owens AKA "Lopez" Fitzgerald told me let's do dang thang . . . Love you babee!

What up doe Charles aka C!

My uncles Kenneth (keep your head up, that's messed up what their tryna to do to you, but look where you're at sc!) Randy, Lennie, Darryl love you guys!

My Grandma . . . VA I love you babee!

To Samuel, the man I've loved my adult life. Wow, it's still hard to imagine, how our lives took a 360 in different directions, wow! Although we didn't make it, (no matter what nobody say, think, or feel) I'll always love you! Keep your head up boo!

My siblings . . . Laquita, Krystal, Zacchaeus, Tron. Although, we haven't been the closest (Not on my part, because I've always wanted a close relationship with my relatives) I love you guys, doe.

Lara, although we haven't spoken in a while I still love you and missing talking to you!

My extended family, Mary Lois, I can't begin to express or find a word big enough to articulate how much it means to have someone like you in my life. I love you lady! Trabia, Latreka, Tyron, Anthony, Pamela, Natalie, Suntia . . . Thanks for welcoming me into your family and treating me like one of your very own. Love you guys!

What up doe Shatara and Miss Bobbie what it do . . . What up doe Rico, Cd, Maurita . . . Elijah and Ceclia, Johnnie . . . I couldn't leave you guys out!

My girl Jackie Chino Vera . . . Love you girl.

Shout outs to my Gray Court Fam Bam, Delvecchio, Doane, Joshua, Garry (see I didn't forget you!) Nick J, Ken, Christopher

My cuzo's Betty Ann, Annette, Shelia, Regina, Tonnette, Shade . . . Love you guys.

My mama Janice and my father Albert I love you both. (when my daddy saw the author copy he was like, I had to read 10 pages of shout outs before I got to my name . . . wow, lol!)

Mary, Bobby, Prince love you all.

What up doe Christopher (Stro) keep your head up dawg!

Lakeisha, Carnel Mosley I know I haven't spoken to guys in damn near a year and some change you guys are family . . . I still got much love for you all.

Shout outs to my girl Sherita Booker, although you talked my head off for hours at a time while I was trying to get this thing complete . . . You my home girl and I love you doe!

What up Quan, Keisha, Londa, Caprice, Fleisha Pulley (aka Flea), Belinda, Teresa Rice, Lafeyetta, Lee Ann, Kemma.

I could not forget Gary and Karen . . . Love you guys

To all my nieces, nephews, cousins, it's to many to even name but I love you all . . . I guess everybody can see that my family next to God means the world to me.

Shout outs to Academy fam bam Jacquetta Fisher, Tascia Jones, Brittany Webb, Geraldine Tolentino, Sonya Deas, Michelle Ellis.

I also wanted to give a shout out to Jeanine V Stringfellow, Rodney Bumpers, Gwen Mueller, Michelle Goodman and Mr Wendell Myers. Also, Mrs. B, Ms Corso, Mrs Kathy. Each and everyone of you were very helpful anytime I needed something, very much appreciated . . . Thanks

Now that I gave a shout out to everybody and their mama, I wanted to give a special shout out to a good friend that has given me nothing but positive words to live by. (In fact, I never once heard nothing negative come from his mouth) Cedric Stewart, everybody needs positive thinkers surrounding them. Every since you walked into my life, it's been great because I now believe that God placed you in it for a good reason . . . love you boo . . .

Last but not least, to my two handsome boys (who's truly my inspiration) mommy loves you both.

I wrote this novel without the help of no one. That means if you see a few typos you'll understand why. I tried to get help from everybody that I knew had a lot of street knowledge, but I guess no one cared or really even took me seriously. Either way I managed to do it alone. I did my best with everything a book entailed, copy edit, content edit . . . Etc (which was hard work, wow!) My personal opinion I think I done a great job. I hope you enjoy this book. Without God I don't think I, well let me rephrase that I know I wouldn't've had the strength to pursue this (so I wanna take a minute to thank you God). My reason in writing this novel is to get all people that are in a messed up relationship, to see you deserve so much better and never have to settle for less than the best. On the other hand, I want people to really sit back and think, at the end of the day is it really worth it to be in the game? Being that it never really last that long. I know all too well, what it feels like to have your back up against the wall. With the economy, the way it is and no jobs for people with felonies. Makes people wanna go out and do the unthinkable. It was times, where I felt like hitting the corner and some mo' shit, but then I weighed my options and said if I do dis' who is gonna suffer, my kids. I know a lot of people may read urban hip hop fiction books or even see it happen in everyday life and say, fuck that me and my kids gotta eat, I'll deal with the consequences when I face them. (When that happens, our kids gonna be the ones who suffer) Or either people will see the end result and decide they don't wanna take that route. At the risk of sounding contradictive, I will say this, I already know in the world today It's like survival of the fittest. From the looks of things people isn't gonna have money to even buy crack, or their drug of choice. This economy is really jacked up! People are doing what it takes to survive. I hope nobody gets it twisted and thinks I'm tryna sound sanctimonious in no way shape or form. I'm happy to say my uncle got out the streets and turned his life

around. He's furthering his education, by going back to school to become a better, father, brother etc . . . I'm proud of you Dawg! You did it! You are truly an inspiration! (Sadly, he missed 3 and a half years with his daughter) On the flipside, all I can say is be safe. Get what you can and get out! (To the ones that's still out there in the game!)

SEVEN YEARS AGO

"Hurry up, niggah. Go straight to your stash spot!" Swagga voice boomed over the loud car engine.

"O-o-okay," Bones stuttered, holding his hand up. "I already told you I don't have no money in there. I just re-upped!"

Swagga pressed the gun harder into his abdomen. "Naw, mahfucka, your ass is about to come up outta your ass with dat loot or your ass is done!" he yelled. The cold steel through the thin jersey he was wearing, sent rippling chills up and down his spine.

"Why are you doing dis', man? We've been boys since we were shorties. Nick-and-dimes days. Man, don't do dis!" he pleaded.

"Shut your sucker whinin' ass up and keep drivin'!" Swagga shrieked. Sure he hated robbing the homie but all the flossing he was doing left him no choice. He had long since convinced himself that Bones was rubbing salt in his wounds and of what had to be done when opportunity presented itself. Everybody knew Bones was getting his money in a major way. He was making enough dough to supply the whole complex with biscuits. Low key, Swagga was tired of being the one in the background watching while he splurged and tricked off wads of money, making him look like a bomb ass niggah.

Fifteen minutes later, Bones pulled into an empty parking spot in his complex. Nervously, he shut the engine off. When the sound of the fan stop spinning, Bones heart sunk to the bottom of his feet.

"Get your bitch ass out of the car and go get me what I came for, niggah!" Swagga slightly raised his voice and nodded his head after every word he spoke. When Swagga sat up to unlock the doors, Bones cringed and nearly jumped up out of his skin.

"Look at dis' ole scary ass niggah here," Swagga shook his head and then they both exited the car and ambled to his crib.

"Don't try no slick shit!" Swagga said in a near whisper.

When Bones reluctantly reached the entrance to his door, an unsettled feeling formed in the pit of his stomach. Which made his whole body fluster. He was so scared; he couldn't find the right key. He knew that once he went in, there was a possibility of him not making it out. Breathing, to say the least.

"Stop fuckin' stalling befo' I put two slugs in your bitch ass right here!" Swagga said through his tightly clenched teeth.

"Aight. I gotcha. Don't trip!" Bones held his hand up. Once they were safely inside, Swagga bashed him in the top of the head twice with the butt of a gun to let him know he was serious. Blood flowed profusely down his face. He let out a loud wail, as he scampered toward his bedroom. Swagga scurried closely behind him. Bones headed straight to his dresser and yanked the drawer open. He cursed himself inwardly for taking the gun out of the drawer just a couple of hours before that very moment. "See, I told you I don't have no money, man!" he dumped all the singles on the bed.

Wham! Swagga went upside his head again. This time it caused a big open gash on the side of his head, just a little above his ear. Warm blood flowed freely outta the wound, into his eyes, and then down to his mouth.

"You must really wanna see how loose steel feel, huh? Who da fuck do you think I am, Slow Joe or some-damn-body? You think you can just tell me anything like my head screw on and off, niggah?" Swagga roared.

"Don't kill me!" Bones pleaded, wiping the blood from his eyes with the back of his hands.

"Next time it won't be no hoe ass slap upside your head!" Swagga warned. "And dat my friend, is a fair warnin'."

Scared that he was gonna be killed, Bones went straight to his stash inside a deep hole in his closet floor. As blood continued to drip from his face like a never-ending stream, he reached in and grabbed all the contents. Five bricks and several wads of cash. While inside of his very soul, he felt as if he was slowly dying because he still owed his connect. *I'm damned if I do and I'm damned I don't* he thought to himself as he handed everything to Swagga, who already had the backpack ready. *Fuck it. I'll just have to find a way to put that niggah lights out before he gets to me.* He thought to himself while watching his once best friend rob him blind. He knew and respected the rules of the game. Which meant even if you have to dig in your shit, by any means necessary the connect had to get all of theirs. No shortcoming was tolerated in the game of do or die.

"Dis' is business. Nuthin' personal. Yea, we started out sellin' nicks and dimes and you graduated to a brick, niggah!"

"We was all eatin' good. I had your back dawg, in whatever you was lackin'. Why man? Why?" he shook his head in total disbelief.

"Niggah, have you forgot the countless times we went clubbin', you always had to be the one to try and out shine me becuz I was still nicklin' and dimin'?" he snapped. "Or what about the time when I walked up on you tellin' da homie, Monty, *dat niggah is cool, but he need to stack his chips. I ain't tryna teach or raise no over grown ass niggah.* Let's not forget about how you boasted and bragged on hittin' licks every mahfuckin' hour. You were getting it and I had to come get it. It's as simple as dat." he said and then turned back to focus on what he was doing. "Fuck! I should just go up side your shit just for breaking a niggah's concentration and shit!" he screamed, trying to salvage as much of the coke as he could that burst when he tried to force it inside the backpack.

"Dawg," Bones yelled out after he turned and started for the door. Swagga stopped in his tracks and turned to face him. "We will meet and greet again. On everything, cuhz! A hundred racks ain't shit to a go getter like myself!" he continued to say. Without raising his voice, even the slightest.

"Are you fuckin' threatening me, homie?" Swagga asked, thunderously. Going under his shirt.

"I merely make threats," Bones said, ominously. With a look of death in his eyes. Bones figured that if he wanted to kill him, he would've done so after he showed him the stash.

"Just think of dis as somebody gotta be on top. And remember I do know where all your people live!" Swagga roared, making his exit out the door. His erratic driving outta the complex made an officer that was cruising through, whip a bitch and pursue him. After a high-speed chase ensued, he unexpectedly turned on to a back road. Thinking that he had eluded the police but, to his dismay that couldn't have been farther from the truth, because he ran right smack into them. Later he was apprehended and whisked off to prison.

BOY, YOU GOT MY HEAD STRAIGHT GONE

Ring . . . ring . . . ring . . . Neeyah jumped up out of her sleep, wiping slobber from her face. *Ring, ring.* The phone continued to ring. She scrambled around on the bed for the phone.

"Hello," she said into the phone with a groggy voice.

"Hey, boo, it's me. What are you doing?"

"What do you do at two in the mornin'?" she retorted.

"Well, I was out in the parking lot but since you woke up on the wrong side of the bed, I guess I'll let you go back to sleep." she cleared her throat and changed her tone. "No, baby, I'm up."

"Well, open up the door, Negro," she hurriedly flung the covers off of her and strutted to the door. "My boo is here, he is here," she smiled and sang along the way.

"Shhhhhhhhh, don't wake my mom!" she shushed him.

When they reached her room, he extended his hand and felt for the light switch.

"Damn, I swear dis' hoe ass light switch be movin' and some mo' shit."

"Boy, you know you trippin'. It's on dis' side. You must be on one!" she giggled, switching the lights on.

"I'm not on shit yet. About to be in a second. As soon as I swallow dis' pill!" he said, taking a sip of water and placing it on his tongue. Then he extended his hand. "Come on baby take one."

"Now, I know you're really on one!"

"Thizz or die bitch!" he said, jokingly in a deep squeaky voice. "I'm just playin' boo, so don't trip." he grabbed the side of her leg.

She knocked his hand off of her. "Niggah, whatever!"

"Damn, like dat doe, boo?" he tightened his eyes.

She grabbed his hand. "Boy, you know I'm just playin'. On da real, your ass better stop talkin' so loud befo' you wake Ms Lara. Trust me you don't wanna feel dat lady's wrath if she haven't had her full 9hrs of sleep. She'll get ignant on dat ass!"

"Nah, not gonna happen. My mother-in-law loves me, so you can miss me with dat. Boo, real talk, take one. I wanna see how you act when you're on one. I heard it enhances sex. Like have you climbin' the wall and some mo' shit!"

"Very compelling. Seems, like peer pressure to me. I'm cool doe! Just sounds too bad for my likin'."

"Dis', shit right hea niggah?" he said, (like Katt Williams) pointing to the thizz pills.

She smacked his hand out of her face. "Boy, move. By the way, what do you mean you heard it makes sex better. You heard or you know, niggah?"

"Oh that's my shit, I'm so cocky with it . . . Teach me how to dougie . . . All my bitches love me . . . All my bitches love me." he sang, ignoring her. "They love the way he do dat . . . heeeey . . . you ain't fuckin' wid my dougie." he smiled and dougied to the floor. "Come on boo, do it with me."

"You so retarded. I don't know what you call yourself doing, but it sure in hell isn't no dougie. How bout I get my lil cousin Itty-Pa-Nitty, to teach you how to dougie!" she cheesed from ear to ear.

"Quit hatin'. You know ain't nobody fuckin' wid your boy dougie!" he two-stepped towards her. "Dump it, boo. Dump it,"

She smiled and giggled watching her boo dance. She loved everything about him. From every strand of hair on his head, down to the sole of his feet.

"Now that's my ish! Heeey," she threw her hands up in the air. "Call me rude boy, boy, gone head and get it up! Take it, daddy take it, love me, love me until you get enough." she sang her own words and grinded on him.

"Oh shit you ain't gotta tell me thrice." he said, unbuckling his belt. "Don't hurt'em, boo!"

She bit down on her lips and danced harder. After he got her all wrapped up into singing and dancing, he handed her the pill again.

"Do you even be listenin' to the words dat be coming from my mouth?" she snapped. He flashed a blank stare. "Do you know what dat one tiny ass pill consist of?"

"No, not really. All I know it gives me the feelin' higher than a giraffe's pussy."

"That's becuz it's made with a gang of uppers. Coke, meth, speed, and some mo' shit." she named them off, one by one. "Do you hear me, bay?"

"Yes, boo!" he chuckled and danced up on her.

"I'm so glad you see the humor in dis' becuz I must've missed it," she flashed a tight grin.

"Give me kiss." he said, holding her chin with the tips of his fingers. When she kissed him, he flipped the pill from under his tongue into her mouth. She tried to break away with all her might, but he kept tonguing her.

"What da fuck, niggah? You little sneaky black bastard!"

"Easy. I just wanted you to feel how I'm feelin'. I don't wanna be the only one thizzin' in dis' bitch."

"Don't trip, umma get your black ass back. But, back to the question I initially asked why you over there tryna switch subjects and shit, you heard it or you know?"

"About?" he asked, uncaringly.

"Oh, so you got selective memory now?"

"No boo, just selective hearin'." he joked.

"So, now you're tryna play on my intelligence, huh? I'm talkin' about the thizz pills."

"Oh, I read it in the source, boo! Come on baby, don't ruin da mood with dat bullshit!"

"Oh it's some bullshit? That's how you feel, doe?" she stared him dead in his face.

"Simmer your ass down lil' girl and come here." he kissed her.

"I guess." she broke away from him.

"You're such a square!"

"What? I can't help my mama taught me to say no to drugs,"

"Niggah, if you don't get yo' square bear ass on somewhere wid dat hoe shit." he said, softly punching her.

"I know one thing, you sock me one more time, umma get ignant on dat ass."

Her mom, Ms. Lara, was a sweetheart. She was always helping somebody. Oftentimes, people would mistake her kindness for weakness. You didn't want to rub her the wrong way as she would say, *You'll see the ghetto emerge!* She was known to reach out and touch a niggah with the quickness in her days. Her complexion was the same shade of of some black licorice. She stood about a good five feet tall and weighed 165 pounds. Although she was on the heavy side, it was proportionate and she carried it well. She never got into her daughter's business. Although, she knew Grievence wasn't shit, but vowed that Neeyah would have to learn the hard way. Just as she did when

she was growing up. She was a very optimistic woman, having something positive to say about everything. People would oftentimes refer to her as a mentor. She hated raising her kids in the projects, but with the cost of living and the economy the way it was, she just could not afford to move out while working on a house cleaner's salary. The state of California was raping people with the cost of living. The apartments they lived in were very shabby, roach-infested, and swarming with drugs. They were actually nice on the outside, but once you step one foot in the door you could see how the maintenance men never did their work. They only kept it looking nice on the outside to keep HUD off their backs, who was also scared to be in the neighborhood so they would drive by every now and then. Neeyah was the oldest of the three, eighteen years old then there's Sonny, fifteen years old lastly, Ricky Junior, five. Ms. Lara was respected in the hood by young and old.

"You look good doe, baby." he licked his lips. "And you already know what time it is,"

"I sure do, daddy. Time for us to lay down and get some much needed sleep," she smiled.

"Play wid it!"

"Whaaaatever!" she grinned. She loved the man that was gracing her presence. It didn't matter that she was pissed off at him for not answering or returning none of her phone calls, because once she saw him, all the hurt and anguish disappeared. He knew the affect he had on her and used it to his advantage.

"You don't have to take them panties off, just slide'em to the side!" he winked. *I Love You Just Because* by Anita Baker came on the quiet storm. "Oh shit the radio is getting off tonight. Just playin' all my shit!" he snapped his fingers and slowly rocked back and forth. "When I think about how much I'm lovin' you boo, there are no limitations. I love you just because emotions more than words can help me say I love you and I love you and I love you. I love you just because I do my darlin' you and it's amazing lovin' you, and there's nuthin' I can do about it and that's just the way it is baby I couldn't take it back if I wanted to," he held her hand and sang to her. This really sent a burst of euphoric feelings all over her body. She admired the fact that he loved and appreciated music just as much as she did.

"By the way, where have you been? You supposed to been here seven hours ago, punk!"

"You already know I wasn't about to wake my ma-in-law up!" he lied.

"Since when did dat stop you from ringin' my phone after midnight?" she tighten her eyes.

He put his finger up to his lip. "Shhhhhhhhh. I'm here now, aren't I? And umma spend the night. So now what, punk?" he lied.

"I'm jus sayin'."

"You're not gonna be sayin' too much of nuthin' becuz I'm about to put dis' dope dick on dat ass and you're about to be speakin' in tongues, ya' digg?"

"Chile, please! You ok, but you're not all dat!" she snaked her neck.

"True story, dawg, you know my shit is off the record!" he said with much confidence. "The best you ever had. Opps my B, I forgot I'm the only one you ever had!" he pushed her down softly. "If you lay back and observe you might, just might learn sumthin'. Although, da' game is to be sold and not told umma go against the grain and make an exception becuz you my boo."

"That's what you think . . . Humph." she smacked her lips. "You're not the only one. Please believe me!"

He wriggled out of his jacket and shot her a look that said keep talking you gone get fucked up. "Relax I'm only playin', so get your tight boxers out of the bunch! I just wanted to wipe dat arrogant smirk off your face. Wid your pompous behind!" she smiled.

"Word? That's how you feel, doe? Don't get your ass Chris Brown'd off in here! That's on my mama, cuhz!" he whispered, spreading her legs apart and tearing her panties off.

"Wait a damn minute!" she yelled. "These are Vickie Secret!"

"Don't trip, boo, it's nuthin'." he whispered in her ear. The *Ed Hardy* by Christian Audigier cologne he was wearing made her pussy wet before he even touched her. "I can buy you hella Vickie Secrets, niggah. I work!"

She hated the fact that she had just caught him cheating on her, with Monie, her first cousin. Meeyah Monie Brown was Leigha Melody Brown twin sister. The two were like night and day literally. In fact, growing up everybody thought the girls were triplets. They wouldn't tell anyone different. As they got older, they went their own separate ways. Monie was liked by few and hated by many. When she got tired of getting her ass whipped for being scantless and messy, she left the state of Maryland for good and moved to California. By the time Leigha turned fifteen, she decided she had enough of moving every time she got comfortable, so she decided to move with her grandma back in California. Although, both girls were identical twins, Monie was thinner. All she did was get high off any and everything

except crack. In fact, her drug of choice was sherm sticks. She was the type of broad that would suck a pussy dry and suck the skin off a dick. Whether it was from a blunt, to a couple of dollars, she never left with just a locked jaw or wet pussy. Both girls stood about five feet seven inches with a light skin tone. Monie weighed about 120 pounds soak and wet. Leigha weighed around 150 pounds, with a washboard stomach. She also had a bad case of acne, which gave her a complex and made her very insecure about her looks. Unlike, Monie, she cursed like a sailor. Every other word that rolled off her tongue was profanity. She had inherited the trait from her Aunt Kimbala, whom also could curse you over and under the table. Although she had a lot of mouth, she was always more than willing to get down with the best of them. On the other hand, Monie wouldn't bust a grape. She was very beautiful with impeccable skin and light green just around the pupil, hazel brown eyes. Which were inherited from her paternal grandmother. Her eyes and silky, hair were the telltale signs that they indeed had Caucasians in their family somewhere down the line. She knew she was the shit and used her looks and thin frame, to get any man she wanted. Outside of her few tattoo's, she had a couple of scars and piercings. One piercing was a Marilyn Monroe, her tongue, clit, and one of nipples. When she got her left nipple pierced, she nearly pissed on herself and decided to leave well enough alone. No one ever knew she had silky hair because she keep a head full of weave. Up under her weave, she had a big scar that she got when she was caught red—handed messing with someone's husband. The wife Emily was working graveyard. For quite some time, she had suspicions on her husband's Anthony infidelity. One night, she got dressed and did everything as she normally did by going to work and calling home from the company's phone. Soon after she got there, she left. On a cold windy morning, with no heat or nothing running in the car, she sat lost in deep thought and praying that she was wrong, while every single time she breathed, it looked as if she were smoking. Fogging up the windows. For about twenty minutes or so, she sat in complete silence and watched her house. Almost ready to return to work, but something told her to wait a few more minutes. She fell back in her seat and listened to her subconscious. Then out of the blue, she seen bright lights beaming through the foggy, misty streets, just as she sat up to start the engine to head to work and the she leaned forward and hurriedly, wiped the windshield with her shirtsleeve. Slowly, the vehicle approached then suddenly, it became clear that it was a taxi. It pulled up and honked the horn twice. Low and behold, her husband came to the door with his wallet in hand and the money that she had just given to him before she left

for work. After she witnessed Monie greet her husband with a long French kiss, she doubled over in pain. Just as he given to her in less than 2 hours from that very antagonizing moment. She decided to let her go on in and get comfortable, so she could make her next move, her best move. She couldn't figure out for the life of her, why her husband was cheating.

"I'm the only one with income. I fuck him in every different position there was ever invented. I suck, lick, and kiss every inch of his body. I mean what? I clean and cook my ass off. Why, me Anthony?" she cried. Her mind raced a mile a minute, to find a reason to justify why her life was suddenly, spiraling out of control and falling apart right before her very eyes. She rocked back and forth looking out the window. Her vision was getting blurry. All she could see was streetlights. *If he didn't want me why didn't he let me go? Why play on my intelligence?* she reiterated over and over in her head. "You can never please an ungrateful ass niggah. Twenty years gone. A marriage of blood sweat and tears!" she screamed inaudibly to the top of her lungs. Finally, she was able to find a little strength from her trembling fingers that was barely able to grip the knob, to unlock the door. She had tried many times before with all her might but the knob just wouldn't bulge. Every time tears welled up in her eyes and streamed down her face, it felt like icicles piercing her skin.

By the time she got out of the car, her whole body was numb. She trudged silently, to the kitchen. Abruptly, she slid open the drawer over the sink and grabbed the sharpest knife she could find. *Everything I Miss At Home* by Alexander O'neal & Cherelle was blaring from her stereo. Her heart sank to the bottom of her feet, listening to the words to the song. After watching like a ghost in horror, her husband of twenty years make passionate love to another woman, he had the audacity to say, "Dis' is the best pussy I've ever had!"

"Better than your wife?" Monie asked.

"Better than my bitch of a wife! And please baby, don't mention dat weak bitch name in my presence ever again. You'll make my shit go limp." he screamed to the top of his lungs.

"What do you mean?" she asked.

"It means, I wouldn't fuck her old washed up ass with my stiff ass daddy's dick. All dat bitch can do for me is slob on my knob. That's for real and not for play." he stretched his eyes wider. This really sent her into a raging maniac. As Emily tiptoed up on them, her knees began to buckle. They were so caught up in a rapture and the music was so loud they couldn't hear her knock the bottle of beer off the table. All of a sudden, it was almost as if her feet weighed a ton. She just couldn't lift them off the floor to save

her life. All she could see was this woman riding the shit out of husband, making him squeal like a field rat and his toes curling in all directions. Then without warning, he flipped Monie over and started long-stroking her from the back. Not missing a single stroke, while her favorite song *Between The Sheets* by the Isley's Brothers was resounding, relentless in the background. *Damn he giving my good dick away, all 10 inches.* she thought to herself. Seeing the horror-show made her squirm. After a while of her standing and looking on, Monie felt her presence and dove across the bed. Emily sliced her from the front to back of her head. Peeling her scalp back on the left side. Unbeknownst to her though. Then she made her move on Anthony, who was horror-shocked and frozen like a block of ice. Monie slipped out of the house. She didn't care that she was naked. All she cared about was being alive. He tried to run. She dove on him like a panther.

"Game over! You shriveled up pencil dick, bitch!" she yelped, calling him every name in the book except the child of god. He racked his brain trying to come up with a way to get the knife.

What am I doing, he thought to himself *she have a knife not a gun.* "Well you gonna have to kill me you psychotic bitch," he bellowed, slinging her off the bed. The knife went flying clean across the room. Straight into the mirror, shattering it into a thousand pieces. Impetuously, he jumped up stuck his feet into his Timbs and stomped her out. She grabbed her side and wailed out in pain.

"You dumb bitch! Yeah, I cheated and have been the whole time we were together! That's right bitch, I was using your weak ass. You often times asked me was I in love with you, well the answer is hell muthafuckin' no, Bitch! I was in love with your bank account. Check book, if you will." he sneered, flinging his hand around in mid air. "And all da shit you did for us. As in the otha women. Yea that's right!" he said, running over to stomp her again. "Ben and Ceddy asked me quite a few times, why do you do dat good woman like dat. My reply would always be, *because I can.* Who can blame me? Hell, I don't slave for it! Dis' shit is over you psycho-bob-ass—bitch!" he screamed, yanking the drawer open. "Bitch you got me all da way fucked up. I should've been took yo' naive, country ass back down to them sticks." he chuckled some. "I'll fuck you up if you ever, I mean ever, pull a knife out on me. Like my daddy always told me, don't pull the shit out lessin' you about to use it!" he yelled, snatching his clothes out of the drawer. "The audacity of dis' bitch . . . humph!"

Had the mirror not been shattered, he would've seen her standing beside the bed, holding a small pearl semi automatic.

"Are you done yet?" he turned to see her holding the gun aimed in his direction. The hair on his neck immediately raised and goose bumps formed all over his skin. "Come on now did you actually, think I was gonna let you leave as easily as you came." she howled with laughter. "In fact, you may leave in a box or a bag? Your choice?!"

"Baby, let's not do dis'. I love you!" he pleaded, while trying his damnest to stifle his tears.

"Ain't dis' a bitch. Your black ass was just all cavalier and shit when you stomped my ass out! I mean you was talkin' big shit." she said, holding her side. "Now you on some beggin' and trying to insult my intelligence type shit! Matter of fact, get your triflin' ass in the middle of the bed, mutherfucker!" she yelled in her thick country accent. "Now!" her voice boomed louder. The more he tried to choke his tears back, the more they welled up in his eyes. With no other choice, he slowly eased down on the bed and scooted towards the center, as told. Making sure his eyes never left hers. Not even to blink, if possible. "Swallow these pills or the fuckin' cops will come in here and find your fuckin' brains splattered all across dis' mutherfuckin' room!" she snarled, throwing him the pills that would instantaneously knock him out. Her voice was becoming more and more ominous. He never saw her so frazzled, let alone cursing. He always heard that everybody gets tired, and now he was staring one dead in the face. Like greased lightning, he scrambled around on the bed for the pills. Shaking like a limb on a tree, he swallowed them. Along with the huge gulp of saliva that had formed in his throat.

"Baby, don't do dis'. 20 years I've loved you. Nobody else!" he said, woozily.

"Shush baby, go to sleep everything is gonna be fine, just fine," she said in a near whisper. Soon after, he drifted off to sleep. When he woke up, he found himself confined to the bed and tasting a dirty sock that she dug up out of the trash. *Ok I'm still alive and not in any pain maybe she's gonna let me go.* he thought to himself.

"Wake up sleepyhead. I thought you'd never wake up!" she kissed him on the cheek. "Would you like some breakfast, Darling?" she said in the sweetest voice, as she grabbed the tuff-a-ware dish from beside the bed. He glanced at the window and saw the sun, glaring brightly through the blinds. "Here baby open up wide!" she said with a big spoon full of Kibbles and Bits.

Is dat dog food? Dis' bitch really got me fucked up! he thought to himself, with a baffled look.

"Oh that's right, I need to remove dis'!" If he didn't know before, he knew at that very moment that she had lost her everlasting mind.

"Damn, I gotta shit! You don't mind if I take shit do you baby?"

"Not at all. Go ahead I'll be right here!" he said, amicably as he forced himself to smile. *Sure bitch, I'll play your little game because as soon as you let me go, I'm gonna dissect your ass and spread your remains throughout the state of California!* he thought as he smiled at her. She flashed a devious smile back.

"Ok, boy you silly. I'll only be a minute!" she said, getting up to get the toilet paper. Seconds later, she returned naked.

Damn dat was the quickest shit I ever seen someone take. he thought to himself.

He actually thought she had come back to her senses. But to his dismay things were about to get nightmarish.

She jammed the sock back in his mouth. "I just want you to lay back and relax!" she gave him a menacing smile. Then she walked over to the stereo and slid Atlantic Starr's cd in and strolled down to *If Your Heart Isn't In It.*

Oh hell. What da fuck is dis' bitch up to? he thought. She turned to the back, as if she was gonna ride him from the back.

"Here comes!" she yelled squatting over him, proceeding to shit all over his body. He squirmed and vomited. But of course, he had to swallow it because it was nowhere for it to go. When she turned around to see his facial expression, she found him choking. "No way you're gonna cop a deal so easy!" she screamed, grabbing his head and removing the sock.

"You psychotic bitch!" he screamed once he was able to get his breath back.

"How does it feel to be shitted on? At least yours was quick and straight to the point, but mine was slow and painful. What da' fuck you thought, Anthony? See, men like you need to be taught a lesson. Just think of dis' as an . . . ahhhhh, what's the word I'm looking for? Exemplary punishment!" she said in calm tone, as she snapped her finger. The heat was up on 90 degrees, so the stench in the room was becoming unbearable. "You know what I don't get Anthony?" she asked. "Why did you do dis' to me when you know my ex Michael, dragged my ass all the way to west hell and back. By cheatin', disrespectin', and everything all in between? You know there's dis' one cliché: *kick me once shame on you, kick me twice shame on me* I think, but it may be the other way around. I really don't know, but who in the fuck cares because you get the picture. So, as I was sayin', I tell you dat niggah dere set the pace, fuckin' it up for all the men dat comes along in my life. Men always gotta play with bitches emotions and shit. And umma gone ahead and tell you right now, shit like dat will get men fucked up real quick like. Just to think,

I was the one who use to work a full 12 hour shift sometimes a double, then come home and cook your fat ass a five course meal, while you sit in the recliner and watch me. Directing me and shit on how much salt to put on it and how to cook it. Then I would run your bath water, wash your back, and then I would eat. After I was done, I would clean the kitchen. After I cleaned, I rubbed your feet, clipped your hard ass fungus-ridden toenails, massaged your cracked scaly ass feet and then I massaged your thick ass back. Faithfully. Every mutherfuckin' night. Like your black ass had just worked the double shift After I got you all squared away, I crawled my tired black ass in bed. But, dat wasn't enough huh, Anthony?" tears streamed down her face. "I was taught to love and please my husband in every way possible. In God eyes, I was doing right. Or so I thought. You were on easy street and got it made boulevard." he remained mute. "Aren't you gonna say sumthin'?" she yelled. Then she snatched the knife off the dresser, drew it back. "Alright mutherfucker, you got 10 seconds to tell me why if you didn't want me, you didn't leave me! 10 fuckin' seconds, you fuckin' ingrate!"

"Please b . . . b . . . babe don't hurt me, I'm your husband!" he studdered.

"Don't studda now mutherfucker. Relax," she said, starring dead into his beseeching eyes. "It's funny how you learn sumthin new everyday, to the statement you addressed earlier. Don't pull it out unless you gonna use it, I do believe those was your exact words, right? So, to dat end, I'm not gonna hurt you, I'm going to kill you!" she let out a long cynical laugh. "Any last words before you go meet your maker?"

"Yeah. Go to hell you callous, bitch!"

"How 'bout I meet you there. And one more thing before you fall asleep eternally, HELL HATH NO FURY LIKE A WOMAN SCORNED," she whispered slowly in his ear. "Yep you're about to go straight to hell in first class. And that's in the front of da bus, my dear. You see I was a changed women and I'll be damn if you didn't make the old me resurface. One more thing before mama rock you to sleep, baby, let Michael know I said hello," she winked.

All of a sudden his heart starting racing really fast. Through it all he remained mute. Once he knew he wasn't live to tell about it, he closed his eyes and swallowed the saliva that rested in his throat. "One . . . two . . . ten!" she yelled, plunging the knife straight through his heart and twisting it twice before pulling it out. Still not satisfied, she cut his dick off and stuck it in his mouth.

"Anthony, now you can slob on your own knob!" she said unruffled, with blood still trickling down her arm. Feeling satisfied, she pulled out a Newport, lit it, and blew smoke rings in his face. When the judge asked her why she committed such senseless, heinous crime, she replied staring off into space by saying, "I wanted to carve a blood-drenched, heart into his chest. You know the funny thing Your Honor, the pain etched on face was a mere understatement of what I felt. You have no idea; I walked in on a horror-show!"

When she scanned the courtroom, everybody either had their jaw dropped or was shaking their heads in disbelief. "What da' fuck?" she snapped. "Yall bitches don't know me. Yall bitches don't feel my pain. Only God can judge me." she screamed with her eyes glinting with anger.

"You morbid bitch!" a female voice yelled from the back of the courtroom. "The sentence should match the crime, you sadistic fuck!"

"How do you even sleep at night you demented, fuck up?" someone yelled out.

"Like a new born baby straight from the womb," Emily yelled out, with a big smile plastered across her face. Everyone in the courtroom stared on and shook their heads in disgust.

"Order in the court." The judge hit the gavel.

"He deserved it, and I would gladly do it again in a heartbeat. With no regrets!" she screamed with her tone quickly switching from audibly to bellowing. Her voice reverberated throughout the entire courtroom. Later, she woke up and found herself restrained to a small metal bed and staring into the unmoved eyes of a savagely flawed patient.

"I've been waitin' on you to wake up! You think you're crazy, you ain't seen crazy. I can't wait to eat you up like a Thanksgiving dinner . . . grrrrrrh!" she roared.

"Oh yeah? You wrinkled up fat bitch, you're right I am not crazy, I am a fuckin' certified lunatic. In fact, you son of a bitch, I can't wait to get a lose so I can rip your eyeballs out and suck your fuckin' skull, you fuckin' twit!"

The woman sealed her lips, turned around, and stared at the padded white walls.

"That's right. Turn your pudgy ass around, bitch before you get fucked up on credit." Emily sneered. "I'm insane in the fuckin' membrane," she laughed a long spooky laugh and then faced the other direction. Vowing to one day find Monie and release the reign of terror she started and eluded on Nov 22th. The day that her or Monie neither one, would forget.

Monie's hair never grew back in the spot, so she keep it covered with a head full of weave. The twins were inseparable at one point. They even got a tattoo of half a heart with each other's name. Leigha had the left side of a heart with Meeyah tatted on her neck and Monie had the right side of it with Leigha tatted on hers.

Here he was, in the flesh as if nothing had ever happened. The truth to the matter, she loved his shitty drawers. He stood a little over five feet ten inches tall and weighed roughly 175 pounds solid with a Midnight Milky Way skin complexion. Tattoos was sleeved up both of his arms along with a couple on his back and chest. His dreads rested neatly, a little past his shoulder blade. A pure goddess that made her pussy tighten at the sight of him. I'm sure all ladies would agree. He had his own unique style. He would wear a fitted T-shirt and jeans with biker chains swooping down underneath his front pocket. You could never catch him without a fresh pair of kicks. Oftentimes, he would wear a bandana or his favorite golden colored, silk scarf around his neck. Neeyah, your average-looking girl. Stood an evenly five feet five inches and weighed 130 pounds. She was thick in all the right places with a set Ds to go with her perfectly shaped body. She was very smart, having graduated valedictorian at age fifteen. She was constantly reading. It was as if her brain was some type of knowledge sponge soaking up everything it could. She was very tenacious and had a photographic memory. Her mom would often say she was the brains of the family. Music was her life. It was like she could feel it deep down in her soul. Old school was her preference and anyone else who understood and appreciated good music as well, was A ok with her. After she caught him with her cousin, all he said was, "Baby, I fucked up. I'm sorry. She saw I was white boy wasted, and she just whipped my shit out and started blowin' me!"

He knew that he had to stop fucking up on her because she was the best thing to happen to him. She never nagged. Half of the time, he could go and come when he pleased without one word said. She may've joked a little with him but she would never let it escalate. She was his cool down-ass chick that never took anything for granted. She was everything he needed in a woman, but he just didn't know how to stop fucking other girls that love to throw the pussy at him daily. The bottom-line was, he was fine, smelled, and looked good. To top it off, he was packing a full eleven and a half inches. He knew a woman's body in and out and he knew how to hit every corner and wall. If only she knew how to work her good pussy maybe things would have been different. Or would it be? She was like an old woman when it came to sex.

She didn't like giving head. She wouldn't kiss all over his body before, during, or after sex. Let's just say, she basically just lay there and let him do all the work. He thought she had to find out the hard way about the cliché *what one woman won't do, another will* because he just didn't have time to teach no grown woman, how to suck a dick or fuck. Especially, when he had professionals handing him bomb head with a side of pussy on a silver platter.

The next day, after she caught him, he surprised her with a teddy bear and a 2-karat diamond tennis bracelet around its neck. Everything was forgiven just like that, she tried to push all the events and thoughts outta her mind that had just occurred two days prior.

"What about the situation with Monie?" she asked, nonchalantly and then turned her head and looked in opposite direction.

"Fuck dat bobble headed, bitch! She just slurped a little on a niggah's dick, and feen for it, but I told her dis' daddy dick belongs to Neeyah," he lied. "Now a niggah already fucked up 'bout it and I don't need you thrown dat bullshit in my face every time were together! Fuckin' up my mood up and shit." he snapped. "And girl, what you trippin for? Dis' dick belongs to you and only you." he pulled her face back towards his and softly planted kisses on her lips.

"Leigha said I should let you just spread your wings and I should find me a new boo," she said, dryly.

"Fuck her. I'm tired of her being in your ear wid dat dumb shit. You always tellin' me sumthin dat crater face bitch done said!" he sat up.

"Damn, I must've struck a nerve or sumthin'"

"I'm just tired of mutherfuckas in my business and shit. I mean damn, am I responsible for dis' recession we're livin' in too? For the life of me I don't know why you always tellin' her shit and then feel the need to run your happy ass back to me wid dat straight bullshit. Fuckin' up my entire mood and shit. Now I don't even feel like chilling, so umma just bounce. Besides who da fuck Leigha suppose to be? Syskill and Ebert or some-damn-body. Dat bitch don't know Adam from Eve, so I suggest she stay the fuck outta mines." he looked over at her. "If you feel she's right then I'll just spread my wings and soar high, cuhz." he sneered.

"No baby, I don't," she said, dryly.

"I can't tell. Every time I turn around you're in my ear wid some shit she done said. Quiet as kept, I don't give a flyin' fuck what a muthafucka got to say about Grievence, becuz what the next muthafucka eat don't make me shit," he pushed her off of him and started getting dressed. She jumped up like a strike of lighting, after him.

"No baby, don't leave I'm sorry," she pleaded. "I don't wanna argue or fight nor do I wanna make you upset so, please bay come lay wid me I'll make it up to you I promise. And I promise to keep people out of our business, boo. Come on, don't go," she cried silently, and tugged at his arm. After five minutes of her begging, he decided to lay back down. She laid on his chest sobbing. Wrong as he was she didn't want him to leave her presence. Grievence on the other hand, breathed a sigh of relief because he had successfully spun the argument and flipped it on her to take the heat off himself.

"Stop cryin' bay, I'm not going anywhere. I'm sorry for getting so upset," he dried her tears. Guilt had started setting in. Deep down, he knew Leigha and everybody else was right. Because in truth, all he was doing was cheating her out of her life. She was too blinded by love to see what Leigha had been saying was true. Although she would tell him what Leigha would say, she had no attentions on ever acting on it. The cold part was he knew Neeyah inside and out and that she would never stray. He knew that he could do anything out in the street, not to deliberately hurt her. Only because he could and she would basically accept it and wouldn't go anywhere. Whereas if she was a hoe, that in itself would keep him on his toes because it would be no way for him to predict what she was doing or with who. He felt that one day he would have it all out of his system and since she was there thru it all, he wouldn't have no other choice but to wife her.

"Ok baby," she smiled, and then they both laid in complete silence. Holding each other. Her mind started flooding with all kinds of images of him and other women.

"We gone be alright, boo." he sat up and stroked her hair. She looked over at him and flashed a smile.

"Bay," she mustered up enough strength to say, after a long moment of silence.

He fell back on the bed. She joined him. "What up doe?" he sighed.

"Do you be giving them skanky ass bitches money?"

"Hell naw! I tell a bitch quick, all you can do for me is slurp on dis' fat dick and break yo'self." he said, quickly forgetting it was her he was talking to.

She sat up. "Scuse me?"

"Babee, I make them bitches break bread for you. I say 99 percent of da time all I have to do is whisper sweet nothings in them bitches ear. For us boo, our apartment." he lied and then popped another pill.

"Is dat suppose to make me feel better?"

"Baby, I'm ready to spend every wakin' moment wid you." he whispered, seductively. Gently planting wet soft kisses on her face. "Niggah, if you don't stop putting questions where it's suppose to be a period. No more questions please. I love you. Believe dat."

"I . . . I . . . I!" she stammered. He shushed her and opened her legs as wide as they would go.

All she really cared about was having him in her presence at that moment. Low key, she didn't wanna get him roared back up. When he stuck his long, fat tongue inside her pussy, it made all her thoughts and insecurities disappear. She let out a soft moan as he started circling her clit and going from side to side up and down and around her clit. Licking it intensely. When he started thizzing, it really turned him into an energetic beast.

"Talk dirty to me, baby. It really turns me on!" he whispered in her ear with a thick coat of her juices glazing his lips.

"Okay, boo!" she purred, pushing his head back down. Then he stuck his tongue all the way in the inside of her hot and ready pussy. As far as it would go. Licking and flicking his tongue all around her walls. "Well damn, dis' niggah know how to eat the shit outta pussy!" she lipped, rolling her hips.

He knew how to make his tongue flip, curve, roll, and some mo' shit.

"Stand up for me baby." he demanded, with her pussy still in his mouth. She stood to her feet. All of a sudden, he lifted her up in the air and put her legs around his shoulder.

"Bay, what are you doing?"

"Just shut up and take dis' shit boo!" he said, sticking his tongue in her juicy pussy, with one hand gripping her butt and the other one on her back.

"Boo, please don't drop me!" she whispered, moaning and grinding her pussy all on his face. *I damn sholl hope my boo can breathe because I got my legs wrapped around him so tight . . . Ahhh dis' shit feel bomb as hell.* she said inwardly to herself praying that he didn't drop her.

"I got you boo, don't trip!" he whispered, holding his head back a little.

Her body tensed and started shaking uncontrollably. "Ohhhh . . . Ahhhh . . . boo dis' shit feels sooo bomb. I'm 'bout to cummmm."

"Cum for daddy, boo!" he panted.

"I ammmmmmm!" she ohhed and ahhed.

She was starting to get a little heavy so he dropped her from his shoulders down to his waist.

"Boo, wait!" she screamed, gripping his back tightly. Fearing he would drop her, but she landed right on his erect dick.

"Didn't I say I wasn't gone, drop you!" he whispered, bouncing her up and down on his dick.

"Yea, bay!" she moaned putting her arm on the bed behind her and wrapping her legs tighter around his waist.

"Then don't doubt me, niggah!" he whispered, giving her deeper and faster pumps.

"I'm sorrrry!" she moaned.

"Don't be sorry, hoe be careful!" he giggled, stooping a little so he could get all the way in it. "Open up boo,"

"Bay, it hurts!"

"Didn't I tell you to take dis' anaconda? You wanted to be a grown ass woman and promenade your ass down dis' murky ass dangerous street. So, take dis' shit." he said in a near whisper, long-stroking her deeper. "I bet dis' will be the last time you take your fass ass down Danger Street!" he said, grinding harder and bending his knees so he could get all the way up in it. "Take dis' shit,"

"I'm takin' it, boo!" she moaned, gripping the bed tighter. *How can somebody so young, be so talented? He is a straight up beast in bed dat keeps me satisfied. The pill was the icing on the cake. Dis' niggah straight ate my pussy in mid air. What da' fuck! Dis' fadamnsho, is going down in the diary. We are not going to get on the subject about his dick. Oh my goodness! He's impeccable! I must say he's by far, the best hands down. Damn did dis' niggah invent sex? He fine as shit, dress fly as hell, give bomb-ass head with a bomb-ass dick. I'd be stupid to let him go. Dis' niggah straight got my head gone!* she was thinking. She long ago, reached the conclusion as well as convinced herself that all men cheated. However, actually catching them was a different story. Without warning, he pulled out, gently laid her on the bed, and buried his head back into her sultry pussy.

"What are you doing bay? That's enough!" she said. Trying to back away from his mouth and scoot up the bed.

"Uh huh boo, don't run from me." he said with his mouth still on her pussy. She started moving her hips faster with the rhythm. Then, all of a sudden, he began fucking the shit out of her pussy with his tongue.

"Dis' shit feels good, bay." she said, letting out a longer soft moan.

"Oooooh, baby, I'm about to cummmmmm!" her body tensed and juddered. The pill had taken full effect, everything enhanced.

"Let me feel it! Cum on daddy dick, boo." he said quickly jumping up and sliding himself inside her while, licking her right nipple feverishly. "Open up boo. Let me get all the way in it."

"Ooooooooh!" she said, with her bottom lip trembling. Suddenly, her whole body quivered with his touch like never before. This time the muscles in her stomach contracted and her back stiffened. Every single time his soft hands groped her body, it sent chills raging through her body and she would just jerk like she was being electrocuted.

"Damn, I'm good," Grievence whispered, and bit down on his lip. "Open up babe, so I can feel it!" he said softly as he watched on, admiring his skills. This really gave him a spurt of momentum. "Hurry and turn dat fat ass over, and let me hit it from the back!" he whispered and smacked her on the ass.

"It's your world, daddy!" she smiled and did as told. He flashed an arrogant smile back.

"Hold up a minute!" he stood to his feet. When he stood up, his dick stood 10 inches out in front of him.

She extended her hand. "Help me!" he hurriedly slid the mattress over, so they wouldn't end up on the creaking floor. Then quickly, he inserted his erect dick inside her pussy that was oozing with juices.

"Throw dat shit back, baby!" he said, with moans escaping from his mouth. He could no longer restrain them.

"Get dis' shit, daddy, it belongs to you!" she said, biting down on her bottom lip. It was a good thing she slept with the radio on every night.

"That's what I'm talkin' about, baby! Dis' pussy is so good, dis' yo' dick boo! Oh, shit ooohhh, dis' shit is so good, baby!" he said in a very low tone while, on the verge of cumming. She started tightening her vagina muscles by using a kegel technique she seen in a newspaper clipping at work. "Dis' shit is tight as fuck!" he said, passionately kissing her. "Damn, you got a niggah whipped fa-shezzzzy!" he said in a near whisper, wanting to scream it to the top of his lungs. "Ohhhh!" he moaned. "Do slugger feel good to you baby?"

"Fadamnsho!" she whispered in ear between moans and groans. *Damn, a niggah must be thizzin' and some mo' shit* she thought to herself rolling her hips harder on his dick, while squeezing her pussy muscles with all her might. "Dis' shit feels hella . . . Damn, I can't even find a word to formulate what I'm feelin'."

"That's dat Obama workin' on dat ass! Boo, you need to let daddy feel how good slugger makes you feel!"

"Fuck dis' pussy baby! Fuck it good,"

"Wanna feel how much daddy loves you?" he whispered in her ear.

"Oh yeah! Baby, let me feel how much you love me!" she panted.

"You have been usin' your patch like—"

"Baaay!" she screamed, cutting him off.

"I'm just makin' sure." he said, coming to an erection. "Damn, dis' bed is stupid small." he fell back on the bed.

She got up and smoothed her hair back into her ponytail.

"Yeah your shit all fucked up and sweated out,"

She flashed a tight smile as she headed to the bathroom. " And niggah, don't even go there about my bed. You want me to have a bigger one, then buy me one butthead. You ballin'!"

"Oh, yea? If I did, where would it fit?" he replied, sarcastically.

She raised an brow. "So you tryna say my room is dat small?!"

"Boo, small is an understatement." he looked around. "Hell, I can barely get undressed without bumpin' into the wall." he chuckled.

"Oh, I see you on some comical shit tonight, huh punk? Cappin' off my room and shit.

"I'm not gonna be too many more of your punks. I done told you, you're gonna mess around and get folded up. Trust and believe me when I tell you, you don't want these hands. Becuz they will reach out and touch you. Anyways, make yo'self useful and go get me a washcloth so I could clean dis' anaconda!"

A smile immediately flashed across her face as she headed to the linen closet. When she opened the closet, all she saw was dingy washcloths ridden with holes. Soon as she walked in her door, she handed him the dampened washcloth. It was a good thing the lights were out. "Here, babe. I know it's a little raggedy, but we haven't done laundry yet,"

"You good." she flashed a smile and turned to walk away. "Babe," he yelled out to her.

"What is it?"

He extended his hand for her to get the washcloth. "Here,"

Ten minutes later, he remembered he was supposed to get up with Monie, so he got up and started getting dressed while she was in the shower.

"Where are you going? I . . . I . . . I." she stammered. He could see the big smile that she had on her face when she walked in the room, quickly turn into a frown. "I thought you were gonna spend the night, tonight?" she whined.

He motioned for her to come sit down on his lap. "Come here." he patted his leg. Without hesitation, she followed his demand.

"Jody my Jody," she rubbed his scalp. As, she sat down her towel fell. The cool morning breeze flowed in from the cracked window. Making her

full double d's stand rigid and perky, at his lips. Her breast was real pretty. Her areola was kind of big and dark. Her nipples was long and thick. He took one in his hand and wrapped his long, warm tongue around it. While thinking of a lie to get out of not spending the night. He watched as her eyes rolled into the back of her head, as she moaned. It was something about her moans that sent him into a passionate beast. "You smell so good boo!" he whispered, pushing both of her breasts together and licking them both at the same time.

"Bay, don't start sumthin' you can't finish!" she turned to face him and planted a huge wet kiss on his lips.

"I love these lips, their so sweet and succulent!" he whispered as he sucked on her bottom lip while, caressing her breasts. Then he unbuttoned his Coogi jeans. "Remember, I'm dat niggah. If I start sumthin' I'll finish what I start . . . ya digg!"

"Awwe, shucky ducky now!" she smiled like a chest cat while, helping him outta his shirt.

"You gotta get on top doe, since I been doing all the work. Let me have the luxury of laying on my back for a change." he said, sliding his boxers down over his feet while, stroking his gifted dick *to make'em rise to the occasion*, as he would say.

Maybe he is going home or sumthin', becuz his ass gonna be too tired to go screw some otha chick! she thought, trying to convince herself that he wasn't as bad, everyone made him out to be.

"It's nuthin', but I have to warn you, sarcasm isn't gonna get slugger licked and stroked!" she whined as she slowly maneuvered her body into a comfortable position. Boy was he appalled. She never initiated oral sex.

"Damn, dat Obama got yo' ass on some otha shit."

"Are you complainin', niggah? On some real ass shit, a bitch got a feelin' of euphoria going on over here."

"Who, not me. Do yo' thang, homie." he said with both of his hands rested behind his head. Although she tried her best, it felt so interminable to him. He was still thizzing, and ready to drop the beginner to get with the professional. He gave her an 'A' for effort. "Come sit on my face, boo." he stopped her. Twenty minutes later, they both came and were dog-tired. She grabbed the towel and lay back defeated. He joined her, while thinking of a way to tell her he had to go, but couldn't seem to do so.

She laid her head on his chest and listened to the rhythm of his racing heartbeat. "Dis' is my favorite song."

He stroked her hair. "Oh yeah?"

"Yup. But dat love spell had yo' ass gone, huh? Just could not resist!"

"Naw, it was dat gushy ushy!" he said, rubbing her wet pussy. "Speaking of which, where did you learn how to contract your pussy muscles and shit? You never done dat shit before!" he asked with his head slightly turned looking at her out of the side of his eyes.

"Bay, you'll be surprised what a book can teach you on how to please your man!" she giggled.

"Uh huh, don't let me find out,"

"Niggah, youz trippin'. Find out what?" she giggled.

"Find out yo' ass cheatin' on me! Why you over there, all ke keing and shit!"

"Boy, please!" she said, smacking her lips. "Ain't nobody even thinkin' about cheatin' on you. I'm sprung and I'm not going nowhere."

"Baby, on the real, Deuces called while you were in the shower and said his BM just put him out. Therefore, I'm going to swoop him up and drop him off at Mom Duke. I'm not tryna have my cousin go back to prison when he just touched down less than six months ago," he lied.

Grievence and Deuces were two sisters' kids. It used to be Grievence, Deuces, and Trees. She was given the name because all she did from sun up until sun down, was smoke weed. Matter of fact, she was the one that got them smoking, at such young age. She was a tomboy that lived beside them, so over the years, they became close. She was the sister they never had; they were the brothers she never had. They formed a click called Crazy '80s Babies. They would use Trees to handle the females if they got out of line.

At ages nine and ten, what did they know? Her mom was a work-a-holic. So, she spent all of her time over to Maryland's house, as well. She had hooked up with this dude named Dro. It was rumored that Dro's name rung bells in the D. these days. He was the man to see. The man was booming on the block. His motto was *"If you want dro, get at me; if you want coke, get at me; if you want dat blow definitely get at me."* When Maryland, Grievence's mother, moved from Detroit, so did Deuces. His mom Kim, was a dope fiend that couldn't seem to stay sober. It seemed as quick as she got clean, she would backslide even faster, leaving him to fend for himself. One day she okayed him to stay with Grievence for the weekend, so Maryland picked them up from school. When he told her about his mom crack binges, she wouldn't let him go back to the roach-infested, crack house. Three weeks later, she'd show up all smoked out and after her tricking escapades, professing that they was trying to take her child from her, so they can use him for food stamps

and a county check. Then one day out of the blue, she admitted that she couldn't take care of her only child, and to prevent him from being in the system, she gave him to Maryland. She welcomed him with a warm heart and opened arms.

"I understand, baby, don't trip!" she said, trying to sound understanding. When inside, she felt like shit. In fact, shit was an understatement.

"I already know you would be on some other shit if dat happens. Wylin' out and some mo' shit!"

"Damn, skippy! That's my niggah, you fuck wid him, you fuck wid me. Straight like dat!" he said, grabbing his shiny Ed Hardy coat that resembled a Member's Only jacket.

"Are you coming back, boo?" she asked. Trying to find some sort of complacency, in not only what she was hearing but feeling. She somehow knew in the back of her mind she wasn't gonna see him no more that night or day.

He grabbed her face. "Babe listen, soon as I handle dis', I'll be right back. I promise."

"Put dat on sumthin'!" she forced a fake smile.

"On every thang boo. I'll be right back so you better stay by the phone and not go back to sleep." he lied.

"Ok, you better go!" she mustered up enough strength to say. Inside she felt as if she was gonna have a nervous breakdown at any given moment.

"Ok, babe! That's why I love you so." he winked and then planted a sloppy, kiss on her lip. She strained a phony smile. While, insidiously dying on the inside. Before he left, he blew her a kiss and disappeared through the door as quickly as he came in. She laid down hurting and feeling real empty inside. When she glanced at the clock, it read 4am.

"Damn, I gotta work in a couple of hours. Dat niggah done kept me up and now his ass done got ghost like Casper on my ass. Love will make you make ignorant choices." she shook her head and muttered. Soon after, she was out for the count.

Knock, knock. "Come in," she said, not realizing she was wrapped in the towel. As she jumped up, it fell to floor. It was her mama's husband, Ricky.

"Ooopppps!" he said, pretending to cover his eyes and darting out of the door but not before getting a good glimpse of her perfect-shaped body.

She grabbed her tattered Victoria's Secret robe that Grievence had bought her for Christmas. The scent of his *Ed Hardy* cologne lingered behind, which made an immediate smile flash across her face.

"Dat, niggah must've taken a bath in dat shit," she thought out loud heading to the bathroom.

Ummmmmmmmm! Ricky thought licking his lips. *She is one bad mutha, titties soooooo perky and pretty.* He and Ms. Lara had been married for going on ten years. They had long since stop having sex for quite some time. That didn't stop him for trying to get her in the mood though. All she would say is, *"Honey, I'm tired."* The truth was he did not turn her on anymore, and she had lost her sex drive. He was like a dad to Neeyah and her siblings. Ricky stood about an even five feet seven inches and weighed about 270 pounds. He had receding hairline that far off he appeared to be bald, but from the back, he had a long ponytail that he kept eight to ten rubber bands on going down the ponytail. Over the years, it just receded farther and farther back. She oftentimes told him he needed to go bald. He always protested. He was working at Larry's pit stop as a mechanic when the owner got busted for running a drug and underage prostitution ring. Every since, he was outta a job, and gaining weight. When Neeyah came out of the bathroom, her eyes shimmered with a golden copper bronze. Her cheeks lit up with darken rosewood look to them. Her lips were sparkling with a glittery coat of Strawberry Fizz from the *Crush* by Victoria Secret collection. Her hair was done neatly in a donkey ponytail, hairstyle. She rocked a black sheer like shirt that exposed her black *Body* by Victoria Secret bra with a short blue jean Ed Hardy skirt that looked tattered. Black Ed Hardy tights hugged her legs, along with some open toe heels. Silver hoops dangled from her ear. She could wear anything to work as long as she made it on time.

"Hey, Ricky, what's up?" she asked amicably, closing her compact mirror shut.

"I was just lookin' for the cordless phone that had been left off the hook all night!" he shot, sarcastically.

"Oh, don't trip I just put it back on charger."

She wasn't at all embarrassed at what happened earlier. She thought of Ricky as a dad and firmly believed that if you saw one, you saw them all.

"Good mornin', mother." she said as she kissed her on the cheek.

"Hi, baby. I'm in a hurry. The breakfast is in the stove. All you will need to do is stick it in the microwave to reheat it," she said grabbing her purse and keys to her rusty bent-up Nova, off the counter.

"Mom, I'm gonna buy you a brand-new Benz one day." Sonny said, looking out of the broken window at the car.

"That'll be nice son, but I'm not into all those fancy cars. Long as it gets me to point A and point B like old myrtle does than I'm good."

"I hear you, Ma. But, you deserve the best." he said, walking her to the car as he did every morning. Ricky was to fat and lazy to even do it. "Drive safe, beautiful lady!"

"Always. Love you, son."

"Love you too and make sure you buckle up pretty lady!" he yelled out.

Sonny stood a little over six feet and weighed 160 pounds, at sixteen years old with long braids that came a little past his neck. Which he kept fresh with sweet designs, thanks to Neeyah. He was also a very humble and respectful boy that made good grades in school.

"Hey, fathead!" he smacked Neeyah upside the head, nearly making her choke on the piece of bacon she was trying to hurry up and eat before her bus came.

"Dang, lanky. You play too much!" she hurriedly swallowed the last of her orange juice. "What time is it, Beavis?"

"Almost time for the Metro to come."

"Are you serious? Why you playin' boy?"

"Naw, sis, seriously the bus will be here in ten minutes."

"Oh shit!" she screamed, grabbing her purse and taking a quick peep to make sure she had her bus pass on deck. "Damn a bitch is lucky Ricky ass knocked on the door."

Fuck, I really dread going to dis' hoe-ass call center, she thought while locking her room door.

"Daaaamn!" she held her breath as soon as she stepped into the urine-reeked, breezeway almost making her vomit.

BEST OF BOTH WORLDS

"Hello, my name is Anita Jones. Thanks for calling KAM Communications. How may I help you?" Neeyah said into the headset, as she sat at her cubicle, taking a quick drink of her iced vanilla Starbucks coffee.

"Yes, dis' is Shirley Jenkins. I saw an ad on TV dat said my cable would only run thirty damn dollars a month for a whole damn year but, every muthafuckin' month, my shit get higher and higher. What da fuck! I wanna know—"

"First of all, ma'am, you need to calm down! No need for all the profanity. You need to start by giving me your address and then verify your name—"

"I want my muthafuckin' money back. All you guys do is advertise shit just so yall bitch asses can get over on them!"

"Ma'am, ma'am!" Neeyah said in attempt to calm her down.

"Haven't you heard the cliché were customers are always right? I want my shit terminated. I'll get DISH Network I'm not fuckin' with dis' janky ass company no more just cut the shit slam off!" the woman yelled without giving Neeyah a chance to speak.

"Ma'am, calm down!" Neeyah pleaded.

"I want—"

Before she could finish her sentence, Neeyah said, "I'm terminating this call thanks for calling Kam Communications and have a nice day."

Damn, niggah's got me fucked up. I've only been here a month, 'bout ready to quit dis' ass-stressing job. A bitch is 'bout ta have a mid-day crisis she was thinking while sitting and staring at her incoming call light blink. *Naw, can't do dat then Grievence, and I want be able to get our own place, damn!*

She began to think about her night with Grievence, but her thoughts were interrupted.

"Anita Jones?!" her manager said without giving her a chance to speak.

"Please log out of the system and report to my office."

Oh shit! What in the hell does dis' tuna-smellin', bitch wants? she was thinking as she was entering the office trying not look nervous, knowing her heart was about to jump outta her body.

Her boss spoke in a disdainful tone that was daunting to everybody, "Ms. Jones."

"Yes, is there a problem?" she asked, nonchalantly.

"As a matter of fact, there is, Ms. Jones. You've been here for less than a month. We've been listening to your calls just to see how you're progressing. It is not just you. It's just something we do to make sure the customers is getting the best satisfaction as possible. As I stated earlier, we have been monitoring your calls and we noticed dat you haven't been sticking to the script. I understand that while you were in training, your trainer could not stress sticking to the script verbatim, enough. So if this happens again, we are gonna have to let you go. If you wanna continue working with this company, you'll make sure you stick to script verbatim. However, we're gonna send you home for the rest of the day because you're not meeting your production. So have a nice day. Oh yeah, customers are always right." she flashed a snide smile rather than friendly. When one of the manger's dorky colleagues Sammie walked in, the tension in the room was so palpable she dropped her mug. It shattered. She immediately dropped down to her knees and apologized a hundred times before walking away.

"No need to be all apologetic klutz, just watch what your doing. Making me lose my train of thought." she said snobbish shifting her attention to Sammie as if she was her boss.

"Dis' bitch is on one." Neeyah muttered to herself.

Sammie stopped dead in her tracks and shot Neeyah a look like I know this bitch isn't talking to me. Neeyah shot her a look back that said yes the hell she is. "First of all bitch who da fuck is you talkin' to, cuhz? I can give two fucks about dis' raggedy ass piece of shit job. I'll sweep da floor with yo' stringy head ass! I'm tryna tell you about me. On crip, cuhz." Sammie raised her tone.

"Hold on you're blowin' dis' all out of proportion. This is all being taken out of context," she held up her hand.

"Bitch, hold on my ass! You got me fucked up. Your ass come in here like you own dis' bitch. Flouncing around dis' bitch like everybody owe

you sumthin' or 'pose to bow down to your fishy smellin' ass. I'm from da hood bitch, and on crips, I will take it up and down thru there on your ass!" Sammie said, getting all up in her face.

"No need to use profanity. It's so unnecessary. This is a professional workplace for heaven's sake."

"You should have thought about dat shit when you tried to belittle me. I can give a fuck less about dis' being a workplace. In my hood you gotta give respect in order to get it, cuhz."

"You must've misunderstood what was said." The manger said scared shitless, stepping back.

"Don't straddle the fence now, bitch," Neeyah said, and then quickly turned her head as if it was someone else had spoken the words she had just breathed.

"Too bad so sad. Check dis' out, I hope you don't misunderstand when I whoop yo' ass!" Sammie said with her fist balled up. No sooner than the word ass rolled off her tongue, she lit in on her.

"Somebody get that crazed woman off her." Another colleague shouted from behind the door. Neeyah stepped back in disbelief.

"I guess today you really found out dat looks can be deceiving huh, bitch? Tryna play me like I'm a punk ass bitch dat gone sit back while you talk to me any kind of way. You may have all these otha muthafuckas in here spooked, but I'm tryna tell you 'bout me, cuhz." Sammie said outta breath while another colleague held her back. "People sholl know how to make us black folks act ignant and take it up and down thru there on their ass!" she looked dead at Neeyah. Neeyah flashed a baffled look. When the manger got up off the floor, she ran her fingers through her hair and straightened out her clothes as if nothing happened.

"Are you ok?" Everyone asked, that could give a fuck less.

"I've been better." she said, with a tight smile.

Neeyah cleared her throat like I guess she showed yo punk ass. *Damn, da homegirl just took da fuck off on her ass.* Neeyah thought to herself. "Sorry dis' happened to you, folks like dat make our race look bad." Neeyah said with dispassion. The manger flashed a fake smile. "But trust me it won't happen again," Neeyah said returning the same crooked half smile. *Some bitches neva learn, I'm a little baffled. If I'm not mistaken, not even 10 minutes ago she got her head whooped for the same shit.* "You have nice day, Ms. Tuna, I m . . . m . . . mean, Ms. Tina!" she stammered. "I think some steak over the eye will heal dat up in no time." Neeyah shot sarcastically before she walked off. *"A bitch just got to work. I'm not trippin' now. A bitch can go home*

and get some shut-eye." she couldn't help but wonder where Grievence was while waiting on the bus to come. "I know next pay period, a bitch gonna invest in a cell phone! Everybody and their mama got a cell phone. Not having one, where they do dat shit at?" she thought out while looking up the street for the bus. "Damn, it's stupid hot."

"Oh shit!" Grievence said squinting eyes while putting his hand over his forehead (as if he was saluting) trying to block the sunlight out, that was beaming down on his forehead. "What time is it?"

"It's time for another round!" Monie said, sliding under the covers and sticking his limp, crusty dick in her mouth.

"What a good mornin' salutation! But, shid I'm not complainin' do yo' thang, homie."

"Your ass is crazy. But, that's why I fucks wid you doe!" she flung the covers off her head and softly massaged his dick. Then without notice, she forced it back in her mouth and put a thick coat of spit on it.

"That's right, drop dat spit right on dis' head," he whispered, guiding her head up and down.

He was supposed to go to work early, but the truth to the matter was, her head game alone was the business. Her mouth was so hot and juicy. The vibrating tongue ring she had, gave him a feeling that he'd never before experienced. She made his whole body quiver and shake, uncontrollably like an earthquake.

"Fuck it!" he grabbed the condom and ripped it open.

"Wait, baby." she held up her finger. "Don't you wanna taste it?" she asked, spreading her swollen lips apart.

"Only if you can tell me if it's triple digits in the North Pole. Look, I'll tell you what, I'll beat it up. Then another niggah can come eat it up! How 'bout dat?"

She licked the juices off her fingers. "Aight, then you missin' out becuz, my shit taste just like burries!"

"Like fiddy, say I'm into having sex not making love so come give me a hug!" he sang with his arms outstretched.

"Whatever!" she sucked her teeth.

"I'll get you the next time!" he lied to make her feel better.

"Baby, do you always have to use a condom? They make me itch!" she whined.

"Hell-to-the-fuck, yeah!" he said in a serious tone while, pulling the tip on his Magnum to make sure there was room inside. "I'm not tryna have

no unwanted babies and damn sure isn't gonna get no tropical diseases, like Fred say!"

"Well, I don't have shit. Hell, I get tested every six months!" she lied, fondling her piercing.

"Nuthin' personal, sweetheart. Besides, your mouth isn't a prayer book. You ought to be glad a niggah isn't tryna run up in you raw. Truth be told, you don't noe what me or the next niggah got. True story!"

"Well, I'm just sayin' I would love to feel how good, slugger feels inside my wet pussy, without the plastic. Shid, I always make niggah's strap on two. That's all babes!" she said, rubbing her engorged clit. Sensing the seriousness in his voice, she decided to drop it. She had purposely missed a couple days of the pill. She surmised her ploy wouldn't work.

"No glove, no love—end of story!" he said spitting on his fingers, then rubbing her pussy with it. Which he didn't have to do to her, but it was something he was use to doing. Then he slid himself inside the best pussy he ever had. Too bad, she was a hoe and his girl's cousin because she did have the best of both worlds, that gushy gushy and bomb head. He did plan to keep her on his team. She jumped on his dick and rode it straight like she was in a rodeo, blowing his mind. She knew she was wrong, but her motto was *a bitch gotta eat and get her groove on,* seeing that it was done to her by her cousin, which gave her the cold heart she had. She figured Neeyah didn't know what to do with all that man that she used to brag about and tell all their bedroom business too. *Sumthin' you should never do! No, no, hell-to-the-muthafuck-no! Because a bitch like me is always waitin', willin', and ready to test it out.* One thing she couldn't get him to do was go down on her or kiss her. On the other hand, do you blame him?

"Oh shit, boy, you got dat bomb-ass, dick! Ooooh, oh, ooooh, oh, I'm 'bout to cum!" she said, very softly and wrapping her legs tighter around waist while scratching his back. Trying her damnest to leave a mark, to fuck with Neeyah. They both came at the same time. Soon after he was done, he hopped up and flushed the sperm filled condom down the toilet. After he pissed, he grabbed his clothes and headed to the shower.

"Damn, niggah, I'm offended. Ain't nobody tryna steal nuthin' from you!"

"Well, boo, when you're from da D, you learn not to trust no one. Blame it on the streets of Detroit. They made me the way I am."

"I'm sayin' doe, I don't have to steal shit from nobody!" she said, knowing all too well that what she specialized in. Plenty of times after sex, she had

rob Peter to pay Paul. That's what she learned from the streets of Maryland. *Love, don't love nobody. Get what you can while the getting is good.*

"No offense, big dawg!" he said drying off. She couldn't help but admire his cut-up rippling physique.

"I guess!" she said, turning her lip up and sucking her teeth. "Let me get a square."

He took the pack of Newports from his front pocket, shook one out and handed it to her and put one in his mouth. "You better take short pulls. These are Newports, shid, I can barely afford to smoke."

"I know that's right in dis' recession."

"Shid, tell me when black folks haven't been livin' a recession?"

"True. Well, I need you to drop me off at the crib."

"Now, you know we can't get caught together!"

"Why not? Neeyah's at work!" she said, snaking her neck.

"Look, don't trip. Here's twenty bucks, call a cab." he snaked his neck and handed her the money.

"Dat's some fucked-up shit! What in da' hell am I pose'ta' do wid twenty punk ass, funky dollars? You came to get my ass at my house, now you're gonna take my black ass home!"

"Look, bitch!" he said in a very loud hostile tone. "Nobody isn't gonna talk to me like dat. Here's twenty bucks, hop your boney ass on the bus!"

She could see the veins protruding from his head and neck.

"You wrong for dat. Where's my banana cush, you promised me!" she held her hand out.

"I'm not giving your hoe ass shit, you bum-ass bitch go suck a fat dick!" he yelled, yanking the door open. He hated cutting her off but was not gonna let nobody disrespect him, good pussy or not, he would have to try and convince Neeyah get her tongue pierced.

Tears welled up in her eyes. "I got you, you punk muthafucka."

"Lose my number you dumb-ass beyatch!"

"Your bitch ass got me bent, niggah!" she yelled before he sped away.

Slow Wine by Tony Toni Tone blared in background. "Slow wine keep it nice and slow it will be so nice baby slow wine." he sang. The Friday morning sun was glistening brightly on the roads ahead. Grievence's 01 Silver Monte Carlo, the car his mom gave him after she bought her a brand new Avalanche, headed south towards the freeway. The loud roar from the dual exhaust pipes, sounded like he was driving his dad '89 Nova.

"You did good, son. Dis' is to be our little secret!" he whispered. "What do you want me to buy you?"

"A whole lotta I mean a whole lot of candy and a game!" Junior replied and then he extended his arms. "Dis' much!"

"Well, you get back in the shower and brush your teeth two times and use dis' mouthwash," Ricky held it up for him to see. "Remember, our secret, son!"

"It's cold, Daddy!" Junior screamed with his bottom lip trembling.

"Well, just get out and turn the water off. Don't forget to brush your teeth." Ricky reminded him the second time.

"These heels are killin' my feet! A price a girl gotta pay for beauty." Neeyah said taking them off, as soon as she stepped in the door.

"Hey, Neeyah, I see you guys got off early, huh?" Ricky said looking like a deer in headlights. Relieved he wasn't just caught.

"Yeah!" she said going to check the caller ID to see if Grievence called. Then, it dawned on her she had been sent home early "Where's Junior?" she yelled while heading to the kitchen.

"He's takin' a shower!" he said nervously hoping she didn't go into the bathroom. He grabbed the mail off the coffee table to sidetrack her. "Oooh, I forgot, you got some mail."

While headed down the hallway to her room, she heard a knock at the door so she doubled back.

"Is someone at the door?" Ricky asked from the kitchen.

"Yeah, don't trip, I got it!"

"Hey, Neeyah. My mama said can she have dis' cup full of sugar?" The chubby girl said, handing her a cup.

Damn, is dis' the biggest cup in 7-Eleven? Big as dis' cup is, she should've asked for the whole damn bag! she thought to herself. "Why aren't you at school?"

"Becuz I didn't have anything clean to wear."

"Are you okay? Do you wanna come in and sit down awhile?" Neeyah asked handing the cup to her. Noticing she was out of breath from climbing two flights of steps.

"No, my mama told me to come right back, or she'll beat my butt, thanks!" The girl said and then wobbled down the hallway. Neeyah couldn't help but shake her head and chuckle at her. She was dressed in a green shirt that was too little. Her stomach was hanging all out, along with some black tiger print tights. To top it off, she had on some shiny gold, spangled looking

flat shoes. After she watched her until she disappeared into the stairwell, she headed to her room and went directly to her bookshelf of many books. "Ummmmmmm, what do I wanna read next? Interesting." she twisted her lips over to the side. Then she picked up *Forever A Hustler's Wife* by Nikki Turner. "I think I'mma go wid dis' one!" She read the back of it. "Sounds very compelling!" Satisfied, she plopped down on her bed and began to read. She couldn't get into the book from thinking about Grievence. Unable to focus on it, she closed it and grabbed the phone, but decided against calling him because she didn't want to be grilled about being sent home early. "Damn, a bitch corns hurt!" she said massaging them. Then she decided to take off her clothes. Once she was comfortable in her pj's, she picked up the mail. The first piece was a letter from a credit card company. After reading the first line, she put it in the shredder. The next was a bill from the cable company. She put it to the side for her mom. The next piece of mail was also, from a credit card company asking for 150-security deposit. "Niggah's got me fucked up sendin' me dis' shit sayin' I'm approved for a credit card, then askin' me to pay 150 . . . humph!" she chuckled, putting it in shredder. The last piece of mail addressed to her.

When she glanced at it, she just knew she wasn't reading what she was reading. The letter stated that her father, Sergeant Omar Jones, died in Iraq while fighting in the army, which she didn't give two flying fucks because she never knew the sorry sack of shit and felt society was better off without such deadbeat. She continued to read.

Your dad has given me your contact address. More to the point of this letter, you and your siblings will share a double life insurance policy totaling one million dollars when you reach twenty-one years of age.

"Damn," Neeyah sighed. *Oh, well, my birthday is in two months. I'll be twenty then. A niggah got one year . . . I guess!* she thought.

I am so sorry for your loss. Your father was an honorable man. Since he died fighting the war, you and your siblings are entitled to $1,000 a month until you reach twenty-five or get married. If you have any questions, please call me at the number listed at the bottom. She read out loud, trying to grasp and retain what was being said.

She sat for a moment to gather her thoughts. It all seemed so surreal.

Never in a million years she would've foreseen a day where she was gonna be the one to get her family up out of the hood.

"Thank you, Mom, for never movin'!" she fell back kicking and screaming. She knew if they had moved, then they would not have been able to get in contact with her.

"Neeeeeyah Neeeeeeyah." Junior sang, running up hugging her.

"How are you feelin', knucklehead?" she asked.

"I feel good!" he screamed, excitedly.

"What have you been doing all day, besides playin' hookey?" She asked as she halfway listened, all the while thinking and rereading the letter to make sure she read it correctly the first time.

"Daddy, had a earthworm like on the Lion King. He let me feel it!" Junior said.

"Oh, big head stop. Have you been on the machine today?" she asked while getting up to get the cordless phone. Her fingers were trembling so badly, till she could barely dial Grievence's number. Her heart started beating a mile a minute as she began to dial.

"Yeah, you reached dat niggah, dat cutthroat niggah dat don't like lames dat's quick to put a slug in yo' brain. Oh yeah," he chuckled. "You gotta grind if you wanna shine niggah so boss up niggah and if you play pussy, you will get fucked niggah . . . peacccccccce!" *Beep.*

"My boo, swear he so hard . . . she said, listening to his voicemail. "Baby, it's me. I got some good news for you. So, as soon as you get dis' message please call me. I love you, baby!" Two hours later, she had left damn near ten messages on his voice mail.

"Damn, a niggah is tired than a muthafucka!" Grievence said putting his key into the door. As soon as he opened the door, Betty Wright's *No Pain, No Gain* was blaring. His mom, Maryland, was sitting on the couch dressed in a thin summer dress with a silk shawl draping over her shoulders. She sat comfortably, bopping her head and snapping her fingers to the music. With a beer and her Newports, watching *Days of Our Lives,* of which she never missed one episode of. She was a cool-ass mom that smoked her weed, and drank her Four Loko. As long as she had two outta three, she was good. She played nothing but oldies relentless. Day in and day out. Therefore, him and his brother knew them and grew to love them as well. She was a very tall petite woman, that had a caramel skin tone with long, pretty red hair which, one would never known, because she kept her shit tracked up. She dressed like a teenager. Matter of fact, if you told her otherwise, you would have to fight her. She would tell everyone who asked her what kept her looking so good and young. She would say, *Ummmm . . . I think it's the bud.* What came up came out. She was never the one to gloss over or sugarcoat nothing nobody, not caring whose feelings she hurt. Her favorite quote, when she embarrassed him was, *I can only be me!* She was loud and obnoxious at times,

ghetto per se. It was going on five years since she last worked. One day, while lifting a patient at work she pulled a muscle in her back. The injury required her to have two surgeries. She was a CNA and going to school to be an LPN. Her dream was to become an RN. It was short-lived. When, the doctor told her that she couldn't work no more; and the best thing to do was apply for social security, so she found solace in drinking.

"Why aren't you at work, boy?" she asked, sitting back crossing her legs.

"I'm off today, Ma!" he said, weakly trying to avoid a lecture. She always gave him when she had alcohol in her. When she was sober, she was quieter than a church mouse, you couldn't get two words outta her.

"You're a bald face lair!" she screamed, with her Newport still intact between her lips. "How da' fuck are you gone insult my intelligence in my face!"

"Oh Lord." he sighed. "What are you talkin' about? I'm off today."

"Don't lie to me, Gerrick Deshad Phillips!" she yelled. Calling him by his government name.

"Ma, just call me Grievence," he said, walking off. "You trippin'." he muttered to himself.

"Bring your ass here!" she screamed, smashing her lipstick-stained cigarette butt in the ashtray that was filled to the brim with cigarette butts.

He did as told. Inwardly cursing himself. He sighed and slunk back down on the plush loveseat. She lit up another Newport. "First of all, I call you what the hell I want, I'm your mother! I named you. Secondly, when I'm tryna talk to you, you're not gonna walk the fuck off on me like I'm one of your little nappy-headed, fast-tale girls!" she said, spitting and dropping ashes everywhere.

"Mama, you're spittin'." he said not tryna piss her off more. *Say it don't spray it* he thought to himself as he watched her lips move, hoping she would hurry up. "Calm down mom."

"Calm down, my ass! Are you tryna hoe me? Don't forget lil niggah, I done been dere and did dat same hoe shit you tryna pull! I didn't earn my stripes for nuthin'." she said, taking a long sip of her beer, savoring the bitter taste it left in her mouth. Then she took a long pull of her Newport. "But back to subject at hand," she said, letting out a huge ring of smoke. "I know your black ass is lyin' because your supervisor called just minutes, before you walked in door and told me to let you noe not to come in to work. Now I told you if you lose your job dat you was gonna have to go back Detroit!" she said gulping down the last of her Four Loko.

"I'm never going back to dat gutter-ass place!"

"Do I have to keep remindin' you dat I'm your mother? You're gonna show me some respect. Dis' house here cost money, and you're not gonna be stayin' here without a job." she flailed her arms around in mid air.

"I'm not gonna have you become a number or statistics like your brother whose been in prison for most of his adult life for being a quote unquote 'hustler'"—with her fingers mimicking—"You're not gonna be bringing no dirty money up in dis' here crib, bottom line!" she said, tearing up.

"Mom, no disrespect but, you didn't feel dat way when you spendin' all dat dirty money, isn't dat how you got dis' house?"

"Looka here boy, I'm your mother. I don't have to explain shit to your fuckin' ass! What I choose and chose to do is my business. I just don't want to see you caught up in these streets. Just look at your brother up in Mounds. Caught a fuckin' ten-year-bid, for what?!" she screamed with tears rolling profusely down her face. Drinking made her very emotional. She drank to take away the pain. She blamed herself for allowing her son to turn to the street life. She was too busy working to keep food on their table and a roof over their heads. She knew deep down inside that, nine times out of ten, when someone gets a hold of that easy money, it wasn't no talking them out of it. It would be irrelevant because it will fall on deaf ears and that the only way out of the game was jail or hell. She vowed it wouldn't happen to Gerrick, but deep down she knew it was something that she didn't have no control over. "For shit." she continued to say. "Because it's not worth it, sure you might ball to your fall with money, clothes, jewelry, women, but look at the end results, never pretty. It's so preposterous! You noe what doe, It probably wouldn't be so bad if niggahs knew how to get in the game—get what they can get and get out. Nah niggahs wanna be greedy, with money comes envy. When they end up in jail, all they have is shoulda-coulda-woulda stories on what they had and done. Fuck all dat hoe shit!" she said, taking a longer pull of her Newport.

"Ma, I hear you. I gotta pee," he pushed himself up from the couch.

"No, you're gonna sit your black ass down and listen, really listen. If you're lucky to get outta the game, then you go to prison. Then sure, you won't have nuthin' but time to sit and reminisce on all the things you had! Son, all I'm saying is an ounce of prevention is worth a pound of cure."

"I'm not gonna end up like them." he said with a little bass in his voice.

She was no chippie, she was a chip off the old block, just like her dad. She had lost her dad and brother to the game she learned from the best. However,

her brother Daniel didn't make it outta the game alive. She vowed to never let her kids fall victim to the shady streets that didn't love nobody. She grew up in one of Detroit's shadiest, grittiest projects on Woodward. Her family was poor, which made her brother stray. Every day, he longed to help his struggling mom. Their dad had already fallen victim to the streets and was doing a double-life sentence for a triple homicide. It was rumored that one of his soldiers was ten dollars short, so he killed three of his relatives—not touching him, just to state a point. The game was so serious niggahs were losing their lives for chump change. *It wasn't the money. It was the point that if I would have let him skate, then* the next *niggah would be tryna do same thing. For some reason, seems like niggah listens to the gun talk clearer,"* their dad would say, who is still to this very day incarcerated in Riker's Island. Daniel lost his life due to a larceny-hearted niggah. She knew deep down it was a lost cause with kids to pursue the issue. Being the mother, she had tried her damnest to steer her youngest son in the right direction. She knew sending him back to Detroit would probably push him to the streets because there were no jobs there, a very poverty-stricken place. She did hope—that by telling him—he would keep his job and not fall victim like so many other young kids with a lot of potential.

"Son, let me ask you an important question," she sniffled. "Where do you see yourself in ten years?!"

"You know, I haven't really given it much thought!" he said.

"Well, do you have any goals?" she paused. "Son, let me crystallize sumthin' for you, you're almost twenty-one years old. You're not getting any younger. Now is the time you sit down and meditate on dat. Time is ticking. Believe me, when I say time isn't gonna wait for nobody, either get with it or get left behind. Now I want you to talk to your supervisor, let him know how much you need your job. I can't handle all these bills alone," she said putting fire to another Newport. "Do you see what yall do to me? Drive me to smokin' two damn boxes of Newports a day!"

"Well, Ma, don't trip. Neeyah and I are getting ready to cop up a spot, so you don't have to worry. I'll be outta your hair soon!"

"You, gonna do what with who—I think I need another beer," she said clearly pissed you could see the smoke coming from her ears. "You and dat little ass girl don't noe shit da first about getting or keeping a place. It'll be like the blind leading the blind! Yall asses is still wet behind the ears. Who's gonna pay the bills? What about all these other little tramps she catches you with? She'll be a fool to move with your ass!" she said low key, scared of her son leaving her.

"I thought dat you wanted your privacy?!" he asked, bewildered.

"Well, I just don't think you're mature enough to get your own place with Neeyah. For heaven's sake, you're still with all these different girls. Son, I'm not tryna belittle you. She really loves you. Why not stay here a while, save some money, then get yourself together decide if she is who you want before you go jumping into sumthin' so fast you'd end up regretting!" she said, raising her tone just a little.

"Mama, you were just telling me, not even twenty minutes ago, I needed to go back to da D!"

"Son, all I'm asking, is just give some thought to what I'm telling you. The sayin' haste makes waste, is tried and true. You're grown, a little wet behind the ears, but you're grown, and it's your decision. And no it's not the alcohol talkin'!" she assured him. "I'm much older and wiser and been down dat road many, many times. I don't wanna see you hurt, dat's all!" she said, popping the top on another beer.

"I hear you, Mama, umma run dis' by her." he said, pushing up from the chair. She let out a long breath, sat back, and started grooving to *Everybody Plays the Fool* by Main Ingredients. He went into his room pondering on what his mom had just laid on him. Even though she was drinking, he had to admit she made sense.

"Everybody plays the fool sometimes. Indeed, they do. There's no exception to the rule," she sang and danced in her seat. After she got tired she sat down and grabbed her can and swallowed the last of her beer, relishing the full-bodied taste. Grievence closed his door and laid back on his bed.

BETTER OFF DEAD

"Hi, Mom, can you explain dis' to me in English. What does dis' means, Ma?" Neeyah said rushing her mom as soon as she walked through the door.

"Dang, girl, can I get in the door first before I get bombarded?" she said, sitting in the recliner. Once she got enough breath, she bent over to untie her shoes. "I'll appreciate if I can get something cold to drink,"

"Okay, Ma, here just read dis'!" she said, insistently. Nearly shoving it in her face.

She took the paper from her. "Let me see what got you all smiley smiley! Now go get my drink." she whisked her off.

"Thank you! Lemme see what dis' is," she said, pushing the glasses up on her nose and then she sat the empty glass on the table next her. "Baby can you pass me my house shoes? Oh my gosh!"

"Yeah, I feel dat society is better off without such deadbeat. He's better off dead! In my eyes, he always was!"

"Stop it, just stop dat!" Ms. Lara screamed. Neeyah jerked her head around appalled, with her jaw dropped. She knew it wasn't at all in her mom's character to condone a deadbeat. This was why she sat still, with a puzzled look on her face. "A human life was lost here. I raised you to be very humble and respectful, young lady, so you need to show some compassion!" Ms Lara continued with tears welling up in her eyes.

"No offense, how could you sit up here and defend him to me. He never done nuthin' for me." she shook her head and looked perplexed trying make some sense out of what was coming out of her mom's mouth.

"Look, there's sumthin' you don't know and I just didn't know how to tell—"

"What is it?!" she cut her off.

"Well, for about ten years now, we have been secretly keepin' in contact. He wanted to be in your life, but Ricky wasn't havin' it. He told him dat

you were his. He clothed you, fed you, and kept roof over your head and dat made you his and ended it by saying, *Anybody can make a baby, but it takes a real man to be a father.* He was right, so your biological dad accepted it and fell back. However, he never stopped writin' or sendin' money for you—"

"Maaaa." she cut her off again.

"Wait a minute, let me finish. I sent him pictures. I must admit he and I became close over the years. He was a very good man that made the wrong decision not to man up. Not long ago we concluded, dat it was time to sit you down and explain dis', since you're old enough to understand. When he decided to fall back and let Ricky handle things, it seemed to be the right thing to do at the time. However, lookin' back, it was wrong because I cheated you outta a father that didn't have no way, at the time to support you. Now I see it wasn't at all about things he bought or could've bought, spending time overrules all dat! For a man dat paid the bills. How do you think after Ricky was outta work the first time you was getting everything you needed and extra? Not because you were the only girl, it was because of him. He loved you, girl. Do you remember dat pretty yellow dress with the pink and green flowers you got for Easter and the big basket?"

"Vaguely?"

"Well, your dad bought you dat I had to lie to Ricky!" she said, reminiscing. "I'm not gonna listen to you ever again talk down on him.

Outta respect for Ricky, he fell back now. You tell me, how do you feel about him now?" she rocked back and forth with tears streaming down her cheeks.

"Geeeeeeee I dunno, what can I say? I know dis' all is so overwhelming. I don't know if I can respect the fact he basically relinquished his rights without fighting. At the same time, I guess it takes a real man to do sumthin' so selfless. What do you say about sumthin' like dat?!" Neeyah asked, feeling a little bad for him.

"Just forgive him, girl. He loved you, baby!" she said, wishing they had more time together. "I remember when you were just a gleam in your father's eye. We had sumthin' special or at least I thought so."

"What does dat mean?"

"It means you wasn't even in the picture. I didn't get pregnant with you until 5 months or so, later."

"Wow. Ma, I do forgive him! I didn't know, Mama." Neeyah said, with tears rolling freely down her cheeks. She knew her mom was a very strong woman, whom she or neither one of her brothers witnessed cry. She hugged her mom.

"What's going on?" Ricky asked, inquisitively.

"Uuuuum, Omar got killed—"

"Who the hell is Omar?" Ricky cut her off.

"If would let me finish, you'd know. Omar, Neeyah's daddy was killed while fighting in Iraq. She and her siblings are entitled to some money!" she said, dryly.

"Whaaaat!" Ricky screamed, as if he had some entitlement to the money. "Wait a minute, I need a drink!" he said, heading to the kitchen.

"So," Neeyah whispered. "Since, you and him kept in contact, I'm sure you knew his status on his marriage and kids, right?"

"Right!"

"So, how many kids does he have?" she asked in a near whisper.

"He has three in all," she said in between sniffs. Neeyah began to do the math. *That's almost 400 g's a piece,* she thought. Ms Lara lifted her head. "That's roughly 340 thousand a piece."

"Yeah, I was just thinkin' dat!"

"I told you he was a good man. He took out enough insurance so his kids could be well off. God bless his soul!" Ms Lara said, rocking back and forth.

"What's with all the sad faces?" Sonny said, walking through the door. "Did somebody die or sumthin'?"

Neeyah looked up at him. "Yes. My biological, father."

"Ooooooooookay and you never knew him, and you're cryin' becuz?" he said, smart alecky.

"It's long story, boy. I'll have to explain it to you later!"

"Ma, are you okay?" he asked very baffled by the fact that his mom was crying. She didn't respond. "Maaa!" he called again.

"I'm sorry, baby. I'm okay, just tryna make some sense of this situation, dat's all! Well, I can tell you that one million was left to his kids!"

"Are you serious? Can you say dat in English?!" he said, excitedly with his eyes lighting up like a Christmas tree. "So does dat mean we're finally finna get outta the ghetto?"

"Yes, baby boy." Neeyah said, as she kissed him on the cheek.

"Dat is what's up, sis." he flashed a happy-go-lucky smile.

"Mommy, you're homeee!" Junior sang, hugging his mom.

"Neeeeeeeeeeeyah!" Ricky yelled from the kitchen.

"Yeeeeeeeeah." she yelled back.

"Pick up the phone."

"Hello."

"What up doe, hoe?" Leigha screamed happily into the phone.

"What's going on?" Neeyah asked, hardly listening.

"Well, I'm getting ready to come thru, a niggah over here bored and some mo' shit."

"Okay, that's what it do!"

"Hey, do you still got some more of them swishas you had the other night?"

"Why?" Neeyah asked, nonchalantly with her mind clearly elsewhere.

"What you mean, fool. I got dat purple, Negro. You know, blow some smoke. Puff, puff pass, niggah. Do you comprende now?" she laughed.

"I'm sorry, dawg, my mind is elsewhere!"

"I know, your ass is on one when it comes to dat niggah, Grievence. Straight got your ass discombobulated like a muthafucka!"

"Bitch, fuck you!" she retorted. "It's not even about him. Now what hoe? You just have your ass ova here in the next twenty minutes, or it's gonna be a misunderstandin'. A niggah really need to smoke right 'bout now!"

"Whateva, hoe, I'll be there and them shits better not be stale and be your ass downstairs in about twenty minutes or some major shit gone pop off," she said and then ended the call.

"What it is, hoe?!"

"I can't call it, gotta lot of shit on my mind, dat's all. Nuthin' I can't handle. But shid, who shit you rollin' in, doe? Lemme get a good look at dis'. What is dis'? Uummm . . . An Infinti G35!" Neeyah said walking around the car.

"I see you called me last night, gurl, but my ass was on one. At da' club. Niggahs was in there whylin' getting hyphy and shit. I was on dat ooooweeee! My ass was feelin' like, oh booooy, thizzin' and some mo' shit wit' da' homeboy J'qwan, posted. Bitch it was stupid niggahs in there too."

"Yea, I bet yo' ass was probably somewhere makin' love at da club!"

"Bitch, I fuck. I don't make love!" she said. They both busted out laughing.

"How 'bout my snotty ass boss got took off on by her colleague in da midst of our conversation, bitch!"

"No better for da dumb bitch. I almost cracked her ass when I brought you dat' money. I knew you needed your job was the only thing dat saved her monkey ass dat day. I was like Woosaaah woosaaah . . . And pushed on."

"I'm already knowing. But, dis' hea is sweeet doe!"

"Girl, you already know dis' is Rah Rah shit. He needed me to run some errands, so I decided to come thru and smoke some of dis' good purp and chop it up with you for a hot sec. You wanna ride over to Crenshaw?"

"Sure, why not." she said hopping in the car. "You look good, girl. What are you using on your skin? It's clearin' up." Neeyah asked staring at her face. Amazed by the results.

"I decided to try Proactive. Shid, I figured it couldn't fuck my shit up no worser than it already was. It is clearin' up, huh?" she asked looking in the rear-view mirror. Soon as she cranked up the car, *No Hoe* by Dlo was blarring.

Dlo he don't give a fuck about no hoe, no hoe, no hoe he'll snatch yo' hoe up and take her to the hoe sto . . . Dlo you already noe doe. You better watch yo' bitch becuz ill repo yo' hoe. They both sang in unison. "Heeeey. dis' my shit!" Neeyah said grooving to the music and looking out the window. *He don't give a fuck about no niggah or no hoe doe. He'll put a bitch on the track . . . I don't care about the weather go get your raincoat, you might get wet but the money is still da same doe.* "Heeeey, you can't be my bitch but you can be my money maker." Leigha sang.

"So what's good with you and dat niggah, Rah Rah? I thought you guys had broken up, Ms. No-nigga-gonna-cheat-on-me-and-I'm-still-be-with-him."

She handed her the bag of weed. "Guuuurl, lemme, tell you." she said, smacking her mouth and snaking her neck after every word she said. "Dat niggah dere he knows he done fucked up a good thing by fuckin' with dat dirty nasty hoe, Kandy. I still fucks with him every now and again when I need the whip or money, doe. There isn't shit else poppin' off doe. Do you actually think I'll fuck behind dat dirty, shady bitch? Hell-to-the-muthefuck-naw! Bitch, you got me fucked up. I look at it like dis', when your ass fuck anything with a dick and believe me, dat bitch doesn't discriminate, probably got all kinds of diseases festering in her shit. I'm talking bout shit dat hasn't been named her nasty ass. I knows how the tramp get down I used to roll wid her ass! Her ass fucked all kinds of stray ass niggahs without protection. I remember one night, we kicked it with Tony and Fred,"

"Bitch, don't tell me you fucked one eyed Fred? Did you girl?" Neeyah asked raising her brow and glancing over at her out of the side over of her eye.

"Google it, you google everything else, bitch. Nah If you shut up and let me finish, you'll know exactly what happened. Anyways, everybody look da same in the dark. In the same essence, I know you done heard da sayin' dat all pussy is pink in the inside. Fuck what you're talkin' about, one eyed Fred, pissed and shitted money.

"Hey ain't no business like hoe business. So I ain't mad atcha."

"Sho you right. Plus on top of dat he had a dick big as my wrist and swung down to his knees so, he was alright wid me. But—"

"Uh huh, he didn't have no horse leg did he, girl?" Neeyah cut her off.

"Tried and true. But, stop interuptin' me bitch and let me finish. Like I was sayin', it was a studio apartment with one bed and dinette chair, right,"

Neeyah nodded her head. "Right,"

"You already know, Fred and I debo'd the bed. I heard Tony say we gone have to do it on the floor, she was like what kinda desperate hoe do you think I am to fuck on a rock hard, cement floor? You got me fucked all da way up. He was like the same slut puppy dat got on all fours, on a dirty mattress in the crack alley and fucked me and my niggah's for a bag of stress. My ass was rollin'. Dat shit was hilarious. Then her only defense was fuck you, you no dick bastard. The moral of the story is, she tried to ack like she didn't know them, but he low key, blasted her ass.

"Just messy! Dat bitch is such a dick magnet. So how did you find out dat she fucked Rah Rah?" Neeyah asked, smelling the weed.

"Yeah, hoe, dat's dat purple urple what you know about them grapes? But anyway, like I was sayin', I had a gut feelin' you noe." she said, looking back to make sure it was clear to change lanes.

"I dunno, homie it smell like dat bunk weed to me."

"Whateva, so you know a bitch like me, is like 007 and shit—as luck would have it, I activated his GPS system and went right to his monkey ass and went smooth the fuck off!"

"Yeah, how did you do dat?"

"Gurl, one day he was sleep, I installed dis' one software on his phone dat would allow me to track him!"

"Damn, I never thought of no shit like dat!"

"Becuz, you're book smart. Go figure! My ass is a bonafied, street-smart chick. You're not smart as me end of story. But, yes gurrrl, I picked up a brick and bashed his shit like, *whoomp*!" she said flinging her fist down in the air. "He was in his bucket too girl,"

"I guess I could learn a lot from a dummy."

"Blow me, bitch!" Leigha flipped her off. "But, how bout dis' niggah comes running outside, after hearing his alarm and shit, with some Timbs and boxers on, I ran straight past him in the house where dat hoe lay, naked. Dis' nasty bitch had cum all in her hair, dried up on her face, and some mo' shit. So, I grabbed her by the long, ghetto, hot-mess ass pink braids—" Leigha started.

"Shit, naw! Dat hoe is black as shit. Where they do dat at?" Neeyah cut her off.

"Dat bitch is so fuckin' unbelievable ghetto, till it's pathetic. But anyway girl, I wrapped them shits around my hand, to get a good grip and snatched dat hoe up like she was a rag doll, and mopped her ass the fuck out!"

"Where was Rah Rah's monkey lookin' ass when all dis' was taking place?"

"Fuck you beauty is in the eye of the beholder, bitch! Besides, beauty is only skin-deep. Anyhoo, like I was sayin' apparently, his ass hopped in his shit and dipped da' fuck off! But, best believe soon as I hit the door, I ran and leaped up on dat bitch and cracked his ass in the jaw a gang of times."

"Rah Rah was like deuces on dat ass. And slow your ass down, and watch out for dat big ass truck!"

"Shut yo' back seat drivin' ass up, I got dis'!"

"You don't ack like it, ridin' his ass and shit!"

Rah Rah stood well over six feet tall, and weighed 215 pounds solid, with a dark skin tone and a baby Afro. People would often say he looked like a turtle. He was definitely about his paper. He stayed dressed in the latest and greatest, with a fresh pair of gym shoes. His jewelry alone was worth half a mil. He wasn't at all attractive. His personality had such magnetism, that it made women drawn to him. Leigha was still in love with him, but her pride wouldn't allow her to be with him after he cheated. He vowed he was gonna get her back one day.

"Well, you know what they say, hoes flock together," Neeyah said licking the blunt.

"Don't get shit fucked up, hoe. I don't even bat in dat bitch's league. You best believe if I'm gonna be doing all dat fuckin', I'm gonna get paid. Niggahs be giving dat hoe a blunt. I'm not talkin' no chronic or cush, I'm talkin' stress. I told her ass to make them niggah's break bread, because pussy is definitely worth a million dollars if you know how to use it!"

"Like my mama always told me, If you're gonna do it, then get sumthin' out of it."

Neeyah couldn't help but think about all the shit Grievence put her through. She was so in love with him. I guess one would say, in too deep. She wondered where Grievence was.

She snapped her fingers in Neeyah's ear. "What's good with you in your niggah? A penny for your thoughts! Helllo, earth to Neeyah!"

"What up, doe? My bad, I'm on one today." Neeyah said lighting the blunt. She knew she couldn't tell Leigha or nobody else about her dad.

"Clearly, well . . ." Leigha said inquisitively. "I wanted to tell you I heard 'bout what my grimy-ass sister did. Dat shit was so fucked up! Her ass came in the house last night, fidgeting and shit. I can tell she must've been tweaking or gone off them sticks! Dat shit was scantless. Point blank period. I went smooth the fuck off on her shiesty ass!" Leigha said reaching for the blunt to calm her nerves. "As you can see, just talkin' about her ass works my nerves."

"You know what, girl, I'm not even trippin' becuz how could I get mad at her for being a scantless ass hoe. A hoe gonna be a hoe, it is what it is. Besides I feel like dis, if any bitch can take my man then by all means get him. But when he comes back fuckin' with me, wanna fuck me and shit, that's when umma go whoop a bitch becuz you took him you better keep him."

"Yeah, girl, I feel you. She did dat shit to you; I know she'll do it to me in a heartbeat if opportunity presented itself. Dat's my sister. I love her to death, but I just can't trust her as far as I can throw her. I dunno doe girl, if dat were me, dat bitch would've been in for a rude awakening becuz she and I would've been strappin'! I would have beaten her like she was a stranger on the street or sumthin'. Dat shit was to file. Straight like dat. Uh huh, how 'bout bitch," she said hitting Neeyah with the palm of her hand.

"Ouch, bitch, dat shit hurt." Neeyah said, rubbing her arm.

"Just shut yo' punk ass up and listen to dis', how bout Keyon bitch Hennesie, was about to dig all in dat ass. It was a gang of them too, gurl. I just so happen to glance at 7-eleven by da house, and see her skinny ass about to get mopped da fuck out. I busted a bitch, and whipped up in there. Threw the car in park and hopped out on them hoes. Straight rolling my fist around in the air, in a circular motion. 'Bout to fire on all their asses. Them hoes was spooked. I was like, all yall bitches was just tryna square up on my sister when she was alone. So square up now, punk ass bitches. What up, what it do bitches. I was talkin' major cash shit. Then dis' one stupid bitch was like, bitch since your ass always gotta be front and centered somewhere, how about she fucked yo' man, Rah Rah, twice! So, whose the stupid bitch, now? I told dat bugged eyed bitch, I could give a fat baby's ass if they were over there fuckin' on a mattress over there. You stupid, retarded ass bitch, family trumps all. That's my sister, she got my blood runnin' through her veins. You got me fucked up. What I want is for one of you bitches to come catch dis' fade and whoop whoop. Hon, I was hella mad. Ready to go dumb on all of them. I felt like I was in retard nation. Not one of them bitches wanted to catch my fade. I was thizz in' and some mo' shit, too. The girl dat was drivin' was like girl I'm still on papers. I can't leave my kids and do

another bid. Next thang I know, she snatched the one girl up and they were
out. It was straight 'bout to be bloodshed. On the way home, I told her she
better call and thank da homie Ej for beggin' me to go swoop up his dough.
I know what your'e thinkin'. So go ahead and say it!" she said, looking over
at her. "Matter of fact, before you even say anything, Rah Rah wouldn't dare
cross those lines and fuck my sista. I know dat niggah."

"I wasn't even gone say nuthin'. You know your man. But, girl yo' ass is
tarded. How you gone fight a group of bitches? And where was Monie's ass?"

"I know. I prolly—"

"Prolly? Girl umma need for you to get some hooked on phonics instead
of hooked on ebonics." Neeyah cut her off.

"Fuck you!" Leigha flipped her off. "My B. I forgot you was raised in
the Valley and you don't know anything about the hood talk."

"Calm down. I'm playin'. Finish your statement."

"You be workin' my nerves too and you know it. But Any ole ways, like
I said I prolly would've had my ass lumped up and some mo' shit, but them
hoes would've had one hell of a battle. You already noe her ass was standin'
behind me. Talkin' big shit!"

"Dat figures."

"Anyway back to what we was talkin' about, you are a beautiful girl. I
don't know why you let him treat you like shit. There's somebody out dat
will treat you and respect you like you deserve!"

"But, I love him." Neeyah said in the saddest voice, knowing that Leigha
was speaking nothing but the truth. "Besides love isn't about finding the
perfect person, it's about seeing the imperfect person perfectly,"

"Yeah, I hear you don't misunderstand, love don't love nobody now. I'm
not tryna tell you what to or not to do. I'm just sayin' you deserve better
dat's all, you're my cousin. I love you. Dat's file how he do you, doe!"

"Cuzo, I know you love me and dat you're just lookin' out for my best
interest. I'm very appreciative for it, but I look at it like dis'—all men cheat,
so if you can't beat them, you'll have to join them. Sometimes, you have
to go thru the bad to get to the good. A piece of a man is better than not
havin' one at all!"

"Bullshit!" Leigha snapped. "Why would you wanna settle for less when
you can have so much more? These days it isn't a such thing as going thru
bad to get to the good, hell it's all bad. Let me tell you girl, don't ever let a
niggah dictate your life or make you wanna settle for less. You deserve the
best, as do I and every other female. Believe me when I say I'm speakin'
from experience! He ain't doing shit but brain fuckin' you wid all these lies

of getting a spot. I wouldn't even wanna move wid his trifflin' ass no way. To be honest, quiet as kept I think he's sellin' you a dream. I'll be damn if a muthafucka gone try and sell me a dream and I can't spend dat shit!" she said irritated by her cousin's ignorance. She was only three years older than her but so much wiser beyond her years. That's what happens when you're forced to grow up at an early age. She saw firsthand how her mom used to chase men that never wanted her, only used her for a place to stay and money, which meant countless times she could recall, when they had to go without. She also at a very early age, witnessed her mom getting beat incalculable times. Quiet as kept, her mom finally broke down and told an inquisitive Leigha. One day, when her mom pimp jumped on their mom in front of them, then nine-year-old, she decided to help her mom. The guy picked her up, threw her against the bricked wall. The incident broke her left arm and fractured some bones in her chest. That was the turning point as well as eye-opener for her mom. "Love don't make the world go round, money does, hoe!" Leigha continued blowing smoke rings out of the window.

"Naw, but it sure makes the ride worthwhile," Neeyah replied, dryly.

"You too gullible when it comes to dat niggah, girl! He be havin' yo' ass discombobulated and some mo' shit. Get some heart like yo' big cuzo." Leigha said, hitting her chest. "One thing I know fa sho—" she started then started coughing. "You can't chase after a man dat isn't worth catchin'. Fallin' down and getting back up is a part of life, and if you never listened to shit else I told you, you had better listened to dis', you are responsible for your own happiness, never look for a man to complete you. Money on my mind fuck niggahs, fuck bitches . . . get money! Get money! Fuck niggahs!" she sang loudly. "Lil Weezy couldn't said it better."

"No offense. But, your man is where?" she asked, sarcastically.

"None taken. Best believe I'm single by choice." Leigha said throwing her hand in the air. "If I went for half the shit you do, I'd still be with dat boo radley-lookin' muthafucka. You're so smart til you're actually dumb. Further more sweetheart, fairy tales don't always come true. In fact, them shits don't exist. So, I can see you're in for a rude awakening as well. Look, I'm not tryna turn dis' into a yellin' match. I'm just tryna give it to you straight, without a chaser. I just wanna see you happy. But either way, it's not gonna affect me one way or the other. Since you wanna be all smart-alecky, then I'm leave it alone becuz if you like it, I love it!" she said turning the music up. Grooving and pumping her fists in the air. "Oooh shit, dat's my shit! Let it go if he's not gone love you the way he should, then let go. If he's not gonna treat you the way he should, then you need to let it go!" Leigha sang along.

Neeyah couldn't help but think she was tryna be low key, funnystyle. The rest of the ride was quiet. All she could do was look dumbfounded and stare outta the window. She was starting to regret hopping in the car with her.

"You're not mad are you, girl? What a bitch need to do, damage control or sumthin'?" Leigha said hitting her on the leg.

"Nah, I'm cool. You know I'm not even studdin' your sanctimonious ass! I'm just chillin' thinkin' about the party at Apple's house, Saturday." she lied, not wanting her cousin know that she got under her thin skin.

"Whatever dat mean, but your ass was just sitting over there quieter than a church mouse and shit. But anyhoo tell me about dis' party and how your ass gonna go from being sarcastic to silence."

"It means you're not fuckin' quote unquote, Holier-than-thou!" she said with her two fingers mimicking it. "Yeah, sumthin' about her niggah is touchin' down."

"That's what's up. Maybe we can slide thru there and make a grand entrance." Leigha said drinking her Four Loko like it was Kool-Aid.

"How them thangs taste? I heard they have yo' ass gone quick!"

"Bomb as hell! They'll indeed get you where you need to be. Them loko's be on my ass. But, how 'bout yesterday when I was at Rosco's dis' busta gone try and holla at me. I'm talkin 'bout dis' fool was hella beat! I can't believe da' audacity of dis' fool. To be honest, I didn't even look at his face, all I seen was them dirty ass crusty biscuits he had on." she said, sticking the can between her legs and wiping the beer from her mouth with the back of her hand.

"Yo' bougie ass!"

"Uh huh, bitch that's not even all. Peep dis' bitch," she said hitting Neeyah on the leg. "So, why when I get my waffles and shit, I see dis' niggah slowly ridin' by, straight rimmed up e-class, bitch!" she yelled.

"So, there you have it, you can't judge a book by its cover! I bet somebody could've knocked your ass over with a feather."

"I guess . . . but money don't make me. I make money, hoe! So get dat shit right. Damn dat beer went straight thru a niggah!" Leigha said pulling up in Neeyah's complex.

"You ain't gotta lie, Craig!"

The sight of the run-down, roach-infested projects instantly, made her depressed. Most of the building were graffiti-ridden. There were bums posted everywhere. Dealers of all ages, was standing around, waiting on sales.

"You are going, aren't you?" Neeyah asked before getting out.

"Already! Well, let's hit the club up tonight while you bullshittin'!" Leigha asked shaking her legs trying to hold her piss.

"That's what's up. I think I got sumthin' to wear. I can use a night out!" Neeyah said, as she got out and reluctantly walked to her building."

"Umma go use you guys bathroom," Leigha said letting up the window.

"Okay, fa sho," Neeyah said in a calm tone. As they were walking to her door, two smokers were fighting over some crumbs. The girls shook their heads in disgrace.

"Lemme make sure it's presentable first."

"Oh, shut up. That's absurd." Leigha waved her off. "Where's my T.T at?" she asked, coming outta of the bathroom.

"I'm right here in my bedroom," Ms. Lara called out.

"Hey, T.T, are you okay?"

"I'm okay, baby, dis' is a tryin' time. I'll get thru it," Ms. Lara said in a soft tone.

"Is it anything I can help you with, Auntie?"

"Naw, baby, I'll be okay. Thanks for asking, baby. How is your mama?"

"She's okay. I talked to her earlier. Work home, work home—you noe how dat goes. Well, T.T, I'm gonna go ahead and take dis' boy his car before he puts an APB out on me. If you need anythin', call me. I love you!"

"I love you, too. Drive safe."

"I will, TT." Leigha said, going down the hallway.

"You leavin'?" Neeyah screamed from the kitchen.

"Yeah, girl, I'm gonna take dis' boy his car back before he gets to trippin'. What yall got to eat? Ah bitch hungry off in dis' piece," she peeped her head in the kitchen.

"Now you know it's the end of the month. Our kitchen is so bare, it looks like one of those sponsor a family infomercials."

"Damn, not even a syrup sandwich?" Leigha laughed.

"Bitch, we don't even have a can of beans," Neeyah joked. "But rest assure, in a couple of days we'll be back poppin'. Fish, chicken, roast, shrimp, and some mo' shit. Matter of fact I'm about to go to sleep and dream about a big home cooked Thanksgiving dinner. Do you think I'd wake up full?"

"You stupid, let me go girl."

"Fa sho."

"Heeeey, Leighaaaa!" Junior sang as he did everybody's name.

"Hey, fathead!" she tickled him.

"Okkkkkkkkkkkkkkkkkkkay, I givvvvvvvvvve!" Junior let out a loud wail.

"Bye yall!"

Not long after Grievence drifted off to sleep, Shari boyfriend D-Nutty rushed in with gun in hand. He had snatched him up so quickly, almost as soon as his head hit the pillow.

"Niggah, you fuckin' my bitch!" D-Nutty screamed, pistol-whipping him.

"Dawg, calm down, I don't know Shari. I mean your bitch!" Grievence corrected himself, trying to shield his head.

"Ooops. Wrong answer!" D-Nutty yelled. "You see lil' youngster, I'm not called Nutty for no reason. And you're not gonna insult intelligence in my face!" he screamed, louder cocking the gun.

"Please don't kill me. I don't know her! I promise I don't. You have the wrong dude. Maaaa." Grievence yelled for his mother. There was no answer. He called out again.

"Don't worry. Dat bitch is dead, but not before slurpin' on dis' fat dick. She was on my shit like a leech, nearly suckin' all da brown off of it!" D-Nutty said, gravely. Grabbing his crouch.

"Noooooo! Not my mama!" Grievence screamed with tears and snot running down his face. He couldn't begin to fathom, how his mother was just lying on the couch, asleep. Listening to her favorite song, *Secret Garden* by Barry White. Then like someone flipped on a switch, where there had been light, now empty blackness filled his world. His mom was his life.

"Don't trip dawg, why you actin' like a lil' bitch right now? Chuck dat shit up lil' homie, you bout to join her, goodnight and have a nice dream!" *Pow Pow Pow* Three gun shots rang out.

Grievence frantically, jumped up. Sweat was dripping from his face like raindrops. He scanned his room, to see it was all thankfully, a dream.

"Fuck dat bitch, Shari. We had a good time in Vegas and she fine as shit with some good pussy, but her ass isn't worth dyin' over!" he said, breathing hard with his heart pounding fast, against his chest walls. After he calmed down, he got up and kissed his mom. Who apparently, passed out on the couch gripping an empty Heineken bottle. *Slow Jam* by Atlantic Star played on repeat in the background. "Ma, what part of the game is it when you start dippin' in my shit!" he said softly heading to the stereo. Still a little shaken up he turned the power off. Soon as he did, she jumped up causing the bottle to fall on the hardwood floor and break. Scaring him almost out of his boxers.

She yelled. "Why you fuckin' with my shit, Gerrick?!"

"Ma, it was skippin' so, I just turned it off so you could sleep ever so peacefully." he lied, heading back to his room.

"Damn, voice mail again, where is dat hoe-ass niggah?" Neeyah thought out loud as she threw the phone on the bed and laid across it.

Later on that night, she was dressed in some blue jeans overalls, her suspenders hang along the side of her waist. With a yellow buttoned-down shirt with ruffles on it and some yellow platform pumps. Big, yellow hoops dangled from her ears. She thought she was the shit. No one couldn't have told her differently. She sported a long ponytail, neatly pulled over to the side of her head, with a long piece hanging in her face. A thick coat of Strawberry Fizz from the Victoria's Secret collection, coated her lips. This particular night, she you tubed instructions on the smokey grey, cat eye look. It turned out good. When Leigha came to pick her up, she was rocking a black skirt with a transparent white laced shirt and a checkered pea coat along with some black calf high Prada boots. When they arrived, they stood in line.

"Damn, I didn't think we was gonna have to stand in a cheese line on a Tuesday night," Neeyah sighed. After they stood in the line of what seemed like forever there was an old man at the door asking for id's. Neeyah presented her id and walked through the door and stood off to the side. Leigha stepped and handed him her licence. She started through the door.

"Hold on ma'am," he stuck his hand out.

"Excuse me?" Leigha looked at him like he had utterly lost his mind.

"Your license is expired,"

"Ok and what da fuck does dat have to do with me getting inside dis' muthafucka?" she sneered. Everybody and line started hissing and getting impatient.

"It has a lot to do wid it. Are you slow? What you can't read or sumthin'? It's posted right there on dat wall in real big green letters. Next," he said, and then shifted his attention to the next person.

"Did you hear what dis' old muthafucka just said," she yelled out to Neeyah. Neeyah shook her head and sighed.

"Don't trip, come on girl let's go," Neeyah suggested. The girl behind Leigha stepped around her and handed her licence to him.

"Hell naw, becuz I'm pissed and I could really use a drink. And hold on, bitch! He's not done with me." she shifted her attention to the girl.

"I know you not gone stand there and let her blast you like dat?" someone yelled from the line. "Check off on dat bitch,"

"Wait a minute . . . Bitch? Who da fuck do you think you're talkin' to?" the girl looked around. She wasn't gonna say nothing but people kept instigating and provoked her. She didn't wanna look like no weak ass bitch

so she entertained the audience. Low key, she was scared as hell. "Is dis' bitch talkin' to you becuz I know for damn sure her ass ain't talkin' to me becuz we can get dis' shit poppin' off." she looked behind her and asked her friend. "It don't make me none, I'm bipolar. I wish a muthafucka would run up, I'll toss their ass up like a salad! Muthafuckas done lost their everlastin' mind out dis' bitch!" she shook her head.

"And I'm schizophrenic, bitch. While you over there talkin' shit like you can whoop sumthin' over here. You got me fucked all the way up," Leigha tried to step to her but somebody got in between them.

"I just wanna go home. I'm too sick I can't be out here fightin'." her friend yelled out. Then she repeated it about four more times.

"Bitch, shut your ole scary ass up. Matter of fact, jump up and click your heels three times!" Leigha screamed.

"You're just scared. If you're sick you should be at home in the bed," someone yelled. "Unlessin' you were diagnosed with scareditis,"

"If you're scared go to church," someone shouted.

"I am sick!" the girl shouted back. "Let's just go, dis' is a just a big catch 22," she tugged at her friend arm.

"Fuck you and everything you're going thru, bitch. I can give two fucks less about you and your quote unquote," Leigha put her fingers up, mimicking it. "Sudden onset illness. I'll give it to anybody dat want it so, what it do? It don't make me no never mind," Leigha screamed, moving her fist around in the air.

"I'm not wid no drama," the girl flailed her arm out and her and her friend walked off.

"Push on then, bitch." Leigha scatted her off and then shifted her attention back to the man. "Looka here you country muthafucka, I don't give a damn about your ass being no senior citizen and shit. On my mama, I'll fuck your old ass up.".

"Don't fuckin' threaten me, I'll go upside ur shit!" the old man said. No sooner than he said that, somebody held him back so Leigha couldn't get to him.

Neeyah tried to calm her down. "Fuck all dat Neeyah. His old antique ass wanna talk shit like he's 21 so umma bust him in his shit like he 21." she yelled. "If a muthafucka step to me, I promise they'll be takin' their last ride to their finally restin' place in a good four days from now. Do da math becuz I don't give ah fuck!" she looked him dead in his face and said. At first everybody was hissing an fussing, but before it was all over they were on Leigha side. A security guard pushed his way outside to see what was going on.

"Is everything ok?" he asked, looking from the man to Leigha.

"Hell naw. Yall asses can have dis' job. I quit!" he walked off. Leigha stepped through the door like nothing had ever happened.

"Bitch, you going to hell in first class . . . In front of the plane," Neeyah laughed.

"And you're seated right next to me for laughin'," they both laughed. "Girl, dat muthafucka done really pissed me off. He lucky I didn't fire on his old ass takin' me thru all them unnecessary ass motions. Ole I love my job tryna be heroic lookin' ass,"

"Come on girl respire . . . whoosaah . . . don't let him rain on your parade." Neeyah said and suggested that they go to the bar.

"Damn, bitch, since when did you become an alcoholic?"

"Girl, lately a bitch just drinkin'. Nerves and shit just gone. Shot all to hell! How 'bout last night I was gone off dat Erkel and Jerkel, straight on face book all night just crackin' up off the drama dat unfolds daily!"

"Umma need for you to stay off face book." she chuckled. "But not, Erk and Jerk, Neeyah? Where they drink dat shit at? Dat niggah got yo' ass turnin' straight to the bottle and some mo' shit. Tell the truth and shame the devil!" Leigha yelled over the loud music. "Hell you already got a beer belly,"

"And it's some good ass pussy under dis' belly too,"

"I guess I bet Gr—"

"Awww shit now. Dat's my shit!" Neeyah cut her off and then started pumping her fist in the air trying not to get Leigha started about Grievence. "Call me rude boy, boy can you get it up call rude boy are you big enough . . . Heeeey! Take it take it. Tonight umma get lil crazy. Take it." she cheesed and sang while was dropping down to the floor, doing her little nasty dance. Then they made their way to the bar and right back to the dance floor.

"Hey!" They waved their hand in the air and rocked their hips from side to side. Neeyah was doing her booty dance and flailing her arm all around. Giving everyone the business, at least in her mind she thought she was. If anyone would have told her anything but, you probably would had to fight her. She was catching a buzz and feeling herself.

She started running her hands thru her hair and rocking her hips faster to the beat. She closed her eyes and danced like nobody was watching. "Damn she finer than a mug!" a boy said walking up to her. "You feelin' yourself, aren't you shawdy?" he whispered in her ear and then walked off. He smelled so good she wanted to dance with him. When she opened her eyes, he was gone.

"Is dat Neeyah?" Grievence thought out loud, doing a double take. "Naw dat ain't her, ah niggah safe." he breathe a sigh of relief.

"Gurl, I'm tired. I done danced three songs back to back!" she said, wiping the sweat off her face with the napkin in her hand. No sooner than she turned around, she spotted Grievence in some chick face. She immediately ran over to confront him.

"That's how you feel, pimpin'?" Neeyah mushed him hard on the forehead.

"What, girl? You trippin', what da fuck are you talkin' about? And what da fuck are you doing here?" he walked off.

"Oh, so you got amnesia now? No . . . wait a minute, let me guess . . . it's selective memory, huh? You know what da fuck I'm talkin' about." she screamed, following him. "Don't walk off on me, niggah!" she yelled, jerking him around to face her. "You hugged up with dis' pop eyed buck tooth, bitch!"

The girl, Nyeisha ran to Grievence's side then suddenly, she stopped dead in her tracks, "Bitch? Who da' fuck are you callin' bitch? You know what let me rephrase dat, I am a bitch, I'm a bad bitch and you bitch, you're a sad bitch!" she yelled to the top of her lungs, staring a hole in Neeyah.

"I'm callin' you a bitch. You fuckin' gawkin' me and shit like I got sumthin' you want!" Neeyah yelled over Grievence.

"As a matter of fact, you do. Your man. On second thought, done had yo' man and can get him anytime I wants to. Dat's right bitch, our man!"

"Bitch, you don't know me. You don't wanna see me. I'll crack yo' ass!" she said, drawing her bud light bottle back.

"It's whatever. Let's do the damn thing! Nyeisha ain't never scared of no punk ass niggah or bitch. Anybody want these hands, can get'em. Believe dat."

"Bitch, you don't want none! I'll mop yo' ass out wid dat raggedy ass, ninety-nine-cent-store weave! Bald headed bitch. trust me when I say, he don't want your musty ass. He may've dicked you down, but he don't like all dat mangy lookin' shit swangin' down a bitch's back. All musty and shit!"

She charged at Neeyah. "I'm not gonna be too many more of your bitches, bitch! And you must don't know what hood I'm from and what set I roll wid?" she threw up her set. "And further more, your man hasn't never asked me for no hair to beat dis' good pussy up,"

"Bitch fuck you, your hood, and your dead homies!" Neeyah said, snapping her fingers three times.

"You got hella shit to say now, but wait til da homies roll up."

"Neeyah, Neeyah!" Grievence screamed, getting in between them. "Chill, dawg!" he shifted his attention back to Neeyah.

"Oh, so I'm your dawg now? Mighty strange I was your boo when you was fuckin' and suckin' all the cum outta my pussy last night!" she yelled in an attempt to make him mad."

"You better check yourself befo' you wreck yourself!" he glanced at Neeyah.

"Fuck you," she retorted.

"Yea, I suggest you handle your bitch befo' her ass get dealt with accordingly!" Nyeisha screamed. Then she sat back with her arms folded tightly against her chest watching and tapping her feet. Waiting on Neeyah to strike.

"Freeze yo' ass up too, bitch!" Grievence said, holding his hand up in her face. "And what da fuck are you flockin' to my side like you my bitch for, cuhz?"

"Bitch? Who, da hell is you callin' a bitch? Muthafucka, since you wanna play me, how 'bout when you ate me out, I had just got finished fuckin' my niggah. Dat's right, he nutted all in my shit, and you came like a human vacuum and sucked it all out. So how did his cum taste? Was it tart or sweet?" she teased adding gasoline to the fire.

"Bitch, I'll smash on your ass, don't ever fuckin' come at me like dat!" he said, walking to her with his fist balled up and fired on her. Nyeisha shrunk back in fear. Neeyah just shook her head in disgust and disbelief.

"Bitch ass niggah, you fired on me?" she yelled, pulling out her cell phone. "You must be ready to die becuz you just signed your own death certificate, my niggah." she screamed to him. "I cant believe dis' niggah done bombed on my ass," she held her face. "Just wait and let me call the homie's up. I bet your ass will think it's the forth of July and some mo' shit off in dis' bitch tonight. Bitch ass niggah, your ass done fucked up beyond all recognition!" she cried. "Niggah, get your ass to the club! Dis' mark ass niggah done fired on me. Get here now, niggah!" she screamed into the phone, pretending to be talking to the homies. "Yeah, niggah all yall bitch asses is about to be dropping like flies! Da homies gone be here in a New York minute!" When in truth, she didn't have a friend in the world because she stayed fucking somebody's man and was known as a shit starter. Which was why she was partying alone.

"Yea, call them niggahs. I don't give a fuck!" Grievence said. Chills went down Neeyah spine. Although he was a no good man she didn't wanna see him hurt or in no pain. She really thought the girl was talking to somebody.

When she shifted her attention to Nyeisha, she was still screaming into the phone, then all of a sudden, her phone started ringing while it was up to her ear. A surge of relief washed over Neeyah. "Just what I thought, fake ass bitch!"

"What's all the commotion about!" Leigha said walking up.

"Oh, you didn't know? Grievence is feelin' really generous again, straight giving out back shots!"

"Huh?" Leigha asked bewildered.

"Yeah, he giving out dick as usual! Straight dickin' bitches down. You know business as usual."

"You really need to be easy. For real, becuz yo' ass talkin' out da' side of your neck! I should've known better than to think tweedle dee would go somewhere without tweedle dum," he shook his head.

"Fuck all yall porch monkeys!" Nyeisha stormed off.

"Yeah, bitch, yo' mouth writin' a check yo' ass can't cash!" Neeyah yelled out to her.

"Bitch, everybody knows your bark is bigger than your bite! I see your punk ass got a little courage now but I'll see yo' ole scary punk-ass on these cold, cold streets, bitch when yo' Captain Save-a-Hoe isn't around!" she said then shifted her attention to Grievence. "And you niggah, you're ass better be incognito. Dat boo, you can take to the bank and cash it!" he tooted up his lips and shook his head.

"What, bitch? You can see me now! You don't wanna see me. I'm telling you, you don't want it!" Neeyah said, pretending like she wanted to go after her.

Neeyah was a big shit talker. The way she talked shit, you just knew she could back it up. She was more of an all-talk-and-no-action-type girl whereas, Leigha was always ready to fight. She talked shit but was always more than willing to put a bitch or niggah head to bed.

"I should've known!" Leigha rolled her eyes in the back of her head. "Same shit different day,"

"Don't even start!" he said, with his eyes trailing from her curvy body up to her sweltering eyes.

"Niggah, fuck all dis' shit, I'm tired of your dusty ass fuckin' up on my cousin! Treatin' her like she some stray ass bitch!" Leigha screamed snaking her neck, stepping to him. "Niggahs come a dime a dozen. For the life of me, I don't understand why you just don't let sleeping dogs lie,"

"Leigha gurl don't even trip." Neeyah said getting front of her, she knew her cousin was thizzing and was belligerent. Like a cobra ready to strike.

"Whateva, man you better gone wid dat hoe shit! I'm a grown ass man. You don't have shit to do with dis', always up in the damn Kool-Aid. You need to fall the fuck back. You, meddling bitch!"

"On the contrary, you fuck wid my peeps you fuck wid me, bum ass niggah! Don't make me get my cousins from da Yay, to fuck yo' pie ass up!" she said then shifted her attention back to Neeyah. "Girl, I don't know why you even waste yo' time on dis' beat-ass niggah for. He's nuthin' but a dog in heat fuckin' everything with a pussy."

"Yep sure do, til the casket drop." he said. Neeyah heard him, tried to act like didn't. "And go get your entourage, bitch. Them niggah's don't wanna see me," he said holding up his shirt. "Becuz, they can say hello to my little friend. Fuck dat, I'll bring the street sweeper out and spray all their hoe asses."

"Leigha, don't!" Neeyah pleaded, waving her off. "Please let me handle dis', he's just talkin' mess, girl," she said trying to justify what he was doing. She looked at Neeyah's beseeching eyes and decided to drop it.

"I'll be back, gurl!" Neeyah said after she got her to calm down.

"Where are you going?"

"I'm gonna go get some fresh air!"

"Aight, gurl, I'll go wid you befo' I open up a can of worms and be done split somebody shit up in dis' bitch!" she said looking dead at Grievence.

"Boss up then, bitch. You billy bad ass and shit!"

"Muthafucka you got me fucked up, I'm not no weak ass, punk ass bitch! You'll get yo' face blew off fuckin' wid me." she stepped to him. Neeyah pulled her back and tried with all her might to pin her against the wall.

"No, girl he's just talkin'!" Neeyah said trying her best to hold her back.

"Nah, boo, let her go. Becuz, if she step in my face like a niggah umma beat her like she one!"

"Homo-thug ass niggah you not gonna put your faggot ass hands on me!" she screamed a long hoarse cry. Nobody would let her get to him. "Dawg, I promise I'll fuckin' make headlines in dis' bitch to-night, on my mama!" she screamed even louder, trying to break away. "Dawg, on everything! Your mama will find your ass stretched out on your back wid your hands folded neatly across your chest!" she laughed to keep from crying more.

"Lee, get your homeboy and take'em home!" Neeyah screamed, happy to see him.

He dropped his cup and scooped him up. "Yo, she's a female, dawg!"

"Fuck all dat. I'll beat his mark ass like I'm the niggah and he's the bitch! Let'em go and watch me!" Leigha shrieked as he disappeared in the

crowd. "Let me go. I promise, once you let me go umma bomb on your ass!" she yelled to the boy holding her back. To their knowledge, Grievence was leaving the club.

"His bitch-ass got me fucked up! On my mama, I'll fuck him up quick and burry his ass in the woods!" Leigha screamed punching the palm of her hands with her fists. Tears flowed freely down her face. "What da fuck, dis' has got to be a fuckin' dream. Muthafuckas wanna test me tonight. On my mama, the next bitch dat so much as look at me the wrong way, is getting these hands!"

"Girl, calm down he's not even worth it,"

"Damn, you done finally woke up and came to your senses. That's what I been tellin' you all along. So hopefully you gonna utilize your own advice and leave his bitch ass alone." Leigha screamed. Neeyah didn't reply she just stared at her with a blank look. She knew Leigha was just talking out of anger. "You know what boo, I'm sorry I shouldn't've said dat.

"You cool, I love you cousin," Neeyah hugged her.

"Right back atcha. I'm not gonna let him rain on my parade!" she said heading to the bar. Neeyah headed outside to let the windy breeze soothe her. She just knew it was about to be some bloodshed. Leigha was so mad she was ready to paint the whole club red, with his blood. While sitting outside on the curb, she tried her best not to cry, but she was over and beyond hurt.

The more she tried to suppress her tears, the more her eyes watered. The sky above was crisp and clear. Also filled with many bright stars, of different shapes and sizes. The moon was full and bright, which seemed to illuminate the entire sky.

"It's not beautiful as you." The boy that was watching her on dance floor said. He noticed she was staring at the full moon.

"Excuse me!" she shot, looking up at him. When she recognized his fragrance she said, "You,"

"Da' moon shawdy." he said pointing at it. "Do you mind if I join you? You look like you can use some company!" he said in a low tone.

She closed her legs and wiped her eyes. "I look dat bad. But, actually, dat won't be a good idea. My niggah's in there."

"Who you talkin' about, at mark dat just played you for ole' girl back there?"

She shot him a look that said *how you know.* "Don't worry, baby girl, I wasn't spying or on no stalkerish shit like dat but you guys caused quite a commotion!"

"Really, wow!" she said, running her pointer finger from the corner of her eye underneath the bottom of it. To stop any tears from running down her face. Every time she talked she looked around, making sure Grievence was nowhere in sight. Where you from anyway?"

"From da A, shawdy."

"A?" Neeyah asked perplexed.

"Atlanta shawdy. Well, look, umma just leave you wid dis' shawdy, let's see how I can delicately put dis' . . . ummm, long as you allow him to treat you wrong; then he's gonna do it. Take it from me, shawdy, I'm a man." he said pushing himself up from the sidewalk. "Let me dissect it for ya shawdy," he said hitting the back of right hand in the palm of his left hand. "It's very simple, real men wouldn't disrespect you. I'm not sayin' they want cheat per se; I'm sayin' you want know about it. Just some, food for thought! In a real way." he said as he turned to leave. After she watch him vanish into thin air, she sat a while pondering what he had said. Then she glanced at her watch and decided it was time to head inside. She stood to her feet to straighten out her clothes, then she open up her purse and pulled out her mirror. "Damn, my eyes is puffy as hell, fuck!" she said running the palm of her hand to the back of her head to smooth out the kinks in her ponytail.

Doing a quick scan of the club, Grievence thought Neeyah had left. So, when he was leaving with some otha chick he had just met, his eyes met Neeyah just as she closed her mirror. Not bothering to say one word, to him she sprinted towards the door.

"Neeyah! Neeyah!" he yelled running after her. She didn't stop, instead she picked up her pace to try to get away from him. Finally he caught her. "It isn't what you think. That's Deuce's boo thang and I was just droppin' her off where he was."

She huffed and puffed picking up her pace. "Just leave me alone!"

"Girl, stop for a minute!" he said, grabbing shoulder. "Just let me explain!" he panted.

"Getcha your filthy hands off of me. There is nuthin' to explain! Dis' shit is not debatable. I bet you fuckin' her too, straight keepin' dat shit in the family, huh?" he shook his head no. "Of course you are? Trust me when I say, dick and pussy don't have a conscience when they come together." she said, shrugging her shoulders and wrinkling up her nose.

"What?" he asked with a baffled look.

"Your dick head don't head don't have a brain." he flashed a blank stare. Still lost. "Uggh . . . I really don't have time to be out here dissecting shit but trust me when I say 9 hours of darkness is a long ass time."

"Stop trippin', ever since you been hangin' out wid Leigha, it's like—"

"It's like what?" she screamed cutting him off. "I'm no longer lettin' you walk all over me like a rug, huh?" she said mad as hell with her hands on her hips.

"Baby, just com'ere!" he said with his arms outstretched.

She looked at him as if he was crazy. "Come on now, I know you're not as stupid as you look and I'm not dumb as I look! You need to reach into your ass and try to find sumthin' new, becuz what worked so well for you before isn't now." she chuckled sum. He shook his head. "What da fuck are you shakin' your head for? I see you're ass is quieter than a church mouse now. But yes niggah, just in case your ass didn't get the memo, as you can see my ass done woke up and smelt da coffee," she said, trying her damnest with every fiber of her being, to repress her feelings. Slowly dying in the inside. He stared at her like she had utterly lost her mind.

"Oh, it's like dat?"

"You made it like dat! Now, run along." she flung her arm around in the air. "I don't want you to keep yo' bitch waitin' on my behalf!"

"Okay, would you like to ride with me to satisfy your insecurities?"

"Insecurities? Niggah, please!" she giggled. "Insecurities, are you fuckin' serious? How many times have yo' bitch ass cheated on me? You know what, get da' fuck on wid dat lame shit!" she scatted him off and giggled some more to keep from crying. She wanted to break down and say, *I wanna roll witd you, boo.*

"If dat's how you feel, I'll call you later!"

"Poof, I hope you gone," she held her hand up in his face. "Do you, boo! Do you, becuz it's yo' thang. I can't tell you who to sock it to!" she said, with tears welling up in her eyes. She was beyond hurt.

"I love you girl, why are you actin' like dis'? I wouldn't cheat on you no more. Not since I fucked up the last time."

"Grievence, why are you takin' me on dis' trip and the cold part is, I didn't even ask to go?!" she seemingly stared a hole thru his body."

"What da fuck are you talkin' about."

"I'm talkin' about you brain fuckin' me with all these lies!"

He flung his arm around. "Whateva, I'm out."

"Push on then, niggah!" she scatted him away.

"You know what, that's your problem if you wanna inflict unnecessary pain on yourself."

"Scuse' me? Come again,"

"If you don't know, just like you just told me, I don't have time to dissect." he chucked up the deuces.

"Keep hope alive!" she yelled out to him. He threw two fingers up as he kept stepping. "I knew your ass didn't give a damn about nobody but yourself no way. I guess every man for himself,"

"And god for us all," he yelled back to her as he disengaged his locks on his door. She stood fuming, with her hands folded tightly against her breast. Her heart started accelerating while she watched as he and the girl got in his Monte Carlo and sped off. It felt like her heart was slowly and painfully, rising up outta her body, like in spirit and trampled on. Five minutes later, she was still in same spot. His car a disappeared in complete darkness. It was almost as if she was expecting him to return in any moment.

Her subconscious kicked in. "Fuck him. Fuck dat niggah!" she mumbled and shook her head. Then she stuck her hand in her purse to find her compact mirror. "I'm about to let these niggah's have it," she said checking her eyes and smoothing back any hair out of place. By, the time she closed her mirror, Leigha was coming out.

"Come on, girl, I'm frazzled! A niggah all thizzed out, and horny as fuck!"

"Whaaaaat? I was just going in to get me a drink!"

"Naw, dawg, I'm about ta dipset!"

"Ugh, you such a party pooper." Neeyah sighed.

"Whateva, hoe, I'm 'bout ta' twirk sumthin'. I met dis' lil' cutie and it's 'bout ta' go down." she said walking toward the parking lot. Their conversation raised over the noise their heels were making, going across the parking lot. "Damn, I didn't realize I parked in the boonies."

"Nasty, hoe. Don't nobody want dat ocean pussy,"

"Bitch you scantless. My shit is so tight I can smoke a blunt with it. I'm in da know, you better ask around,"

"More like an big ass Garcia Vega," Neeyah coughed. "But, true story, dat's not what I heard. Loose cootie, Judy."

"Don't hate on me, becuz a bitch 'bout ta' get her swerve on. If yo' ass would've been inside the club instead of out here rackin' yo' brain 'bout dat lame-ass niggah, then you could have found you a lil' boo thang too! Or then again, I know yo' ass ain't bout finna mess with nobody, but his busta-ass!"

Wishful thinking! Neeyah thought. She wasn't gonna hardly fuck nobody but Grievence. "Whateva, just because I don't hoe and tell, don't mean dat dis' booty don't be movin' boo. I'll move sumthin'—"

"Yeah, from your mouth to God ears. Like I said, your ole scary ass ain't even gonna venture out and fuck nobody else." Leigha cut her off.

"Girl, you just don't know me as well as you think. How bout low key, one night me and the home girl Jerrica, linked up with some dudes from face book—"

"Um where was I ma'am?" Leigha cut her off.

"Boo'd up. But, anyway we agreed to meet at Apple Bee's. He told me what he was wearing so I would notice him, right,"

"Right,"

"How about soon as ole boy walked thru the door, I was like oh hell to the naw and we ducked our asses down until they left."

"You scantless for dat, bitch,"

"No the hell I'm not. His ass looked like a pudgy ass Umpah Lumpah. Twenty minutes later, he sent a text to Jerrica's phone talkin' bout some yall bitches flaked. I was like how your ass gone have a profile picture up of you before all the big macks and chicken sandwiches you scarfed down. To make matters worse, he sent me hella pictures of a his toned and ripped body. My ass was too heated. Dat very incident proved that anybody could be hiding behind the computer screen. Anyways, your ass just go by 7-Eleven. So I can get me a twelve-pack of Heinekens."

"I told your ass about face book. But you're tryna be blowed and some mo' shit, huh?" Neeyah didn't respond. She was too busy thinking about Grievence. Wondering was he gonna eat the girl out like he did to her. Or was he kissing her ever so passionate, like he did to her.

"Uggh!" she sighed.

"Damn, bitch what's your problem? Blowin' and shit."

"Nah niggah, don't trip. I'm just havin' a moment."

"I guess, bitch! I'm bout ta' twirk sumthin'." Leigha said doing her little thizzle dance in her seat at the red light.

Neeyah remained mute and forced a big smile to her face. "I'm happy for you. I'm just elated!" she said, wriggling out of her thin jacket.

"Damn, do I sense some hater-ration in the air, dawg!" Leigha grabbed Neeyah's arm.

"Fuck you!" Neeyah sneered, jerking away from her.

"As a matter of fact here's a flick we took!" Leigha delved through her purse to find it.

"Damn, bitch, don't you know what it means to clean out your purse!" she noticed how she was flinging stuff everywhere.

"Here, hater!" she said, handing her the photo. Then she started singing, and waving, "Hi hater hi hater bye hater bye hater."

"Are you fuckin' serious, hate on you? He must be . . . what? Sixteen?" Neeyah asked inquisitively looking at it.

"What are you insinuatin'?" Leigha asked looking over at Neeyah, out of the corner of her eye.

"I'm just makin' an observation, boo and stating the obvious!"

"He's eighteen, I believe. Why? Damn all dat. Check out our thizz faces!"

"Becuz, I wanna know, dat's why. He look hella young. Yo' old robbin' the cradle lookin' ass!"

"Hey, I'm wid da no child left behind committee, I take'em at sixteen and a half!" she laughed.

"Bitch, you silly!"

"I'm playin'!"

"Naw, hoe, don't try and switch up. You for real, don't let me find out."

"Find out what?"

"Dat yo' ass is a tree jumper and shit!"

"Bitch, fuck you." Leigha said flipping her off.

"Do he work?"

"Damn, bitch, you cross-examinin' me or sumthin'?"

"I'm just curious!"

"I'm beginnin' to feel like you interrogatin' me wid all these pointless ass questions. Becuz, all you need to noe is at a bitch is about to get her swerve on. His ass is at the club, so he has to be at least eighteen. If not, then oh fuckin' well—but judgin' by the way his dick was bulgin' outta his slacks, he has ta be grown!" she said biting down on her bottom lip. Having a flash back on when he came up behind her and started grinding on her on the dance floor.

"Hot ass!"

"Call me what you wanna, but you will neva call me brozoke! Cause a bitch definitely make them niggahs break bread befo' anything go down. Like my niggah Weezy say, *It ain't trickin' if you got it.* Furthermore, I screw'em one day and fuck'em da next day. Not puttin' my heart in shit, becuz bastards these days rip dat shit out and stomp on yo' shit right in your face. And then on to da next bitch, as easily as they came in your life, they'll leave as fast as their feet will carry them."

"You couldn't've used a better choice of words."

"Yup, that's why my ass say, fuck'em and feed'em grapes."

"I feel you. But, it's sad becuz there's still dat 10% out there dat isn't like dat."

"To bad so sad. I'm shittin' on all their asses and not feelin' no sympathy for none. I'm like fuck you pay me, bitch! Trust me when I tell you, I tell a niggah quick, fuck you and everything your going thru."

"Dis' a cold cold world. Roll with it or get rolled over."

"Sho you right. Becuz a bitch like me can give a fuck less." Leigha said, pushing the cigarette lighter in.

"If you can't beat'em—"

"Join'em," Leigha cut her off.

GUESS WHO BAZZACK

Ring, ring. Grievence mounted his head. To his dismay, his mom had purposely put the phone beside him. *Damn, I thought I was dreamin'*, he thought as the phone continued to ring. He narrowed his eyes and glanced at the caller ID. It displayed an unavailable call. By then, it had stopped ringing. He buried his head back into the many pillows on his bed. Ring, ring.

"Ain't dis' a bitch, as soon as a niggah get comfortable!" Ring, ring. "What the fuck, another unavailable call?" he pressed the end button. No sooner than his head hit the pillow, the phone started ringing again—quick reflex caused him to answer the phone. "I swear if dis' a hoe ass bill collector, on my mama they gone get da business!" he said, pushing himself up. The recording had already started when he put the phone to his ear.

"Hello, dis' is Evercom from Mound Correctional Facility with a collect call from Swagga." the recording said. Swagga got his name because people loved his swagger. Antonio "Swagga" Phillips, stood about six feet two inches, medium build caramel skin tone that would put you in the mind of Trey Songz with a haircut. He kept a low haircut with waves. He was definitely a ladies' man. The recording continued to play, "Please listen to this message and its entirety before making your selection as there's a new system. If you would like to accept the call, please press 2; to refuse press 0 for rates press 1. Thanks for using Evercom. Standard rates apply. Your call is now being connected."

"What up, doe niggah?" Grievence cheerfully spoke into the phone.

"What's good witcha, bruh bruh? A niggah was beginnin' to think my call was gonna get refused and shit!"

"Naw, dawg, the number was comin' up unavailable. I thought it was a bill collector. But at any rate, how have you been?"

"Man, tryna survive and maintain my sanity. That's all, but I do have some great news!"

"Word?" he said, anxious to hear the good news.

"There was a new law passed dat all cases dat of related to crack can get your sentence reduced two to three years. Being said, I got my approval back not even ten minutes ago, and, niggah, I'll be touchin' down in two days, my niggah!" he screamed happily into the phone.

"That's what's up, doe!"

"Tell moms, don't trip on the bill, I know dis' call is costin' twenty-five bucks, but I'll double dat in a sec!"

"I see," he said not wanting to rain on his brother's parade. However, he couldn't believe what he was hearing. He wasn't no-slow leak, by far. I *guess some things never change* he thought to himself. You see, the streets were his glue and he didn't know no other way of life. "So are you gonna come to Calli when you touch down?"

"You already know I'm D'in dis' thing out. I'm gonna stay true to my roots."

"Well, I'm true to my roots. That's my home, never ran neva will. But, Detroit is not da' business right now. It's hella gutter—."

"Okay, you act like you just now findin' dat out." Swagga cut him off.

"Naw, it isn't like dat. There's no jobs there and I'm tired of dat cold-ass weather. You should come out here. Its very beautiful and jobs pay hella good!"

"I don't mean any harm or disrespect, but miss me with dat getting-a-job shit! I work for myself. Picture dat, me workin' a nine to five. Dat shit is such a derisory."

"De-fuckin' what? You know what never mind I wonder why niggahs always wait 'til they go to the penitentiary and then become all educated and shit!" Grievence said. They both fell out laughing.

"It means it's fuckin' hilarious, niggah. Get a dictionary pimpin'. On a more serious note, I'm good on movin' out there, the D. is all I noe. Besides, umma link up with dis' sweet tender thang thang, dat live over in River Terrace."

"Aren't those apartments?" Grievence asked. "Off what?"

"It's off Jefferson and Grand." he said after giving him a few seconds to respond. "It's across from Belle Aisle. I intend to use her until I can see straight again. Right now, shit is just a little obscured. Besides, I have dis' Italian guy, dat made me a promise dat once I get outta here, he was gonna look out for me. 'Bout two weeks ago, my celly and I saved his son's life when a pack of mahfuckas, tried to shank him to death. I got shanked twice, in the stomach and the other one in my side." he added.

Grievence scratched his head. "Damn, brut, them niggah's tried to take you out the game."

"They tried but you know I'm soldierin' dis'. But, as I was sayin', I don't really know what it's gone be, but I do know it's gonna be sweeeeet!" he said, rubbing his hands together. "I can just taste it already. I'll tell you more 'bout it face-to-face."

"And you need me for . . . ?" Grievence asked still a little puzzled.

"I need you to come to the D and help me for a hot min while I get things poppin'!"

"I dunno, man. I have a girl and a job out here."

"Lemme, ask you dis' lil' brut, how much are you getting paid? Never mind dat. I can promise you'll be able to quadruple it in a week's time. Well, look I'm not askin' you to answer now, but I don't trust anybody else. I thought who else better than my little knuckleheaded brother. It'll be nice, we'll be able to catch up on old times. So how's Ma Duke?"

"She's okay. You know long as she got her beer and Newports, she's a happy camper. She been stressin' a lil on her truck payments, doe."

"That's my mama. Damn, she ain't gotta stress imma pay dat thang off. Find out how much she need but, It's really good hearin' your voice, man!"

"Likewise, Brut and I will!"

"Moms ridin' high in da big boy Avalanche all rimmed up, huh?"

"Yup, it's candy painted. Candy apple red at dat. She thinks she's the business."

"Leave my mommy alone. She is sumthin' else doe,"

"Hell, I wanna be like her when I grow up." Grievence said and they both laughed.

"She gave you da Monty didn't she?"

"Yup."

"Well, stick some shoes on dat baby."

The operator interrupted the call, "You now have sixty seconds left on dis' call."

"Well, you go ahead and link up with Deuces to see if he's game. Sleep on what I said, weigh your options. I'm not asking you guys to move out here. It's just temporary. Tell Ma the good news and I'll be—" The phone cut off.

Grievence picked up his cell phone and noticed that he forgot to power it up. He did so, heading to the bathroom. As he got closer to the living room, soothing sounds of *Let's Get It On* by Marvin Gaye filled the room. His mom was lying on the couch dead to the world while, the music played unremittingly in the background, as usual. Music was her world, she would

fuck somebody up quick for her cds, records and tapes that she keep neatly stacked on two big stands. When he made it up the hallway, the scent of fried chicken hit him. He went directly to the kitchen, "Giving your love to me could never be wrong if love true ooh, baby, let's get it on come on, baby, I don't wanna rush let your love come down." he sang his own lyrics while, two-stepping. His mom had cooked fried chicken, macaroni and cheese, mashed potatoes corn bread and okra.

"Now that's what's up," he said, looking in each pot on the stove. "Hot water cornbread, now dat's what I'm talkin' about!" he said noticing it in the microwave. "Now, Maryland put her foot in dat mac and cheese!" he said putting the last of it in his mouth. There was nothing left on his plate, not even a crumb so he put it in the sink and headed to the refrigerator. Soon as he opened it, he spotted his favorite, a caramel cake. "Oh hell naw!" he snatched it up. When he walked out of the kitchen, he was full and rubbing his belly.

"I love my mama," he said softly as he kissed her on the forehead while she slept as if she didn't have a care in the world. He and his mom had a good relationship. Although, she talked a lot when she was drinking, they were still very close. Maryland had been thru a lot and not only that, she grew up surrounded by a whole family of street niggas. That in itself made her street smart. He knew his mom meant well and that she was tryna to radiate tough love. All and all, she was his number one lady and Neeyah kind of envied it. When he looked at his phone he noticed a lot of missed calls from Neeyah.

"Hi, Ms. Lara, how are you today?"

"I'm okay, and you Gerrick?"

"I'm good. Is Neeyah around by any chance?"

"Wait just a minute, baby"

"Neeeeeeeeyah," she screamed. There was no answer so she called out again.

"Yeah, Maa." she said, drowsily.

"The phone."

"I got it."

"What up, doe?" Grievence said in a sexy tone.

"Babe," she said in a raspy voice.

"Was you sleep, boo?"

"Yeah, I had a long day. So how was your night, incognito and shit?"

"Whoo weee, I can smell yo' breath. Boo, I don't want to argue. I'm havin' a good day. I went straight home. I asked you to roll and you turned

me down, so what can you say? I should be askin' you 'bout dat niggah dat was all in yo' grill. But dat's the difference between you and me. I trust you and you need to trust dat I won't let nuthin' or nobody come between us." he flipped it.

"Yeah, I hear you!" she said dryly. Just like that she had let it go.

"What's dat 'pose ta' mean?"

"Yeah, niggah, you talk a good game!"

"Keep on talkin' mess, umma box yo' ass out!"

"Whateva, niggah. I ain't neva scared. I can whoop you wid one hand tied behind my back! And dat, boo is a fair warning." she giggled a little. Just that quick she had let go of the night before at the club.

"Keep on when I see you, you're gonna have to put your money where your mouth is, chump! Just play wid it that's what I want you to do. You do not want these hands, trust and believe. But shid, what's good, doe? You blew a niggah phone up. What's the good news?" Without giving her a chance to respond, he started guessing. "You preggo, got a new better-paying job, I mean what? I'm hyperventilating over here,"

"That's how you feel, niggah?" she asked sleepily.

"Naw, I'm playin'. I'm anxious to hear dis good news of yours!"

"Well, to answer your question, no and no!" she decided against telling him about her entitlement just to see how would their relationship play out. Sorta like a probationary period. "I just wanted to tell you dat I loved you sooo much and—

"And?" he cut her off.

"I can't wait to suck your long hard dick!" she blurted out. Grievence took the phone from his ear and looked at it to make sure he it was her, that he was talking to. "Hello, are you there, punk? I'm tryna give some good Becky," she teased.

"I'm here, boo."

"Well, are you gonna respond, Negro?"

"I'm just appalled. Speechless, would be a better choice of word. Well in dat case, Becky, Becky marry me."

"You silly," she giggled. She was so in love with him to the point where all he really had to do was apologize and the were back on track.

"What time is, baby?"

"It's a little after seven," she squinted her eyes to see the time.

"I'll tell you what, I'm gonna hit the gym up, shower, and then I'll slide over there."

It was music to her ears. "Okay, babe, I'll be waitin'. Love you,"

"I love you more," he replied. She immediately got up and powered on the stereo to get her in the cleaning mood.

"Damn, let me clean dis' tiny-ass room. My ass done procrastinated long enough," she looked around her room in disgust. *Damn, what am I gonna wear to Apple's party, all these clothes is so obsolete.* she thought.

Whenever Grievence went to her place and intended to spend the night, he'll let Deuces drive him over. He learned the hard way about the projects. One night after work, he went to her crib to spend the night. He awoke the next morning to find some dull-ass hubcaps. Whoever did it, done it to profession. To the point of picking out some that looked just like his rims. It was like a dagger in the heart because he had never worked so hard in life to pay for something he wanted. He'd worked over two months of overtime to pay for them. Hell, he worked longer to get them than he had them on his car. Oftentimes when he walked out of Neeyah's apartment, he would have flash backs of how he use to park directly under the street light, because he loved the way the it coruscated on his rims when he was walking up on it.

"Good mornin', sleepyhead!" Grievence said, kissing her on her forehead.

"Likewise, boo."

"Whoa," he said catching a whiff of her morning breath. "Warn a niggah before you start whisperin'," he said holding his head back and then he leaned in to kiss her. "I'm jokin', but you do have dat dragon just dancin' on yo' shit!"

"Whateva, you been havin' hella jokes lately. Just feelin' yourself, huh?"

I know one thing, say sumthin' else and we gone lock up!" she said, with her voice deeper than his.

"Girl, please. You don't want none. I already owe you a fist sandwich for talkin' all dat mess on the phone, but umma let you pass since I beat dat thing up hella good."

"Boy, please! I done told yo' pompous ass."

He showed her his muscles. "Play wid it lil girl. Just keep on, umma have yo' ass all lumped up in dis' bitch and please turn your head toward the wall when you talk."

"Whatever, boy. My little brother's muscles are bigger than dat'!"

"Boy?"

"That's what I said. Little-ass boy dat live at home with his mama!" she joked.

He grabbed her arm and put it behind her back.

"Stop, boy! You play too much then you tryna take my words and shit. Get yo own shit, swagga jacker!" she laughed.

"Dis' is a citizen's arrest!" he said in a deep squeaky voice. "Say man."

"Boy! Boy! Boy!"

He tightened his grip on her arm. "Okay, we can do dis' all day. I ain't got shit else to do."

"Okkkkkkkay, man."

"Dat's what I thought."

"You still a chump, punk!" she said, pushing him softly. She just loved everything about him. He made her laugh and smile even when she felt like shit inside. She loved his dirty drawers.

"Ok now, umma crack yo' ass. On some real as shit, you did your thing last night."

"Yeaah," she said coyly.

"What time are you gonna pick up your check up?"

"I dunno, are you takin' me?"

"Yeah, I can shoot you over there and swoop it up. It's nuthin', boo," he said with a seductive look. "Damn, I got cramp in my neck—fuck! Dis' dis' tiny-ass bed," he massaged his neck trying to soothe the pain.

"You always got jokes. Ha ha ha, very funny." she laughed.

"Naw, dawg, I'm serious as cancer. There isn't shit funny about wakin' up to cramps."

"Whatever, stop being so sensitive."

"Can you get a niggah some juice or sumthin'? Besides have diarrhea of the mouth." he said. Soon as the words rolled off his tongue, she hopped up and did as told. On her way out of her door, she grabbed her robe that was ridden with holes. "Damn, girl, time for another one. Seems like you've worn the threads outta dat one."

"Hint, hint," she smiled.

"Don't trip, babe I'll get you another one."

Soon as she disappeared through the door, he powered up his phone; to call Deuces to come swoop him up. He never had his cell phone on in her presence. She often wondered why it never rang while they were together, but didn't speak on it because she didn't wanna self inflict no unnecessary pain on herself. She felt like all men cheated and did things and what he did when he left her door, she had no control over.

"Boo, you go ahead and take your shower. Umma go wait for Deuces. I'll be back in one hour, so be ready." he said imperatively.

"Fa sho, I'll be ready."

When he left, the scent from his dreads lingered behind.

"Damn, I almost forgot to call Leigha," she dived across the bed to get the phone.

"What it is boo?" Neeyah said happily into the phone after Leigha answered.

"Nuthin' much, shid just woke up, not too long ago. But shid what's good, doe?" Leigha replied in a masculine tone.

"I'm just tryna see was you still going to ole girl's party tonight?"

"Hell yea. Shid a niggah gotta go hit Rah Rah's ass up for some dough, I really don't wanna go fuck with his ass. I'm not tryna mislead his ass!"

"I hear you girl. Well, I'm getting ready to go pick my check up. Maybe later we can get up and hit da Galleria up."

"Okay, fa sho."

"So, how are you wearin' your hair, Neeyah?"

"I had my mama perm it last night. Probably just a body wrap, and you?"

"I dunno, I'm tryna debate on going to dis packed-ass salon. I want me some twists and spiral curls, over to the side. But, umma see what's good and keep you posted," she said, and then ended the call.

I WANNA DO SOMETHING,
FREAKY YOU

"Honeee, honeee," Ricky whispered, as he slowly scooted towards her back, kissing it multiple times. She was still in mourning over Omar. As she laid lost in thought, she wondered what it would've been like to share her bed with him once again. Her thoughts quickly diverted to the day she'd met him. It was a cold, snowy day. Her mom asked her to go the corner store to get her and her younger siblings something to eat. Being that it was knee high snow out, she put on three layers of clothing and a big wool coat to top it off. Back then, coats had big buttons the size of quarters, that you fasten with latches. Before she walked out the door, she stuck her feet in her mom's size ten iron toe boots. She never would forget, how she tussled through the snow and how big of a mistake it was to be dressed in three layers of clothing. When she stepped one foot onto the icy sidewalk, it gave away. She tumbled down the hill. She was so mortified. When she looked up, she saw a group of teenage boys standing by the store. They were having a snowball fight. All of a sudden when they noticed her, they started throwing them at her while, she laid helpless on the ground. Then out of the blue, one of the boys motioned for them to stop, as he ran over to her. When their eyes met while he was helping her up to her feet, she knew there was a deep connection. It was Omar; he then 14 yrs old. She still remembered his beautiful starry eyes and how perfect and white his teeth were. Being that he was two shades past a Hershey bar. Most important of all, how his huge gleaming smile would lighten up the darkest night. In the beginning, everything seemed so perfect. He walked her to school every morning, and even carried her books to class for her. Not long after she gave up her virginity, she started seeing less and less of him. Before long, he completely stop going to see her. When she found out she was

pregnant, her mom made her learn the hard way about being grown and fast. Which she didn't care, because she was so euphoric, to be having one of the most popular boys in school, child. Unfortunately, the feeling wasn't at all mutual because when he saw her coming, he would quickly go in the opposite direction. She just knew having his baby would keep him gracing her presence, or so she thought. "What's up, baby?" she said dryly, with her back still turned.

"You already know, I'm feeling kinda . . . you know . . ." he said, licking and blowing her ear. "I wanna do something freaky to you, baby right now baby," he sang softly in her ear.

"I don't feel good, baby," she said, before it went any further.

Everybody, knows when you're not no longer feeling a person you don't even want them to touch you in no kind of way. Having sex with you is like reading the Reader's Digest. So fall your fat humpty dumpty ass back. she wanted to say.

"What's wrong now? Matter of fact, turn toward me!" he demanded, grabbing her shoulder. "I mean you've taken two days off of work, I mean what?!" Ricky said throwing his hands in the air. As if he was surrendering.

He looked into her eyes. She returned his stare, with a blank look, as if she hadn't fully clutched what he said. She was thinking of a way to answer. She knew he was about to lose his tetchy temper, the last thing she wanted to happen. He tapered his keen eyes, smaller. "Don't tell me it's dat niggah, Omar? Hell yeah, of course dat's what it is. Your ass been moping around here since you found out. I can't believe dis' shit you on," he said jumping up outta the bed with his little pecker sticking straight out. "I'm going to sleep on the couch," he grabbed his pillow.

She didn't say one word. Instead, she got up and started getting dressed. On his way to the couch, he caught a good glimpse of Neeyah coming outta the bathroom with her hole-ridden robe on. As soon as the air hit her, it made one of her nipples protrude from one of the holes.

"I thought you guys were sleepin'?" she said, brushing past him with water still dripping from her body. Oblivious that her nipple was sticking out. This made him hornier.

"I'm going downtown to pay some bills and visit my sister," Ms. Lara said grabbing her keys from the kitchen counter and heading towards the door. "Can you please feed Junior when he wakes up?" she said, closing the door behind her, without giving Ricky a chance to respond. "Neeyah, Neeyah!" she yelled back inside.

"Yeah, Ma."

"Grievence is out here waitin' on you."

"Tell 'em I'll be right out." she yelled back. Not completely dry, she sprayed on some body splash and then she slipped into her *Pink by Victoria's Secret* tracksuit.

"Maa, wait!" Sonny shouted. "Where are you going?"

"I gotta go downtown and pay some bills. Why, son?"

"I need to ride with you, becuz Auntie Pam is giving me forty dollars for raking her yard."

"Well, you better hurry your behind up. I'll be in car."

"I wanna go," Junior said rubbing his eyes, barely awake.

"No, you stay here, wid yo' crusty face," Sonny teased. "Always somewhere smellin' gas."

"Leave me alone," he whined, with his bottom lip poked out.

"Uh huh no you're not. You're too old for dat, boy!" Neeyah said turning the TV on Saturday cartoons. "Go wash all dat crust outta your eyes and brush your teeth. Your dad is gonna fix you some cereal," she said, grabbing a comb and heading for the door.

"You're back early." she said, closing the car door.

"Yeah, I went by the crib and moms wasn't home. I had left my key on my dresser. So what you got up for today, boo?"

"Nuthin' much, Leigha and I suppose to get up sometime today. But, dat's about it. Why, what's good?" she asked, cheerfully.

"Calm down boo, just tryna make conversation," he said, looking back to make sure it was safe to switch lanes. "Oh yeah, I told my mama about our plans on getting our crib," he continued.

"Yeah?" she asked, interestedly. "What did she say?"

"Dat we wasn't ready yet."

"So, what do you think?"

"Honestly, I think we should continue to stack our paper. We still gonna do what it do, don't worry." he said, stroking her face. "Baby, I'm ready to move you up outta them raggedy shits. It's just gonna take a little more time doe." Her face lit up like a Christmas tree.

Damn, my boo look oh so good, she thought staring at him. His lips continued to move. All she could think about was how lucky she was to have such a fine man, of his caliber. To call her man and how nothing could ever take his love away. She tried to concentrate on what he was saying.

"Bay, you heard me?"

"Yeah, I heard you." she lied.

"Oh yeah, I meant to tell you dat Swagga is touchin' down today."

"That's what's up!" she replied. "Is he coming out here?"

"To be honest, I think hell would have to freeze over before my bullheaded brother came to these here parts. Another thing . . ." he paused, debating on whether to tell her about Swagga's request.

"What is it, baby?" she asked in a concerned tone.

He decided against telling her. "My bad, boo, I just lost my train of thought for a moment. I just wanted to tell you how nice you look. Your hair is so pretty!" A big smile flashed across her face.

"You think so? It look okay, I permed it myself."

"Girl, stop being so modest and give yourself credit." he said stroking her hair. That really put her on cloud nine.

"Babe, I was thinkin' on the way home, you can stop at Sprint—"

"What do you need to go to Sprint for, Neeyah?!" he said cutting her off with veins protruding out of the side of his neck.

"I-I-I," she began to stutter. "Thought I would get a cell phone."

"You supposed to be stackin' money, not spendin' it on a hoe-ass cell phone. You got me fucked up, if you think for one minute I'm gonna be saving while you spendin'. But, at the same time, it's your money, do you." he said sticking in his favorite CD, none other than a Lil Wayne mixed cd. "The best rapper alive. Weezzy babee. Hello, muthafucka hey hi—hi, you're doing it's wezzy f. baby, come to take a shit and urine on the toilet bowl bitches, puss ass niggah's." he rapped. She sat still thinking of a way to make her boo talk to her.

"Is dat da one song of Lil' Wayne wid Drake and nem?" she asked, trying to make conversation.

"Yeah, dis' shit go hard!" he said dryly. The rest of the ride was quiet.

"Juuuunior!" Ricky yelled.

"Yeah, Daddy." he said, running out with toothpaste all around his mouth.

He motioned for him to kneel down. "Come here, son."

"I'm not even done brushin' my teef!" Junior yelled holding the toothbrush up.

"Dat's okay, just come over here." Ricky said, jacking himself up and down. "Get on your knees." he said in a very low tone, sitting up on the edge of the couch. "Here put it in your mouth, just like other day," he said, thinking about Neeyah. Imagining it was her. The phone rang very loud startling him, causing him to jump. Scaring Junior, making him bite down hard on his it. "Fuccccccccccck!" he screamed, pushing Junior off of him and doubling over in pain. "Helllllo." he said into the phone, cupping himself tightly.

"Is you all right, honey?" Ms. Lara asked in a very concerned tone.

"I'm okay, just havin' one of them damn back spasms again." he lied.

Junior started to cry. She was calling to apologize for the way she had been acting, realizing that over the years, Ricky had been good to her and the kids.

"What is dat boy crying for?"

"Oh, he's still crying wantin' you." Ricky lied with tears welling up in his eyes.

"Tell him if he doesn't stop crying, he's not gonna get these toys his auntie Pam got him."

"Junior, your mom said if you don't dry those crocodile tears, then you won't get the toys your auntie bought you," he said still in pain. Junior immediately stopped crying. Almost as quick as they rolled down his face.

"What kind of toys?" Junior happily screamed with his nose running down into his mouth.

"Go, clean your nose, boy and finish brushing your teeth." Ricky said pointing down the hallway. "Ok honey I'll see you when you get home." he said, ending the call.

Ricky unlocked the door then headed back to their bedroom. When he removed his hand, all he could see was swelling. "Oh my gosh!" he panicked.

Then he immediately ran into the kitchen to get some ice cubes. Scared shitless, he decided to use a plastic bag from the grocery store. He placed the bag in his boxers and got dressed.

"I love you, baby." Grievence said kissing Neeyah.

"You do?" she said, bashfully.

"Even though we don't agree on everything doesn't mean I don't love you," he grabbed her face and squeezed it. That really sent her to heaven. She felt that if she died the next minute, she'd die with pure happiness.

"So, we just gone agree to disagree, huh?" she smiled. Then she lipped, "I love you too, baby." While reaching into her purse, pulling out a crisp one hundred dollar bill and handed it to him.

"You didn't have to do dat, babe." he said quickly putting the money in his glove compartment before she changed her mind.

"It's okay, baby. Really. I made a fat eleven hundred on my check!"

"Is dat right?" he said with a mischievous look, stroking his goatee. "Dat's what's up. But, boo, check dis' out, why don't you let me put four hundred of them dollars up for our crib?" he asked, cleverly. But, really

had other plans at the moment, for it. Such as, buying a new outfit and gym shoes.

He gave some thought to Swagga's offer and decided he was game. He just had to run it by Deuces. That wasn't hard. He was a go-getter. Anything that paid the bills, clothe and fed his daughter. He didn't get along with his other child's mother so he didn't do nothing for his kids.

"Okay, boo." she said amicably, and flashed a smile as she a handed it to him. She wanted very badly to live her man. Come hell or high water, that was gonna happen for them.

After she watched her boo Monty disappear, she sashayed through the complex like it was all about her. Nothing else mattered. Not even the crack head lying in the breezeway, that she had to step over to get to her apartment. Not even the unbearable smells, oozing from his body. It was mind over matter, all she smelled was Grievence's scent. When she got into her apartment, she almost slipped in a puddle of water. Her eyes followed a long trail of water leading to her parents room.

On her way down the hallway, she glanced into the kitchen, the cracked tile and broken window that the maintenance men never bothered to fix, made chills wash over her body. "I guess not bad after living here for damn near 15 years." she shrugged. "What am I trippin' fo'? Me and my boo gone be like deuces on dat ass." she threw up two fingers, going down the hallway.

"Where did all dis' water come from?" she yelled.

She didn't get a response. So she walked into her mother's room; where she found Ricky asleep with a big wet spot underneath him. Apparently, he dozed off and forgot about the bag of ice in his pants.

Damn, I just know dis' overgrown ass muthafucka didn't piss all thru the house and on the bed my mom sleep in! she cursed inwardly while looking at him. When he turned and walked away, she stepped on one of Junior's toys. Startling Ricky.

"N-N-N-Neeyah," he stuttered, with a very sheepish look on his face. Then he realized that he and the bed were wet. "Dis' isn't what you think. I was havin' muscle spasm and I filled a bag with ice," he explained.

"What? Where's Junior?" she said a little bemused.

"He's in his room, sleepin'."

"Well, did he eat?"

"Well, not to long after you guys left he went back to sleep,"

"Ok. I'm going to my room." she said, dryly sensing something was wrong because of the intangible feeling she had but couldn't quite put her finger on it. Quickly dismissing it, she decided she'll get back to that later and

that nobody was gonna steal her the joy she was feeling. The phone began to ring. She dove across her bed to get it. "Oh, Leigha," she said pressing the talk button. "Whudd it do, hoe!" she spoke cheerfully into the phone.

"Why are you so happy-go-lucky today, niggah?"

"I'm residing on cloud nine today," she said, twirling a couple strands of hair.

"In love yall, just be your butt outside in five minutes. I'm already in area," Leigha said and ended the call.

THE PARTY

"Yeah, I'm gonna be da bomb in dis' Apple Bottom suit tonight. On dat ass!" Neeyah said, looking in the mirror holding the suit up to her. "I'm not gonna let nobody rain on my parade," she danced in front of the mirror. "I better call my boo to see what he got up for tonight,"

She picked up her cell phone and started dialing his number, but quickly decided against it. She didn't want him to know she had a cell phone. Not quite yet. Instead, she called him from their landline. He answered on the first ring. "Dang, boo, you expectin' a call or sumthin'," she said, into the phone.

"Actually, I seen it was my boo, so I hurried and answered." he lied. Khia, Apple's cousin, had just hung up on him, so he was thinking it was her. She was a hoodrat, known for tricking niggah's out their weed and money. She stood about five feet three and weighed about 135 pounds with caramel skin tone. Her beautiful green eyes, complimented her round, baby face and a little fucked up in the head. As a child, her mama passed her off to anyone for sex. Even her own daddy. Underneath her clothes, she wore an ugly scar that would scorn her forever. When she was about seven years old, she got tired of her stomach growling and her brother crying from hunger so she turned a skillet that was on the stove on. Her mom was laid out, naked on the floor in her room. Smoked out and dead to the word. There was enough grease to fry a whole pack of chicken. At seven, what did she know? So, she cracked 2 eggs and it started popping causing her to touch the handle and tip it. The whole pan fell on her. She ended up with second-degree burns over 30 percent of her body. Before she was fully healed, her mom made her lie in excruciating pain to have sex with two men. That really fucked her up in the head so, as she got older she felt that she was an ugly freak-show. And that no man in their right mind would want to be with her, especially with a hideous body. At least that's what her mom instilled in her. When in actuality, she was very beautiful. One day when she was ten years old,

she vividly remembered how her mom Paula, called her in the living room. When she got in there, she immediately noticed an old drunk white man and his dirty fat girlfriend.

Her eyes quickly sidetracked to Paula, who was in the corner inhaling as much crack, from the dirty crack pipe as she could. When she noticed her watching, she motioned for her to go ahead. Then she shifted her attention back to the couple who were getting undressed.

"I should go first!" The musty white man slurred unbuckling his belt. He was dressed in a pair of dirty wrangler's and an old plaid flannel button down shirt.

"Mutherfucker, now you wait a cotton-pickin' minute, you always go first!" the woman said in a deep country accent, plopping down on the couch.

"Bitch, shut you fuckin' yappin' and look in my front pocket, dere's a surprise in there." he yelled over his shoulder. She hurriedly snatched his jeans up and rummaged through his pockets, until she found some crumbs.

When Paula saw the crumbs, it made her eyes sparkle. "Girl, come over here I already got the fire ready!" she said motioning for her to join her. The man quickly shifted his attention to a very scared, shivering Khia.

"Don't worry I want bite, you're old enough to fuck like a woman now, so come on over hea, gal. he said grabbing her and pushing her down on the bed. Then he aggressively tore her panties off and tried to force his soft dick inside her. He smelled really awful. She closed her eyes and silently prayed that the musty smelling man on top of her would soon do what he had to and get up. He was perspiring profusely. Sweat was dripping from his body into her mouth. Finally, after minutes of tussling, he got a hard on. Before he came to an eruption, he hurriedly pulled out and came on her stomach. As soon after he was done, he got up and started getting dressed. She never forgot the smells that exuded from his body and how rank his cum smelled. His naked girlfriend saw him and decided it was her turn, but he waved her off.

"I knew you was gonna bullshit me Ray Earl, hell I wanted the purty young thang too!" she screamed, slipping her dress over her head.

"Just, bring your hillbilly ass on here, before I leave your ass down yonder in the boon docks, somewherze!" he slurred, pointing toward the ceiling.

She quickly scurried behind him. That night, Khia hopped in the shower and nearly scrubbed all her skin off her body. Tears dropped from her eyes like raindrops. Later that night, she ran away and decided, by any means necessary she would survive and she never looked back. She had her aunt alarm the CPS (child protective service) for her siblings. After that, she did

it moving. She had three kids by three different niggahs, Her body wasn't at all, what ran niggah's off it was her youngest son Sam.

A three-year-old, that was still in diapers. He was bad as shit. One day, Grievence went to kick it with her, she asked him to watch him while she hop in the shower. Lil' Sam told him to get the hell outta his mama's house.

When Grievence asked him to say the alphabet, he sat on the couch next to him and said, "You not my daddy, punk." Then stuck up his pointer finger and licked out his tongue. "My mama don't like yo' ugly self. Ha got a man!" He continued to say. As soon as, he jumped down off the couch, Grievence got a whiff of the shit in his diaper.

I know dis' grown-ass niggah didn't shit on himself? he thought to himself.

"Did you use the bathroom?"

"Leave me lone. Umma tell my mama." he said hitting him with the wrought iron candle holder across the knees. Catching him off guard. Grievence screamed and massaged his knee.

"Oh shit. What da fuck! Umma fuck yo' lil ass up. Come here," he said through his tightly clenched teeth. "Where dis' bitch at so she can come get his lil' bad ass befo' he be done got fucked up!" he said peeping down the hallway.

He had never seen anything like it before, a child that knew all the words to a song and talked to him like he was the child, was still in diapers. Fifteen minutes later, she appeared from the hallway. "Next time I come over here, make sure dat lil' niggah is sleep." He said as soon as he saw her, heading to the door. "Damn, I just feel like crackin' his lil' ass." Grievence mumbled when he glanced over at him. She stood with her jaw dropped for a minute or two. Then she walked right over to sleeping Sam and beat him black and blue.

"Is dat right?" Neeyah grinned from ear to ear. "I was tryna see what you got up tonight?"

"Shit, nuthin' much. Probably go hoopin' and hit the gym up, afterwards. Dat's about it. Why, what's good with it?"

"On a good Friday night?"

"Well, my mama want me to go with her to get some furniture in the mornin'. So, I'm chillin' tonight," he lied. "You already noe how ma duke be on some staying in the store all day, type shit. Don't let her have to go to Wal-Mart, oh lawd! You may as well get a sleepin' bag and some mo' shit. Then she only bring out two hoe ass bags." he emitted chuckles.

"Uh huh, boo you ignant for dat."

"For the life of me, I don't know why yall females go in Wal-Mart and stay for hours. I just can't see giving Uncle Sam all my money."

"At any rate, I was kinda hopin' you could come through tonight, but I guess I'll see you tomorrow."

He palmed rolled his hair and sprayed it with some Mango spray. "You sure will, baby. Our night tomorrow is gone be crackin'. But don't trip, I'll hit you back before I go to sleep doe."

"Boo one more thing, do you remember that night when we was suppose to be going to Vegas for our Valentine's Romantic Getaway?"

Oh hell, he thought to himself. "Yeah, boo. I had got sick so we couldn't go."

"Yeah, you had the swine flu so I couldn't come around you right,"

"Right. I really hate dat because I had planned a special night at the Palms. I'm talkin' rose petals and all. Dat fuckin' swine flu fucked up our romantic vacation. But we will do it again as soon as I save some more bread," he lied.

"Ok baby I know we will. I just hated the fact I couldn't be around you for a week to pamper you. It really hurt me deeply, you have no idea. I remember callin' you and you could barely talk. At one point you had completely lost your voice. I'm glad that scare is over. But I'll be waitin' for your call. I love you!" she whined.

"I know baby, the last thing I wanted for my boo the love of my life to catch it. But boo stay by the phone so I could hear your sexy voice befo' I go to sleep," he lied. A big smile flashed across her face.

"And you know dis' man," she said and then ended the call. Feeling completely satisfied, she headed to the shower. She was high off of love she felt like she could touch the sky.

Her robe had shredded up so, she had to trash it and use a towel. Just as she started putting a coat of clear polish on her nails, her mom called her to get the phone.

"Hello," she said into the phone as she shook her hands dry.

"I'll be there in fifteen minutes!" Leigha said without giving her a chance to speak and ended the call.

"Oh shit!" she screamed. "I'm not even dressed yet," she blew her nails. Then she hopped up and combed her down hair down. "Damn, I look good." she said, putting her earrings on in the mirror. Before leaving out her room, she turned around and glanced at her butt. "Say she got a donk!"

While outside waiting for Leigha to come, a smoker walked up to her trying to sell her a pendant and earring set.

"I see you like jewelry, huh, lil' mama?" The rancid-smelling, smoker said. Every time he talked, she got a whiff of his all-day morning breath.

"Hold up, playa respect da boundaries." she pushed him back. His teeth looked as if he actually brushed and gargled them with shit. The smells that emanated from his body was making her gag.

"What's wrong, lil' mama?" he asked. Clearly in total oblivion about his bad body odor.

The audaciousness of dat question, did he even had to ask? She thought to herself while trying to sniff her perfume, to keep from barfing up the pepperoni hot pocket she had just eaten to coat her stomach.

"Well, check dis' out," he said, licking his thumb and pointer finger, smoothing down his moustache. "I got dis' one-karat diamond ring I was gonna give it to my girl, but since I thank it'll look betta on yo' fine self, I'll give it to you for da low, low, sixty bucks." he smiled like he was advertising for Colgate.

Niggahs always somewhere tryna run game, she thought as she let out a silent chuckle and then she flashed him a cruel smile.

"Hell naw, I'm not payin' no sixty dollars for no hot ass ring, dat I don't even know if it's real or not," she snapped.

"Look right here, baby girl. It says 14-karat gold!" he said, pointing to it with his fingernails that looked like he soaked them in motor oil.

"Lemme see," she examined the ring. Actually, liking it. "I'll give you thirty-five!" she sighed.

"Baybeee, you killin' me! Okay give me forty," he said throwing his hands up, looking paranoid.

"I'm givin' you thirty dollars and dat's dat. Take it or leave it?"

He weighed his options and snatched the money. "Black bitches." he muttered and then he scampered off.

"Fuck you! You cruddy dusty muthafucka." she yelled out. She did wait till he had vanished into thin air, though. She was no dummy. She surmised that he had just boosted the ring from somebody, from the way he was acting all paranoid.

"Looser's keepers and finder's keepers. So oh well, their loss is my gain!" she thought out loud slipping the ring on her finger. After, meticulously wiping it off with the hand sanitizer and feminine wipes, she kept in her purse at all times.

"Where is Leigha, hoe ass?"

Just as she pulled out her phone to call her, she was pulling up, honking the horn. "Damn, I thought you flaked out on my ass or sumthin'." Neeyah said opening the car door.

"My bad, girl, dat niggah held me there, literally beggin' me not to go out tonight. He wanted to patch things up until I went off on dat bitch. He just leave a bad taste in my mouth. Damn, bitch why you battin' yo' eyes like dat?"

"Becuz, I just got dazzled by your bright ass headlights."

"Halogen lights, bitch?" she shook her head. "Any-ole-ways, like I was sayin', I told dat niggah we was finished, finito . . . done. Dat niggah knows I'm a good, down ass bitch and he got none, zilch . . . nada mo chances."

"Umma tell you like you told me, from your mouth to God ears."

"Black folks. Always somewhere using what you tell them against you. But dat bitch had the nerves to tell me don't go indulgin' in his past unless I wanted to be hurt."

"Whaaat?"

"Yeah girl I told dat bitch, I'm not indulgin' in shit. I'm just not gone fuck wid you on dat level no more since you fucked Kandy's nasty ass." Leigha said.

"I have yet to figure out why men will never live shit down dat you do, but the moment their bitch asses do sumthin' you dare not throw it up in their face more than once."

"You know what, fuck them bitches. I ain't tryna figure shit out. Two tears in a bucket,"

"Fuck it," Neeyah chimed in. When she closed the car door, she got a good glimpse of her ring as the street light radiated from it.

"Heeeeey, I'm so icy."

"What are you all heyin' about?" Leigha asked lighting up a blunt.

"I just copped dis from a booster." she showed her.

Leigha grabbed her hand. "Lemme see. Dat's what's up! I see the clarity, gurrrl." Leigha said blowing smoke rings outta the window.

"Girl how bout I was on face book and dis' bitch gone post on her status, she just found out her man was fuckin' her sister, mama, and aunt. Her mama came to her and told her dat she was in love wid him and dat she had to move out so he could move in. Shaking my damn head."

"What da fuck?"

"Yeah girl she went on to say, he's the father of my three kids and I love him. I think umma fire on her ass."

"Ok she lived there and had no clue, get da fuck out of here. Bitch, I don't know why your ass stay on face book like dat reading dat Jerry Springer type shit. Face book is so childish becuz all people do is post their business and wonder why a muthafucka check off on their ass. Clearly all it's doing is turning your brain to mush!" Leigha laughed.

"Whateva! But ole girl ass is stupid for real and not for play. I would've been checked off on all of their asses." Neeyah said all geeked up.

"Not to mean or rude but you know me I have to speak my mind—"

"Speak your mind," she cut her off.

"That's said in the same essence of how my sista did you. It's seems like it's hella easy for someone to see someone else's faults and overlook their own. I been guilty of it plenty of times, myself trust me. I've said she's stupid dis' dat and the other. Not tryna be low key funny style, but the moral of the story we can't cast stones then throw our hands becuz well never know what well do until were in the situation. Not talkin' bout ole girl from face book either." she glanced at Neeyah who was sitting in passenger side quieter than a church mouse. "I'm not tryna be mean. Are you mad?"

"Nah, girlie you good, I'm just listenin' to you make a valid point. I can't get mad becuz your just stating the obvious, your opinion. Besides, opinions are like ass holes, everybody has one," she busted out laughing, not wanting Leigha to know she got under her skin, once again.

"I guess,"

"What are you listenin' to?" Neeyah switched the subjects.

"Girl, dis' is the Friday-night mix. They be bangin' on the weekends!" Leigha said in between puffs.

"Oh hell, naw!" They both yelled in unison. "They took that shit all the way back. Doin' the butt. Awwww, sexy, sexxy!" They both sang, facing each other.

"Straight old school," Leigha said passing the blunt.

"Dis' party is packed like shit," Neeyah said. "Our ass gonna have to park out in da boonies."

"Hell-to-the-no the fuck I'm not. I'm ready to party like a rock star!" Leigha yelled to the top of her lungs. "Come on bitch, keep dat shit in rotation. Puff puff pass, niggah." she said, reaching for the blunt.

"Do your ass ever say anything without cussin'? Dat is so not lady like."

"Absolutely, fuckin' not!" she laughed. "Besides, it's not like your ass have virgin ears, bitch!"

"I guess . . . Anyways, I'm about to get it in!" Neeyah said grooving to the music. "Man, it's stupid packed!"

Cars were lined up the entire street. Leigha circled the block about three times before spotting somebody peeling off in a hurry.

"That's what's up, doe!" They both said in unison.

Neeyah held up and pressed the button to disengage the door. "Wait, girl!" Leigha said pulling out some Grey Goose and grapefruit juice. She

handed her a cup and quickly downed hers. "We gotta get prelocked, don't we?" she said. Then she poured herself another drink without the chaser.

"Damn hoe, youz a true alcoholic!"

"Yea bitch, pure unadulterated! I told you I plays noe games." Leigha said putting on a fresh coat of tinted Mac lip gloss.

"Girl, you crazy," Neeyah said guzzling down the drink like it was water. "Ahhh . . . dat shit burnt my throat." she grabbed her throat.

"You such a faker. You never ceases to amaze me! Dat was more juice then goose, niggah. While you over there tryna be like me. I been drinkin' since I was a toddler." she said taking a long swig of the blunt.

"Dat shit was strong bitch. I can't help I'm not an alky like you. But you funny as hell."

"Cut dat shit out. You know dat wasn't even potent enough for you to be all dramatizin' dat shit like dat. But dat's for real and not for fake. One day, my curious ass tasted my mama's drink when she left da room. I still remember like it was yesterday. I think I was four or five, but she caught me red handed and was like you little fast ass black, bitch, now down the rest. My ass turnt da shit up and passed out. Every night afterwards mama gave me a good cold beer to knock my ass out."

"Get da fuck outta here."

"Oh bitch, that's no worse than T.T Lafa givin' us Benadryl for the whole week straight, I stayed at your house dat year!"

"But our asses was bad. Any sane person had to do dat to keep their sanity, bitch."

"Don't try to gloss over shit. We were not dat bad, bitch." she looked over at Neeyah.

"What about when I stayed with you guys for spring break one year and your mama gonna sit all seven of us down on the couch and she literally went down the line and smacked all of us in a row. I forgot what we done, but I know dat memory is forever seared in my brain." Neeyah said.

"I remember hon. My mama was sumthin' else. But knowing her ass it was becuz she didn't have no alcohol in her system."

"Oh, fuck!" Neeyah screamed.

"What happened, girl?"

"I just got burnt by the blunt," Neeyah said, blowing her finger and rubbing the black smut off.

"Oh, you mean the roach. You see when it gets down to dis' point, I think you're suppose to throw it away!" Leigha chuckled, handing Neeyah some gum.

"Blow me, bitch!" she said taking the gum. "Oh, I need you to go by Vons on our way home so I can get a bottle of Hennessy."

"Well damn, you gonna pay forty-five dollars for a bottle of henny, bitch?"

"Actuuually," she said stretching the word. "I have 25 dollars, I was hoping my big cuzo could loan me the rest!"

"Damn, why you got to always have champagne taste and beer money? Where they do dat shit at, bitch? Your ass betta get you a bottle of Moscato and call it a night."

"Uh huh, I need sumthin' way mo' stronger than that. But, don't trip, umma give you yo' lil funky, punk ass 20 dollars back! On me, with interest."

"Nuh huh bitch, you're better off snatchin' one of these niggah's up and using their ass as a crash dummy. You, do do dum for dat!" Leigha chuckled. Neeyah twisted her lips and rolled her eyes. "Chile ain't no need for all dat, becuz you gotta get in where you fit in. Naw, I'm playin'. I got you. On Friday my face will be the first one you see when you walk out dat bitch."

"Damn, for 20 punk ass dollars, dawg! It's like dat?" Neeyah faced her.

"Bitch, I would maul your ass down for 5 dollars! Gotta get all mine." Leigha giggled, unlocking the doors.

"By the way, you look nice, girl" Neeyah said.

Leigha was dressed in a Baby Phat denim, sleeveless outfit. Her diamond nameplate necklace complimented her tube top. The big gold double braided belt, with a big gold Baby Phat emblem, set her whole outfit off. She was rocking the hell out of her golden colored, Babyphat calf high boots. Her hair was pretty as usual. Curls trailed along her shoulders and down her back. Big gold hoops hung from her ears. When she stepped out, better believe she was on point.

"You talking 'bout, me. Why, thank you. You're not lookin' bad yourself." They both laughed. "You need to give me some of them double Ds," Leigha said, squeezing Neeyah's breast and sticking a thizzle in her mouth, catching the attention of a group of boys.

"Um finna get it in and find me a 10 inch angus smoked sausage." Neeyah licked her lips.

"Don't nobody want no drunk pussy, bitch! All impotent and shit."

"Fuck you." she flipped her off.

"I remember one night me and Rah Rah's ass had got so drunk, how bout in da midst of him eating me out, dat bitch just threw up in my shit. I was to drunk to even tell doe. All I know is, when I woke up, I kept smelling whiffs of garbage and it didn't take long to conclude what it was and I just fired on his ass two good times. I was like you whiskey dick muthafucka

and whoop whoop and he was like bitch your ass was drunk too. You kept begging me to fuck you so I had to try to eat it becuz I sure in hell wasn't fuckin' no limp pussy." Leigha said.

"Ewwwe . . . what an asshole. He just let your ass fire on him."

"Nah bitch, I was stickin' and movin'." Leigha laughed.

"You not gone drink nuthin' wid dat pill you just scarfed down?" Neeyah asked.

"Naw, beezie, that's called survival of the streets. Just da secretions of my mouth. I can see if you was put out here on these cold, lonely streets you couldn't survive one night. Let alone, find your way out of a brown paper bag. Becuz a you act like a white girl from the Valley. I know what it is, you need to hang out wid your big cuzo more."

"Bitch, I'm from the hood."

"Shid, I can't tell. It's ok becuz one day when I have da time umma teach you hood and streetology." she said, rubbing her back.

"What da fuckeva, don't touch me," she shrugged her off.

"I'm playin' boo you know you hood, but I need some of your chi chi's while you're bullshittin'." she said, pushing her breast up.

"You can use some of mine with them prunes you got."

"Bitch, at least I do have a mouth full. A muthafucka don't have to pick my shit up off the floor to put them shits in his mouth." she continued. "He can suck 'em all night long, standin' attention."

"Whud it do, shawty?" A boy with a deep Southern drawl said, looking dead at Neeyah. "You finer than a mutha." she flashed him a coyish smile that said, I know!

"Dat's how yall get down on the westcoast?" One of his homies with dreads and a mouth full of gold teeth said.

"Whatever dat means! Where are you guys from?" Leigha said being the people person she was.

"Why, we can't be from here, lil' mama?"

"I was just askin' Gold Mouth, Dreads or whateva your name is becuz you guys have a thick country accent!" Leigha shot sarcastically.

"Gold Mouth, huh? I like dat it has a nice ring to it. But my name is Dreadlocks, sweetheart." he smiled. "Are you tryna stereotype us, doe?"

"Hunny, are you slow? Naw I'm fuckin' wid you but If that's you're interpretation then, what can I say? But you know what Gold Mouth, you're not about to blow my high becuz I'm thizzin' and feelin' damn good."

"Don't pay him know mind boo, he's playin' but we're from Naw Leans [New Orleans], Miss Lady!" One of his other homies said.

Neeyah stepped back, pondering whether she should get the boy's number that kept undressing her with his eyes. *Maybe I should get his number just in case Grievence kept up with his bullshit!* She thought to herself.

"We're in town for my big homie dat touched down today. What are you fine ladies doing later on tonight?"

"I dunno, why, what's good?" Leigha asked. "I try not to plan things. Them shits never work out. Well, lemme ask you, how long are you guys in town for?"

"A week, but dat depends on if there's sumthin' here can make me stay. Well, let me slide you my number, call me. Maybe you can show me round town," he said, winking at her.

"Maybe," she said, slipping the number in her black D&G purse.

"I like you becuz you're a cold piece of work."

"What in da hell do dat 'pose ta' mean?"

"It means you're a direct person and speak yo' mind."

"Uh hum, sho'll do. Glad you know it. And dat's for real and not play." she said tooting up her lip like she was hard. He chuckled some.

The one boy slid his number to Neeyah. She looked at it and tore it up.

Leigha shot her a flabbergasted look. *What the fuck, the gall of dis' girl, she could have at least waited 'til them muthafuckas were outta sight to tear it up!* She thought, opening her purse checking to make sure she had her razor within reach.

"Dat's how you feel, lil' mama. You just gonna be dat bold and tear the shit up in my face." he said, with a grimaced look.

Leigha hurried and guzzled down the rest of the drink in her hand.

"I have a very photographic memory. I'll remember especially if somebody worth rememberin'!" she winked.

Leigha was relieved, to say the least. Although she was talking cash mess to them, she was messing with their pride.

"Dat niggah, was like I know you're not gonna be dat bold and whoop whoop . . . For a second, I thought he was about to sock the shit out yo' ass, for real dawg! Just keepin' dat shit one hunnit!"

"He was about to get his shit split fuckin' wid me!" Neeyah retorted knowing good and well she wasn't gonna bust a grape.

"You already know I was ready to fuck somebody up. Blade in hand, bitch!"

"Did you see the short chubby one? His ass has to be gay!"

"You got gaydar or sumthin', bitch?"

"As a matter-of-fact I do. Girl you can't tell me you didn't see them tulips and gardenias dat flowed out when he opened his mouth and plus I could tell by his posture with them long ass pinky nails!"

"Ewwwe, where they do dat at?!" Leigha scrunched up her face. "Your ass crazy, talkin' about flowers came from his mouth when he spoke. Now dat was some funny shit,"

Then both fell over laughing. "I hate gay muthafuckas!"

"Stop gay bashin',"

With that, they both walked off. "I see you got game!" Leigha said punching her softly catching her off guard causing her to stumble.

""Damn, girl, you're on one. You see dat goose got a bitch leanin' and some mo' shit, already!" Neeyah said looking around to make sure nobody saw her stumble.

The girls pushed their way through the crowded party. Straight to the alcohol. Leigha convinced her to have another drink. Giving in, she got a cup of Corona. She was kinda eerie about drinking,—her gut told her not to—but figured what the hell. Apple went all out. She had Hennessy, Grey Goose, Patrón, Crown Royal, José Cuervo, and two kegs of Ice House. You would have thought she robbed the liquor store or something. She also had hella food, catfish, chicken wings, and barbecue wieners.

"Chug! Chug! Chug! Chug!" Leigha screamed as Neeyah guzzled down two cups of beer. The whole time Leigha was screaming *chug*, she was guzzling down some herself.

"Dat's enough!" Neeyah screamed, wiping her mouth with the back of her hand.

One boy stared at Leigha, biting down on his bottom lip.

"Look at dis' ole cakin-ass niggah right here!" his friend teased, licking barbecue sauce off his thumb.

"Well, I know ole girl, you better be ready to break bread!" his other homie said.

"Fuck dat! All a bitch is getting from me is henny and the dick. Maybe just maybe some chronic if the pussy is good!" he shot sizing her down from head to toe.

"Fuck!" Leigha screamed. "Girl, I gotta pee. Here hold my cup!" she said, shoving it in her hand. Before, Neeyah could protest, she had disappeared in the crowd. Neeyah smacked her teeth and stumbled over to a chair. "Damn a bitch is really leanin'."

"I know dat isn't who I think it is," Leigha said in awe. Coming outta the bathroom. As she got closer, she couldn't believe her eyes. *But then again, it's*

to be expected out of a lame-ass niggah, she thought. With her high immediately blown, she made her way back to Neeyah. "Neeyah, you gotta see dis', the audacity of dis' sucker-ass niggah!" Leigha grabbed her arm strenuously and pulled her through the crowd, not giving her a chance to respond.

"Wait a minute! Where are we going?" Neeyah asked, very loudly because the music was up so loud you had to scream to be heard. Leigha was mad because her high was blown. She turned her around and told her that she saw Grievence hugged up with some trick. Her stomach started churning.

"How could you be sure, it's very murky over there?" Neeyah asked looking at her like she was crazy, hoping she was wrong.

"Look if you don't go over there and check dat bitch, I will. I really don't mind putting the two knuckle shuffle down. On my mama! I'm tired of muthafuckas playin' you like you're a punk ass bitch. Dis' shit 'bout to get cut! Becuz, a bitch like me will slice a niggah throat and sit back and watch their ass shiver and take their last breath. I don't give a fuck!" Leigha screamed over the music, **w**aving her hand under her neck. Knowing her cousin, she walked a little closer.

Her heart began to sink. She knew Leigha seemed very adamant it was him. The more the music roared, the more her head thumped and her heart raced.

"How will I know it's him?" she asked, not wanting to cause a scene. The alcohol was telling her to walk over there and see. Then it hit her she had her cell phone. She walked closer to see if he would answer or his phone would ring or something. Sweat balls began to pop up on her face and run down the side of it. Her heart started racing a mile a minute. Her knees got all weak and wobbly. Most of all, her fingers were trembling so bad she could barely dial his number. She looked back at Leigha who was getting angrier by the minute.

Please, God, don't let dat be him, she prayed silently feeling all the enthusiasm draining outta her body. She pressed the talk button. Leigha stood back fuming and tapping her feet. Then all of a sudden she saw girl get up and he pulled out his phone.

USE OR GET USED

"What up, my dude?" Kadaafie said in a very serene tone.

"Shid nuthin' much, 'bout to go hoopin' and shit, but what's good witcha doe, cuzo?" Amauri asked.

"Umma be very concise, what do you know 'bout dat niggah Rah Rah?"

"Rah Rah?" he reiterated. "I don't really know too much about him, but he's getting dat paper in a major way. I hoop with him every now and again, dat's about it!" he said a little puzzled. He hadn't spoken to Kadaafie in months. All of a sudden, he calls him out of the blue.

"I don't wanna go into too many details over the phone, but I will say dis' much, dat mark got my lil' sis pregnant. Then when she told him, he kicked her in her stomach and told her, either she get rid of it, or he would! Dat's my little heart, man. Dat niggah gots to pay!" Kadaafie said with tears welling up in his eyes.

"Wow! Dat crab-ass niggah need to be taught a lesson. Dat shit was file." Amauri said pretending to care, when he really gave two flying fucks all he seen was money. *Ching ching!*

"I haven't figured out how yet, but he will see how loose steel feel," Kadaafie said in a very harsh tone. "Mom duke may as well get her black dress ready, because I'm sending her ass a wreath!" he said with no remorse.

"I know his bitch. I fucks with her twin sister. She was always on a niggah's bumper, wantin' me to fuck her and some mo' shit!"

"That's it!" Kadaafie said thoughtfully. "I need you to get real close to dat hoe and have her get close to him."

"So we just use her ass to make him our target?" he asked.

"Bingo!" Kadaafie said. "You will be well compensated for your help. I'll be in touch with you in a couple of days! In the meantime, holla at ya' girl." He said imperatively. Amauri hung up smelling money and immediately flipped through his sidekick, found Monie's number. He knew his big cousin

had money out the ass and that he paid well. Dat's all he was thinking about as *Why You Bullshittin'* by Sugar Free played in the background.

"What's good, baby girl?" Amauri said seductively into the phone.

"Shid, you pimpin'! What cha' got a lil suntin' suntin' for your girl?" Monie asked baffled.

"Looka hea' boo, a niggah gonna get straight to the point, cancel all your plans for tonight because we're going out to dinner. I'll call you later for directions to your house." he said, imperatively.

"Cocky, aren't we?" she said, trying to make sense of the call. "First of all, my man won't like it if I cancel our plans tonight." she lied.

"Well, you just tell dat niggah he gonna have to fall back becuz you got a new niggah to take care of you." he said, then blew her a kiss into the phone. He could tell she was falling for the lies. He could just tell she had a big smile plastered across her face.

"Well," she paused. "Since you insist, I don't suppose me breakin' one date will hurt. All right, umma fuck wid you tonight." she said gladly.

"So you gonna fuck wid yo boy, tonight, huh?" he chuckled a little.

"That's what's up. Say no mo', sweetheart, I'll call you in a couple of hours," he said with a big smile spreading across his face, ending the call. "Dat bitch is do do dumb." he said, powering on the computer.

Twenty minutes later, he called the most elegant restaurant and made reservation and asked for a private seating area. He stood about five feet nine inches and weighed about 180 pounds with a dark skin tone, about the shade of a hersey bar. He was mixed with Mexican. His short wavy jet-black hair accented his baby face. He kept a neatly tapered goatee. Definitely, fine as fuck with a six-pack to go with his nice toned body. With, *pay me or pay me no attention tatted on his neck,* not only was It his M.O, he lived up to it in every way. A typical, nickel-and-dimer, looking for a quick come up. Every week, he would go to the Garment District and get brand new items. He sold everything from clothes to CDs, movies, dope and pills—anything you could think of. However, he still found time to work out and hoop. He had a very deep sexy voice that sounded like he was whispering. That alone made panties drop. He was also very smart and persuasive. He could crack any code. Hell, he could even steal the stink outta shit. He was good at what he did.

He was pissed about having to go into his stash but quickly, cooled off when thinking about his big payout.

"Ching, ching. Chyea!" he said, heading to his stash. Then he reached inside and pulled out a large stack of money. He counted out $650 and put the rest back. He had managed to save over six Gs. With future plans of

opening up a Laundromat with an cleaners in it, starting with one, then a chain. Looking, in his closet, he selected two of many, brand-new outfits. After pondering for about twenty minutes or so, he decided to go with black-and-red pinstriped (everything Roc-a-wear) blazer, buttoned-down shirt and black jeans. Next, he laid them on the bed and he hopped in the shower. Once he was out the shower, he did his daily regimen. As he did after every shower, doing ten of each—jumping jacks, sit-ups and push-ups—which didn't make sense. Why take a shower then exercise? *Go figure*!

An hour and thirty minutes later, he called Monie to get directions to her home and then instructed her to have on a just a robe when he got there. When she hung up the phone, a big kool aide smile flashed across her face. In her nasty mind, she thought he was coming to give her the dick that she longed for, so she was practicing what to do and say to him. She heard around hood, that he was a hung, paid niggah, or so she thought. Now she had one foot in the door. She was *happy!* He took his time to get dressed. Starting by, taking his du-rag off and sprayed on some *Fahrenheit* Cologne on. Before leaving out the door, he slipped his chain over his head. After taking a quick glimpse in the mirror, he grabbed his 04 Honda Accord off the end table by the door. He headed straight to the Slauson's swap meet and bought Monie a black dress, only paying fifty dollars for a dress, shoes, costume jewelry set and nylons. When he got back inside the car, he took a quick peek into the bags and seemed pleased. The good thing about it was, the dress had a tag for two hundred dollars on it. He knew all about shopping for women's clothes because, he done it for his other women. Then he made a quick stop by Dillard's Department Store and bought two gift boxes. An hour later, he pulled up to Monie's home. She had been in the window looking for him ever since they had hung up. She had everything all planned out, with her toys, oils, and creams packed in her overnight bag. When she saw his car pull up, she was about to run to the door, but saw him exit the car. "What is dat? It looks like a cake or sumthin'." she dumbly, asked herself.

"Hey, stranger!" he said, kissing her on the cheek and handing her the box. "I was beginnin' to think you were gonna flake out on a niggah!"

"Don't be silly boy." she giggled. When he leaned over to kiss her, her pussy began to jump. "What's dis'?" she asked disbelievingly, knowing good and well that wasn't the same man she conducted business with. "You look and smell so good!" she continued. "Oh my god!" she screamed with her jaw dropping to the floor. She was appalled. She never had a man to buy her nothing. She only ran across niggah's wanting to fuck her. "Wow!"

"Will you excuse me for a minute, Miss Lady?" he politely, asked running to the car to get the bag with the shoes and other things. She was too speechless to say anything. He caught a glimpse of her looking at the price tag through the cracked door. All she could see was dollar signs. He chuckled at the dumb gold digging broad, but at the same time, they were both hustler's looking for a come up.

He handed her the bag. "Here, sexy lady,"

"I dunno how to thank you." she managed to say.

"You can thank me later!" he said in very low, soft sexy tone.

Again, she was thinking how she was going to fuck the shit out of him. That could not have been farther from the truth; that was the last thing on his mind. He was a niggah true indeed, but a careful one. Her name rang plenty of bells in the streets.

"Now go get dressed," he bit down on his lips seductively and whispered.

She took the things and really felt like she was walking on clouds. When she came out of the room, she was looking stunning. The dress was looking every bit as captivating as she was. He couldn't figure why somebody so fine, could be so slutty and scandalous.

"Could you do me da honors?" she handed him the necklace. They both stood looking in the mirror. Her heart was about to jump outta her body as he touched her, sending chill through her body, she wanted to scream *come fuck me baby!*

"You look nice," he whispered, in her ear running the back of his hand down her face. His palpable touch, was ever so soft and delicate. Making her weak and unable to respond. *What size is dis?* she said inwardly, sticking her feet into the shoes. The dress fit perfectly, but the shoes were too little. Putting on a facade, she grabbed her knockoff Louis Vuitton purse, and they were on their way. He opened the door for her. Once she got into the car, she pinched herself to make sure she wasn't dreaming.

Damn, I'm glad to be in the car. My feet is killin' the fuck outta me! she thought. *He said these shoes were a size 8 and a half, but what are they measured in? Dick inches?*

"Are you okay, baby?" he asked, pulling off into traffic.

"I'm good." she replied. Trying to act as if she was used to that type of treatment.

"Just relax. The night has only just begun." he said with a mischievous smile as he reached in the backseat and picked up a rose from the backseat. *Dis' all has to be too good to be true,* she said silently to herself.

He handed her a single lavender rose. "Here you go, beautiful!"

"What's dis'!" she said, stretching out her hand to take the rose. "Oh a rose, you never cease to amaze me. A purple rose what does it mean?" she glanced back at him.

"Well baby, a lavender rose means, love at first sight." he said, winked and gave her a malicious smile.

She cheesed from ear to ear. "Oh is dat right? Love at first sight, huh?" *Did he have to park all the way out here? In West bubble fuck?"* she was thinking to herself as she looked around. Not seeing a restaurant nowhere in sight from where they had parked. "So where's the restaurant?" she asked, looking around at all the houses.

"It's up there, boo!" he said, pointing up the street. "Would you like for me to carry you up there?" she wanted to shout *"hell yeah!"* instead said "Your good!" swallowing a big gulp of spit that was in her throat. He actually parked so far off because, his baby mother lived in the area.

"You sure? It's nuthin'!"

"Oh hell-to-da-no, a fuckin' hill, he got my ass fucked up!" she thought to herself, dreading the long walk in the too little shoes to the main entrance. No other choice, she forced a smile to her face as she reach up to unlock the door.

"No, boo, allow me!" he screamed, jumping out of the car to open her door. She sat back and took a deep breath.

"You sure know how to treat a lady,"

"Lady, humph, shittin' me mo' like hoe!" he said, inwardly. "Especially when they're as fine as yourself." he winked and continued to run game. He was the king of running games, scams or anything that had to do with money. He was down for the crown, use or get used. Above all, when he had been hurt by the one true love of his life, which made him stereotypical about all women. Funny how one bad experience from someone can fuck shit up for everybody. She was instantly was blown away to be at The French Laundry. One of the most expensive restaurants in California. The outside appeared to be that of an old house but, the inside was breathtaking. She tried to act like a woman, but her smile were slowly disappearing. She felt like cutting her whole feet off.

"Reservation for Mr. and Mrs. Carlton!" he said, shifting his attention back to her to check out her facial expression.

"Oh my gosh! she wanted to shout. *"He already is givin' me his last name! Does dis' niggah have an agenda? Have he had feelings for me but was scared to act on them?"* she thought as her mind raced a mile a minute.

He had given them a fictitious name. He couldn't help how good he was and how well he devised everything on such short notice.

"Right dis' way!" A thin-framed white woman said, vibrantly.

They followed her lead.

"Dis' is so romantic," she whispered, to him as they walked to their table. He flashed a smiled, and then grabbed her hand and kissed it.

"Oh yeah, dis' is only the beginning of a beautiful relationship!" he whispered, back sending chills up and back down her spine.

She decided from that moment on she had potentially found her soul mate and that she was gonna leave all the no-good niggahs alone and focus all her attention on her new man. After all nobody ever spent so much money on her to fuck so, she automatically assumed he always wanted her.

"Ladies first," he pulled out her chair,

"Can I get you guys anything to drink?" The unattractive woman asked.

"Yes, umm . . . we'll take a bottle of your finest Dom Pe'rignon."

Ten minutes later, she returned with it. "Here you guys go our finest wine!" she sat it in a bucket of champagne, surrounded by ice along with two flutes on the table. "Are you guys ready to order, by any chance?"

"Yeah, I'll have the creamy Beets & Leets with a side of carrots and cucumbers!" he said handing the server the menu. Then she looked to Monie, who still had a look of indecisiveness on her face. Nothing on the menu looked appealing or worth eating. Expensive as it was.

"I'll have what he's havin'!" she blurted out. "Sounds very good!" she closed the menu and handed it to the waiter as well.

"Are you nervous?" he asked, staring at her.

"I'm okay," she stammered.

"Just relax and enjoy your evening sweetheart."

"Ok. Intriguin' I must say!" she scanned the restaurant.

There were mirrors surrounding them. The seats were made of soft Italian leather. The lights were dim with candles lit everywhere. Fresh flowers were in a vase at each table. The restaurant was very elegant and every bit enchanting. She was awe-struck.

"I'm still having a hard time trying to figure out whether dis' is real, or am I dreamin'?" she said, starry eyed.

"Well baby, you will see I'm dat niggah, dat walk what I talk." he said pushing himself up from his seat "Dance with me!" *Slow Jam* by Atlantic Starr was playing, softly in the background. She hated slow jams and most of all, oldies. They were so depressing to her. Suddenly, they sounded so good to her.

"Outta all dis' time I've known you, why didn't you say sumthin' to me?" she asked, out of curiosity.

"Well, for one, I'm all-action-and-no-talk niggah. I felt you were fine and when I stepped to you, I had to have my game and paper up," he whispered in her ear, she could feel the juices emanating out of her pussy. Knowing he had her going, he decided to add fuel to the fire. "Besides, I'm a lonely niggah with a lot of money and nobody to help me spend it. Are you okay? I'm not overdoing it am I?"

"No not at all. I'm just a little overwhelmed,"

The two chopped it up while the music played relentless in the background. Upon making the reservation, he requested to have R&B play.

An hour later they arrived back at her house. He got out like a gentlemen and walked her to the door and kissed her on the cheek. Her pussy started thumping when he leaned in to kiss her. "Aren't you gonna come in for a bit?"

"Nah pretty lady. Dat want be a good idea."

"Why not you don't have self control or sumthin'?" she laughed.

"To be honest, fine as you are I know I wouldn't. Plus I'm not ready to take it there with you. Ah niggah wanna show you dat he's not using you for sex or a one hitta quitta. I'm genuinely tryna be your niggah." he ran game and flashed a seductive, mischievous smile.

"In dat case then ok." she blushed and bit down on her lip. *Is you slow or sumthin? I'm handin' you da golden ticket to dis' bomb ass pussy.* she thought while looking at him.

"Well damn, ain't dat a bitch. He didn't want da pussy, damn I a bitch need a wet stick now," she said, watching him drive off.

FOR EVERY ACTION,
THERE'S A REACTION

"Grievence!" Neeyah shouted.

Startling him, he pushed Khia to the floor. Her dress flew up, which revealed to everyone that she wasn't wearing any underwear. The Thizz pill that Leigha had convinced her to take gave her an adrenaline rush. Normally, she would've just talked shit but, she was fed up She pounced on Khia so fast and started taking off on her. You would've thought she was Bionic or something.

"What's going on?" Apple yelled.

"They're fightin'!" someone shouted.

"I'll be damned, black folks can't go nowhere without showin' their asses!" A drunk girl said, stumbling to the alcohol before everything was shut down.

"Bitch, move your drunk ass outta the way." one of Apple's home girl's screamed, shoving the girl down. She was running in the opposite direction from the fight. Low key, she was scared to help.

"Don't run bitch, come catch dis' fade." the girl slurred, once she was able to get up off the floor. "Fuck you then. You can suck out my drunk pussy!" she screamed out to her. Khia had tore Neeyah's shirt and bra off.

"Titties and ass!" A tall funny-looking boy with dreads yelled. Shifting the lights from dim to bright. This made Grievence snap outta the trance.

"Neeyah, get off her!" he yelled. He knew he was wrong but figured he could always apologize to Neeyah later. After all, he was on a mission to get the chronic that Khia had just jacked off one of her tricks. Which was over a thousand dollars worth.

"No the fuck you didn't say no sucka-ass shit like dat? Niggah, you got shit all fucked up. Neeyah 'pose ta' be your girl, instead you playin' her for

dis' washed up, worn out, cold pussy bitch!" Leigha screamed reaching for her blade. Apple pushed her way through the crowd and saw her lying on the floor.

"Eat my pussy, bitch!" Neeyah screamed, putting her pussy all in her face.

She wasn't naked or nothing. When the crowd cheered her on, she started socking Khia in the face. Khia lay, defeated.

"Oh hell no!" Apple screamed when she realized it was Khia.

"It's one on one!" Leigha screamed. "But, if you wanna check it, you can check it, bitch." she said, pulling out her blade. Unbeknownst to anyone else though. Apple grabbed Neeyah by the hair and gave her three uppercuts. She tried to do it the third time. Leigha grabbed her hand and said.

"I said one on one, bitch!"

Apple hopped up and leaped on Leigha and began socking her.

"Somebody break them up!" Apple's boyfriend yelled. He had just got out of outta prison and didn't wanna be nowhere around when the rollers came. They somehow ended up outside. What nobody realized is that Leigha was slicing Apple's shit the whole time. Apple didn't feel it. She was so drunk.

Neeyah sat on the ground holding herself, crying uncontrollably with mascara lines running down her face. Her hair was all sweated out. She looked a hot mess. That didn't matter; nothing mattered at the moment. By then, the man from Louisiana, had come back and put his shirt on Neeyah. Apple thought she was sweating because, she tasted a salty liquid. She soon found out it was blood.

"She's bleeding!" someone shouted. While everyone turned their attention on Apple, Leigha them made a run to the car.

"Neeyah!" Grievence bellowed.

She stopped dead in her tracks and turned to face him.

"No, girl! Come on, leave his trifflin' ass!" Leigha shouted, sweating profusely.

She looked from Leigha to Grievence then back to Leigha.

"Bitch, I don't have time to play the do I stay or do I go game. You can't be straddin' da fence. Dis' is a no brainer, Let's go!" Leigha screamed. After pondering on it a moment, she asked Leigha would she be okay and told her that he just wanted to talk. Then she scampered off toward's him.

"Don't fuck wid his lame ass, girl. Let's go. Don't do it!" she said, banging on the hood of the car with her fist.

"I'll call you later. I'll be okay!" Neeyah yelled over her shoulder. She was dumbly in love in there was no use in trying to steer her no other way.

"How da hell can somebody so smart, be so damn dumb? Dis' some bullshit! I guess you can't squeeze blood out of a turnip after all!" Leigha shouted to the sky as she got into the car and sped away. She cursed herself for even telling her and vowed she'll never tell her dumb ass, nothing else. As she looked in the rear-view mirror, she could see them peeling out. When her chest started burning, it was then she realized her nameplate was gone.

"Fuck!" she shouted at her carelessness. Then she called her aunt Lara and told Neeyah were in a fight without going into detail. She did say it was because of Grievence and that she was with him.

"Babee, it wasn't what it looked like. I was just tryin' to get some money outta dat hoe for us, boo. She just had gotten a settlement. She was gonna give me two racks and I was gonna use it to buy us an apartment, like I promised!" he lied. Even though it didn't justify his actions, she sort of felt bad for causing such tumult. "Do you hear me, boo? Dat bitch is just an ATM machine." he said, shaking her arm. She didn't respond. "Neeyah!" he shouted.

"I hear you, bay," she said, in a near whisper.

"I know you hear me, but are you listenin'?" he said pulling into the empty K-Mart parking lot.

She nodded her head yeah. *Umma have to teach his ass a lesson!* She thought to herself. "Look, just take me home." she said in between sniffs. "I'm tired. I've had a long night. We can continue dis' tomorrow." It truly hurt him deeply to see her crying the way she was.

"Babee, I'm sorry. I didn't mean to hurt you!" he said wiping her tears.

"I dunno why I keep cheatin' on you. I'm fucked up in the head, boo. I need some help. I can't help it, but it's almost like a sickness I got where I go out and fuck all these bitches." he said, grabbing her hand. "Please baby, don't leave me. I'll go try to get help!"

She jerked her hand back from him, in disgust. "What do you want me to do? Anything, I'll do it, boo." she sat still, and listened, not saying one word. "I hope you're listening. I mean it. I'll do whatever!" he begged. "I'm saying doe, I'm sitting here pouring my heart out telling you everything and you're ignoring me. I don't like dat hoe shit, please say sumthin'—fuck you muthafucka, son of a bitch, or sumthin'!" he said, getting a little angry with her, for disregarding him. "Look, all I'm sayin' is, all the cards are on the table. It's all on you. The ball is in your court, boo."

"I need some time. Can you please just take me home?" she said. Wiping her nose with her sleeve.

"Restate dat please?" he said, pushing his earlobe up.

"I wanna go home. There's nuthin' to talk about." she said, trying be hard. The minute the words rolled off her tongue, she regretted them. She couldn't take it back so she took in a deep breath. *Woosaaah Woosaaah . . .* she said to herself.

"Say no more!" he said pulling back into traffic.

She couldn't help but wonder if she was making a mistake by not talking to him. He pulled up to her complex, let her out and peeled off. She just stood there crying uncontrollably, watching his silver Monte Carlo disappear into thin air, wondering if she was ever gonna see it again. Her vision became more and more blurry. She broke the heel off her shoe, when she was running. She was a mess. All she could say was, "How did it come to dis'? My day was going so good, why me?" She stumbled to her apartment with the broken shoe on, not bothering to take it off. As soon as she opened the door, her mom walked up to her with arms outstretched.

"Oh, baby! I'm glad you're okay. I was worried!" she said rubbing her back.

"Oooh, Ma, how did you find out?"

"That's not important. I'm just glad you're home." Ms. Lara said moving the hair outta her face.

"It's over, Mama. I thought he loved me. How was I so stupid? Do you think I'm crazy, Ma, for still lovin' him so deeply? Honestly, I think I'm strong enough to walk away, but too weak to stay gone."

"No, baby, I don't think you're stupid. Love is blind, sweetheart. You have a lot to learn, that's all."

"Why, does it hurt so bad? You would think I would be used to dis' by now. I been hurt so much by dis' boy," she chuckled, to keep from screaming out in agony from the piercing pain in her heart. "I dunno, maybe it's me."

"Listen to me!" Ms. Lara said, grabbing both of her shoulders. "If a man wants you, then nuthin' can make him leave. If he doesn't, then nuthin' can make him stay. Stop making excuses for a man and his behavior. You should never live your life for a man before you find out what truly makes you happy. Don't sell yourself short or settle for less when there's always someone out there more deserving of your love. Baby, please don't stay in a relationship thinking things will get better because, trust me, you'll regret it later when they only get worser. Believe me, you could be blocking your blessing. Believe me, when I say there's somebody for everybody." she smiled, and thought about her birth father. "You'll be fine! You're a very beautiful intelligent girl." she said, hugging her.

"Don't forget, with great attributes!"

"Of course, baby. Dat goes without sayin'. In the same token, If you keep doing what you've always done, then you're gonna keep getting what you've always gotten. It may take a while but you're gonna realize it later on all your mistakes. I also believe there's good and bad in everybody. I cant pick and chose who you decide to live your life with, but I can say you're a beautiful black queen and you should be treated as such. I also know everybody gets tired and when you're tired you're tired."

"In all seriousness, the wisdom that you attribute, is so . . . beyond remarkable. Matter of fact remarkable, is an understatement. I can't find a word big enough to express how strong and powerful, of what you possess. You're the best. You always noe what to say to make me feel better. How come you so strong and I'm so weak?" she said staring in her mother's eyes.

"Hummmmmmm, let's see," she said, with her thumb and pointer finger cupping here chin. "I think you get the weakness from your dad."

They both chuckled a little bit. "See, there's a smile I've been waiting for. You're gonna be just fine, baby, just fine," she said, rubbing her hair as she did when she was younger. "It's like when life throws lemons at you grab'em and make lemonade."

"Ok, you lost me. I don't follow?"

"In other words baby girl, use your struggles and obstacles life throws at you and make opportunities, positive out of negative's."

"Yeah right my wrongs, huh? Dat does make a whole lot of sense. It seems like everybody else is so pessimistic. Especially when it comes to me and Grievence."

"Baby, you're still learnin', you'll be ok," she said as she pat her only daughter on the back. "Let me say dis', misery loves company. Nine times out of times when people are being negative, is either because things in their life is all messed up or their plain jealous. On dat note, I'm going to bed. You try to get some sleep and most important, I don't worry 'bout things I can't change. Dat's another reason I still have my sanity. You'll just have to pray on it and leave it up to the good Lord. Another thing I've always lived by and firmly believe, you change your thinking you change your future. But you're strong too. You just don't know it yet!" she winked and walked off.

"Maah!" Neeyah yelled.

"Yes, baby, what is it?" she said, turning to face her.

Neeyah ran up and hugged her. "Thanks for not passin' judgment or scoldin' me to make me feel worse than I already do,"

She kissed her on the forehead. "That's my job, isn't it? To pick you up when you're down?"

The talk with her mom made her feel a little bit better. She decided to hop in the shower; all she could think about was Grievence. "Why can't I just let him go?" she asked herself out loud. "Then again, I'm damned I do and I'm damned if I don't?" she said, as tears started running down her face; then she slid down the shower with her back. Stooping down, with her arms gripping her knees with water hitting her all in her face, she didn't care. The water started to get tepid. She didn't budge. When the water quickly got freezing-cold, it caused her to snap outta her trance. She got up, stepped out of the bathtub and wrapped herself in a towel. Not, bothering to dry off, she headed to her room. Laid on the bed and dialed Grievence's number. It went straight to voicemail all ten times. Then she balled up in a fetal position and cried herself to sleep.

"Who man is my sister fuckin' now?" Leigha said inaudibly, watching Amauri drive off.

When Grievence got home, his mom was on the phone with Swagga. *Maybe Tommorrow* by the Jackson 5, was playing in the background.

"Here's your brother!" she said, cheerfully handing him the phone so she could get back to her song and beer.

"Thanks for rescuin' me from ole' mama duke. Wow, she was lecturing' me the whole time!" Swagga sighed.

"You know, I know all too well how dat goes!" They both laughed. "So how does freedom feel?"

"I'm feelin' blessed, ole girl picked me up and straight took me on a shopping spree spent a couple of racks on a niggah. Then we went out to eat. I ordered breakfast, lunch, and dinner!"

"Is dat right?" Grievence said with his mind on what just happened to him.

"Well, at any rate, I'm not gonna keep you, my kitty is purrin'. I'll get up with you soon, man!" he said to make her happy because she was staring dead in his mouth.

"Fa sho, I'm not tryin' to be no cock-block-ass niggah ya' digg!" Then he ended the call.

When he got off the phone, his mom had dozed off. So, he kissed her softly and whispered, "I love you, Ma Duke."

"I love you too, baby." she said in a very soft whisper.

When he powered up his cell phone, he had a message from Khia crying hysterically. He laid back on his bed with his right hand cupping the back of his head. No sooner than his head hit the pillow when Khia called again, still crying. "Dat bitch cut my cousin a gang of times!" she screamed into the phone.

"Calm down, I can barely hear you!"

"Calm down my ass! Dat bitch sliced Apple's face wide da fuck open! She had to have an emergency surgery to stop the bleeding. She's so gonna pay. Who the fuck was dat pizza-face-bitch?" Khia screamed.

"I don't have shit to do wid dat. Leave me outta of it!"

He didn't care for Leigha, but he wasn't no snitch-ass, gossiping-ass niggah either.

"Niggah, you have a lot to do with it!"

Grievence just chuckled to himself out loud.

"Yeah, niggah, laugh now cry later. Bitch-ass niggah." Khia said then slammed the phone down.

"Bitches!" he garbled, before knocking out.

KILL OR BE KILLED

Swagga immediately put his plan into action by going to see Bruno's dad, Salvodore better known as Sal. Which he found out to be part of the infamous, Natalli family. The biggest drug cartel, family that ever walked on the Mid West streets.

He was instructed to come alone. When he got there, he personally thanked him for saving his son's life.

"Where's Bruno by the way?" Swagga inquisitively asked, quickly scanning the room.

"Oh, he couldn't make it, but he sends his love!" he sat emotionless. He couldn't tell him that Bruno let his friend sell drugs in front of one of their properties, which made them a target. As a mob boss, he knew that he had to be killed and he felt that he should be the one to carry out the hit. That was the one of the rules of being in the mob. You had to be a stand-up guy and die for yours. An hour had went by and they were still puffing on cigars. They made small talk until the food was served. Sal had his cook prepare a big dinner that mainly consisted of pasta and different types of sea food. There was also three women waiting to satisfy his every need. Shit wasn't at all that sweet, because what he didn't know was that he was gonna have to prove his loyalty first. While Swagga was soaking up everything, a big burly man that weighed at least 350 to 400 pounds tapped him on the shoulder to let him know Sal was ready to see him. An uncanny feeling washed over his entire body. With no other options, he put his game face on and pushed himself up from the leather sofa. He followed the man down a long, creepy hallway and down some unstable old, wooden steps to the basement. Each time the step creaked, chills went up and down his spine. He wanted to go in the other direction from whence he came, but when he turned around all he saw was pitch black darkness. Which made an instant onset of queasiness.

"Swagga!" Sal said in his deep Colombian accent.

"Boss!" Swagga scanned the room. First off, he noticed a chain saw and a huge machine that he later found out to be that of a meat grinder. Then in another corner, he saw a man whimpering like a wounded dog. He was bound, gagged, and duct taped. Swagga stomach started churning.

"As you know, nuthin' in life comes without a small price. I'm sure my son gave you the scoop on our family."

Swagga nodded his head yes. Sal instantaneously diverted his eyes back to the man. "Well, you're at a point now of no return," Sal motioned for his bodyguard to get the gun. Swagga caught an instant migraine. The dull pain in the bottom of his stomach told him not to ask questions. Just listen, and do as told.

Please, Lord, don't let me have to kill nobody. he prayed silently to himself. *Bruno never mentioned dis'. What have I gotten myself into!* he thought while putting on his game face.

"I want you to put two to the head, in dis' fuckin' rata!" he yelled. He let him know that when you shoot someone, always do so by putting two behind the ear with a .22 because it would rattle around in their head.

"I fuckin' odio a ratas! Dis es lo que pasa cuando usted se chiva, hembra!" he screamed, hitting the man with an iron crowbar. Blood started flowing drastically, down his chunky cheeks. The man let out a loud wail. Swagga was scared shitless! He had never killed anybody nor, witnessed one. He may have smacked a couple of niggahs up in his time but, never murder.

Then his thoughts immediately flashed back when he was around six, his uncle Daniel took him up 17 flights of steps. To a roof top, where there were two men were waiting around a bonfire. They were arguing about money, and then it escalated. He remember how Daniel's voice shook with suppressed anger, all of a sudden, he pulled out his gun and shot them both, execution style. Then he picked up a bottle of kerosene and doused them with it. He also remembered, one of the men, didn't die instantly. And how he squirmed and made piercing screams, when he threw the match on them. "Tony, Tony," he heard his uncle call out, but he was aghast and unable to move. So, he swooped him up off his feet and carried him down the steps.

All those memories were repressed until that very moment. He was a street pharmacist! Now faced with being in a murderous game, Sal could sense his nervousness and assured him that once he did it once that he'd be able to do it again and again without thinking twice, as he took the gun from his bodyguard. When Swagga reached for the gun, he could barely hold it because his hands were quivering very badly. Clearly dithering, as he shifted

his attention back to the tied up man, Sal told him that he should never let his victim see fear. Then he leaned over, amicably whispered to him, either he do it or they were gonna put two slugs to his brain. *I'm damned if I do and I'm damned I don't* he thought to himself, as he hurriedly swallowed the huge chunk of saliva that rested in his throat. As, he put the gun up to the man head he caught a glimpse of the man's beseeching eyes. After seeing them, he closed his eyes as tight as they would go and squeezed the trigger twice. *Balm Balm* After the first shot, he felt the adrenaline rush and it actually didn't feel so bad. When he was done, Sal stuck a canary in his mouth and said, "Cante ahora usted fuckin' parásito!"

"Why did you stick a bird into his mouth and what was dat in English?"

"Well Swag, it's sing now you fuckin' parasite. But It depends on what message the mob is trying to send is how they dispose of your body. For instance, the hit dat was just carried out, the guy snitched. So, we wanted him to be found with a canary stuffed in his mouth. Then again, if someone vouched for you, you may be found with your hands cut off, for the simple fact you brought him in shaking hands with everybody. On the other hand, if they wanted you to simply disappear, they'll chop your ass up with the chainsaw, put your ass through the meat grinder and throw your ass in the Lake Michigan, for the sea animals to devour!" It was rumored that Sal has killed more men than cancer. See it in the mind, he was one of the most ruthless, cutthroat gangster. If the man had a warm spot for any living thing, it was for his dog, Sammy. "See, my man, Swagg, it wasn't dat bad, huh? I promise, the next time you won't even flinch," he said in his deep Colombian accent, with his arm wrapped around his neck.

Swagga's mind started racing, trying to find the right words to say; he kept coming up blank.

"Piece of cake. I guess you can't learn how to swim without getting into the water!" Swagga said making small talk. The bodyguard returned with a duffle bag.

"Here's your goody bag, your lifeline." Sal reminded and handed it to him. It contained three kilos and ten thousand in cash to get him started. "I want a sixty-five grand back. Welcome aboard!" he continued, hitting him on his back. Although he could potentially make forty racks off of one key alone, Sal wanted to reward and help him stand alone.

"The point of no return." Swagga replied, turning to leave. He felt like jumping for joy; he was so happy. *Damn I just killed a man!* He thought and quickly pushed it out of his head. He was driving Angie's '04 Neon. Which he no longer needed but decided to keep her on his team a little

while longer. He had other plans for her. "Damn I hope these birds fly in the same night," he said putting the duffle bag in the trunk. He immediately set his plan into action, starting with getting a spot that was referred to as "*The Trap*" that he sweet talked Angie into getting. He knew he was seven years behind and he wasn't gonna let time pass him by anymore. Angie was so vulnerable to the point, he could've gotten her to do anything. Although she got the spot, she wasn't allowed there. She didn't care because she was happy having a man of Swagga's character living with her. She stood about five feet five inches and weighed about 255 pounds. She was black mixed with Puerto Rican. She had a real pretty face with some extra baggage and a funny shape. Her nieces would oftentimes tease her, telling her that her butt looked like SpongeBob and maybe if she sat in some water a little bit longer, that it might swell up a tad bit. Within a few days, he had his operation up and running. He ran into one of his old homies, who had two homeboys that was starving and ready to eat. Being said, he had his lieutenants and he just needed his fam, Grievence and Deuces.

Neeyah continued to call Grievence; he pressed end and sent her straight to the voice mail whenever he number showed on his phone.

When he went to talk to Deuces, he told him that he was still on the papers.

While, Grievence was laying across his bed, his phone started ringing for the fourth time in a row, just as he was about to cut his phone off he noticed it was his brother. "What up doe?" he said into the phone.

"I need you niggah." Swagga said with sincerity in the phone.

"You up and runnin' already?"

"Up and runnin'." he reiterated.

"Damn, you don't waste no time, do you?"

"Time is money. If you aren't sure about nuthin' else, you should noe I'm all about my money." Swagga said seriously.

"Tru dat, tru dat," Grievence retorted. "Shit I haven't even told Ma Duke yet, or Neeyah! I don't even have no money. I have to wait 'til I get paid to get a ticket," he said, looking for all types of excuses not to go.

"Niggah, stop. Don't even trip. You make the reservations and I got you. Matter of fact, I'm gonna send you five racks now. Just give Ma four, for her truck and you take one. Believe me there's more, much more."

"Word?" Grievence said in a loud tone. He was beginnin' to think it wasn't a sacrifice after all, especially if his brother just got out days ago and was already shelling out that type of money.

"It's nuthin'!"

"Say no more. I love you, man. No homo shit." he said, giving in.

"Likewise. Umma go because like I said, time is money." he chuckled, ending the call and. The conversation with Swagga gave him a lot to think about. He just didn't know how he was gonna break the news to his mama. Neeyah, he didn't really care about, so he headed over to see her.

"Hey, Ricky." Grievence said extending his hand. Ricky sneered. He took a look at his own outstretched hand, and wondered why it hadn't been acknowledged. No mattered what happened to him and Neeyah, Ricky was always cool with him. "Is Neeyah here?" he asked, slowly putting his hand down, hanging his head low. Ricky snorted and walked away.

"Baabee." he yelled down the hall. Almost, immediately she appeared in the hallway.

He hung his head low. "Hey, Ms. Lara is dere any way I can talk to Neeyah. I know you're probably upset with me, huh?"

"I don't like seeing my daughter hurt, but as long as it doesn't get physical, then umma stay out of it. Understood?" she said, with a very stern look.

"Understood." he nodded his head.

"How are you doing by the way?"

"In a word?" he asked dryly, trying to avoid eye contact. "Bad, because I love her. I would never physically hurt her. I don't intend to hurt her at all," he said, looking into her eyes.

She knew he meant well and was the typical boy that wasn't ready to settle down. She didn't condone his behavior but what could she do. That being said, she was not gonna get into their business. She looked deeply into his confused, beseeching eyes; and actually saw that he had a warm heart. "Come here." she said with her arms outstretched. "Neeyah's in the room, go let her know how you feel." she said letting him go, but still having his shoulders in her firm grip.

"Thank you for listenin' and not judgin' or chewin' me out!" he said, walking toward Neeyah's room. She smiled.

"Neeyah," he whispered, quietly easing the door open.

"Grievence!" she yelled. Appalled to see him standing in her doorway.

"W-w-what are you doing here?" she stammered, grabbing the covers and pulling them up to her chest.

He was shocked to see her looking the way she did. She looked like death warmed over. Her hair was mangled; her eyes were all bloodshot and puffy and it was all his fault "I had to tell you sumthin' and wanted to do so in person."

"Why are you staring at me like dat?" she asked with an attitude.

"Don't trip, I just haven't never seen you look like dis', dat's all!"

"I wonder why I look like dis'!" she said with a very soft creaky tone while, looking at the ceiling.

"Look, I just came to tell you sumthin' and felt it was only right to do so in person. But, if you're gonna give me a funky ass attitude, I'll leave." he said starting to get up.

"No, please don't leave, baby. I miss you sooooooo," she begged.

"Umma keep it real. I miss you like shit too, but there's sumthin' you need to know,"

She feared it was gonna be bad news. Her gut told her so. "I'm listenin',"

"Well, I see you still wanna be with a niggah. Damn, girl, you must really love a niggah."

"Spit it out!" she demanded.

"Ok, I see I'm just cheatin' you outta your life and I think you deserve someone dat's not gonna keep hurtin' you,"

Tears flowed freely down her face as she listened to the painful words that came from him mouth.

"Why? Why are you doing dis' to me? I've loved you for my entire adult life. Please don't do dis' to us. I need you in my life. We can get through dis'. We've been through so much together," she sat up crying.

"Don't cry, it's not your fault. It's hurtin' me to see you cry. That's why I gotta let you go, all I do is hurt you. You deserve so much better!"

"I need you, baby!" she yelled. "Please, boo, I love you. We've weathered plenty of storms together. When it was cold it was real cold. But, no matter what the sun always shined thru the clouds." she smiled a little, for a moment she felt like there was an ounce of hope. He remained mute and listened to her talk. "Even when it seemed so far away, it shined. Let me hold you close, boo. Just lay right here and when you wake up tomorrow a and it would be a brand new day."

She flung the covers off of her body and hopped up. "Don't go, we can fix dis'. Let's compromise." she said, dropping down to her knees to look him in the eye.

"You right. The sun hasn't always shined and sometimes it has to rain boo, but think about it for a minute. The bad outweighs the good. You deserve so much better than me. Please get up!"

"I can't, I love you sooo."

"If you don't get up, I'm gonna leave because I can't stand seein' you like dis'!" she ignored him and continued to beg.

"I love you too, girl, but I'm tired of hurting you," he said, with tears welling up in his eyes. But, being the man he was, he vowed that no one

will see him cry. After all, his grandfather told him crying was for sissies right before he took his last breath. He thought back on the day. How tears welled up in his eyes when his grandfather told him that they gave him a week to live. Later that night, he was stood over him and stared at all the tubes and machines he was hooked up to, tears started flowing down his face. His grandfather opened his eyes and said, *Don't cry, cryin' is for sissy boys*, Moments later, he gasped and took his last breath.

"Who knows, maybe we need a little bit of time apart. Dat way I can clear my head, and if we're meant to be, we will be. And just like the sun rose dis' mornin', it's gonna set tonight. You need to go on with your life, because you deserve better," he continued, contradicting himself. He loved her, but he was young and lost to continue taking her on the rollercoaster to hell and back.

"What does dat suppose to mean?" she snapped.

"It means life isn't gonna stop becuz of us taking a break from each other. Just use dis' time to heal and get yourself together. I can assure you, one day you're gonna thank me for closing dis' door,

"Don't make decisions for me. I know what I want and need!" she snapped.

"Dat wasn't all I wanted to tell you." he sighed. Then he paused a minute.

"I guess when it rains, it pours," she said as she rocked badk and forth.

"I'm going to Detroit for about a month or so." he continued.

She sat spaced out, rocking back and forth on the floor and crying. "Take me with you, baby," she stared at him.

"You would leave everything and everybody to follow me to da D.?" he looked down at her.

"At the drop of a hat." she flung her arm down. "Baby, I'll follow you like twitter. To the ends of the earth,"

"Wow. That's nice to know but unfortunately I gotta make dis' move alone. But don't worry I'll be back and we can proceed with getting our place."

"So, in other words, you're just gonna leave me here in misery? How do I breathe without you, Grievence? How am I gonna get thru the night without you? I want to know, damnit?" she screamed. "You're my world, my heart, my soul! What kind of life will it be without you?" she cried and begged. He choked back the tears that welled up in his eyes. "There isn't gonna be a sun in my sky. Why? Why? Why me, Lord?" she looked up at him. Snot was running down from her nose to her mouth.

He kneeled down on one knee, grabbed and pulled her closely to him. Nearly squeezing her to death. She didn't care because without him she felt like she was gonna die. He didn't care that she was slobbering all over his

Coogi outfit that took damn near his whole check to buy. Without warning, she flipped and started hitting him in the back. "No, let me go."

"Don't fight me, baby!" he whispered in her ear. "Breathe. Come on say it with me bay, wooosaah woosaah."

"Fuck dat shit! It's for da birds." she said breaking away from him. "Gone on. Go." she screamed to the top of her lungs. He pushed himself up from the bed.

"I gotta do dis' for me. I mean, for us." he corrected himself. "Let's see how dis' works out. We just gonna take some time apart to clear our heads and see where it goes. Besides, my mom always says, absence makes the heart grow fonder." he whispered in her ear. When he got up to leave, she snaked her arm out and grabbed him.

"Please, don't leave me. I know what I want, and it's you!" he didn't look back. He just took his sweated-out Coogi bandana off and hurled it over his shoulders and shut the door.

"Nooooooo!" she shrieked. Then she felt a piercing pain in her stomach. She balled up in a knot. The pain was a mixture of hunger and a broken heart.

Nothing mattered to her. She just grabbed the bandanna and squeezed it with dear life. As, Sonny saw him rushing out in a hurry, he heard her scream and rushed in her room. He was so mad you could see smoke coming from his neatly done cornrows. "I noe dat mutha—," he said and stopped mid sentence when he saw her laying on the floor in a fetal position, sobbing like a hungry child. "Sis," he screamed. "Did he lay his hands on you? I promise you, I'll kill dat mutha—"

"No, he didn't touch me. He don't want me no more, Sonny. My baby don't love me no more." she blubbered. All he could do was hold her. He felt bad for his sister and vowed that he was gonna pay one way or the other for hurting his sister.

"Don't cry, baby girl." he said, trying to console his sister. Then, he helped her get in bed and whispered, "Dis' too shall pass."

Grievence heard her scream before he left. He hopped in his car, opened up his armrest, and grabbed his blunt. After sitting out in her parking lot thinking, he cranked up and drove straight to the only other person that could take his mind off all his problems. A woman named Shelly, whom always had a revolving door, for him twenty-four hours. She not only offered him sex, she gave him advice and support. Upon seeing her, he thought back on the one time he did try to have sex with her. He made sure it was pitch black dark. "Let me hit it from da back," he whispered to her.

She turned around and bent over. When he stuck himself inside her, it felt like he was in a cold ass abyss. To make matters worse, when he felt her flabs flapping against his legs, it instantly made his dick limp.

"Damn, baby I know what it is, it was dat damn Remy I just drank." he said to protect her feelings.

She took his limp dick and stuck it her warm secreted mouth. "Don't worry daddy, mama's got a remedy for ole whisky dicks."

"Damn, if her pussy felt anything like her mouth she'll be da shit." he muttered. Guiding her head as she went up and down on his dick putting a thick coat of spit on it. Then all of a sudden, her lips covered his entire head and she started sucking it vigorously. She licked from his head down to his balls. For about fifteen minutes, almost in a pattern. His whole body began to tremble. By the time she was done, he had busted two nuts. Those moments would forever be seared in his brain. She stood just over five feet tall and weighed 110 pounds, soak and wet. She was around his age, but looked much older than what she was. Judging by the way she looked, you could tell she had a rough life. The only thing that looked appealing on her was her shoulder-length dreads, dyed honey blonde. Her whole body was wrinkled and flabby, from the weight she had lost. Her butt looked as somebody pushed it from the back to the front. He only used her for somebody to talk to or to get head from because her coochie was all worn out, with no walls. She couldn't even pay a crackhead to fuck her. Matter of fact she proved the cliche about *another's man trash is another man's treasure* to be dead wrong. Men often times, referred to fucking her, like sticking their dick in a big, dried out well. Besides that, she was a cool ass female that was not only book smart, but also street smart. If he ever needed anything, she was dere. No matter what it was.

THINGS THAT CAN HAPPEN
WHILE UNDER THE INFLUENCE

Monie was laying on the bed with the phone right next to her. Where you could've found her for the last couple of days, waiting for Amauri's call. Wearing a thin, satin chemise and letting the breeze from the fan soothe her.

It's been four days. I haven't heard from him, she thought. Scared she was gonna miss his call, she decided to just wait. She didn't have a number to reach him on. She even turned down dates, which wasn't at all like her.

Amauri was in a deep sleep when he was awakened by his vibrating cell phone.

"What's up, my nigg," Kadaafie said into the phone in a very deep voice.

At first, he was a little disoriented. "Hello!" he said a little louder. Amauri had been up all night popping pills with this little hood rat named Yatta, he'd just met.

"My bad, dawg, I was yawnin'!" he lied.

"Well, I tryna see, can you meet me at dat joint we talked about the other day, off of MLK (Martin Luther King)?" Kadaafie spoke into the phone without his tone changing.

"Yeah, fasho, give me an hour." Amauri turned over to find Yatta still in his bed.

"See you in an hour." Kadaafie ended the call.

He looked at her. "Damn, she looked finer than a muthafucka last night. Look at them big-ass ears sticking from her braids. I never in my life seen no shit like dat before. Damn, I thought we had thirty-two teeth? Her ass has to have at least fifty-two, damn." he sneered. "Dis' bitch is a walkin' creepshow!" he shrugged his shoulders as if he'd gotten a chill. She stood about six feet tall and weighed about 150 pounds. Her dark, ashy skin tone made her look Haitian. Long, nappy tie knots, swung down her back to

her butt. She was skinny and black as shit! His mind started racing, trying to find a quick way to get her out. "Fire!" he yelled.

She jumped up with her eyes bulging out of her head and slob was running down the side of her face. "Where?!" she screamed, thunderously. Wiping the slob off her chin. "Oh my fuckin' goodness, I don't wanna die today! I'm way to young to die," she said. Clearly, still on one. When she just up out of his bed, she left a couple of braids behind.

He helped her gather her things. "Hurry and get your shit before dis' muthafucka burn down. Run!"

She fell about two times trying to put her shirt on, running half-dressed trying to get the hell out of dodge.

"You run dis' way and I'll run dat way!" he yelled. Closing and locking his door behind her. She never looked back.

"Ewwwe!" he shrugged his shoulders. "Damn, she looks like she hit every ugly branch, falling out of a tree. The things dat happen when you're under the influence!" he said hopping in the shower. Then suddenly, it dawned on him that he didn't find no condom package. He punched the wall but didn't feel the pain, at least not right away.

Thirty minutes later he pulled up in a parking spot and shut his engine off. Kadaafie was already inside.

Soon as he hit the door, Kadaafie stood to his feet to greet him. "What's good? Long time no see, huh?"

"Yeah fam. But ole girl fell hook, line, and sinker. I planned it oh so well though." he said, popping his collar. "I started by getting her a dress and shoes from the Slauson's and I put it inside of a Dillard's box. She bought it and ate the shit. Then we went to the most expensive restaurant I know. I spent every bit of five hundred on her dat night."

"Yeah, sounds like you gave her ass the red carpet treatment. The main thing is she feed right into the trap. But, that's what's up, doe!" he said content with the results. "So have you spoken to her since?"

"No, I got dis' over here on my end. Don't trip, umma have her bum ass eatin' outta the palms of my hands. Dat bitch was like I've always wanted to fuck the shit out of you and whoop whoop, so trust me I got dis'."

"Well, I gotta head off to Kingston in the morning, come walk with me to my car." Kadaafie said getting up from the table. Amauri did as told.

Once inside the car, Kadaafie went inside a special compartment in his car and pulled out a small manila envelope. "Dis' should be enough to replace the money you spent the other night, and here's a couple of dollars for your pain and suffering. Why don't you take ole girl on a vacation to

give her more assurance." he said handing him the envelope. "There's more where dat came from, so play your cards right."

Amauri's eyes stretched wider than a crack head's eyes, fresh off the pipe.

"Oh, cuzo, dat niggah Rah Rah's days are limited,"

"Yeah, I know. Well, umma go handle dis' business before I leave. You know if you need me, I'm just a call away."

Amauri nodded his head yeah. "And you go butter dat bitch up. I'll be in touch with you," Kadaafie said with a stern look on his face.

He got out of the car. "Fasho, cuzo. Have a safe trip."

"Always," Kadaafie said, throwing his hand out of the window and driving off.

"Now that's what's up, doe!" Amauri said with a happy-go-lucky smile. His thoughts quickly diverted back to Yatta. *Damn, I don't even noe how or where to find her to make sure she didn't get pregnant.* Almost as quick as the thoughts entered his mind, he quickly dismissed them. Then he opened up his armrest and took his knock Cartier's from the case. "Fuck it, I'm not gonna worry about something I can't change." When he got there, he counted the money. It was seven racks. "Damn, I wanna be like you when I grow up."

While, heading to the computer his cell phone started vibrating. He pressed end and sent it to voicemail. It was one of his regular customer's trying to cop the new Taker's movie that had just hit theaters. "Fuck dat funky ass bitch and her punk ass 20 dollars, I'm on some otha shit now!"

He searched the internet and found a cruise to a remote island. As luck would have it, he caught a last minute special. Buy one get one half-off ticket. He snatched it up. "Two racks. Not bad, not bad at all."

He pulled out his prepaid visa card. The ticket included all meals, for a four-day-three-night cruise and a bonus stay at another remote place for three days and two nights. Two hours later, he headed back to Slauson's. This time he bought her eight outfits including two swimsuits, underwear and lingerie. "I freakin' love the swap meet!" he yelled walking to the car. On his way home, he stopped by the mall and headed straight for the Famous Foot Ware. Soon as he walked in, he grabbed the first pair of shoes on display. Upon paying for them, the cashier told him that the shoes were on a buy one-get one free deal. "That's what's up!" he said heading towards the sandals. "I noe she'll like these joints right here." he said picking up a pair of tan sandals that had the long straps that you tie up to your calf. "Hey Miss Lady, is there any way I can get these in a size 9!" he asked noticing

the other shoes he got her were too little. He wanted her as comfortable as possible. After he shopped for her things, he went shopping for himself and then used his bags to put her things in.

Monie woke up looking at her watch. It read 8:00 p.m. So, she flung the covers off her body and hopped up to make sure the phone was plugged into to the wall. It was. Then, next, she checked the ringer to make sure it was on. It was. Lastly, she checked to make sure there was a dial tone. There was. *"Damn!" she said to herself, why haven't he called me? How he gonna come do all dis' shit and not call me no more? I wonder was it sumthin' I did?* she thought to herself. Her mind began to race. "I guess a watched teapot doesn't boils!" she said falling back on the bed. Finally, the phone rang. She scrambled around on the bed until she found it.

"Hello," she spoke into the phone, in her sexiest voice. On the first ring.

"Sounds like you were expectin' my call." the voice on the other end said.

"You!" she sighed.

"Yeah, baby. Who else would it be and where's all the enthusiasm I usually hear when I call?"

"Whadda you want, Brianyant?" she said dryly.

"Damn, it's like dat? I didn't sleep with your monkey ass last night. Your ass been jolly, jolly when a niggah called."

"I was sleep, damnit!" she snapped, clearly pissed because it wasn't Amauri.

"I was tryna see did your bummy ass want some of these sticks I got. But, fuck it. Matter of fact, fuck you, lose my number wid yo' stanky-ass pussy! You can go suck an AIDS dick and get sick, bitch!" he screamed into the receiver. With that, he ended the call.

"Fuck you, little ddd—" she retorted but stopped in mid sentence when the operator said, of you would like to make a call. Any other time, she would've jumped at the opportunity to kick it with him, because he smoked countless blunts with her and gave her a couple of dollars to go in her pocket. But, she just wasn't even trying to feel that, at the moment. She sure as hell didn't feel like holding his little dick tryna suck it. "Two tears in a bucket! Shid, fuck you and yo' punk ass sherm. I said I didn't wanna be fuckin' bother so get the fuck over it!" she said, zooming the cordless phone across the room. Her thoughts sidetracked back to her date with Amauri. After their date, he demanded to have her house number so he would know she was home.

Amauri headed home to pack. After looking around, he decided to tidy up a little bit. He started with his room. He found about five of Yatta's

mangy-looking plaits. Which, made all the thoughts of her, come flooding back. The hair smelled so bad, it made him gag.

"Damn, did dis' bitch ever wash her shit?" he said holding the hair by his fingertips and tossing them in the garbage. "Damn, how did a bitch catch me, a G, slippin'?"

When he got out the shower, he glanced at the clock on the bathroom wall, it read 10:45 pm. He was exhausted so, he wrapped the towel around himself and headed to his room. Leaving a trail of wet spots behind on the carpet. His king-sized bed was calling him and he couldn't get to it quick enough. He had just made it up with his brand new 1020 thread count sateen sheets. Soon as he got into his bed, he grabbed a pillow and stuck it between his legs. Almost as soon as his head hit the pillow, he drifted off to sleep. Like a newborn baby, just out of the womb. An hour later, which seemed like eternity, Amber, his baby mama sister was trying to wake him up.

"Amauri, Amauri." she whispered. He didn't budge. He was dead to the world. So, she decided to splash some water on his face.

"What da fuck!" he screamed, thunderous, as he tried to jump up. But, was quickly forced back down. She had him handcuffed to each pole on his high-post bedroom set. Hands and feet. "How the hell did you get in here?" he asked with a bewildered look on his face.

She ripped the towel off of him so she could see his dick. "Listen, here it's like dis', you told me I was never gonna catch ya' ass off ya' guards."

"Get da fuck out of here, lil girl!"

"Kill dat noise. Renée, sent me over here to give you some pictures of Kamauri. However, when I knocked on the door, there was no answer. So, I banged on the door; I called your cell phone a gang of times, there was still no answer. I seen your car here, the lights were on and then it dawn on me how klutzy your ass was and figured, you had a spare key. I was afraid you were hurt!" she said trying to sound concerned. "Then, I called your name and shook you hella times, you still didn't respond. I even checked your pulse."

"Well, as you can see I'm perfectly fine, now unlock me and take your fast ass home." he said imperatively.

She jumped on top of him. "Uh huh, homie, opportunity has presented itself fa' me to make you eat your words. Therefore, I ran and got my handcuffs outta my trunk!"

"Youz a little fuckin' psycho bob!" he yelled.

"If I were you, I would stop all dat yellin'. You're gonna need all ya' energy. Besides, stop tryna ack like you don't fantasize 'bout me. I be seein' the way you eyeballin' and undressin' a niggah, with them big sexy eyes of

yourz. Like you can eat me up." said rolling her hips. "Becuz ya' ass finna see dis' gone last all night long, so you may as well lay back and enjoy,"

"If you don't fuckin' uncuff me umma—," he started.

"You gonna do what, spank me, daddy?" she cut him off. "Meow!" she purred like a cat. Then she started slowly, undressing. Enticing him. Every piece of clothing she took off, she hurled it at him and said, "Meow!"

Damn, she's very tantalizin'. Look at her body, I know it's definitely, sumthin' in the milk now. he thought to himself, getting aroused.

Then she pushed her breast up and started licking her right nipple and fondling the left. She purred and watched him with a sexy, seductive look.

"Girl, you need to take these fuckin' handcuffs off and carry your young fast ass home!" he wiggled his arms and feet to try to loosen the handcuffs.

"Come on, you know you want dis' young (*moans*) virgin, (*moans*) hot pussy." she moaned and rolled her lips in a circular motion.

He shot her a look that said, *Virgin, shittin' me!*

"Okay, virgin may be a little overrated, but I've only been with one person!" she said, slowly running her hand up and down her nice thick curvaceous body. Her titties were every bit of compelling, they sat up so perfect. Her ass was so nice and curvy, that you could probably set two cups on it without her knowing. She definitely had a body of an adult and was only seventeen. He tooted his lip up. "Okay, fine! Five. Niggah, damn, but they were jus' little-ass boys dat teased me. I need a grown-ass man to make my body scream, oooowww!" she said. Then she whirled around and bent over as if she was picking up something from the floor. Soon as she turned back around, the first thing she seen was his big dick, standing erect in the air.

"I'm glad somebody wants me, showin' me some love. I was beginnin' to feel unwanted," she said. Then she continued teasing him, by sucking and licking her left and aggressively, squeezing her right nipple. Without notice, she hopped on his bed and opened her legs as wide as she could. Slowly she opened her pussy lips, and then inserted her pointer and index finger in and out. Moaning as if she was being fucked. Louder and louder. Then she started flicking her sticky clit back and forward.

"I know you want dis' hot," she moaned. "Wet, juicy pussy." she continued to taunt him for ten minutes or so. "Don't you wanna find out why they call me Aquafinna, baby?"

"What I want is for you to let me loose and go home, lil' girl!" he cleared his throat.

"Damn, niggah, stop being so narrow-ass-minded and recognize you got a real, hot woman in front of you dat's ready to give you the business."

she leaned up to make eye contact with him. Just as he was about to say something but there was a knock on the door.

She licked her finger and jumped up. "Hold dat thought!"

"Don't you dare go to my fuckin' door." he screamed to the top of his lungs. Ignoring him, she kept pushing. First, she looked out of the peephole, then she took the chain off of the door and unlocked the deadbolt. "Niggah easy." she waved him off with one hand and slowly eased the door open with the other one.

"Why da fuck did you go to my—" he stopped in mid-sentence, when he saw her homegirl Passion. She walked in the room wearing only a black-and white checkered Deron pea coat and stilettos. As she ambled towards them, she slowly unbuttoned her coat, revealing a red-laced Victoria's Secret underwear set, matching her red stilettos. Passion, was her stripper friend that turned her out.

"Now dis', hea' niggah, gone be on the house and next time you gotta pay before pump!" she said, taking her coat off and slinging it in the chair.

He thought he had died and gone to heaven. The handcuffs no longer hurt. All his pain was numbed, by pleasure.

"Damn, Passion girl, why did it take you so long to get here? And where's the radio?" Amber asked.

"I had a hard time finding dis' spot. I've never been on dis' side of town befo'. Dat and you know I had to find the Thizz kids. But, the radio is by the door." she said, pouring some Grey Goose and cranberry juice in a cup.

"Girl I done told you, you gone get enough of messing wid them lil' pill pushers on da corner. Anyways what you sippin' on over there?" Amber asked plugging the radio in, playing track 5, which was *Sticky Face* by Trey Songz.

"Girl, you be knowing, dis' right hea' is my doctor-feel-good medicine. Hea' girl, take a swig." she handed her the cup along, with an pill. Then she walked over to Amauri and forced one in his mouth.

"Dat, Grey Goose be having your girl all loose and some mo' shit." Amber said.

"Loose as a goose don't get her started." Passion sang, waving her hands in the air.

"Heeey. That's my ish," Amber flailed her arms around and then she started guzzling down the rest of the drink that was left in her cup. Before she could finish, Passion grabbed her hand and slowly led her over to the bed. Once they were close to the bed, she pushed her back on it and leaped on top of her like an tiger. Then she started sucking her lips slowly, making her

way down to her right breast. Kissing, biting, and licking every inch of her body along the way. Then she made her way over to the left harden nipple. Knibbling, sucking, and flicking her tongue all around it. With her free hand, she grabbed her right breast and squeezed it very aggressively. Amber screamed out while directing Passion's head over to the other nipple.

"Do it baby!" Amber said, leaning up to kiss her passionately. Passion flashed her a seductive look and broke loose from her, hungry for something else. She made her way down Amber's soft body. Gently, planting soft kisses along the trail to the nest. Amber grabbed her head and held on to it. Every time the metal from her tongue ring touched her body, she trembled and jumped. She was in pure bliss. It felt so good her; she had forgotten Amauri was even in the room.

"Uh huh, niggah don't flinch, be still" she said, running her tongue down her body. Licking and sucking her navel.

"Yeah!" Amber screamed to the top of her lungs, as the e-pill began kicking in. "Are you hungry, baby?"

"Voracious. Grrrrh," she roared like and tiger.

"Yall some ole' freaks!" he said, licking his lips while the veins in his dick were expanding. Passion teased him by getting on her knees, and making her cheeks jiggle in his face.

"Let mama see it smile for me!" she said, slowly spreading Amber's swollen lips apart and sticking her long pierced, tongue in her wet pussy. Gently sucking on each of her lips. Then she flicked her tongue all around her walls. Starting slow, and then as she moaned louder, she got faster with it as she watched her face for reaction. "Don't stop!" Amber screamed and moaned in ecstasy. All the while slowly, scooting up towards the wall. Amber started breathing heavy.

"I done told you, don't run from me. Bring dat ass to me!" Passion said in a near whisper, pulling her body back down to her tongue. She listened on as Amber, moaned and breathe heavily, admiring her skills. When she began to cum Passion, tooted her ass up higher and plunged her face into her pussy. So she could suck all the creamy juices that emanated out. All he could see was her ass jiggling and Amber's toes wiggling. Passion didn't stop there, with her fingers she rolled her nipple in a circular motion. Her tongue was lodged in Amber's wet pussy. With her other hand, she used her fingers to trigger her g-spot. Amber screamed, wiggled and gripped the sheets very tightly. Passion relaxed her body, so she could get all up in her pussy with her tongue and fingers. Then suddenly, Amber whole body tensed and her back stiffen. She quivered like she was having a seizure, "I'm cummin'!"

she said deafening, as she began to squirt cum all into Passion face. When she was done, she stuck out her tongue and licked around her mouth. In a circular motion to get all of the natural sweet creamy juices.

"Well, Damn!" he said out loud, seeing the cum on her face when she turned around. She shot him a look that said *now top dat.* Then he glanced at Amber, who was on the bed still jerking. With juices emitting, from her throbbing pussy.

"Sorry you felt a little neglected mama's here. Best believe she take care of all of hers." Passion grabbed Amauri's throbbing dick, and deep throated it like a pro. It was almost as if it disappeared in her throat. He knew she was use to it because she didn't gag one time. He guided her head up and down.

"I see you did your homework in school, huh?"

She took his dick out of her mouth. "Niggah, I had a 4.0 in sucking dick and eating pussy. In fact, I was so good I got triple promoted to a professor." she looked up at him. Then she shifted her attention to Amber, who was cheesing.

"Dat was a good one.

"Baby, I'm good at what I do. A bonified pleaser." she massaged his dick gentle with her free hand, while licking continuously around the head of it. Then she put a thick coat of spit on it, and made popping noises as she pulled up on the tip of the head with her lips. He moaned and groaned. Before he got a chance to cum, she quickly slipped a condom on his dick and rode him like a pro in the rodeo from the back. Amber rushed over like ravenous lion that has caught it's prey slipping, and sat up on her knees, and then wrapped her warm tongue around Passion's nipple. She was riding so fast to the point the condom popped. When it did she quickly hopped off.

"Switch," Amber yelled, quickly hopping on his erect penis that stood twelve inches in the air. Passion laid down and scooted all the way down in front of Amber. First, she licked and sucked her lips. Then she whispered, "Don't trip I'll kiss every lip, don't flip!" Seconds later, she buried her head into Passion's fat, hairy pussy. Like a rhythm, Passion rolled her hips. All the while, still bouncing up and down on Amauri's dick. He could no longer restrain his groaning. All of a sudden, Amber spun around on his dick to face him.

"Niggah, do you still think I'm too young?" she whispered in his ear. Passion stood back to watch them.

"Yo' sis' gonna beat mine and your ass," he said in a soft tone in between oohs and aahs.

"Fuck my sister!" she bolted her head up.

"I mean, what can I do, you guys raped me. Look at me, I'm defenseless!" he joked.

"Cut it out. Kill dat shit and take dis' good pussy!" she said, bouncing up and down on his dick. She didn't care if Renee walked in the room and saw her fucking his brains out. In fact, she would've gave her left leg for her to walk thru his double doors. Low key, she anxiously awaited the day when she could tell her, and rip her heart out and dangle it up in front of her. In her eyes, fucking her sister's first and only love, couldn't hold a candle to all the pain she felt and endured over the years. She knew her sister loved Amauri dearly and wouldn't let another man touch her since they had split up. The whole thing was bittersweet, because Renee nor Amauri knew how she felt and hid very well. She loved her Amber terribly and would have quickly, without second guessing, taken a bullet from her. Every chance she got she reminded her how pretty she was. On the other hand, Amber would put on a facade with nothing but devious thoughts running through her mind. *Simple minded, bitch* she thought to herself, starring at him. Then she thought back on their many conversations on her sister telling her how much she genuinely loved Amauri and wanted him back. Amber would pretend to listen and wait for her cue to bash him and make up lies on him every chance she got. It never failed, as soon as she heard the words from her sister's mouth, *I love you and value your opinion so umma let him spread his wings,* A big wide grin would spread across her face as she hugged her and then she would help her dry her tears. Amber really festered off her sister's pain and she enjoyed every moment of it. Even when she was in a wreck and made it out without a scratch on her body. Amber would often say, *Dat lucky suppose have died in dat car wreck,"* Lo key, Amber had cut her brake lines in her car. She wanted her dead and out the way. All the hatred stemmed from when they were younger. She had a complex and envied her sister because of her lighter skin complexion and she thought she was much prettier than she was because everybody ate Renee up. Over the years, the anger and resentment multiplied. They were both conceived by the same parents and raised in the household with. She thought her father showed favoritism, because she was darker with short nappy hair. Whereas, her sister was pretty with long silky hair. Although dark, she was just as pretty as Renee. Amber loved her father to death and couldn't understand why she never got sit in his lap or on trips with him. All her father would say, *You're to little go and you're just gone be crying for your mama,* Come hell or high water Renee was gonna pay dearly for the lack of her father's love and attention. Little did she know the real reason

why her father paid more attention to her. If she knew the deep dark secret that ate at Renee like a monster living inside her.

Amauri could no longer hold his bestiailty in, he held his head up a little bit to suck her breast, aggressively. She smelled so good he wanted to taste her. Passion sat back and watched them go at it while she played with her swollen pussy. *Damn, dis' pussy feel so good . . . so tight . . . hot . . . juicy!* he thought to himself. Then she sat up and positioned herself like she was squatting and started going up and down. When they let him loose, he stood to his feet with his dick sticking rock hard out in front of him.

"Ummm . . . I wanna taste," Amber whispered seductively, leaping on Passion. Then she buried her head between her legs. Amauri on the other hand, started gently stroking the shaft of his dick as he watched on.

"Oh do you feel neglected again?" Passion said, getting up on her knees and grabbing his erect dick, wrapping her warm tongue around it. Amber was on her nipples like a parasite.

"Yea, he was feelin' a lil' neglected. I heard 'em say there ain't no fun if da homie can't have none." Amauri said, running his hand thru her hair. Amber kneeled down and joined her. They were on his dick and balls like a pack of rats on cheese. His knees begin to get weak, his body juddered. He began to nut all on Passion face and breast. Amber licked her body clean. Then he grabbed Amber by the hand. "Come sit on my face, I wanna taste dat." he whispered, seductively in her ear. She cheesed and followed his lead. They sucked and fucked each other all night until they fell asleep. They freaked him so good that he went into the stash and gave them five hundred dollars each.

"Damn, look at my brand-new sheets!" he said, looking at the cum stains on them. "Oh well, I'll just take 'em to the cleaners."

Monie woke up the next morning, at the crack of dawn, feeling like a fool.

"I'm not trippin'. I knew dis' shit was just too damn good to be true," she said, hopping in the shower. When she got out, she threw on some cut of sweats that revealed her pussy print with a wife beater and no bra.

"Fuck dat niggah too! Dat's why I be jackin' their bitch asses every time opportunity presents itself!" she cussed and fussed, pulling her hair back into a ponytail. Once she had it pulled back neatly, she slapped a thick coat of gel on it to lay it down. When she was on her way to the kitchen, she heard a knock at the door. She figured it was Rent-A-Center, because they had came all that week for a payment on her bedroom suite that she only

made one payment. And that was to get it to her house. After that, she was incognito. Ducking and dodging from them every since. "Bitch fuck you and your punk ass contract. Dis' is a recession, bitch ass crackers. You ain't getting shit because I aint got shit, and if you come try to take the shit, you'll get your face blew the fuck off!" she cussed and fussed. As she pushed the curtain back, and lifted the blind just enough to peep out of. But, didn't see anything with their company's logo on it. The knocks at the door became a little louder. So, she looked out through the peephole. All she could see was someone walking away holding flowers. Slowly, she opened the door. It never dawned on her it was Amauri. He was looking and smelling hella good. He was dressed in some plaid, baby-blue-and-yellow Roc-a-wear shorts with a yellow Roc-a-wear shirt with a big blue R stretched across the front and some straight out of the box, blue and yellow Forces. As soon as she opened the door, the air hit her. Causing her nipples to jut out. He greeted her with a dozen of pink roses and a kiss on the forehead. When he bent over to kiss her, she could feel his dick bulging thru his shorts.

Damn, he's makin' my pussy thump! she thought. "You're so sweet thanks for the roses."

"No, thank you for our lovely evening at the French Laundry. By the way, that's what the pink roses symbolizes. Anyways, I missed you, baby!" he said with a devilish grin.

"I can't tell. Seeing as doe I haven't heard from you in a week and a half!"

"Baby, umma tell you like dis' here, I'm not a phone person. Besides, I didn't wanna scare you off by callin' you too soon or too much for dat matter. I been told by females dat it can really be a turn off!" he lied.

Oh my fuckin' goodness, she wanted to shout to the top of her lungs.

"So are you gonna invite me in, or we gonna stand out here and socialize?"

"My bad, I'm sorry, babe!" she said, letting down her guard.

"Where your manners, young lady?" he joked.

"I know right. I'm on one today. You're so full of surprises, huh?"

Damn she look good even on her bad days! Dat camel-toe is just sitting out, uuuuuummm, yes indeed I'm have to beat dat up! he was thinking while walking inside.

"So what do you got up for today, boo?" she asked. While, putting the roses in a vase of water. Hoping he was going to say her.

"Well, I was kinda hoping we could go get a room and lay up all day!"

Her eyes stretched and lit up like a child on Christmas Day. She didn't want him to think she was so geeked up or pressed so It was a good thing

she was turned in the opposite direction where he couldn't see her facial expression. "I'd be honored to accompany you!"

"On dat note, you don't need to bring nuthin'. Just yourself." he said glancing at his brand new, diamond studded watch. Their plane was scheduled to leave in less than two hours. "Okay, I need you to go slip on some clothes because I gotta go pick da homie up at the airport in less than an hour!" she strutted through the living room purposely, teasing him. He smiled and watched her until she disappeared. She headed to her room and threw on some skin tight Apple Bottoms jeans and a white shirt to match with some white-and-gold Nike Shox. Then, she splashed on some Victoria's Secret Love Spell body mist. After grabbing her handbag, she took a quick glimpse in the mirror.

Twenty minutes later, they arrived at LAX (airport), he asked her to get him a Pepsi from the vending machine, on the other side of the airport. While she was gone, he took their luggage in and had it checked in. By the time she came back, everything was handled. He grabbed her hand. "His plane will be landing over here."

"I dunno. I don't think we supposed to go all the way back here by the gates, do we?" she asked, scanning the crowed airport.

"Sure, we do." he said, with a firm grip on her hand. When they reached the gate, she was looking at the number when they announced, "Now boarding from gate 2b." However, it still didn't dawn on her. He pulled out two tickets and gave them to the agent. *I'll be damn, a muthafucka can't pay me a million dolla to fly on shit. If I can't get there by car or bus, then my ass want get dere.* she leaned over and whispered to him, watching everybody in a hurry to catch the boarding plane. Still in oblivion about what was going on. She didn't realize they were leaving, until they were on the plane.

She grinned from ear to ear. "Are you kidnappin' me? Where are we going? I done got bamboozled. You stay on your shit don't cha?" she said, like she never breathe the words, *no one could make her fly.* Although scared shitless, she took a window seat beside him and put on her facade like she wasn't.

"If you stay ready, then you don't have to get ready. You feel me? Just relax, I got dis'!" he wrapped his arm around her neck.

"I don't even have no clothes or nuthin'. My sister is gonna go ballistic and put an APB out on my ass!"

"It's all taken care of. I told you, I was dat niggah dat was gonna sweep you off your feet and take you from your niggah!" he winked.

She fell in love, instantly. *Where have he been all my life,* she thought to herself as she stared at him. *I guess they say good things come to those who wait!*

"We'll be arriving in Miami at 6:00 p.m. Now you can take off your seatbelts, it's now safe to move about the coach. Enjoy your flight." The flight attendant announced over the intercom.

"Miami! We're going to Miami! Oh, thank you, baby. You been so good to me." she said, planting a big wet kiss on his lips.

"Don't trip. It's nuthin'. The best is yet to come." he said, pulling out his brand new touch I-pod connecting the two way headset.

When they arrived in Miami, there was a black sedan waiting on them to take them to the dock.

"Oh my goodness, how long have you been plannin' dis'?" she said, smacking him on the butt.

"You better stop. Dat shit turns me on!"

"We're going on a cruise!" she screamed, taking off her knock off, Chanel stunna shades. The view was breathtaking. She was utterly, blissful.

There was a woman waiting as they boarded the ship that took them to their room.

"Mr. and Mrs. Carlton, your room is right dis'way in a nice non-smoking cabin, enjoy your stay."

Monie was in awe. The room was so exhilarating. A big king-sized round bed that rotated and vibrated at the touch of a button, was centered right smack in the middle of the room. The cabin was also equipped with a Bose music system that had stored music of all kinds. It included a remote that would work from any area in the room—with speakers mounted to the wall in the bathroom. A big forty-two-inch plasma was mounted to the wall in the corner just to the right of the bed. There was also a big plush oversized love seat with big fluffy white pillows cornered in the room. The mirrors on the ceiling and behind the bed set the romantic scene off. Most important of all, there was a big, oversized Jacuzzi surrounded by candles, varying in different shapes and sizes. When she looked in the vanity area, there were two baskets—one had scented bath oil, bubble bath, body wash, and beads. The other basket had an array of oils, massage and edible oils along with a tag that read, "Compliments of the Soffshore Cruise Lines. The room was so enthralling she didn't wanna leave.

He really had hit the jackpot with the special for the room because normally it would have been a little over 3,500 dollars.

Not long after they got to their room, there was a knock on the door. It was a concierge who handed him a big tray with a covered dish with a bucket of Moët surrounded by ice, along with two champagne flutes. He told him that it was compliments from Soffshore for all arriving guests.

"They sure know how to take care of ah niggah." he said, quietly to himself.

"What's dat, babe?" she asked, prancing outta the bathroom.

"Sumthin' I ordered just for you!" he lied. "And you better eat up, dis' shit really hit my pockets deep."

She plopped down on the bed and lifted the top off the dish. "Dat's what's up!" she panted. There were huge strawberries with assorted chocolate dipped tips, a side of whip cream, and some chocolate syrup. *Too bad I'm not with somebody worth all the stuff,* he thought. Ten minutes later, there was another knock at the door. They both looked at the door.

"I'll get it," Amauri ran to the door. It was the concierge again with roses he pre-ordered. When he turned around, he put them behind his back and slowly walked towards her.

"Here beautiful lady," he handed them to her.

"Oh my goodness! You're spoilin' me."

I told you. Girl you better listen to a grown man with hair on his chest, when he talks." he said in a near whisper. Biting down on his bottom lips.

"Ohhhh sexy, sexy. Ummmmm dark red and blue . . . I wonder what these lovely colors can possibly mean?" she said with her pointer finger on her temple.

He flashed an mischievous smile. "Dark red means that I thought it was impossible to get you and here you are,"

"Here I am," she shrugged her shoulder and smiled like a chest cat. He returned the smile.

"Yup my boo is here. Mama I got a keeper," he shouted to the ceiling. "I got her, how bout dat. But, back to what I was sayin', boo, blue means you are unconscionable beautiful," he grabbed her hand and kissed it. From that moment on she was caught up in a rapture.

"Umma go take me a long hot bubble bath. Will you be joining me?" she purred with a seductive look, grabbing her suitcase to see what goodies were in there.

"Nah, umma go hit the craps table up!"

When she opened it, she gasped holding her chest. "You really outdone yourself, didn't you? Come here, give me a hug." she said, with her arms outstretched.

"Boo, dis' moment is priceless." he said, deviously. He really orchestrated everything to profession. From that moment on, he knew he could get her

to rob the president if he needed her to. He had everything she needed and more, packed neatly in her suitcase.

"Thank you baby!" she smiled, lighting the candles. It was ever so beautiful. It looked like a scene straight from a movie or something. Then she her way over to the vanity area and clipped her hair up. Then she undressed and stepped into the tub. That was huge enough to fit five people.

"Ooooh, dis' feeeels hella good!" she oohed and aahed, sitting on one of the jets as the warm water was shooting straight up to her coochie.

"Amauri!" she yelled.

"What it do?" he stepped back in the bathroom.

"Can you put on some relaxin' music?" she asked. Then she laid back and closed her eyes and enjoyed a nice hot bubbly, bubble bath. Instead of going through the trouble of trying to find a song, he just stuck his I-pod in the dock and fixed it so the it could play through the speakers in bathroom.

When he walked back into the bathroom to make sure it was loud enough, he couldn't help but be taken aback by her beauty. After he stood and watched her for a while, he decided to take his clothes off and join her. She had this certain comeliness about her. Slowly making his way over to her without her noticing, he kissed her very passionately.

"Wow!" she said, opening up her eyes. "Where did dat come from?" she broke loose for some air.

"You were lyin' here so beautiful and I just wanted to kiss those juicy lips of yours!"

"Well, kiss me again!" she grabbed his face and deep-throated him.

"Have anybody told you dat you were a good kisser?" he asked, looking into her beautiful hazel eyes.

"No, becuz I don't kiss no one. Ever!" she lied.

"Oh, so I must be special!" he said, rubbing her lips with his fingers.

"Baby, you're over and beyond special!" she said, laying back on the pillow. Her harden nipples, projected through the bubbles and stood attention. As he bent over to lick her nipple, she could feel his thick long dick pressing up against her stomach. He was the first to ever lick and suck her breast very delicate without grabbing them with aggression or biting them. He took his time and did it very gentle and slow. First, he started the left breast licking, then sucking the silver barbell that was through her nipple. Her small breasts were beautiful and still perky because she didn't have no kids. She had a big darken areola surrounding her thick nipple.

"These nipples are big and nice, just like I like them." he said, nibbling on them softly. Then he started pulling on them softly with his lips. Then

he made his way over to her right breast, sucked, and flickered his tongue on her harden nipple. She screamed and moaned in pure bliss.

"You must be a titty-man?" she asked, looking down at him. He was on one nipple like a baby calf on a cow and twisting the other one with his free hand.

"Yea baby, I'm more or of a titty man. Is sunthin' wrong with dat?"

"No not at all. I love getting them sucked. I would've thought being black you would be more of an ass man, lawd knows all I have is two hand fulls, but by all means have your way with them!"

"Yours is just perfect. I like them just like dat!" he lied. They made love in the Jacuzzi and then he picked her up and carried her to the bed. Right off hand, he noticed she knew how to tighten her cootie muscles. So that in itself, on top of her bomb head she slurped him down with, he knew why her name stayed in a niggah's mouth. After they made love for hours, she laid exhausted in his arms.

"Boy, yo' shit is off da Richter!" she said as she bit down on her bottom lip and glanced over at him.

"You know I had to put it down. I said my baby deserve dis'. No half steppin', you feel me?" she nodded her head yes. "So, I gave you da business."

She closed her eyes and bit harder down on her lips. "Dat you did. Bomb ass sex."

"So, boo I want to know everythin' about you!" he suggested, halfway listening.

"From A-Z?"

"Yea, niggah A-Z!" he said. Waiting to Leigha name came up. "Get the fuck out of here, Leigha is not your twin sister, is she?" he said, going in for the kill. "I use to sell movies to her niggah." he lied.

"Who, Rah Rah?"

"Um humm!" he said, but wanted *to say is a pig pork, bitch!* All he wanted to know, was about Rah Rah.

But she kept going on and on. *Bitch, will you shut da fuuuuck up. I can give two flyin' fucks on why you're and Calli and your dreams of becoming shit. I just don't give a fuck,* he said, inwardly as she talked his head off and back on. Somehow, he had an preternatural ability to persuade people to do things they normally would not do. She would have never crossed Rah Rah in a million years, but he had her head so gone.

"Tell me 'bout Rah Rah?"

She jerked her head around and stared at him with a puzzled look. "Rah, Rah?!"

"Yeah, I heard dat niggah got the block boomin' and some mo' shit. I wanna be down with his dream team, but he's not gonna just fuck with me like dat. Dat niggah might think I'm the feds or some shit like dat. You feel me?"

"Yeah, I feel you. Rah Rah and my sister isn't together no more. Sometimes he pays me to do little shit for him like clean and run errands and shit like dat, but I haven't done that shit in a minute though,"

"I heard dat, I'm just tryna be part of his money-makin' team,"

"Okay, baby, I'm not slow by far. It's okay if you be honest with me because we're probably thinkin' the same thing, because I been in all thru dat niggah house except he have dis' one room dat nobody's allowed in. I've helped him count five hundred racks, niggah on me. I know dat niggah is paid. Low key, I wanted to put two to his head and swoop all of it up. But you need me to?"

"Okay," he paused. Pondering whether he could trust her or not. "Fuck it. I want you find out where's dat invisible room is! Baby, if dis' all turn out right, we can be rich and ride off into the muthafuckin' sunset and probably get married and some mo' shit, at dat niggah's expense. I'm already falling in love; you got a niggah pussy whipped." he kissed her very passionately, one would've thought it had to have some meaning or feeling behind it.

"Dat sound good to me! Say no mo' consider it done. So how are we gonna pull dis' off?"

"Baby, the less you know, the better off you'll be! Anyway dat's neither here nor there." he said running his fingers through her hair. "You have a tat lemme see?"

"Yeah, it's half of a heart with my sister's name. She has the other half with my name. I never liked dat arrogant-ass niggah, no way." she lied. "But outta respect for my sister, I dealt with him!" The whole time there, they gambled and had sex. She was in love.

THE TRAP UP AND RUNNING

Grievence stumbled off the plane, drunk as fuck. After getting a whiff of the cold air, he quickly sobered up. Especially when it was damn near ninety degrees in Calli. He was afraid of flying and had to face his fear. When he got inside the airport, his brother was waiting.

"Long time no see," Swagga nearly squeezed the life out of him.

"Look at dis' niggah here, wearing a sick ass Al Wissam Urban Legends jacket. Wrist all froze, VVS studded and shit, already and haven't been out but a few days. Damn, homie I'm tryna be like you when I grow up. Come home all swollen and some mo' shit!"

"Yeah ah niggah, been going super hard since I touched down. So, how did escape the lion's paws?" Swagga asked, as they walked up to retrieve the bags from the conveyor belt.

"She have been known to be domineering at times but, I told her I was only gonna be gone a couple of weeks or so and gave her the money you sent. She tried, actin' like she didn't want it at first, then finally gave in to temptation. She was like my bills is kinda behind and cried but, then gave me her blessin'," Grievence grabbed his bag and they headed towards the car. "She has a guy friend she met at church, so she'll be all right,"

"Does he know how much she smoke and drank?" Swagga looked at him quizzically.

"As do he!" Grievence said, putting his bags in the tiny trunk. "I know one thing I don't miss,"

"What's dat?"

"Dis' damn cold-ass weather!" Grievence said, blowing into his fist. He had on a hoodie, T-shirt, and a down feather coat with the fur on the hood and was still freezing.

"Your body have to adjust to dis' weather, dat's all. It's thirty degrees, and dat's kinda warm compared to yesterday. It was below zero out dis' bitch!" he said lifting his hood up from his head.

"Damn, just look at dis' niggah. Got so many waves in his shit, makin' a niggah sea sick."

"You already know. Niggah, ain't shit changed. I got an image to uphold." Swagga rubbed his hair.

"I see dat not much has changed around here since, I was last here!" he said, looking at all the abandoned homes and buildings.

Swagga glanced over at him. "Yeah, dis' here city is one of the poorest, grittiest cities in America by far. Enough about me, what's up with you cuffin' these hoes and shit? Didn't you learn anythin' from your big brut? Let me find out you lettin' them hoes drain your pockets, niggah."

"If you don't miss me wit dat hoe shit. Ah niggah ain't cuffed nobody and nan hoe can ever cuff me." He let out a few chuckles.

"Don't let me find out." Swagga smiled.

"Picture dat with da digital, baby." he chuckled.

Twenty minutes, they pulled up to the Trap. Swagga, introduced Grievence to everybody. There was Trigga and Bread, who grew up together, homies from way back when. Trigga was given the name because of his eagerness and readiness to squeeze the trigger at any given time. He was death to anyone who crossed him or somebody he loved. He would oftentimes say that his trigger finger itched, and the only way to relieve that it was to release a slug or two in you. Bread got his name because that's all he chased all day. His motto was *Money make me cum bitch*. There was Stubby who got his name because of his funny-shaped physique. He was shorter than the average male. A little chubby, but quick and swift with the hands and feet if need to be.

Upon meeting them, Grievence got a bad vibe about Bread and made a mental note to keep a close watch on him.

"What's up, mayne?" Trigga extended his hand.

"Ain't nuthin' just tryna get my share of dis' big pie, that's all!"

Trigga gave him a pound, fist to fist. "That's what I'm talkin' 'bout, mayne. You don't want all of it. You just want your share, huh, mayne?"

They chopped it up and put a couple of blunts in the air. Within a week, he felt good about his decision to go to Detroit. Being there seeing all the money that was made and still to be made, he didn't wanna leave. *I see why it's so hard to get out of the game. The shit is too addictive!* he thought,

looking at all the money his brother had piled up in his hotel room. His job was relatively easy—his brother's extra set of eyes and ears, as well as collect all the money.

He took up with Trigga quicker than he did with Stubby and Bread.

When he looked in Bread's eyes, he saw envy and greed. He never mentioned it because you can't always judge a book by its cover, so he just paid close attention to his actions as well as what he spoke.

Grievence sat down and made small talk. "You been to any clubs, since you touched down?"

"Fuck a club. Niggah, I'm tryna get my paper up. Straight stack my chips! Fuck it, I'm tryna be the one responsible for making it snow in Detroit. Ya' gotta grind if you wanna shine, niggah. Ya' digg?" he said, unsmilingly hurling a stack of money at him. The truth was, he was well on his way. He figured if he could sell his product dirt cheap, he'll keep them coming and coming for that good, 80's like dope.

"I hear you, Mr. Young Black Entrepreneurial!" he said, flipping through the cash like he was flushing cards. "Three hundred racks in less than one week, not bad, not bad at all,"

"Just think in a couple of months time, we can own dis' city!"

"Well, umma go ahead and hop in shower and get some much-needed sleep." Grievence yawned.

"You do dat, I'll come thru a lil later and swoop you up. Right now, umma go to Trap and see what's good ova there!"

"Niggah, do you eva close your eyes and sleep?"

"Not really, I be thinkin' I'm gonna miss out on sumthin'. Besides, idle hands are a devil's tools. I'll sleep when I'm dead!" he walked toward the door.

When Grievence woke up, he got in the shower. After he dried off, he laid on the bed and thought about his homegirl Trees.

"Now what is her grandma's number? Fuck, I used to know it." he said, thinking out loud. Then he picked up the phone to look at the numbers on the keypad. He knew the first three numbers.

"What's the last four? Her ass done had the same number for damn near 30 years, 8303. Yes that's it," he smiled from ear to ear, as he dialed the number.

"Hello," the voice on the other end said, in a cracking voice.

"Ms. Johnson!" he spoke, excitedly into the phone.

"Yeah, baby, dis' is she. Who's dis'? Is the Sam?"

"No, dis' is Gerrick!"

"Jerry, I don't think I know no Jerry. Jerry who?"

"No, Ms. Johnson, I'm Gerrick, Maryland's son. Lisa's friend!"

"Hold on, baby, let me turn my hearing aid up so I can hear you. Okay, now say your name one more time." *Beeeeeeeep*. "Oh, I'm sorry, baby, I turned it up too loud."

By then, he was regretting the call. He didn't wanna be rude and hang up, so he waited for her to adjust her hearing aid.

"I'm Gerrick, Lisa's friend!"

"Ooh, you Maryland's boy." she said. Her hands were shaking so bad she could barely hold the phone.

"Yeah!"

"How's your mama, baby?"

"She's okay. Is Lisa there?"

"No, baby, Lisa live ova there on um umm . . ." she said, trying to think. "Oh over on 8 Mile with her boyfriend. I got her number on a piece of paper right here on my end table. Hold on a minute, baby. It's gonna take me a little while to find it because my sight ain't dat good anymore," she placed the phone on the table. He wanted to say he'll speak to Trees when he speak to her. After five minutes, she got back on the phone and said, "You still there, baby?"

"I'm here."

"I found it." she said and read the number off slowly, "It's 555-6556, you tell your mama I said hello." Then she hung up before he could respond.

"She couldn't have did dat shit soon enough." he breathe a sigh of relief. He decided against calling instead, he dozed back off.

An hour later, Swagga was back. "Wake your sleepyhead ass up! It smells like straight budussy in dis' muthafucka. Wake yo' cakin' ass up niggah!"

"You need to chill with them pillows, dawg. I'm tired than a muthafucka!"

"Niggah, what? Man, get yo' weak ass up! You have been sleepin' all day. In dis' game, if you sleep too long, you gonna miss out."

"What time is it?"

"It's two pimpin'."

"Huh, what time is it? Two in the afternoon?"

"It's two in da mahfuckin' mornin', niggah. It's money to be made. Da fuck you being doing in dis' mahfucka? You been going in somebody's back door instead of front, niggah?" Swagga tighten up his nose.

"Shut your corny ass!" Grievence said, as he got up and did as he was told. When they arrived at the Trap, a neighborhood smoker named, Shooter, was trying to sell Bread a VCR.

"I'm good on dat, man!" Bread scatted him away.

"You don't understand. Dis' thang right here, niggah." Shooter pointed to the VCR. "Is what's happenin'. It's high-def, man! I heard you had dat straight butter. Listen here dawg, I get paid tomorrow and you already know umma spend wid you all day, baby!"

"If you don't get dis' hoe ass, old VCR outta here, umma bust yo' shit with dis' bottle, niggah!" Bread yelled.

"Just give me a bump, a hit or anything, and it's yours!" he continued to beg.

"Okay, lemme see it." Bread said, taking it from him and then he cracked him upside the head with it.

"Man, whacha do dat for?!" Shooter screamed, with blood trickling down his face. When he saw that he was bleeding, it really sent him into a frenzy.

"Get yo' beggin' ass on, niggah, befo' I stomp yo' crackhead ass out!" he said, releasing smoke from his lungs.

"Bread, I don't need you causing no scene making us hot and shit!" Swagga said, walking up.

"My dude, dat smoker violated me. I can't stand a beggin'-ass niggah, but I feel you. It won't happen again."

"That's all I'm askin'." Swagga said, going into the apartment.

Trigga was sitting up sleep with the controller glued to his hand.

"Niggah, wake yo' ass up." he yelled startling him, causing him to reach for his gun.

"Damn, my bad!" Swagga said.

"Yeah, niggah, gotta stay on my guard at all times out dis' bitch." Trigga rubbed his blood shoot eyes.

Bread was very ostentatious. The money he was making was starting to go to his head whereas, Trigga was more laid-back and mellow.

"Where's dat niggah, Stubby?"

"Oh, he stepped out to go holla at some broad!"

"See, mahfuckas always claim they 'bout their money, as soon as they get couple dollars in their pockets. They get to splurging with bitches and shit, ole cupcakin'-ass niggah. Dat niggah stay on a bitch's bumper." Swagga said, raising his tone. He was clearly upset because he had called a meeting.

When he spoke, he knew what he was talking about and everyone would listen. It was as if he was so much older and wiser with a charismatic personality and allureness. He had the eye of the tiger and was hungry. Very ambitious and nothing or nobody was gonna take it or fuck things up for him. After all, he killed once and was ready to do it again, if necessary. He

went into the area with a broom and swept up all the bullshit. People didn't have no other choice but to love him because it wasn't like he was moving in or trying to take over nothing. He was just simply making sure everybody ate. Power emitted from every pore of his body. Just as he was about to start the meeting, Stubby came sauntering through the door, with a happy-go-lucky smile. Like he had just gotten his first piece of pussy. His smile instantly turned into a frown when Swagga chewed up and spit him out.

"Okay, I want Trigga and Bread over in dis' area." he said, pointing to a map, he had all mapped out. "You are the head of dat area."

"That's what's up!" they both chimed in unison.

"Stubby, I need you to handle dis' area, but I need you to focus more on getting your paper up. Always remember dat you lose money chasing hoes and you could never lose hoes chasing money. Believe me when I tell you if you stay focused on your money, the bitches will come! Trust me when I tell you, aint worse than havin' money and losin' it without havin' shit to sho for it." Swagga said—giving him a look that said, *I'm telling you, not asking you.* After he was done talking everyone sat quietly, lost in their own thoughts.

Swagga, lieutenant, all had purple tops that were sold for twenty dollars when everyone else in the game, were getting no less than fifty for it. Each vial consisted of two big chunks. The smokers would say they had that '80s dope. The green tops were straight powder. They were the only ones using the vials. When you walked through their area, all you would see were those tops everywhere. He was up and out at the crack of dawn, every morning. The money was pouring in very fast. Everyone was eating and content.

DEPRESSION

Ms. Lara was worried about Neeyah so, she asked Leigha to come over and talk to her. Leigha didn't wanna fool with her because of how things went down at Apple's party, but agreed. When she knocked on her room door, there was no answer. So, she quietly eased the door open and went in. As soon as she opened the door, a bad stench hit her right in the nose. Neeyah was laying on the bed staring at the ceiling, looking very disheveled.

"Neeyah, girl, why are you doing dis to yourself? You're here lookin' a hot-ass mess thinkin' about dat niggah, who is probably somewhere lookin' fly ass hell and I'm willin' to bet my last blunt, he wid some hoe. All he does is brain fuck you." she said, easing on the bed and setting her Chloé purse down. She tried to stifle her tears, but they started rolling down her face at the sight of her cousin. For somebody that was always bubbly and never came out the house without looking her best. There she was, her hair was matted down to her head and what wasn't matted down, was sticking out in all directions. Her lips were cracked and scaly with blood that had long since dried. Her eyes had dark circles around them. She had lost weight and had a very livid look to her skin. She looked frightening. Her room looked like a pigsty and was so stank to the point Leigha had to hold her breath. There were dirty period drawers laying on the floor, dried-up food her mom brought her, that she refused to eat. She had really let herself go for a man. The smell was unbearable, but she still toughed it out. Leigha was beginning to think she made a grisly decision in telling her about Grievence at the party. She knew talking bad about Grievence wasn't gone help the situation.

All I want to know is where he goes, what does he see in them otha bitches dat he doesn't see in me. Can you fill in the missin' fuckin' pieces to dis puzzle? Neeyah thought.

Leigha continued talking to her, Neeyah laid uncaring. "Neeyah, do you remember the summer's at Grandma's? Boy, did I love going to Inglewood.

The last day of school couldn't get here fast enough for my ass," she paused, a minute then let out a few chuckles thinking back. "I used to have my shit pack a week befo' school let out and just slept the days away. You remember how she put the fear of God in us about going down 115th." she let out a few more chuckles. "She was like you guy's see dat street right there, don't ever go near it. there's all kinds of things going on down Danger Street. Rape, murder, and drugs you name it, it's done on dat street." she smiled, thinking back. Neeyah laid mute listening. "Every summer, she was like Danger St. is so bad . . . and well say we know Granny, it's so bad dat the sun want even go down dat street. We use to sit on porch all day and watch all the kids play up and down the street til, one day Monie who always has been the fast, hardhead one. Just quick to test people, had said come on guys let's go play! We shook our heads. She was like you guys are some scary punks. I said you know what Grandma said about dat street. Monie said quote unquote "Hello, the reason the sun never shines over there is becuz the street is lined with trees!" then she toddled her fast ass off. Grandama really had our little asses scared. We had to be what . . .?" Leigha asked Neeyah, knowing she wasn't gonna get no response. "I think, 9 and 7. You were skinty. I was always the thick one." she smiled, as tears flowed freely and abundantly, down her cheeks.

Leigha tried going down memory lane. She reminisced on their childhood. Neeyah just stared at her as she cried. She couldn't cry no more, she had cried all her tears out. She wanted to say, "*Don't cry!*" But was unable to find the strength to verbalize those two words. She listened as her cousin talked.

"Girl, you need to get cha yo' ass up and go hop in the shower. I'll help you clean dis' room, and let's go hit the Galleria up. You got me all up here getting all emo and some mo' shit!" she sniffed and wiped the tears from her face. Although she didn't have no intentions on going nowhere, Neeyah still didn't budge. She tried to sit up but, couldn't muster up enough strength to do so. In her mind, she was trying, but her body just couldn't do so.

She was essentially, immobile. She had fallen into a deep depression. "You deserve so much better. He cheated on you. Dat niggah should be crying. He don't deserve you, baby." she said, hugging her. "You have to wanna let go. You'll feel so much better. Instead of using your eyes to cry, boo use them to find somebody else. Oh," she reached in her purse and pulled out *Still Dirty* by Vickie Stringer and placed it on top of the bookshelf. Tears continued to fall freely from Leigha's face. Neeyah was her best friend, cousin, and sister. She was hurting deeply and so was she. Neeyah never saw her cousin have a meltdown before and although on the outside she appeared to be unmoved

and emotionless, if Leigha could see through her soul she'd see how she was dying on the inside. "I thought you might like dis', seeing as thou you was waiting on it to drop. And remember dis'," she said, zipping her purse and putting it on her shoulder. "Every cloud has a silver lining." she said and then turned to leave. "One more thing," she turned back to face her. "Bottom line boo, life all comes down to a few moments and dis' my dear is one of them. And its up to you to make those few moments count On that note, what don't kill you will only make you stronger," she turn and walked through the door. Neeyah watched as she quickly made her exit. It didn't hit her until Leigha left.

"She's right. She's right. He don't deserve me! Please give me strength, lord to get up when I move my legs," she closed her eyes and prayed silently. She tried to get up for twenty minutes straight. Her mind was even tricking her body into thinking she could, but no matter how much she tried her body just couldn't find enough strength to do so. Suddenly, a burst of momentum washed over entire body and it was almost as if she was never immobilized because she mustered up enough energy to get up. Although, still a little weak she headed to the bathroom. "Thank you Lord," she glanced up at the ceiling and stared at herself in the mirror. For the first time in nearly two weeks.

She was frightened at what she saw. Although she loved Grievence, she vowed not to drop another tear because of him.

A couple of days later, Leigha decided to swing by and see Neeyah. Soon as she opened the door, the smell of her favorite mixture of Strawberry and Satsuma oils came rushing at her. She had cleaned up, showered, and washed her hair. She looked a little thin but, healthier.

"Why are you lookin' at me as if you done seen a ghost?" Neeyah asked, standing in front of the mirror brushing her hair back into a ponytail.

"Naw, dawg, you look good. I mean, I have to admit you scared the shit outta me." Leigha said, awe-striken.

"Girl, I was horror-shocked my damn self. Honey, when I tell you it felt like a bolt of electricity shooting thru my body and all I could do was ball up in a fetal position and cry like a baby. Straight from the womb. You just don't know how bad it tore me up inside cousin to see you drop tears like dat."

"Yea bitch, I didn't think you was gonna come back from dat one. I just knew you were MHALA bound," (Mental Health America of Los Angeles)

"Girl, you stupid. I was going thru the motions. Hell I didn't think I was gonna make it my damn self," Neeyah laughed.

"Damn," Leigha chuckled. "But, bitch you hold my bloodline and I love you. Dat's from the bottom." she hit her chest.

"I sure do, but girl, last night I said to myself, Grievence's ass got me fucked all the way up. I woke up feeling hella liberated. When you were here I was just laying numb, soaking up everything you and my mom said, and you guys were right. You know it seems as if it takes a minute to have a crush on somebody, an hour to like somebody, a day to love somebody, but a whole lifetime to forget someone. I'm here, inflicting unnecessary pain on myself. Literally slowly, killin' myself. While his ass is probably stretched out on a beach somewhere with some other hoe not even studdin' my ass. Just like you said. I wanna thank you for the kind, encouraging words."

"Com'ere," Leigha said, with her arms widely spread. "Girl, I knew when you had enough you were gonna see dat he isn't worth you health. I also knew you were strong, and there was only a matter of time before you would realize it!"

"Yeah, I use to ask myself how much is enough? Girl was walking around blind without a cane, but I'm gonna somehow get thru it all. It's a very good thing you cannot relive the past. I'm not gonna say it doesn't hurt because love hurt like hell, but now I'm able to avow it. That's the first step, isn't it?" she asked. She was torn but she had to get on with her life. Just as he did. One thing she never understood was, how could men move on to the next woman so quickly and easy. Almost if things don't work out in their current relationship, it's like they yell, *Next.* And keep that shit pushing. Hell, it was probably something they couldn't understand either. Her aunt once told her one way to get over somebody, was to get up under someone else.

"Yep, that's the first step, admittin' it to yourself and others. And you got me too girl. Love begins with a smile, grows with a kiss, and ends with a tear. Being in love is not easy!"

"Churccch! Tell me about it girl, I do look a little thinner, huh?" Neeyah said, looking in the mirror. "Why is it dat your ass is the first to go?"

"Girl, you silly, I dunno, maybe because it leaves the back and goes to the front!" They both fell over laughing. "In all seriousness, it's really good to see you're laughin' again, girl. I was really worried!"

"No time to talk about dat. You're gonna make me all emo and shit. Let's talk about dis' Flawless dude!" she said, hoping that he would be able to take her mind off Grievence.

"Girl, I spoke to his homeboy yesterday. They're back in New Orleans but, is supposed to be back out here in the next week or so. You should call him, oh shit!" she said, remembering that Neeyah had tore the number up.

"What? What's good?" Neeyah asked, a little bemused.

"I forgot you don't have the number. I'm tryna think how I could get it, girl, becuz dat niggah there got dat bread out the ass." Leigha said, with her pointer finger on her cheek.

"Oh yeah?!" Neeyah opened her cell phone and dialed his number. "Flawless," she winked at Leigha.

"Speaking. Who dis'?" he asked, baffled by the unknown area code.

"Dis' is Neeyah, the girl you met at the party while you were out here—"

"Oh, hey you!" he said, cutting her off. "I see you do have a photograph memory, huh?"

"I told you, niggah, I don't be playing. I'm real wid it!"

"Is dat right?"

"Yup, for real and not for play. Don't know no other way to be!"

"That's what's up!"

"What is he sayin'?" Leigha lipped. She stood eagerly, in front of her trying to find out what he was saying.

Neeyah put her finger up, telling her to wait. "When are you gonna be back out here?"

"Well, dat depends on if I got a reason to come back there." Flawless said, in a deep Southern accent.

"I got your reason right here!" she said, with a big smile spreading across her face.

"Well, check dis' right here, lil' mama, I'm be out there dis' weekend and I'll hit you when I touch down!"

"Bet it up."

WHATEVA HAPPENS, HAPPENS

"See, dat wasn't so bad, was it? Oh, girl, lemme tell you," she said, putting both hands on her hip. "Ole' boy told me dat Apple ass got two big ass lacerations. One down the side of her face and the other on her neck. Dat bitch had to get stitches, staples, and some mo' shit! And tell me why, their tryna find out what's my government name?!"

"Really?!" Neeyah screamed. "Damn, that's fucked up. He didn't tell them your name, did he?"

"No, but dat skanky, scantless bitch snatched my necklace off."

"The one with your name." Neeyah asked meekly.

"Does a bear shit in the woods, bitch?"

"Damn, dat is not the business. Them hoes still don't know Adam from Eve, so don't trip."

"I'm not even trippin! Umma go ahead and handle dis' business, but I will call you later!"

"Fa sho, my mom is takin' me to get some kinky twists ova to Tasha's crib. Any ole ways, so I'd better be getting ready because she said if she have to come in the house dat she wasn't gonna go back out. You noe how dat goes!"

"I know all too well, I can take over there. It's nuthin'!"

"Mama gonna take me because she's gonna wait for me."

"All right, if you need me, I'll be only a call away," she headed for the door.

Soon as Leigha left, Neeyah threw on a pair of black Baby Phat petal pushers and a black-and-grey shirt to match with some all black Forces. While looking in the mirror, she said to herself, *I love myself. Dat niggah don't deserve me.* It was something her mama suggested she do. Although at first, she thought it was a little quirky, but decided to do the affirmations anyway. Then she grabbed her bag of hair and put Grievence's hat that still

reeked of Jamaican Oil, on. She sniffed a long hard sniff then exhaled and took off.

"Neeyah, I wanna go, I wanna go!" Junior ran up to her.

"You can't go. Mommy said you have to stay here until we come back."

"No fair!" he dropped his head. "I never get to go no where!"

"Awwwe, you and me will go to the park tomorrow."

"Just you and me?" he asked, with his eyes lighting up.

"Just you and me, buddy!" she said, touching his nose with her fingertip. Then she sprinted out the door.

The next day, she kept her promise by taking him to the park. The conversations with Flawless grew more and more. She looked forward to his calls. As soon as he got into town, he called her and instructed her to be ready in two hours. When he arrived, he greeted her with some roses and a gift.

"Oh, you didn't have to do dat!" she blushed.

"Oh, it's nuthin', lil' mama." he said, with his thick Southern drawl. "You look so exquisite."

She had on a black Chanel dress, thanks to Leigha. Rah Rah, bought it for a birthday present, but it was cut too small and she figured it would be perfect for the occasion. With some Prada black suede bow detailed, peep toe pumps. Her lips glimmered with a glittery bronze color.

"You don't look bad yourself!" she sized him up from head to toe. He was wearing a Prada navy blue suit, pinstriped navy and white buttoned down-shirt, with a pair of Prada leather moc toe, loafers. The three and a half karat, canary yellow diamond earring in his ear shimmered, thru and thru from the lighting of the restaurant. His low cut, wavy black hair complimented his very smooth pecan tan skin tone. He wasn't a hustler or nothing like that, he was just lucky to have inherited his family business. He was also a philanthropist that had a soft spot for helping people that wanted to help themselves and just couldn't do so because of their unfortunate situation. Back in New Orleans, he had a foundation set up for the Katrina victims. His friends all had money. Dreadlocks was the renowned one, with the most money. Being that, he moved weight than the law allowed, without touching it. When they arrived at the five-star eatery, he was so polite to her. He did things for her that Grievence wouldn't be caught doing.

"I see you have a very exquisite taste!" she said, looking around the restaurant. Focusing in on the live jazz band. Although he had the money, he didn't look as good as Grievence. She couldn't seem to stop thinking about him.

"I actually looked dis' joint up on the Internet."

"What would the world be without the internet?" she said, stirring the ice around in her cup.

"Right, right!" he agreed.

"So, I bet you have women practically throwin' themselves at you all the time, huh?"

"You'll be surprised. So you never told me what kinda of work you do?" he said, unfolding his napkin and laying it in his lap.

"Right now, I'm currently lookin' for work. The jobless rates in dis' city have astronomically skyrocketed."

"Yeah, I know dat seem to be the problem in damn near every state now."

"Yep, the economy is so jacked up now. Definitely, a bad recession. Let's see can Obama save us!"

"I can save you!" he said, licking his lips and biting down on them, with a seductive look.

"With all due respect, I'm not no welfare charity case. I can work and handle my own." she said, wanting him to think she was this independent woman.

"Well, if you play your cards right, you may never have to work." he winked.

Niggah, please, game recognize game! she wanted to say. "Like I said I got dis' don't trip!"

"Well, let me ask you, miss-she-got-her-own, where do you see yourself in ten years?"

"Ummm . . . I see myself finished with school, having a career thing going on! And possibly a mother, if I'm financially stable."

"What kind of career? What do you want to be? What do you have a passion to be?" he asked inquisitively, swooshing the Moscato around in the flute.

"Well, I really wanna work in the nursing field. I love helpin' people!" she said.

"So, let me ask you dis', what's hinderin' you from doing it?"

"To be honest, nuthin'. I do not have no excuse and not trying to make one. I was enrolled in school once. But, I never got to finish the course and its entirety!" she smiled. He sat still and mute. "Yep my life is not as quite exciting as your. No fireworks or standing ovations. Just a poor girl born and raised in the projects."

"Ok. I wasn't born with a silver spoon in my mouth either. Most of my childhood life was spent in projects in New Orleans. Does dat make

you beneath me? No it don't," he grabbed her hand. She shied away a little bit. He leaned in and whispered. "Then another thing I never shared with anybody, I peed in the bed til I was eleven in a half. Does dat make me beneath you? No it doesn't. Becuz none of dat matter. Besides, how can you learn to appreciate something without strugglin' to get it and keep it. I look at it like dis' when something that's handed to you, you want appreciate or value it quicker than sumthin' you've worked for!"

"True dat. You're funny you did not pee in the bed until you where a teenager, did you?" she giggled a little.

"If it's ever repeated I'm comin' for you." they both laughed. "Low key, from time to time I still tinkle a little bit, so if we're married you have to go buy me some depends. I'm just fuckin' wid you." he smiled.

He was so impressed with the way she spoke. She enunciated every word properly. He could tell that she wasn't pretentious, she was really smart.

"But back to our conversation, boo, it's never too late. Let me give you some food for thought, never put off tomorrow what you can do today!" he said. She remained mute and listened to every word that rolled off his tongue. Even though she had heard it all before, she was just mesmerized with the way he licked his lip like Nelly, after every other word he said. After they had dinner, he drove her to a nearby park. That could be seen out the eatery's window. As they meandered through the park, he hugged her from the back. She enjoyed the cool, refreshing breeze that blew gently on her face as she walked barefoot through the sand, enjoying every moment with him. He made her feel good and safe.

"Are you a little nervous?" he spun her around and asked.

"No, why you ask?" she asked, making eye contact.

"Becuz, you jump every time I stroke your beautiful face. You need to relax and let the sounds of the flowin' water wash away your stress and soothe your frazzled nerves," he said, and then shifted his attention to the waterfall that was centered in the middle of the park.

"I'm not nervous, really. You make me feel so safe. As if I don't have a care in the world. The water is trickling, gently in a never-endin' stream, very captivating and relaxin'!" she squeezed his muscular arms that was wrapped around her tightly.

"Wow! I didn't know I had dat type of effect on you. Mama, I'm overwhelmed!"

"I'm just being real. But, isn't it funny how the moon is illuminatin' the whole sky." she asked, looking up at the moon.

"Yeah, it's a full moon!"

"Ok tell me dis' what's the name of dat star?" he pointed to it.

"It's the north, boo!"

"That's correct. If ever your lost if you're and don't see dat star, you're going in the wrong direction. So, what are you lookin' from me?" she asked, curiously. "Sex?"

"I mean, whateva happens, happens, baby girl. But, I'm not lookin' for sex. Do you noe how many girls throw themselves at me daily? Who knows what dis' might manifest to. Besides, I know you're still in love with dat niggah!" she couldn't say nothing because he was right. "You are still in love, aren't you?"

"I'm like beyond hurt, I have feelings of ambivalence right now. But, to answer your question, yeah I love him. At the same time, who knows maybe you can help me forget about him."

"Awwe, bittersweet. So you're in love, huh!"

"What? Are you psychoanalyzin' me or sumthin'?" she laughed, trying to make it seem like she was joking.

"Naw, I'm just tryna get to know you, dat's all!"

"Don't trip? I'm just playin', no need ta get all sensitive on me."

"Girl. I'm spank you!" he scooped her up in the air and delicately, spanked her.

"Put me down! Put me down!" she giggled, softly punching him.

After they walked, what seemed like infinity he dropped her back off at the complex. She really enjoyed talking to him. It was like he cared about her well-being. He asked how her day went, little things like that mattered, things Grievence very seldom asked. She tried calling a couple of times over the weeks. If he wasn't sending her to the voice mail, he'll answer and say, *Let me call you right back.* And never did. She still missed him terribly, but tried her best to maintain a normal life. It was hard, but hey nobody said it was gonna be easy. At least, she had her newfound friend Flawless, which always found a way to make her smile and laugh. When she opened her gift, it was a little crystal angel with a message that said, *When you're feeling down and blue, just know I'm watching over you,* she hung it over her bed and smiled every time she looked up and saw it. She couldn't wait to see him again.

Her phone started vibrating. It was him.

"Speak of the devil!" she smiled.

"Oh yeah?"

"I was just sittin' here thinkin' about you!"

"Is dat right, good or bad?"

"I dunno, it depends on your interpretation of what good or bad. It could be either or!"

"Oh yeah, how so?" he said, eagerly awaiting her answer.

"Well, I was just sitting here thinkin' how I wanna fuck yo' brains out!" she said, twirling a handful of braids on her finger. "You see, I talk like dis' cause I can back it up. I walk like dis' because I can back it up!"

"Sounds like someone got a big ego!"

"Yea, I'm feelin' myself ova here! Ready to give you da business." she popped her collar.

"Ooooow, dat's bad. Are you trying to seduce me, young lady?" he said, impressed by her straight forwardness.

"If dat's how you look at it. So, how soon can you make dat happen?"

"Girl, you wild. You're serious, aren't you?"

"As cancer, baby!"

"I dunno, baby, my sex isn't just sex. It's like crack, boo. You'll be up tryna find a niggah in the wee, wee hours of the night and shit. Straight feenin' for dis' dope dick. I'm talkin' about gettin' rid of back spasms and shit! Yezzur!"

"Don't worry, daddy, I'm a big girl. You talkin' all dat shit when you hit dis' I'mma havin' you talkin' like ow, ow, ow, baby I, I, I, in a falsetto." she sang.

"Well, I'll see if u can put yo' money where yo' mouth is, Negro!" he said, turning into her complex. "Becuz, I know how to make dat thang squirt, you know what I'm talkin' about?"

"Don't trip, you don't won't have to worry about dat becuz I walk what I talk, boo boo!"

"Well, I was initially callin' you becuz I wanted to see you before I left!"

"You left," she snapped. "I thought you were stayin' until next week?"

"Calm down, lil' mama. Sumthin' came up, and I'm leavin' tonight. But I'll be back da' weekend. I would love for you to come outside so we can talk face-to-face!"

"Now?" she yelled.

"Now!" he said, hanging up the phone.

She hurried and snatched the rest of the rollers out her head and slipped on her red velour *Ed Hardy* track suit. Which, made her ass look fat. Before she left out the door, she stuck her feet in her high-top all-white Forces. Then, she quickly checked the mirror to make sure she looked good.

"Sorry, it took so long?" she said, getting on the passenger's side of his rental charger.

He leaned in to kiss her. "Nah, you good. Do wanna ride with me somewhere?"

"Where?" she replied.

"Over to my hotel?"

"Okay, that's what it do!"

"What you know 'bout dis' joint right hea'? Dis' dat grown folk music you know what I'm talkin' 'bout?" he said, turning the volume up on the radio.

"Boy, bye. I grew up on oldies," she sucked her teeth.

"Shhh, dis' my part," he shushed her. Then gave more volume to the radio.

"Walk wid me becuz the door is open, talk with me come on, baby, loooove me don't you wanna gooooooo," he sang, along with the O'Jays's *Stairway to Heaven.*

"What is it you say you do again?" she cleared her throat.

"Stop hatin', girl! I didn't know you had such foul mouth!"

"There's a lot you don't know 'bout me?" she said, licking her lips seductively.

"Oh yeah? Fill a niggah in then."

"I would love to enlighten you, but I'm more or less an all-action-and less-talk kinda girl!"

"Um, hummm." he pulled into a parking spot.

Just as they were getting outta the car, it started to drizzle, then suddenly it poured.

"Damn, I do not feel like getting wet, smellin' like no damn wet puppy and shit!" she muttered.

"Don't trip, lil' mama, I got you!" he said. Then he covered her with his leather coat that was lying on the backseat. As he got closer to her, she got a strong whiff of his *Fahrenheit* cologne. It made her pussy wet.

As soon as she got off the elevator, her legs began to totter. She started getting nerves because, she knew she had just talked a lot of shit and had to walk it out. He opened the door and put his hand out to switch on the lights. She was in awestricken. It was a suite that had big glass windows that you see the outside, but no one could see inside of it.

"Can I get you anything to drink?" he asked, removing his shoes.

"I'm good!" she said, feeling like a virgin on prom night.

"Suit yo'self!" he said, popping open a Sprite can and guzzled it down. "A Sprite a day helps keep da doctor away!" he burped.

"Eww, where are your manners. But, I do believe dat's an Apple!"

"Whateva, but sorry." he said, peeling off the wet clothes. He stripped down to only a wife beater and some gym shorts. "Man it's coming down in buckets out there, isn't it?"

"You so country!" she smiled and chuckled a little.

"Well what do yall city folks say then, miss city girl?"

"I say it's rainin' hella hard!"

"Well, scuse' me then, miss thang! I see low key, you tryna to clown a niggah shorts."

"They do look a little feminine." she giggled.

"Come here," he patted the couch next to him.

She did as told. "Naw, but what up, doe?"

"What movie do you wanna watch?" he grabbed the remote control off the end table. "Let's see what's on!" he said, powering the TV on, and flipping through the pay-per-view channel.

"It doesn't matter. But, to keep it oh so real, I would much rather be watchin' you, let alone feelin' you!" she said. She could feel her panties getting wet, looking at his rippling, physique. That screamed to be touched after he peeled off the wife beater.

"Are you comin on to me? Umma tell my nana!" he said, placing the remote on the couch beside him. Suddenly, one thing led to another. He slowly undressed her. As soon as he unfastened her white lace bra, her nipples fell out and stood attention-screaming, *lick me*. He gently, pushed her back on the couch, and then began nibbling on her breast. For once, her mind left her body and she was no longer thinking about Grievence. As he licked and sucked every inch of her body, she laid back in pure bliss, enjoying every moment. She let out soft moans as she stared at the window, watching the rain teeming up against it. It was so relaxing making love to the sound of raindrops hitting the ceiling. Then, he picked her up and laid her on the bed. "Showtime!" he whispered, pushing all the pillows on the floor. Then he very quickly flipped her over and gently opened her butt cheeks, and started sucking her pussy from the back. Then he ran his tongue up and down her ass, causing her to quiver and shake uncontrollably. He placed one finger in her asshole.

"What da hell you do dat for? That's an exit not entrance." she whirled her head around.

"Relax boo, I wouldn't disrespect you like dat." he whispered. She turned back around and he buried his face back into her pussy. She was begged him to stop and gripped the sheets tighter. He loved hearing her squeal, so he opened up her butt cheeks wider then blew and her ass. Which really made

her wanna climb up the wall. Every time, she moved an inch, he'll be right behind her with his face embedded in her ass. Out of nowhere, he aggressively flipped her over and started sucking her pussy while, fingering her.

"Damn baby! What are you trying to do to me?" she panted. He remained mute. He was too busy sucking everything out her pussy, like his mouth was a vacuum.

"No, no, that's enough. Noooo!" she begged, trying to move away from his mouth.

"I warned you. I told you, but I was gonna straight give yo' ass da business." he whispered, in a low tone.

"Let me do you?" she blurted out. Not meaning to. But, wanted him to let her up.

Of course, he ignored her and continued to give her da business. By the time he was done, she had snatched all the covers off the bed. Then he slid his gym shorts and boxers down. With his feet, he threw them across the room. Then he laid back on the bed and motioned for her to suck it. "Ok, baby I'm ready for dat Becky."

"Huh?"

"I want you to swallow my babies!" he whispered, running the back of his hand down the side of her face.

"Naw, niggah! I'm on a diet. Before you say anything, let me simplify it, sperm has 35 calories per teaspoon. My ass don't need to get no bigger."

"Put dat on sumthin"

"That's on everythang I love. Goggle it."

He rubbed her scalp. "Well baby, a few calories isn't gonna hurt, becuz I'm 'bout to help you burn them shits right off. Besides, I read where sperm has calcium in it and it will help strengthen your teeth and bones." he smiled.

"Well you know you can't be believing everything you read,"

"My ex has teeth so strong; the dentist has to use a crowbar to pry them shits out!"

"To dat end, ok." she said, giving in. She swallowed the big lump in her throat. Every time she went down on it, she would gag. So, she decided to just lick around the tip of the head instead. Sensing she was an amateur, he told her to bend over so he could hit it from the back. Then, he reached in the drawer beside the bed and pulled out a Magnum.

As soon as he put it in, he started oohing. "Damn, baby, dis' shit feels so—you're so good, so tight, and wet!"

"Fuck me, baby. Fuck me, baby!" she yelled. "Damn he can eat the fuck out of some pussy and finger fuck the hell out of it but damn, I'm lookin'

to be pleased not teased." she lipped silently, rolling her eyes back in her head, while he did his best. To make matters worse, the faster he got, the more he would sweat. The more he sweated the wetter she got. *I quess I must fake it to I make it, I heard it'll make'em cum quicker* she thought inwardly as she moaned and screamed boasting his ego like he was actually giving her the business.

"How you want it, fast or slow pumps?" he asked, holding on to the back of her head.

"Slow, Daddy, slow!" she said, letting out moans. After they were done, they both collapsed on the bed.

"Wow, dat was amazin'!" she lied, trying to catch her breath. *He's definitely no Grievence, oh well I'll take what I got and work and work with it. Damn, I miss my daddy, big dick!* she thought as she laid and looked at him, with him having no idea what was really going through her head.

"You walk what you talk, right?"

"I never felt like dis' before. Dis' gotta go down in da diary?" she said, ignoring him.

"You heard me, big head!" he said, picking up the pillows off the floor. When she glanced at the nightstand, she saw her Palm Pre vibrating. It was Leigha.

"It's nobody but Leigha. I'll call her back later!"

"You should get dat. It might be important."

"All right." she said, pressing the talk button. "Whattup!"

"You hoe! I done called yo' raggedy ass a gang of times!"

"I was on some other shit. But, what's so important you keep ringin' my phone, dawg?"

"Hellllo, you and I was 'posed ta be going to the mall to cop the new Forces!"

"Damn, I forgot. Like I said, I was on some other shit!"

"Yo' hot, ass gettin' yo' shit played in. I Ain't mad atcha, doe. Hit it up when you're home!"

"Aight, girl!"

"Neeyah!" she screamed.

"What up, doe?"

"How was it? Is he packin', girl?"

"Bye, girl, you silly!" she chuckled, placing the phone back on the nightstand.

That Monday, she went to the library to do some research on colleges to pursue her career. She knew the money she was getting wasn't gonna last

forever. It was teacher's workday at Junior's school, so he had to stay home. She told Ricky that she wasn't gonna be home too late, because she was gonna kick it with Leigha.

"You want some candy, Junior?" Ricky asked, peeping outta the window to see if Neeyah had left yet.

"Yeeeah!" he said, happily.

After giving them a little while to be gone, he took Junior into the room. He knew Sonny was staying after school for basketball practice and wouldn't be home for a while.

"Dis' time, we gonna try sumthin' new."

"What, daddy?" he asked, with the chocolate from the Kit Kat paper, all around his mouth.

He didn't respond. Instead, he walked out. Making a quick scan, he nervously checked the lock.

When he returned, he had some Vaseline and another Kit Kat. Then he instructed Junior to lie on his stomach and gave him the Kit Kat. Junior knew what was happening wasn't right. He let out a loud wail, "Daddy, don't. It hurt!" he pleaded.

"Shuuush, son. I'll be gentle." he said, in a very low whisper with sweat dripping from his face onto Junior's tiny back. He knew that he was wrong. But, in his twisted mind, he figured that having him suck him off was no less than penetration. Junior continued to cry louder. Fearing somebody was gonna hear his loud cries, he cupped his mouth with his hand. Somehow, Junior managed to bite down on his finger, causing him to remove it. Still in excruciating pain, he cried out, catching the attention of Sonny who was just walking in the door, from a cancelled practice.

"What da fuck! You twisted fuck!" he screamed, snatching Ricky up. It all happened so fast Ricky didn't have time to react or nothing.

When Sonny pulled him up, blood was oozing outta poor Junior. Keeping in mind that Ricky is much bigger and with solid weight, that didn't matter because seeing what was happening to his brother at the hands of his own father, gave him this power he never knew he had.

Ricky couldn't say nothing, all he could do was surrender. "Go ahead and call the cops. I fucked up!" Sonny wasn't trying to hear none of that shit; it was like he was zoned the out or something, he heard nothing but, however saw visions of him on his baby brother. Ricky pleaded for his life. His cries and pleas went unheard. Sonny just kept beating him with the bat until his body was limp and lifeless. Tears were streaming down his face. Then he looked at his brother who was in the corner shivering and crying

with his hands gripping his knees. That's when it dawned on him what had just taken place. He immediately rushed over to him and picked him up. Held him tightly; blood was everywhere. He stepped over Ricky's dead body, and walked through his blood, making his way to the living room to call the police. Not even ten minutes later, they were there. When the cops put the handcuffs on Sonny, he broke away.

"I hope you rot in hell. You fuckin' pedophile-ass niggah!" he yelled to the top of his lungs while, kicking Ricky's lifeless body. A short buff cop intervened and escorted him out the door.

"The boy will be going to Child haven!" one of the officers said.

"He was raped. My brother was raped! He needs to go to hospital! I love you, Junior. I love you, baby boy," he screamed, looking back while tears were still streaming down his face. It was so sad everyone was out their doors standing around, looking. Junior was wrapped inside a sheet and taken to the nearest hospital.

IT IS WHAT IT IS

As soon as Monie got back home, she had set her plan into action. She started by going over to Rah Rah's house. When she pulled up, Rah Rah glanced at the monitor. He wasn't alone. He had a neighborhood hoe named April, over. Giving him bomb head.

"Hold on," he pushed her back.

She continued to suck his balls, like a baby calf sucking the milk out of a cow. "I said hold the fuck on, bitch!" he snapped, yanking her by the hair and forcing her to the floor. She let out a loud wail. He watched the monitor to see who the unknown car was pulling in to his driveway. April laid on the floor holding her head, sobbing. Then all of the sudden, she saw him reaching for his gun.

Damn what part of the game is it when a niggah wanna shoot you for going down on them. She thought balling up and shielding her head with her hand, as if they could stop bullets. Realizing he was looking at the monitor, she hopped up to her feet and straightened her clothes. When he saw that it was Monie, he put the gun back on coffee table and headed downstairs.

"What the hell! Don't ever come to my shit unannounced. You got 1 minute to get yo' stanky ass off my shit, befo' I stomp yo' raggedy ass out! Word to Mama, yo!"

"It's not like—" he slammed the door in her face. She scurried off to the car. Once she was safely in her car, she locked the doors and peeled off, running over one of his sprinklers and mailbox. Safely, out of harm's way she pulled out her Cricket phone.

"How did it go?" Amauri asked.

"It didn't go well at all!"

"Well, where are you now?"

"I'm on my way back to the crib! I'll meet you there,"

"Bitch, don't meet me there, beat me there!" he muttered, switching lines.

"Hello? I didn't hear you. Hello," Monie repeated and then glanced at the phone. "Oh he must've lost signal."

"What's good witcha, fam?" Amauri said into the phone.

"Nuthin' much, tryna see what you know good?"

"Shid, just tryna set our plan into action, that's all. I got ole girl workin' on dat as we speak! You feel me?"

"That's what's up, so how was your vacation?"

"Dat shit was the business. We went on a cruise, and then continued on to a hideaway. It was lovely. She figured out my ploy,"

"She figured out what?!" Kadaafie snapped.

"It wasn't like dat doe, cuhz!"

"You know what, fuck it becuz I don't even gotta waste my breath tellin' you what's gonna happen if she fuck dis' up. What if she goes to tell his ass? Dat hoe might be playin' your weak ass. Just make sure dat bitch don't cross you." he said, ending the call.

Amauri pulled up to Monie's house and shut off the engine. She was standing outside her rental car waiting on him. "I got dat, niggah. I'll be dat." he said.

He sat in the car a minute or two, to gather his thoughts. She glanced over at him. "My boo is so sexy," she smiled.

When he saw her staring at him, he exited the car and greeted her with a yellow rose with a red tip. "Hey sexy." he said. When he really wanted to choke the shit out of her.

"You don't ever quit do you? What do dis' one mean?" she said, looking at him.

"Never. I aim to please. I told you I'm dat niggah. A yellow rose wit a red tip means I'm falling in love with you." he said, giving her a peck on her lips after every lie dat rolled off his tongue. She could've died right then and her life would've been complete. "Enough of all dis' we'll have all the time and the world for these elated moments. So, what happened with ole' boy?" he asked, standing directly in front of her with his arms folded.

"Well, when I showed up, he was on one. He was like, bitch don't be comin' to my shit unannounced and whoop whoop, I thought he was about to pistol-whip my ass,"

"I thought you guys were cool like dat."

"Apparently, not." she said. "I shouldn't have showed up unannounced."

He hugged her, but low key he wanted to strangle her. "Don't trip, boo, we'll think of sumthin',"

"Oooh, I know how I can get at him!" she broke away from him and rubbed her hands together.

"What? Let a niggah in. Don't be keepin' a niggah all in suspense and shit?"

She decided against telling him her real stratagem, on fucking him.

"Umma just call him and talk to him!"

He shot her a look that said, *get da' fuck outta here.*

"I was blessed with the gift of gab, niggah. You didn't know? Umma pull some strings."

"Well, you do dat. Pull some strings, make it happen. Umma go handle some business. I'll hit you later." he said, giving her a peck on the lips.

"Will do. You be careful, baby!"

He didn't respond. He just threw two fingers up in the air, got in his car, and sped off.

She pulled out her phone and pressed her luck with Rah Rah.

While waiting on to answer, her heart started beating fast against her chest wall. "Who da' fuck is dis'?" he screamed into the phone, not recognizing the number.

"I-I-It's me, Monie." she stammered. "Don't hang up, please. I really need you right now." she pretended to be crying.

"What's good, witchat Word to mama, you were seconds away from taking your last ride." he said, softening his stance. He had a soft spot for crying women, especially somebody that he loved, being that he loved Leigha.

"I know," she said. "I wouldn't have never done dat. You know me. You know sumthin' had to be wrong."

"Well, you kinda caught a niggah off his guards and shit, but what's good? You need some money or sumthin', but you know a niggah ain't just gonna give you shit. You'll have to work for it, nah mein!"

"No, nuthin' like dat!" she said. "Can I come over and speak to you face-to-face becuz I really don't like talkin' on cell phones."

"Yeah, you can come thru in about an hour and a half. A niggah is out and about, getting my haircut and shit. Who shit you rollin' in anyway?"

"Oh, dat's just a rental, but I'll see you then!" she said, excitedly and hung up.

He made a mental note that something was definitely off with her from the way she ended the call and if she was crossing him then, *pow!*

As soon as she hung up, a big Kool-Aid smile flashed across her face.

"Checkmate!" she screamed, to the sky. Then she scampered toward her house, heading straight to the bathroom to shower. When she got out, she applied some lotion and oiled herself down. Once she was done, she put on her red lace underwear set, along with a short black button-down dress. Before heading out the door, she sprayed on some of Leigha's favorite perfume *Halo* by Victoria's Secret.

Soon as she got in the car, she adjusted the seat and straightened out her dress.

While adjusting her mirror, she noticed Hennessie and her entourage, walking by. So, she quickly put on her stunna's and adjusted the volume. *Miss Me* by Drake blared from the speakers.

She hoped the light would catch them, so they wouldn't have no other choice but to see her pushing the silver chromed-out 2011 Impala.

"Hate it, bitches!" she said, peeling off. Luckily, when she got back to Rah Rah's house, he was just pulling up.

"What's good witcha?"

"Are we gonna talk in your driveway or can we go in?"

"Nah, I'm straight. We good right here."

She put on a sad face and then told him that her boyfriend was beating her, and that she was coming to him for a loan on a gun.

"Maybe we ought to go inside." she followed his lead. Once inside, she sat down while he disabled the alarm. He returned with a glass of water.

"You don't have nuthin' stronger than dis'?"

"I got some Henny. You'll have to excuse my place. My sister's kids were just over here."

"Oh boy, please, I'm not trippin'. I know how kids can be, trust me. I've seen way worse and no kids in the picture." she said, looking around. *Honey, stop, a child didn't do all dis'!* she thought to herself. "You got dat Henny, huh? I could really use a drink!"

He handed the drink and sat next to her. He smelled so good. She wanted to suck all the skin off his dick.

"Now you know I couldn't give you no gun. Even if I wanted to. Yo' sister will kill the both of us, yo',"

She loved hearing his New York accent and was a sucker for them up North niggahs. After talking to him a while, she was begining to feel a little sorry that she was plotting against him but quickly dismissed the idea and convinced herself that it was business, nothing personal. Nothing more nothing less. He was a very genuine person. She also knew that he would

never make a pass on her or even look at her like that for that matter. She swallowed two thizz pills along with any doubts of guilt she was having.

"What's dat girl?!" he asked, baffled.

"Oh, it was just Tylenol for dis' migraine headache I'm havin'," she lied, taking a big gulp of the drink. Caught off guard by the question.

"Well, you know you can't be takin' no medicine with no alcohol, nah-wha-im-sayn'!" he scolded her.

"Ok, daddy!" she said, sitting the empty glass on the coffee table. He was so caring; she could see why her sister had gotten past his looks and had fallen deeply in love. Allureness radiated from his body. After a while of sitting, she asked for another drink.

"Okay, only one more becuz you're drivin'!" he said, walking towards the bar. When he left the room, the scent of his *Curve* still lingered behind. When he walked back toward her, she was thinking, *he look so damn good with dat wife beater he's wearing along with them gym shorts exposing his print, down to his knees . . . Oh lawd . . . breathe. His teeth look like his toothpaste came with bleach.* His smile was so beautiful, she wanted to straight fuck his brains out, her pussy was thumping a mile per minute.

"Well, I guess umma go fuck with the court for a hot second."

"Alrightie, dat's my cue to get out!"

"Naw, it's nuthin' like dat, nah meen? I just thought you were done."

She scanned the room. Not at all surprised to see how dirty his crib was. It was mostly dirty dishes and clothes thrown everywhere except in the basket where they needed to be. She made a mental note to go at that aim if all else fail.

"Donald Goines, huh?" she said, noticing all of his books neatly on a bookshelf. The only thing that seemed to be in order.

"What you know about him? Youz a youngster, nah-wha-im-sayn'!"

"I guess . . . but, truth be told, I know a lot more than, a lot of people tend to give me credit fo'!" she said, getting a tingling sensation from the way he kept licking his lips every time he spoke. "I know he was the Greatest Street Legend to ever walk the streets."

"Dat he was! A damn shame how a mahfucka murked his ass befo' he could see how much of impact his books had on mahfuckas now and days! Nah-wha-im-sayn'!"

All she could do was nod her head at everything else he said. She seen his lips moving but heard nothing else. She was taken aback by his knowledge and was very much drawn to him. A good feeling washed over her while watching him talk.

"Well, umma go ahead, go shoot some hoops!" he said, pushing himself up.

Her mind started racing a mile a minute, trying to come up with a legitimate excuse to keep him there, but it kept coming up blank. Suddenly, she asked to use his restroom. When he turned his back, she unbuttoned two of her buttons, revealing her laced bra. Then she dropped down to the floor. *Bloop!*

"Are you okay?!" he yelled. "I knew your ass was more than a little tipsy!"

"I hope you have some insurance becuz I'm suing you niggah. Naw, I'm just playin', but I tripped over dat top in yo' flo', Negro. Are you gonna help me up or what?"

"My bad," he said, running over to help her up. He couldn't help but notice her shirt was opened, revealing her breast. So he closed it.

Are you fuckin' serious! she wanted to shout. *Here I am practically handing you the good pussy on a golden platter, and you don't want it. Get da' fuck outta here.*

She was thinking while looking at him. He loved and respected Leigha too much for that. He knew Monie was a hoe, and damn sho wasn't gonna fuck off what he had with Leigha. The realest female that came into his life. When she got on her feet, she planted a big wet kiss on his lips.

"You trippin', dawg, I mean, yo' ass really buggin' da fuck out," he said, breaking away. "I think it's time for you to leave."

She dropped down on her knees and impulsively grabbed his dick and forced it in her mouth. Her mouth was so hot and moist, that he decided that it would not be in his best interest to protest. Instead, he let her gum him down. She was sadly mistaken, because after giving him some bomb head he pulled his gym shorts up, and escorted her to the door.

"Damn, damn!" she said, hitting the steering wheel with her fist, feeling like an ass. "Dat's it!" she said, snapping her fingers.

The next morning, she called Rah Rah and apologized with the usual excuse. She blamed it on the alcohol, telling him that she needed to make a couple of bucks. And asked him was there something she could do for him. He told her she could clean for him and instructed her to be there at 10:00 a.m. sharp. When she arrived at his crib, he threw on some blue Sean John sweats, with a wife beater and Prada house shoes.

Damn, dat walk she thought, watching him walk towards her. "I wanna apologize for my actions yesterday. I was on one, dat pill had a niggah trippin'!" she said, with a sheepish look.

"Don't trip, you good!" he said, using the bottom of his shirt to wipe the sweat beads off his forehead. She immediately noticed his Cavalli boxers as she sized him up and down. He apparently, had just finished working out. "Damn, I need to go hop my ass in the shower!" he said, showing her what needed to be done. "I noe it looks like a lot, but you don't have to finish all in one day. Umma take care of you, nah-wha-im-sayn'!" he said, heading upstairs.

She pretended to be cleaning, but was snooping around trying to find the hidden room and what it consisted of. Her search turned up empty, so she hurriedly cleaned the kitchen. Fifteen minutes later, he appeared outta the pantry.

"Looks good!" he said, scanning the kitchen.

Damn, I know I seen dat niggah go up the stairs, she thought. Then it dawned on her. *The secret room must be inside the pantry,* she thought acting as if she wasn't paying attention where he came from.

"Well, it wasn't dat bad in the first place!"

She was doing such a good job he let her stay while he went out to meet with his connect. Of course, he told her he was going to handle some much-needed business and that he would be back in less than thirty minutes and that upstairs was forbidden.

"Come on, you know me better than dat. I have no reason to go upstairs!"

"Well, I'll be back in thirty minutes." he said, grabbing his keys off the island bar. "Do you want sumthin' to eat while I'm out?"

"Nah, I'm straight!" she turned to sweep the floor.

"Are you sure becuz I don't have no problem stoppin' by Mikky D's and getting you a fat, double cheeseburger off the dollar menu." he joked, walking towards the door.

"Mikky D's . . . Eeewww who eats from there!" she joked.

"Girl, them shits be bangin'," he said, going out the door. Fifteen minutes later, she went back and inquisitively searched the pantry. Nothing struck her as odd or unusual but, once she walked over to the wall and flicked the hidden switch, which she thought to be a light switch, the whole wall opened. She was utterly awestruck. The room looked immaculate compared to the rest of the house. It was neatly, decorated with everything by Scarface. Everything from pictures to rugs and lamps. There was a custom-made pool table flown in from Italy, with Tony Montana holding his machine gun, engraved in the center. Just to the right of it, he had a big comfortable black leather couch, adorned with Scarface pillows. The room also had a

spiraling staircase leading up to his bedroom. There was a 75-inch plasma television mounted to the wall. When she glanced at the monitors, she saw Rah Rah pulling up so she quickly flipped the switch down. It closed as quickly as it opened. Then she ran and grabbed the remote and plopped down on the sofa.

CROSS ME ONCE, SHAME ON ME
CROSS ME TWICE, SHAME ON YOU

When Swagga arrived at Sal's house, he was instructed to wait in the living room. When he walked by, he could see men eating dinner and having what appeared to be a friendly conversation. Thirty minutes later, the bodyguard told him that the boss was ready to see him. He picked up his duffle bags and headed in to greet him. As soon as he walked into the kitchen, qualms hit him. Two people were shot; one was slumped over on the table, and the other one was sprawled out on the floor.

"Swag, come on help me move these fat fucks!" Sal screamed, out of breath. "Fuckin' scumbags."

As soon as they picked the man up from the floor, pasta fell from his stomach. That really made him sick. Sal didn't have to do nothing; he simply chose to. After all, to ensure something is done the right, you have to do it yourself. Once they were inside the basement, there was a team of men waiting, with their chain saw. Afterwards, he followed Sal back upstairs to conduct their business. Once in the great room, Sal motioned for one of his men to grab the duffle bag and count the money. Upon finding out it was the right amount, he gave him fifteen more bricks. He was now officially in "bed" with Sal. Once he got the duffle bag in his possession, he headed fro his car.

"With any luck, these birds will fly tonight." he said, getting on the highway. To the home he shared with Angie. Luckily, she wasn't home. After he showered, he headed to the Trap. When he pulled up, he saw Stubby chopping it up with some female. When he spotted him, he tried to walk off fearing that he was gonna feel Swagga's wrath. But Swagga was on some other shit. By the time, he stepped one foot in the door Stubby was right behind him.

"Damn, you really on a niggah's bumper."

"Nah, ah niggah gotta pee." he lied. Swagga had recently purchased a town home. The only person knew about it was Grievence. Money was pouring in, left and right. His scheme to sell his products dirt-cheap had really paid off.

"Time to get down to business!" he said, placing the bag on the table that contained three bricks. Just as he was about to sit down, there was a knock on the door. Swagga was closer to the door.

"Don't trip, I got it, dawg!" Bread screamed, jumping up.

Swagga knew something was wrong but couldn't put his finger on it. So, as the guys were filling the vials, he decided to see who was at the door and immediately got heated. He saw Bread slapping some hoe, out in the parking lot. He knew Bread was gonna be a problem, and he had to be dealt with. As soon as Bread stepped back into the apartment, all the cutthroatness was revealed. Bread sat down like nothing was wrong. Swagga slowly got up and pistol-whipped him.

Bloom, bloom. The forceful hit from the gun caused him to fall back over the kitchen chair, breaking it into pieces. It all happened so fast he started gasping for air like he'd actually been shot.

"I told your mahfuckin' ass you're not gonna be havin' mahfuckas comin' round hea' makin' a scene and shit makin' my shit hot, bum azz niggah!" he said, in a very loud hostile tone.

"My bad, it won't happen again." he said, in a weak voice as blood was dripping from his face like water. He was just glad he wasn't shot. Trigga looked on in terror. They were friends, but he wasn't trying to feel Swagga's fury. Right was right, if Bread made the spot hot and the joint got knocked, that meant he too would have to go back to sticking niggahs up. He wasn't tryna feel it. Bread caught a glimpse of Trigga looking at him. When he looked at him, he quickly turned away. Besides, what could he do, Swagga was the boss. Whateva he said went, and if you had a problem with that, then you'll just simply disappear. That was the rule of the game. They all went into the game with their eyes wide open. After he busted his shit up, he helped him up and said with no remorse like shit didn't just happened, "Shall we continue?" Bread was sitting at the table bleeding, liberally.

"Maybe you ought to let us do dis'." Swagga suggested, fearing he would get some blood on the product. "Just go clean yo'self up! Next time I hope you think twice about your childish antics."

The next day, Bread and Trigga went to their spot on Gleason, as if nothing had ever happened.

"Mayne, what was dat all about yesterday?" Trigga asked.

"Low Key, dawg, I got dis' thing going on the side. I was gonna mention it to you earlier, but I wanted to see how it would pan out." Bread spilled all the beans, unable to hold them.

"What thing, mayne?"

"I got a couple of hoes wanting me to be their pimp. Then I got some dope of my own. I'm tryna be a boss myself, ya digg?" He went own telling the friend he could trust with his life. "Dawg, I got dis' shit boomin'. I made five hundred dollars in less than forty-five minutes and still makin' money."

"Didn't you learn your lesson?" he said, angrily not wanting nothing to happen to his friend. However, he picked and chose his own path of life.

"Fuck dat puss-ass niggah. Low key, I got sumthin' fo' his puss-ass, just watch!" he said, barely able to open his mouth from being all busted up.

"Mayne, you buggin', youz eatin' good. It's not dat serious, yo'!"

"I'm tryna have dis' hea city on locked. No' just dis' hoe-ass block!" Bread waved his hand at the skyline.

"Patience. You are movin' too fast, dawg. I think you need to slo' yo' role!"

"Fuck all dat! You can just miss me wid dat hoe shit, dawg! Dis' is an every-man-for-him-mahfuckin'-self-world, ya' digg? You can't be movin' too slow out dis' bitch you'll get left behind, fasho!"

Trigga knew that his friend was bullheaded and wasn't no sense in talking to him. He really felt bad, but he knew he had to tell Swagga about his strategy, because if the ship went down he didn't wanna go down with the captain. Trigga, decided to go to Blue Jays to get a cigar. Then, he ran into his old homeboy Shady, who was now a smoker "low key."

"What up, doe, my niggah?" he said, giving his old homie some dap.

"Shid, nuthin' much 'bout to bust dat hoe-ass niggah, Rich up!" he said, so mad you could see the steam coming from his cornrolls.

"Word?" he said, low key pissed he ran into him.

"Dat weak-ass niggah gonna try to nut up on me fo' five punk-ass dollars. I was 'bout to give his bitch ass da business, Smith & Wesson style, you know how I do!" he said. The truth was, over the years he had lost his touch and all of his street cred. A couple years prior, he was known to murk a niggah within a blink of an eye.

"Straight 'bout to give homie da business, huh?" he said, trying speed up their convo, knowing dat Shady wasn't about nothing but pop off at the mouth. "Well, lemme go get dis' niggah shit befo' he put an APB out on my ass," he said, walking in the store. Word on the streets, was that Shady

was a snitch because he had been to jail about twenty times and didn't do no more than three years at the most. Trigga remembered back in the days when he was just a youngster, Shady used to be the man to see until he met this one broad that had his head gone. Sent that niggah straight to sucking a glass dick. Right doing his own product. That is the number one rule in the game, never get high on your own supply.

While lying on his bed, Grievence decided to call Trees. When he picked up his cell phone, it started vibrating. It was Neeyah. He simply pressed the end key, sending the call straight to voice mail. He waited a few moments; then, he dialed Trees's number. There was no answer, so he left his number on her voice mail. Fifteen minutes later, she called back without listening to the message.

"Did anyone just call my house?" she said, erasing the number off the caller ID.

"What up, doe, punk?!" he said, geeked.

"Is dis' dat niggah, Grievence?!" she yelled, excitedly into the phone, recognizing his voice.

"Da one and only, baby! Long time no hear, Negro,"

"Yeah. What's been up, doe? You da one a stranger and shit,"

"Naw, dawg, you know it's not even like dat. I have been caught up in dis' thing they call love, but shid, it's been the same shit different day out dis' bitch. So how did you get dis' number?"

"From yo' granny, niggah. Well I'm in town for about another week or—"

"Dat is what's up, doe! I bet she had your ass on the phone for 'bout an hour, huh? So where are you stayin'? Umma come thru and fuck witcha." she cut him off.

"I'm over at the . . . what da fuck is the name of dis' roach motel?" he said, trying remember the name of it.

"Damn, niggah, on second thought, I think you need to lay off the chronic. They say your memory is the first to go. Onset of early Alzheimer lookin' ass." she joked.

"Picture dat? I need my weed like I need air to breathe," They both laughed. "But, it's the one Murray Hill off of 8 Mile."

"Oh, dat's right up the street from me. I'll see you in about fifteen!" she ended the call.

It had been over five years since they saw each other, so he wanted to shave and look good for her. He threw on some Evisu jeans and a fitted

white T-shirt with some brand-new fresh-outta-the-box white Forces. Then he dashed on some his favorite *Ed Hardy* cologne. Thirty minutes went by, she wasn't there. Three hours later, he got up and decided to head to the Trap. She called wanting the room number. He pulled his hair back in a ponytail, and unlocked the door for her.

"What up, doe!" she said, with her arm outstretched.

"You, stranger. That's have to be the longest fifteen minutes, ever!" he joked. "Let me get a look at you." he stepped back. She stood firm, waiting to hear what he had to say. "You look gooder than a muthafuka," he said, looking at her from head to toe. "I see you traded in your Forces for some pumps, huh?"

"Why, thank you!" she blushed. "Well, you're easy on the eyes yourself look atcha grill all gleaming and shit!" she said, walking over to sit down. True enough, she had switched up her whole style. She went from wearing sweats and jeans to dressing professional. She was dressed in some black dress pants, a red-black-and-white shirt with ruffles and bangles, all from Chanel. Along with some black square toe pumps. The all black Al Wissam pea coat she was wearing set her whole outfit off. She stood about five feet six inches, and weighed about 130 pounds. Her skin was a light tone and smoother than a baby's ass. Her hair was full of reddish, honey blonde curls that complimented her eyes. A honey brown color, which was contacts. She was definitely on her grown woman.

"Look at Ms. New York!" he said, starry-eyed.

"Yeah, my niggah like it when I dress like dis', getting my grown woman on and shit, but what you brings you back to da D?" she asked, giving him bag of weed.

"Shid, I'm out here fuckin' with my bother, going hard on these niggahs!" he said, probing and smelling the purp.

"Yeah, niggah, dat's dat good good. When did his ass touch down?"

"He has been out for a couple of weeks. Go ahead a roll it up, you know rolling a blunt has never been my forte." he handed it back to her.

They reminisced for a while and then he headed to the Trap.

She headed home. No sooner than she walked through the door, Dro jumped up and lit into her. "You tryna to fuckin' hoe me." *Wham! Wham!* "You fuckin' slut puppy!" *Wham! Wham!*

"What are you talkin' about?!" she cried, trying to shield her face. Not having a clue. He was like a walking time bomb. Anything could set him off. That's why she was a homebody, that is as long as she had weed.

"Bitch, I'm talkin' about dat hoe-ass niggah you cheatin' on me with!"

"I'm not cheatin' on you, baby. I love you!" she cried.

Everything she said went into one ear and out the other one. He just smacked her. "After all dis' shit I do for your slutty ass, get yo' shit and get the fuck out! You worthless piece of shit!"

"No, please, baby, please don't do dis' to me. You know I have no place to go," she pleaded.

"Well, bitch, you should have thought about dat shit befo' yo' slutty ass decided to have your tricks callin' my shit. Matter fact, you're not takin' shit, just get what your yo' bum ass came wid and dat's nuthin' and get da fuck out!" he screamed, to the top of his lungs. She dropped her head and cried uncontrollably. With no other choice, she put her pride in her pocket and left. He had smacked one of her contacts out; she didn't care. She was just worried about not having anywhere to go. Going to her grandma's wasn't an option because she didn't wanna hear no "I told you so's." While, sitting on the steps crying and shivering, she started to wonder, *was the lavish lifestyle worth it?* She figured she could take the mental abuse that he constantly lash on her until she could get on her feet, but on the other hand, she was tired of pretending. Outside looking in, hoes would probably kill to walk in her shoes, but no one knew her pain or how her heart ached. She wanted more. She was tired of walking on eggshells knowing he could break at any moment. After a while, her mind went blank. It was so cold outside; she was numb and couldn't think no more. She vowed that he would get his. Three and a half hours later, he saw her sitting outside in the cold and felt sorry for her. He knew she wasn't cheating; he just had a guilty conscience.

"I want you to know I'm not cheatin' on you!" she said, shivering. He just shushed her.

"Baby, you're freezin'. I'm so sorry!" he whispered, undressing her. Planting soft wet kisses along her body.

"What are you doing, baby?!" she asked in a soft, weak voice.

"You need body heat, or you'll go into hypothermia or sumthin'," he said. Then he carried her into the bathroom and placed her into a tub of warm water. Twenty minutes later, he took her a sponge bath.

"I got it bay," she said, tryna lift herself up.

He lifted her up out of the water. "No, baby, allow me, After all it's my fault dat you were out there and I'm so sorry, baby!" he said, with tears welling up in his eyes. She just stared at him as if he was crazy. "You, do forgive me don't you baby? I promise it will never happen again."

"Yeah, baby I forgive you," she said, planting a kiss on his lips. "Look at the floor boo, it's gonna stink in here from all the water."

"Fuck dis' hoe-ass carpet." he pointed to the floor. "I'll have da carpet men come lay some brand new shit down, I'm concerned about my baby now." he said, rubbing her face with the back of his hand. For a moment, she got lost in his web of lies, and they had head-banging sex after he apologized for hitting her. She forced a wicked, mischievous smile on her face, thinking, *you gonna get yours.* Once they were done, she lay back in his arms, thinking of all kinds of ways to make him pay dearly.

Grievence went on the Internet to find a good strip club.

"Club Lexx."

"Hello, I would like to speak to your manager."

"May I ask what is dis' concerning?" The woman on the other end of the phone spoke, enunciating every properly

"Well, if you're not the manager, then it doesn't concern you, ma'am!" she sighed, and then slammed the phone down. Five minutes later, he came to the phone.

"You guys are pretty busy, huh?"

"Excuse me." he said, with an attitude. "What do I do you the pleasure of dis' call?"

"Well, I'm going to keep dis' concise. I wanna know how much it will be to get four of your best girls."

"I'm sorry sir, but we don't make house calls. Dis' isn't an escort service we're running here. Now if you don't mind, we're busy!"

"Sir," Grievence screamed into the phone, "Look, I'm willin' to pay top dollar for four of your finest girls for one day!" That caught the money hungry manager's attention.

"Say hypothetically, if I was to maneuver around some things and bend some rules, how much are we talkin'?"

"Well, first off, I need to fly the girls to Detroit Friday mornin'."

"Detroit?!" he screamed.

"I mean, it's nuthin'. I can pay top dollars. You name your price!"

The greed took over and he said, "All-expenses paid?"

"All-expenses paid," Grievence repeated.

"Well, let's say about a one thousand five hundred apiece. Now that's cuttin' you a deal because the girls make triple dat in one night!"

"Say no more."

"One more thing, just how are you plannin' to make dis' transaction?" he asked, bemused.

"Well, I was gonna give you my credit card number." he called off the number on his prepaid green dot of which he had just dropped ten racks on it. Before he hung up, he made sure to tell the manager he was part of the mob. After that, he knew what that meant. When he hung up, he noticed Deuces had called. He called him back.

"What's crackalackin'?" Deuces happily said into the phone.

"Shit. About my money, you betta come get yo' slice of the pie, baby!"

"I heard yall had the block boomin' out there. But, shid that's what I was callin' to tell you, a niggah is finally off da papers, ya digg!"

"That's what's up. So why aren't you here then, niggah?"

"Well, my plane touchdown tonight at 8:00 p.m sharp. Show up or hoe up!"

"Don't trip, I got ya!"

ORANGE JUMPSUIT, WHO WOULD HAVE EVER THOUGHT?

"Fuck! What do their bitch asses want?" Leigha glanced into her rear view mirror and pulled over to the side of the road. "Is there a problem, officer?" she asked with heart beating outta her chest. *Damn, I hope they don't smell dis' gunja I just smoked because if they do, they'll search dis' muthafuka and find my fat ass chronic sack I just copped!* she thought to herself tryna to look like nothing was wrong.

"License and registration!" the officer said, with a stern look on his face. Her heart dropped because she didn't have his registration.

"Can you tell me why you pulled me over? I was doin' speed limit, damnit! Oh, I know dull, because I'm black in a nice car!" she said, hitting herself upside the head. She wanted to just fuck with him because he was ignoring her. He remained mute and emotionless. She kept on popping off at the mouth.

"Ma'am, I'm gonna have to ask you be quiet while I run your license, or we gonna have to take you into custody."

"Well, do you know what the First Amendment states? I think it says you have da quote unquote right [putting emphasis on *right*] to freedom of speech," she said, putting her pointer finger on her temple. She could've shitted bricks when the officer told her that the car she was driving was involved with an incident and that she was gonna be taken in for questioning.

"I need you to step outta the car slowly with your hands on your head, ma'am!" he said, stepping back toward his cruiser.

Her heart raced, so she did what anyone under the influence would've done, just crunk up and dug off.

"Suspect is at large. We need backup. She's heading down Crenshaw Avenue!" the officer yelled, into his radio. Then jumped into his cruiser and pushed the pedal to the floor, doing one hundred miles per hour.

"Damn, ain't dis' a bitch!" she screamed, with tears streaming down her face. "What the fuck did I get myself into?" she asked herself. Rah Rah warned her to stay away from that side of town.

"I located the suspect. She just turned onto a dead-end street!" he yelled in his radio.

She got outta the car as if she was going to surrender "Fuck it!" she said, kicking off her pumps. There was no egress, so she ran and hopped over the wall. The alcohol she had just guzzled down told her she could out run the police and that's what she listened to.

"She just hopped over the wall. Where's the backup I requested? I need some backup!" he yelled into the radio, out of breath.

She had almost gotten away, but was actually relieved when the cops found her out of fear she was gonna be mauled down by the vicious barking pit bull.

"Suspect apprehended!" he yelled into his radio. *Wham, whamp.* "Bitch, dis' is for makin' me run after your stupid ass after I had just finished eatin' my donuts!" he hit her with his black stick.

"You two-sandwich donut-eatin' muthafucka, umma sue yall crooked asses," she laughed to keep from crying.

"Yeah, same thing dat make you laugh, will make you cry!" he replied, tightening the handcuffs. She tottered to the cruiser.

As soon as Ms. Lara arrived home from a hard day of work, she saw a coroner van and a lot of people standing around. Which, was nothing outta the ordinary. As, she got closer to her building, everybody was staring at her but, nobody said nothing.

"Damn, I sure hope they're not blockin' my whole building. I'm ready to lie down." she said, walking up to her building.

"I'm sorry, ma'am, but there's been a homicide in dis' building. Nobody's is allowed to go up." the short stalky officer said, holding her back.

Homicide, I really hope dat boy didn't kill dat girl, she said to herself, never imaging in a million years it was at her very own home. Nobody breathed a word to her. She actually overheard a smoker telling somebody.

She just took off toward the building, straight through the tape. Her heart sank. Tears flowed freely down her face when she saw they were at her door. "Excuse me, ma'am, you're not allowed in here!"

"Dis' is my home, let me thru," she yelled. He could no longer hold her. When she broke free, she saw all the blood in her apartment and the black bag, she passed out. Twenty minutes later, Neeyah was walked up. Her neighbor told her. She rushed inside.

The officers tried keeping her out, but they couldn't hold her. She was just too strong. When she got there, she saw an EMT (emergency medical technician) fanning her mama who was passed out in the hallway. As, she rushed to her mother's side, they were bringing the body out. "Who is dat?!" she screamed, with tears streaming down her face.

"I'm sorry, I'm have to asked you to step back," the cocky EMT said.

"Answer me, I wanna know. Is dat my brother, you stupid fat fuck!" Neeyah screamed. "Where is my brothers, damnit?" she rushed past the EMT and unzipped the bag. "Ricky?!" she yelled, puzzled.

"What happened?" Ms. Lara asked, coming to.

"Mommy, it's Ricky. Sonny killed Ricky, Ma!" she said. Still a little vague about what happened.

"Why?" she screamed. "Where's Junior?" she asked, looking around. Just then, her neighbor came over.

"Ms. Lara, I can't begin to fathom what you're going thru. If you need me, you know where to find me," the phone began to ring. Neeyah rushed to it.

"Hello, am I speaking to the parent or guardian of Ricky Jr?"

"No, it's my brother. Where is he?"

"I need to speak to the parent or guardian!"

"That's my brother, you racist bitch! I wanna know what's wrong with him! Where is he?" she snapped.

"Neeyah, baby, who is dat? Give me the phone!" Neeyah handed it to her and stood directly in front her waiting to hear what was said. "Where is my son?"

"He's here at the hospital, ma'am. We can't release no information over the phone. He's gonna be transported to ch—"

Dat's was all she heard and needed to hear. When they arrived at the hospital, the doctor told her that extensive damage had been done to Junior's anus and that he had to undergo emergency surgery to stop the bleeding.

"My baby!" she screamed out in agony. "How could he do dis' to his own son?! My poor baby!"

Normally, Neeyah didn't use profanity in front of her mom, but she was mad, hurt, and baffled.

"Dat fat pedophile muthafucka, he got exactly what he deserved. I knew sumthin' was off!" she said, pacing back and forth.

"Why did I leave my baby with him, oh my gosh?!" she said, with pang forming in her stomach. "All the times I left him with dat monster, he always wanted to go. Why didn't I let go, Neeyah?"

"Mommy, it's not your fault. Please don't blame yourself. I need you to be the strong one for Junior and Sonny!" she said, looking at her crying uncontrollably.

"The Lord isn't gonna put no more on me dat I can bare," she said. *Lord, please watch over Sonny, and please Lord, let my son make it thru this tryin' time* she prayed silently.

Junior was admitted to the hospital due to losing too much blood. He actually lost consciousness, shortly before arriving at the hospital. Two days later with his mom and sister by his side, he regained consciousness.

"He's woke!" Neeyah screamed, startling her mom who was taking a catnap after she was given some meds to calm her down by the nurse.

"The Lord is good!" she glanced up at the ceiling and yelled to the top of her lungs.

"Mommy, mommy, daddy's dead. Sonny did it with my bat," he said, weakly.

"Shush, baby, it's okay. Mommy's here and I'm not gonna leave you. Just rest, sweetheart."

When Neeyah went home to shower, she listened to her messages. She noticed one from Leigh calling her from the county. She figured she might as well make a trip to go see her and Sonny both at the same time.

WHEN BAD THINGS HAPPEN
TO GOOD PEOPLE

Amauri was sitting in front of his fifty-inch plasma, on his new black leather sectional sofa. Watching the Grammy's, a recorded program from his DVR. "Dat was tightest one yet." he said, outloud after looking at the *Swagga Like Us* performance. He glanced at his phone, it vibrating. Monie number displayed on the screen.

"Hey, baby, I missed you!" he said, in his sexiest voice, crossing his legs at the bottom.

"Awwwwe, I missed you too."

"So what cha' know good?"

"Well, I found out a grip of shit on dat niggah, but I was wondering, can we talk over some breakfast? A niggah starvin' like marvin', I'm tryna get my grub on!" she said, rubbing her belly.

"Only if you are treating, I'm playin'. I'll meet you at IHOP over by your crib in about let's say, forty-five."

She hopped in the shower and when she got out she splashed on somebody spray and slipped in her black-and-gold Apple Bottoms tracksuit. Since it was a little chilly out. Forty-five minutes later, he greeted her with a hug, a kiss, and a single red rose, that he picked up from Vons along the way. He was definitely on his game.

"You look and smell so good, boo!" he whispered in her ear, handing her the rose. "I just wanna eat you up." he nibbled on her ear.

She blushed. "Okay, dat's gonna get you in trouble! A red rose umm . . . I wonder what that symbolizes."

"You already know it goes without sayin'! But, if you must know it means I love you, boo. No one ever showed me they genuinely cared about me like you have." he lied.

"Awwe, I think I wanna cry. I'm touched!" she said, planting a big wet kiss on his lips. "I'm in awe!"

"Well, like I said babygirl it has only just begun." he smiled, like a chest cat and then continued with his web of lies. That she got entwined in.

She was so in love with him to the point all she did was stare at him and smile, whenever in his presence. "You look nice."

He was wearing a cream-and burnt-orange Sean John tracksuit with some burnt orange Timbs, which really looked good on his smooth cocoa butter skin tone. While they ate and had a little discussion, she told him that her sister was in jail, being held on outstanding warrants. The minute she told him, she regretted it. She wanted to back out, but since she played the important part, she had to be there.

"Dat man, dat man . . . Ahhh so refreshin'. A tall glass of water." she smiled, watching him drive off.

"Damn, I'm hella nauseas!" Leigha said, to herself massaging her stomach, as she thought back to the letter she was gonna give Rah Rah.

"Breakfast!" the C/O yelled. Leigha continued to lay and think about her next move, and how she was gonna make it her best move.

"Aren't you gonna get up and eat your breakfast?" one of the inmates asked looking at Leigha like she had utterly lost her mind.

"Hell no, I'd rather have some Kibbles and Bits or some Goulash and some mo' shit, befo' I eat dis third world country bullshit!"

"Well I'll take it!" her celly said, with her eyes lit up.

"Be my guest," she said, getting up making her way over to the sink to wash her face and brush her teeth. Once she was done, she made her way to the phone. She didn't have to stand in line because everyone rushed to breakfast.

"Don't worry I'll get you back later with a spread,"

"Spread?" she shot her blank look.

"You never had a jailhouse spread? Get the fuck outta here," she asked Leigha. Leigha just looked at her as if she had lost her everlasting mind. "Girl, them shits too bomb. I be smashin' them,"

"I guess," Leigha walked off. "Yall asses can have dat slop! Better them than me!" she said, picking up the phone and dialing Rah Rah's number. "Hey baby." she whispered into the phone as soon as the call was accepted.

"When they set the bail umma have my sister come thru and swoop you up. Dat's my word, ma."

"Please, baby, I can't take dis' shit." Leigha cried. "Nasty, smoked-out, bummy bitches in my cell, and shit I'm not cut out for dis'!" she sniffled.

"I know, baby. I know." he said, in his sexy New York accent, in attempt to calm her down. "Just hang in there, boo. I'm here for you, nah-wha-im-sayn!"

"I know baby, I just can't believe I'm sittin' in jail for attempted murder and shit. The bitch just got sliced in the face, how the fuck is dat attempted murder? Next time, it won't be attempted. It'll be successful!" she said, out of anger. "Dis' shit is so barbaric!" she screamed, catching the attention of an officer.

"Yellin' is not admissible in here sweetheart!" An officer told her. As soon as she turned her back, Leigha flipped her off.

"Don't trip, boo, I'll handle everything. You need to watch what you say. Dis' shit is recorded, nah-wha-im-sayn, ma. I told you, as a matter of fact, I pleaded with you not to go to dat party."

"Fuck dat 'pose to mean, what are you insinuatin'?" she snapped.

"Look, I'm just sayin' I wished you would've stayed with me dat night, then you would not be in dat hellhole, nah-what-im-sayn, dat's all, boo."

"I know, baby, I'm sorry for snappin'. I guess I'm sorta' lookin' for a scapegoat. When in truth, there's no one to blame but myself. But, bay, dis' is inhuman the way you're treated here."

"Don't trip, you good. I love you," he said, before the phone cut off. Three hours later, she was shackled down and led to the courtroom.

"Leigha Brown, how do you plead?"

"Your Honor," she glanced over at Apple. "Please try to understand I wasn't at all myself that night. I'm terribly sorry for what happened. I just reacted; because I thought they were gonna kill my cousin! Please, don't misconstrue Your Honor, I wasn't sane. I lost my ability to think. I just looked up and seen a crowd of people on her. I'm from the streets of LA were you're taught to do what you can to get somebody off you." she said, with tears streaming down her face.

"Okay, Leigha, I'm gonna ask you one more time. How do you plead?" she tried not to look at Apple, but it was hard seeing through she was sitting directly across from her. "*Damn, I didn't know it was that bad. I really fucked her ass up on credit. Her fuckin' ass looks like the bride of chucky!*" she said to herself.

"Ms. Brown?!" the judge said with a little more bass in his voice. "My patience is wearing thin."

"I plead guilty," she said, swallowing a big glob of saliva that had formed in her mouth at the sight of Apple's wound. "But, if I could rectify dis', I would!" she said, looking at Apple.

"Well, I'm gonna try to show some leniency. Since, I see you're very remorseful about what you've done. Seems, as if you've made a trenchant argument in your own defense," the judge said, solemnly. "However, there was a terrible mishap. I just can't let this go unpunished. If I did, I'll look up, and see you soon in this very courtroom. I'm hoping this will serve as an exemplary punishment for you and others dat decide they wanna make an attempt on someone's life. Sentencing will be held in six months, and your bail is set at forty thousand." he said, hitting the gavel. Apple sat still with her arms folded on top of her breast, hissing.

"She's a threat and a menace to society. She needs to be put under the jail for what she did to my baby!" her mom, yelled.

"Order in the court." the judge said, hitting the gavel. Her mom's sarcastic outbursts, during the trial got her removed from the courtroom; especially when she thought Leigha was gonna go scott-free. Rah Rah, got her the best lawyer. His shrewd courtroom tactics made him a highly sought-after attorney. She was just happy to have her bail set. She knew that Rah Rah was gonna make sure she was straight, and she couldn't get back to her cell soon enough to call him. After her case was heard, it was time for the next case to be heard. She sat back and twirled her hair around on her pointer finger, daydreaming about what she was gonna do to him when she got out. Next thing she heard was, "We, the jury, find the defendant guilty on all three accounts of capital murder." Although the man sat with an impassive look and remained emotionless while the verdict was read, no one could've predicted such pandemonium would ensue. When his lawyer stood to greet him, a cop accompanied him. The man impulsively, grabbed his gun. First, he shot the lawyer execution style. "That's for takin' all my money and sellin' me a dream, you sucker-ass cracker." he yelled. Then he pointed, aimed and pulled the trigger at the judge, killing him on site. Then he shot, the unarmed cop in the chest. "I will not spend one more night in dat hellhole!" he said with the gun up to his head. He pulled the trigger the gun jammed he fixed and before he could pull the trigger again, a bailiff rushed him from behind causing the gun to fly clean across the courtroom. His family looked on in horror.

As soon as, Leigha got back to her cell, she called Rah Rah. He told her that his sister would pick her up on one condition that, if she could drop the kids off while she went out. Which this was no problem because he loved his nieces and nephews. Five hours later, his sister picked her and dropped the kids off. He also had his sister get the car out of pound and had her park at

her mom's house. He knew that would be the perfect surprise for Valentine's Day. Leigha, figured she would tell her family later, that she was out after she got some much-needed sleep. When she arrived there, he had a bathtub full of rose petals and filled to the brim with bubbles. *He was so good to me; why did it take me so long to see it,* she thought to herself. He sponged her down with the pink by Victoria's Secret sponge. Allowing her to relax a little, while he went to check on the kids. When he returned, she had drifted off to sleep.

"Wake up, baby." he whispered.

"I'm not sleep. I'm just lyin' here thinkin' with my eyes closed," she lied, without opening up her eyes.

"Do you love me?" he whispered in her ear, sending chills up and down her spine.

"Is dat a rhetorical question? You know dat goes without sayin'!" Her eyes were still closed.

He watched her for a few moments until she started snoring, then he got her out, dried her off and laid her on the bed. Fully dressed he laid next to her. He knew she was exhausted. He didn't care about getting no pussy because, he could get that all day every day if he wanted it. He just wanted to lie facing her. He watched her, as she slept ever so peacefully. He loved her. She was with him from the day when he didn't have shit, when he was nickel-and-dimer and for that, she held a soft spot in his heart.

"Uncle Raheem, Uncle Raheem," the kids said, running and jumping up on the bed.

"What do you two knuckleheads want?"

"We scared to sleep by us self. Can we come in here wid you?"

"Well, not tonight?"

"Please!" Diamond, his niece said holding her head down, looking up at him.

"You think them big brown eyes can get you anything, huh?" he said, pulling the covers back on the big custom-made bed.

"Now when you fall asleep, I'm puttin' you guys back into the other room."

"Okay," they said in unison.

"Where were you last night? Moms called worryin' me," Kadaafie asked his sister.

"I was with Raheem."

"Why was you with dat snake-ass niggah?" he snapped.

"There is sumthin' I wanna tell you. I sorta lied. I'm not pregnant. He just told me he loved that bitch, Leigha, so I was hurt. So, I made it all up." she said, waiting on his reaction.

"You did what? So he didn't kick you in your stomach? Do have any idea of the trouble you caused?"

"What you mean trouble? You didn't hurt him, did you? So help me God if hurt him." she screamed. Before she knew anything, he drew back his hand and backslapped her so hard; she went flying across the sofa.

"You punk muthafucka, you not gone put yo' hands on me. You got me fucked up, niggah! I got sumthin' for you!" she yelled, bouncing up like it didn't hurt and stomped outta the room holding her face He knew she was mad and was just venting. After an hour of crying and wondering what kinda trouble she got Rah Rah, into knowing her brother he was gonna kill him, she tried calling him to warn him, but his phone kept going to voice mail. She didn't know his house number or where he stayed.

On the other side of town, Monie lay on her bed pondering on whether to call Rah Rah or not. After twenty minutes, she decided to do so. It went straight to his voicemail, all ten times.

"Damn! I'm damned if I do and I'm damned if I don't." she yelled, throwing her cell phone on the floor.

Five minutes later, the house phone rang.

"Hello." she said, with her heart beginning to race.

"Where have you been? I called you a gang of times?" Amauri said, with an attitude.

"Calm down, boo, I was making some phone calls for my sister. Don't trip?" she lied.

"Well, I need you to meet me over at the IHOP because it's about to go down,"

"Okay, babe," she said, dryly regretting her part.

"What's wrong, boo?"

"I'm just thinkin' about my sister. You know dat feeling the other twin feels when something's wrong, that's all!" It was partly true. She did have a gut feeling something was wrong with her twin, sorta' of like her sister got when she was hospitalized.

"I'm sure your sister is okay. She's a big girl," he said, in an attempt to make her feel better. "I'll say a small prayer for her." he lied. He could've cared less about her or her sister. *That's what happens when you're in the game. It's a cold, cold world. After all, I didn't choose the game, it chose me,* he

thought to himself as he slipped on all-black hoodie. A half hour later, he pulled up. She was already waiting on him. He instructed her to leave the car parked and get in the car with him.

"Where to?" he asked, approaching the busy street. As she gave him directions, he kept looking at her in the mirror. He sensed her nervousness. "Relax, babe, we need to handle dis' so we can get married." he said, handing her a small, Tiffany box along with a dozen of white and red roses. "I'm tired of living dis' way. I just wanna go somewhere and start fresh!"

Once she opened the box, all the nervousness she felt, went out of the window. "Will you marry me?" he asked, pulling off the road into an empty parking lot.

"Yes, yes!" she said, with warm salty tears rolling down her cheek.

"Yes, what?!" he said, holding his hand up to his ear.

"Yes, I'll marry you!" she screamed, hugging him.

"Put dat on sumthin'?"

"I put dat on my life. I will marry you Amauri Carlton!" she screamed, like she just knew that was his last name

"Well, can I get a kiss?" he asked. She gave him a small peck on the lips.

"Uh, ummm, you gotta do better than dat to make your future husband happy, Mrs. Carlton." she leaned over and planted a big, fat wet on his lips. "Ooh, baby, I love them juicy delectable lips of yours, or shall I say mine!" he could see her blushing. "Now we gotta take care of dis', so we could make dat happen."

"Let's do the damn thing!" she chimed, sliding the—two-karat princess cut ring on her finger. "I like it, babe, I like." she said, moving her hand from side to side so she could see the light reflecting off of it.

"Be careful, boo, you gonna blind a niggah! Lookin' like crushed ice over there!" he teased.

"You musta' paid a grip for dis', huh?"

"To make my boo happy, priceless! Let me just take a minute to tell you how beautiful you are. Absolutely mouth-watering . . . ummm," he said, biting his bottom lip. Stroking her face. "I could go on for hours telling you how much you mean to me. But, fortunately, I have you for a life time to do so." he continued to stroke her ego. Then he let down the window and screamed out to anyone that was listening. "My boo said yes she's gonna marry me, making me the happiest man in the world. We're fuckin' gonna be united as one . . . Where to next?!"

"You really tryna ice me and wife me, huh?"

"Why, are you having second thoughts or sumthin'?"

She hit him on the leg. "No, boy, don't be silly!"

"Well, I was about to say, a niggah still got da' receipt to dat ring,"

"White and yellow . . . hummm," she smiled and glanced over at him.

"It means were gonna be one. You have no idea you've made me the happiest man in the whole world," he lied, with tears rolling down his face. One would've thunk it was real and genuine.

"Awwwe, baby don't cry. You gone make me cry." she said, with tears streaming down her face.

"Don't trip, boo." he dried her tears with the palm of his hand. She grabbed his hand and kissed it three times. Entwining herself deeper in his web of lies. He was so good that even the unbreakable, shielded woman would crumble and fall. It just didn't take her long because she was already liking up on him, as well as vulnerable.

Bitch these tears rolling down my face is as fake as your hair, use or get used. Dis' bitch believes anything under the sun. he thought looking at her. Nothing she did made him feel even the slightest bit of sympathy for her. He was the type of man to never mix business with pleasure. And that's what separated him from the typical man that spent time with a female on a consistent basis and not develop nothing for them.

Twenty minutes later, he arrived at Rah Rah'. He drove by twice to check out the scenery. Most importantly, to ensure an escape route. Satisfied with his plan, he pulled up alongside of a dimly lit street and turned the lights out.

"Befo' we go in, you need to put the ring in the case 'til we come back "Why?" she snapped. "I'm not takin' dis' off, no way Jose'!" she examined it.

"Girl, you crazy, I just don't want you to get no blood or nuthin' on it!"

"Blood? Why would blood get on my ring?!"

"Don't trip, if yo' shit gets messed up, then don't say I didn't warn you," he snapped, deciding to let her at least keep the ring.

"You right. Calm down boo," she said, kissing it and then putting it back in the box.

Churrrrch! he wanted to scream.

"You game?"

"Wait a minute, I didn't know you were gonna hurt him!"

"You didn't think he was gonna let me prance in there and let me take his shit, did you?"

"You right," she said, tensing up. Not wanting to become his victim as well. *How did I get myself into dis' shit?* she thought to herself, watching him put the silencer on the gun.

"Baby, I want you to beat on the door real frantic like!" he ordered. She nodded her head yeah as she was walking toward his door. Each step, she took was a step closer to her being a conspiracy to murder. Her heart started racing, her vision became blurry and butterflies began to toss and turn in her stomach. When she reached his door, her knees began to wobble.

"You need to relax, or you gonna fuck dis' up for us! Now I'm gonna stoop down right here beside the door so when he open it up umma take'em out. Now, knock!" he said, imperatively. She stood frozen like a block of ice. "If you keep stallin', he's gonna come kill both of us. Is dat what you want?!"

She shook her head no and proceeded to do as told. She was in a no win situation. It wasn't really all that hard to pretend, because in truth she wasn't performing, she was scared shitless. Hoping that he was on his guard and was looking at the monitors, she stood right in front of it shaking her head.

"What da fuck are you shakin' your head for, bitch? You tweakin' or high off them sticks or sumthin', huh, bitch?" he asked, through his tightly closed teeth.

"I was just boppin' my head to the beat in my head, boo." she said, in a near whisper. They were all inside sound asleep. When he heard a knock at door, he glanced at the monitor and saw it was Monie.

"Where are you going, babe?" Leigha asked, with her eyes still closed.

"I'm thirsty. You want anything to drink?"

"I'm okay," she said, then turned in opposite direction. Rah Rah slipped his arms inside his nice and thick Dolce & Gabanna robe. The knocks became louder at the door. He hurriedly stuck his feet in his house shoes and made his exit through the door, closing it behind him. Halfway sleep, he made his way downstairs and opened the door.

"Why are you here at dis' hour?" he asked, rubbing his eyes.

"He beat me! He beat me!" she screamed.

"Well, your si—," was all he said when he saw Amauri aiming the gun. It was too late to react because he had put two slugs in him before he could say anything. Before he collapsed, he shot Monie a look like, *Why!* Soon as he hit the floor, Amauri stepped over his body, and then he instructed her to go to the hidden room while he go upstairs to make sure they were alone. The first door he came to he opened it but nobody was in there. On down the hall there was another door. He slowly and quietly eased it opened and found three people sleeping. He went over to where they slept peacefully and shot them one by one. Execution-style. Soon as he shot Leigha, a gust of queasiness washed over Monie's body. A feeling she couldn't shake. A familiar feeling that came over her when something was wrong with Leigha.

"My sister is safe," she reassured herself. Before Amauri left the room, he glanced at the monitor and saw Monie was still in same spot. He thought about putting a slug in her, but decided he had other plans for her. After he checked all the rooms, he headed back downstairs.

"Why fuck aren't you doin' what I asked you to do?" he said, in a loud tone sending bone chilling, chills through her body. For a moment, she stared at him as if I know this isn't the same man that just gave me the ring.

"I-I-I was waitin' for you, boo!" she stammered. After a brief moment of silence.

"Baby I'm so sorry for callin' you outta your name earlier. I was just scared he was gonna come murk us both. I should not have taken it out on you. I promise to never do it again." he said, planting a kiss on her lips.

"I forgive you bay." she smiled. He flashed a smile back and lipped, *I love you, baby.* She forced a smile to her face and led him to the pantry. He was enthralled, when he looked around the Scarface themed room. It didn't take him long to locate the safe behind one of the large pictures. She was so shaken up, she couldn't even see straight. He pulled out his special device that could crack the code. "Bingo!" he screamed, as it popped open. "Come on baby and help me. We did it boo we did it! I fuckin' love you!" he lied, swooping her off her feet. Together, they collected half a million dollars and twenty bricks. Then he instructed her to go to the bedroom to takes the tapes out of the surveillance system of which, he already disabled. "Here, take dis' gun in case you run into somebody."

With her hands shaking, she took it and did as told. *Why didn't he do it when he was up there,* she thought. As soon as she reached the doorway were Rah Rah lay, her mind immediately started tripping. Her mind was telling her that soon as she try to step over him he was gonna snake his arm out and grab her leg. She looked from kitchen to outside to kitchen, trying to decide whether to leave or not. *Damn, he know where I live, he'll hunt my ass down and maul me like a werewolf.* she thought all the while saying softly to herself, "He's dead, he can't hurt you! Do as Amauri say or you'll be laid within a feet from Rah Rah! I'm so sorry, Rah Rah." she said, silently then she closed her eyes, took a deep breath, and stepped over his inert body. Slowly, she made her way up the steps, holding on to the wall of her every step. When she made it halfway up the steps, she noticed unfortunately she wasn't wearing gloves, like he was. As soon as she opened the first bedroom door, she was relieved to see no one in there. She closed the door and made her way down the hall. Soon as opened the door, the smell of death hit her in the face. She immediately started vomiting at the site of three stiff bodies.

"Dat heartless, sadistic son-of-a-bitch!" she said, to herself covering her mouth with her shirt. *At least they were sleeping* she thought to herself. She noticed two were kids. Then stepping back, she noticed her name on the girl's neck. That's when it dawned on her that it was Leigha.

"Noooooooooo!" she screamed, dropping down on her knees. Grabbing her sister's lifeless. Her body had already started losing heat. "I'm sorry. I'm so sorry! Leigha, wake up. I said wake up, damn it!" she shook her. "I didn't know. I didn't know. You were supposed to be safe in the county." she screamed, with tears streaming down her face. As soon as she left the room, he ran to the staircase and placed a black rose there. Then he picked up the Scarface phone, pressed 911 and hung up and then made his exit. Leaving Monie with the gun in hand.

Fifteen minutes later, the cops showed up. Upon seeing Rah Rah's stiff body sprawled inside doorway, one of the cops put two fingers on his neck to check for a pulse and called for backup. Cautiously, they walked up the steps with their gun drawn. They discovered the murder weapon, in Monie's hand. Where the three bodies lay.

"Drop the weapon ma'am!" One cop yelled getting down on one knee aimed and ready to shoot. She couldn't say anything. However, her mind functioned well enough for to drop the weapon. She was unable to move, speak or anything. She was in total distress.

"Ma'am are you responsible for these fatalities?"

Her mind was telling her they were asking her did she wanna go home. She nodded her head yes.

They rushed her, slamming her to the floor. The big 200 lbs plus police officer held her down with his knee in her back while he slapped the handcuffs on her. Her mind was gone, it had left her body when she seen the tattoo with her name on it. She laid defeated, whimpering on the cold hardwood floor, face down. When she was being lead to the police car, she noticed on the table by the door, three black roses. Of which she didn't recall seeing there before.

Still it never dawned on her it was from Amauri. He was long gone. He had vanished like a thief in the night.

I'M IN LOVE WITH A STRIPPER

Grievence woke up to loud knocks at his door. "Da fuck is dat?" he jumped up. He knew it wasn't Swagga because he had a key card. With his heart pounding fast against his chest wall, he got up and stumbled half sleep to the door. He could barely see out of the peephole. "Who is it?" he asked groggily.

"Ur homegirl, Trees!" he opened the door to let her in. "I hope it's not to early." she scrunched up her face.

"Girl, get yo' butt in here!" he pulled her into his room. "So, what bring you by at," he asked, glancing at his Cartier watch, and then back to her. "Five thirty in the morning?"

"Well, I'm so sorry. You're my bestie, and I need you." she whined.

"For?"

"Are you trying to be sarcastic? I'm serious over here."

"Can I get you sumthin' to drink?"

"Whadda you got?" he asked, getting up. When he got up, she couldn't help but admire his perfect six-pack and his heavily chiseled, tatted-up body that instantly made her pussy wet. The *Ed Hardy* cologne, he was wearing didn't make it no better.

"Pop or good cold water?" he held them both up.

"I thought you had some Nuvo or sumthin' way mo' stronger? You already knows how I get down. Ain't shit changed but my age."

"Niggah, your square ass. G's like me don't be drinkin' no hoe ass Nuvo. But you ain't said nuthin'. Ciroc or Patrón." he said, slipping his wife beater over his head.

"Awwe shitt, now! You got dat shit dat goes down extra smooth, huh? But, I'll have some Patrón on rocks, please?" When he walked back toward her, she could see his dick print swinging through his thin gym shorts.

Hangin' and swangin', she bit down on her lip and thought to herself.

"Where are you coming from at dis' hour!" he said, handing her the drinks. She didn't respond her eyes were glued to the mass that was bulging from his gym shorts. "Trees," he called out. He watched as her eyes trailed from his shorts up to his sparking eyes. "Hello, is anyone home?" he stretched his eyes.

"Shut up! And lemme see, the last time I checked I was grown!"

"Excuse me then, Ms. Thang!" he snaked his neck. Then without warning, she impulsively, kissed him.

"Wow! Where did dat come from?" he asked, backing away.

"I'm so sorry!" she exclaimed.

"You good."

"So, I bet you think less of me now don't you?" she glanced at him out the corner of her eye.

"No, I don't. Just a little caught off guard is all,"

He couldn't have gotten dat out of his mouth soon enough. She pounced on him like a lion.

"What are you doing?" he whispered. "Dis is wrong. Are you tryna seduce me? Umma tell Maryland," he joked.

She pulled him closer to her lips. "Shut up and kiss me." He did as told. She slowly used her mouth to pull up his shirt, kissing and sucking each of his nipples slowly and gently, making her way down his navel and planting gentle, wet kisses along the way. When she reached his gym shorts, she used her lips to pull them down. While she was taking his shorts down, his dick sprang out like a jack-in-the-box and hit her in the eye.

"Be careful now, slugger is ready to beat sumthin' and I definitely don't want it to be your eye." he teased. "Umma just keep it one hunnit."

"I got dis' hea, don't even trip. I been cravin' dis' dick for a long time!" she said, taking his dick in her hand and putting it in moist mouth. "Not to mention all the times you were on the court and all I could see was dat shit swinging from side to side. Making me wanna sprint out there and suck it in front of everybody," she licked her lips.

"Have your way with him. Don't let me stop you." he said, as he put his hand on her head and gently, guided it up and down. *Oh shit, I think I done found me another Monie . . .* he asked himself. Her head game was on point. She licked from the top of his dick down to his balls. Once she made her way down to his balls, she gently massaged his dick and slurped on his balls for at least ten minutes straight. She was on his on his balls like a vulture mangling his prey.

"Are you ok down there?" Grievence asked, looking down at her.

"You just relax and let me do what I do," she backed away from his balls.

"By all means, do what you do." he flailed his hand out. Slowly, she sat up on her knees and made her way back up to his throbbing, rock hard dick and then she started licking up and down and all around the head. His eyes just rolled back into his head in pure bliss, sending him into rapture. Moans escaped his mouth as he felt he was about to have an eruption.

"Turn over!" he whispered.

"No!" she replied, continuing to suck his dick. "I want you cum in my mouth, baby!"

"Huh?"

"You heard me niggah!" she said, removing it from her mouth and gently massaging it. "I want to swallow your babies! You comprende now?" she whispered, and then made her way back down to his balls. He never had a woman that stayed on his balls the way she did.

"Say no more"

"Lay back and enjoy the ride because it's about to be long and bumpy," she whispered. A good calm feeling washed over him. It was just something about the way she said it. She maneuvered her body into a comfortable position. Then she lifted up his balls and licked the area that separated his balls from his ass. Every time her warm tongue touched it, he cringed.

"Oh shit now," he yelled out. Unable to restrain what he was feeling. It was indeed a no brainer, she had Monie beat. Hands down. Every single time her tongue stroked his body, it sent rippling jitters up and down his spine. Within seconds, cum shot out from his dick like a volcano. In all of his years of having sex, he never seen so much cum shoot from his dick. If only he knew, that was the very reason her niggah, Dro was sprung and jealous. Then she released the soft grip on his dick. When she did, it stood elongated in the air. His eyes widened when he saw the increase in size.

"Jackpot!" she bolted up. She jumped and watched her work for a split second and then she forced it back in her mouth. "Yeah, babee!" she said, engulfing every drop of the creamy cum that emanated out of his erect dick. She loved giving head.

"Stand up," he demanded, out of breath.

"Are you ok? Come on respire," she chuckled.

"I'm good. I'm a G." he said, jittery. "What you think you done did you sumthin'. While you over there all giggly giggly?"

"Nah, niggah you think I have. In fact, I do think I deserve a twenty-one gun salute, doe while your bullshittin'." she giggled, feeling herself.

"Oh really I didn't hear the star spangled banner or see no fireworks going off?" he teased.

"I'm confident in mine sweetie,"

"I'm jokin', you did your thang," he whispered, gradually undressing her with his mouth. He unbuttoned every button, with his teeth and lips. Then he took both of her arms out of her shirt and slowly, slid her pants down over her ass. Revealing her brown body by Victoria's Secret bra set. "Damn, dis' look and feel like your skin, girl!" he rubbed and squeezed the bra. Then he turned her around and undid her bra. She slipped her underwear down over her heels, revealing a neatly shaved pussy. When she started to take her heels off, he stopped her. "No, keep'em on. I wanna fuck you with your heels on." he whispered, pulling his hair back with the twisty from his wrist.

"Ok, you runnin' dis' show! It's your world, daddy. I'm just a squirrel tryna get a nut. And that's for real and not for play."

"Glad you know who is the king of the castle!" he said, kissing her slowly from head to toe. He noticed when he sucked her right nipple; she moaned and gripped the sheets tight. So, he paid special attention to that nipple, making his path down the center of her body down to her perfectly shaved pussy. Spreading her legs apart, he dove headfirst. He started by licking it then sucking it gentle. She moaned while rolling her body and pulling the sheets tighter and tighter.

"That's right; eat dis' pussy, boy. Eat dis' shit like it's a Thanksgiving Dinner!" she screamed, grasping the sheets tightly. Her legs began to get weak and tremble. "Oh yeah, dat feel good. Oh my fuckin' goodness I'm 'bout ta' cuummmm!" she screamed out in pure bliss. When he felt her body contracting, he put his mouth closer to her pussy so he could suck all the sweet juices flowing out.

"Yo' pussy taste gooder than a muthafucka. Whacha been eating, juices and berries?" he backed away from it and started fingering her. Once his finger got tired, he reached over to the side of the bed where his Roc-a-Wear jeans lay, dug into the pockets, and pulled out a magnum. She watched impatiently, as he put it on and secured room in it.

"Hurry up, niggah. I'm ready for some good penetration!" she said, eager to feel it.

"Hold on," he held his hand up.

"I just know dat shit is bomb too." she bit down on her lip and stared at it. "What da fuck niggah you don't know how to put on a condom?"

"Of course my shit is good. I got dat dope dick, you finna see in two point two seconds," he smiled. She was stroking his ego and he was enjoying every single moment of it.

"I been waitin' for dis' day for a very long time!" she said, running her fingers down his deeply tatted chest.

"Oh is dat right?"

"Geah!" she hopped on his erect dick.

"Turn around," he ordered. She did as told.

"Oole, right there!" she moaned and groaned.

"Right there?" he asked, biting down on his bottom lip.

"Yeeeeeeeees!" she screamed, out in pure bliss.

"How does slugger, feel?" he asked, as he pumped faster. The condom broke he didn't stop instead he pumped even faster.

"It feels so good!" she screamed "I like it like dis', right there boy! Oooooole dat shit feels good uuuuuummm." she said, giving it back to him. When he was about to cum, he hurriedly pulled out and squirted on her ass cheek. They both collapsed, drenched in sweat and sticky from cum.

"Lay on my chest," he ordered. "Do have any idea of what we just did?" he asked, rubbing his fingers through her hair.

"You seduced me, Negro!"

"You knew what you were doing, niggah. Seeing you in them gym shorts was tantalizing. All inked up and shit knowing I'm a sucka for a fine inked-up man!"

"I bet you been had a crush on a niggah, huh?"

"Okay, let's not get full of yourself, Mr big ego," she joked. "Naw, but in all seriousness, I've loved you since I was ten and secretly envisioned us together!"

"Wow, dat's deep,"

"I never acted on it, doe. Although, I know we could never be and it felt good but, can never happen again!" With that, she got dressed. Feeling mortified she went to her grandma like she was initially supposed to do. She didn't get to tell him that she needed his help to take her Dro out the game.

He couldn't say nothing; he laid back appalled and speechless. After an hour or so, he drifted off to sleep. Soon as he heard *Single* by Lil Wayne, he knew it was Deuces.

"What up, doe?" he said, sleepily.

"Niggah, wake yo' sleepyhead ass up and come get you some of dis' bread!"

"You need to be easy, homie. I just left yall asses not even three damn hours ago. A niggah need his beauty sleep!"

"Whatever, hit a niggah up when you're on dis' side."

"Fasho."

Two hours later, his cell phone started vibrating. It was his alarm; it was almost time to pick up the strippers from the airport.

While Bread was at the spot, Trigga went to Swagga.

"Boss can I holla at you for a minute, mayne?"

"Sure, what's good witcha?"

"In private?" he said, with a little more bass in his voice, shifting his attention to Deuces.

"Dis' sounds important, give me a second!" he said. Then he sent Deuces to the corner store to buy him some cigars.

"Okay, we're alone now, so what's on your mind pimpin'?"

"Well, you know Bread and I, been homies from way back when."

"Yeah. Go on!"

"Well, more to the point, he got dis' side thing going on where he has his own dope and he also suppose be pimping a couple of hoes." he stared at Swagga and watched for some type of gesture, but Swagga remained emotionless. Trigga got up to leave. "And what you choose to do or not do with dis' info is up to you, mayne. I just wanted you to know. I didn't have nuthin' to do with it."

"Aye," he said, in a loud tone. "Good-lookin'. Good-lookin'. That's love, dawg!" he stopped him before he reached the doorknob.

"Anytime, it's nuthin'. Greed is an ugly disease. Dat's my niggah but, he's an avaricious ass niggah!"

"Fuck, took you so long, niggah?" Bread asked, taking the cigar from Trigga.

"Damn, I didn't know a niggah was being timed and shit?" he shot, with his voice dripping with sarcasm.

"Niggah, as long as your ass been gone, I could've been done fucked and busted two nuts!"

"Shut yo' corny lookin' ass up!"

"Oh, let me go holla at Sherry?" he said, setting his Corona down on the ground. His very intention was on having her bring all the customers to him, but as soon as he made it across the street and called her name, she took off running. "Sherry! Sherry! Let me holla at you for a minute!" he yelled out to her. But, she didn't look back. Instead, she sped up thinking it was somebody wanting to get a free hit. There was no use in trying to catch a crack head especially when they had just copped that hard raw.

"Damn!"

"I don't even know why you even hoed yo'self like dat, mayne. You know there isn't no use in tryna catch no smokers dat just copped dat hard raw!"

"Dat cruddy bitch must've had some wheels on her feet or sumthin', dawg!" he said, trying to catch his breath.

Low key, Trigga felt bad for telling Swagga what happened, but what was done, was done. *No since in crying over spilled milk* he thought to himself. "Niggah, yo' ass be wildin', you need to be rolling up dat purp instead of tryna recruit smokers and shit!" he joked.

He flipped him off. "Niggah, fuck you!"

"So what are you wearing to the club tonight?" Trigga asked tryna make small talk.

"Yo, dawg, I don't even know. A niggah need to go hit da mall up. I did cop them new tinted Cartie frames, doe. Them bitches sweet!" Bread said. When he glanced across the street, he noticed a girl named, Chardonae he had met three weeks prior. It fucked up his entire mood. His mind went back to the day when they met up. A day that went down in history. Although, over three weeks had past, it seemed like it had just happened. She was a bad bitch. He had spent most of the day preparing for their date. He started by going to the liquor store picking up some Ciroc and Hennessy. He even paid his cousin 300 dollars, to borrow his car and apartment for 3hrs. When he picked her up, he took her shopping at Victoria Secret. Being the bad bitch she was niggah's knew they had to come correct stepping to her. After they left the mall, they headed back to his cousin place where he ordered Chinese food.

She scanned the room. "It's so nice and clean in here."

"Yea, you know all niggah like me gotta be on my shit!" he said, with a smile spreading across his face. The food will be here in 45 minutes!" he said, looking at his watch trying to calculate the time he had left. "Let's see, we stayed in the mall about 45 minutes to an hour. The food gonna take 45 minutes. So, that's gonna leave us about an hour, damn!" he muttered to himself. Brown or white?" he yelled out, holding them up.

"Damn, you sholl know how to treat a bitch. I mean you got all da party favors, huh?"

"For a fine bad bitch like yo'self, you can get it all!"

"Sounds good to me. I'll have some Ciroc on ice please."

He poured her a glass. "Don't trip boo, I got you."

Fifteen minutes later, she asked to use the bathroom.

He pointed down the hallway. "And you already know baby. It's down the hall and the first door on the right."

Along the way, she admired all the black and white theme pictures. Soon as she got up, his eyes was glued to her ass until she disappeared into complete darkness. "Umma tear dat pussy up." he said, biting down on his bottom lip. "It looks like it's just good; while I'm bullshitting I better call cuzo for another hour." he licked his lips. When he did, he agreed.

"You live here alone." she asked, straightening out her clothes before she sat down.

"And you know dis' mann!" he lied.

"Very good taste!" she said, nodding her head. Just as he was about to make a move on her, the food had arrived. After they ate, she washed her food down with a shot of Hennessy.

"Boy, I know I'm bout ta' tear dis' shit out da frame!" he said softly to himself, cleaning the food up. When he returned, he made his move. "Come on baby, don't you wanna see how my room looks?" he asked, gently taking her by the hand and kissing it.

She grabbed her purse. "I'm good. I think it's time for me to go. I enjoyed my evening."

"What? I'm sorry come again?" he pushed his earlobe out.

"You heard me niggah! I know you didn't think you was gonna fuck, did you?!" she asked, scrunching up her face.

"Listen baby, baby." he chuckled and clapped his hands. "Anytime a man spends money on you, dat means your signin' a contract to give the pussy up at the end of the night."

"You trippin'. I said I'm not ready. You got the wrong bitch now! I don't know why muthafuckas think just because they spend a lil money or smoke and drink wid a bitch, dat I'm fuck. Hell no! Yes, I'll smoke and drink yo' shit. You buy me sumthin', hell yea umma take it. I can tell you it's gone take a hell of a lot more to get dis' good pussy that's between my legs! Fuck all dat hoe shit, just take me home?!" she screamed, getting up heading to the door.

"Aye, simmer your slutty ass down,"

"Oh I'm a slut, but you wanna fuck me, huh?" she chuckled. "I don't know what da fuck you thought anyway?"

He was fired up and wanted to knock fire from her but took her home. When they pulled up to her house, she tried to grab her bags before she got out.

"Uh huh, bitch I'm not ready to give them to you yet. Yo' funky ass better be glad I didn't make you cough up my Chinese food and my henny bitch," he said, peeling off.

"Fuck you niggah and yo' hoe ass shit." she yelled out to him. He remembered just like it had just happened. He wanted to strangle her on sight.

Swagga sat in front of his plasma TV, playing Grand Theft Auto IV. "Man, dis' shit here is tight!" he said with *No Hands* by Waka Flocka blaring in his ears. His thoughts diverted back to Bread. He decided he knew what he had to do, from the moment he was told and the perfect person to do it. His cell phone started vibrating, interrupting his thoughts. It was Angie. "What up, sexy?"

"Don't what-up-sexy me, niggah! Where are you?!" she said with an attitude. Fed up with Swagga's bullshit.

"Damn, that's how your greet your man. Your future husband?"

"Fuck all dat overrated bullshit, niggah! I'm tired of never seeing you. I want you to come get your shit da fuck outta my crib, and I'm takin' dat one spot outta my name. Life is too short for dis' bullshit!"

"Whoah! Whoah," he paused the game and placed his controller on the table. "Where is all dis' coming from? You never had a problem wid it in the beginnin'. You came into my life wid yo' eyez wide da fuck open. Dis' shit shouldn't be new to your ass."

"Whatever! I guess the sayin' how you start is how you end is true." she sucked her teeth.

"Yo' fat ass don't be complainin' when I peel your ass off wads of cash do you, or what about me spendin' all dat money on your grown ass kids, who don't even like my ass."

"You right. I'm sorry—"

"Naw, niggah, I'm not done." he cut her off. "I'm out here makin' money for you, and you wanna talk shit, but, if dat's how you feel then it is what it is." he lied.

"Boo, I'm sorry. I . . . I . . . I," she stammered. "Didn't mean it. I'm just sexually frustrated."

"What your fat ass studderin' fo'."

"I knew it. You do think I'm fat, don't cha?!" she cried seeing how heated he was, trying to switch the convo up.

"Look, I don't have time for your bullshit. I'll send my brother to come thru and swoop up my shit up and do what you gotta do about the apartment, I don't give a flying two fucks!" he said, slamming the phone down on the table.

Grievence arrived at the airport, thirty minutes late due to backed-up traffic. He pulled up to the valet and handed them their tip as he stepped out of his 2011 rental all-black Malibu. He was dressed to kill with some Red Monkey jeans with the biker chain hanging down, a fitted tee with some custom-made red, blue, and white Forces to match his tee. On this particular day, he pulled his hair back into a ponytail, revealing his fresh line up and his neatly trimmed small beard. A pair of tinted Cartier frames adorned his face. His wrist gleamed with a diamond Cartier bracelet. It sparkled like a rainbow every time the sun hit it. A diamond chain swung almost down to his navel. A set of five-karat VVS studded, princess cut earrings gleamed brightly from his ear. When he walked, he knew he was da shit. The women walking by smiling confirmed it. He smelled so good, that when someone walked past him, they had to do a double take. He looked every bit like a million bucks.

When he walked up, he saw two girls outside looking fly as hell. One was smoking a cigarette and tapping her feet while the other one was looking at her watch.

"I don't know where da hell dis' fuck-ass niggah is at but I'm getting heated."

"I feel you, girl. Our ass could be at a club makin' some money!"

"Well, I'm 'bout to go back inside and find a bar or sumthin'. A bitch like me needs a drink right about now," she said, smashing her cigarette butt inside the ashtray on top on the bin.

"Damn, who is dat fine angus meat there? I sholl can squeeze and pull on dat meat all night! I'm beginnin' to love Motor City already!" One of the girls said, pushing her breast up. When he finally made it to the area where the girls were waiting, he noticed only two girls from a distance. They were fine as fuck from a distance, but when he got closer, he was like *oh hell naw*! To himself.

"Oh, you must be dat niggah, Grievence!" the girl said, smiling from ear to ear, as she extended her hand for him to kiss. "I'm Wet Wet!"

"Oh, is dat right? Yeah, I'm dat niggah." he smiled, baring all thirty-two.

Then she continued, "And dat's my homegirl, Juicee."

She flashed a tight smile with her mouth closed. But, when she opened it, he started to yell, "Damn!" Her teeth were so long, he couldn't begin to figure out how she closed it. "And dat's Xtacy." she said, pointing to her walking up. "Oh, you're dat sexy niggah walking in front of me," she said, licking her lips in a circular motion.

"Don't pay her no mind. Her name needs to be Hot Cooty Judy!"

"Fuck you hatin' hoe!" she shot.

"And last but, not least that's Pleasure."

"Well, since we all greeted, shall be on our way."

Wet Wet flung her arm around in the air. "You lead the way."

"Do any of you lovely ladies need help?"

"Naw," they all said in said in unison. "I can think of a couple of other things you can help me with," Pleasure said, while licking around the Coke bottle.

I think I'm in love wid a stripper, he thought to himself while he seductively undressed Wet Wet with his eyes.

"Girl, sit yo' hot cooty self down somewhere." Wet Wet said, picking up her Louis Vuitton luggage. Wet Wet stood about five feet two inches, weighed bout a good 125, milk-chocolate skin tone with a head full of curls that rested neatly on her shoulders. She was wearing white, ruffled button down blouse with a red vest that instantly pushed her breast up and a black jumpsuit by G-Star. Her six-inch shiny red pumps by Miss Sixty made her his height. Big red hoops dangled from her ear. She just knew she was shit, because when she walked, she looked and smelled just like money. When they decided to leave, she put on her red Just Cavalli stunna shades and pulled the handle out on luggage led the way. As soon as she hit the door, the wind was blowing. It reminded her of why she never wanted to leave Miami. It was a very breezy day in early March. She was really enjoying the cool crisp breeze as the wind instantly blew through her hair full of body. When they reached by the entrance, she closed her eyes and enjoyed the blissful moment.

"It feels rather nice out here! Not as cold as I expected it to be." Pleasure said enjoying the sun as it shone on her face.

"While ya bullshittin', I heard how one day it be eighty degrees out dis' bitch, and the next day it be snowin'! Ain't dat a bitch!" Wet Wet spoke up. Grievence was taken aback by her. She was so beautiful.

Juicee was dressed more or less like a schoolteacher with a short hairdo. She was wearing tight-fitting light grey Chanel vest and some dress-type capri's to match and some Dolce & Gabanna reading like glasses. She had perfect measurements, 34-26-34. She was more of a platinum kinda girl. Two platinum D&G bracelets dangled from her wrist. When Grievence saw her butt, he was really like, "Whoah. Do you need a wheelbarrow to move all dat ass?"

"Boy, youz a fool!" she blushed, with her hand covering her mouth. Xtacy stood an even five feet seven inches and was 130 pounds. She was rocking

some black Guess capri's with a golden colored, button-down shirt along with a pair of Salvatore Ferragamo tiger-print five-inch heels. Pleasure was just rocking a pink Roc-a-wear tracksuit and white-on-white Forces.

"Damn, are yall movin' to da D.?" he joked.

"Naw, a bitch just gotta be prepared for whatever!" Wet Wet spoke up.

She was very loquacious at times. She looked like she couldn't be no more than eighteen years old. "Can I ask how old are you, lil' mama?"

"Well, how old do I look?" she blushed.

"Ahh let's see . . . eighteen."

"Nope, close doe. Seventeen,"

"Youz just a baby, huh?"

"If dat's what wanna call me, but I don't think dat no baby will have no big, juicy, and hairy pussy!" she whispered in his ear, sending chills down his spine.

"Oh yeah. I bet yo' shit wet now, huh?"

"It's not polite to whisper!" Xtacy said, secretly envious because he wasn't paying her no mind.

"Yeah, dat shit there ain't da business doe." Pleasure instigated, pulling her Chanel stunna shades down to her nose.

"N-t-way, as I was sayin'!"

"You know what, hold dat thought, lil' mama!" he said, holding his pointer finger in the air, when he noticed his car approaching. While he was walking up to it, his phone started vibrating with a text message from Neeyah. He accidentally erased it when he powered off his phone.

THE EVIL TWIN

Ms. Lara sat in a little chair beside her son bed, watching him sleep ever so peacefully. She was waiting on the nurse to let her know when he was gonna be released. She hadn't had no sleep since the nurse gave her the dosage to put her to sleep. Her thoughts were quickly interrupted when a social worker walked through the door.

"Ms. Lara!"

"Yes, dis' is she," she extended her hand.

"Hi, I'm Nancy with CPS, (child protected services)" she said, extending her hand. Ms. Lara snatched her hand back.

"And you feel you need to speak to me, because?" she snapped, looking from her hand to her face as if she was crazy.

"Well, I'm not here to make things harder, but I'm here because when Ricky Junior is discharged—"

"Hell to the naw. Yall asses ain't takin' my child nowhere!" she yelled, cutting her off with tears rolling down her cheek.

"Ma'am, calm down. I can't even begin to fathom or know what you're going thru, but I'm just doing my job!"

"Calm down my ass! Over my dead body. I'm not lettin' you do it." she said, rushing to his side.

"Okay, either we're gonna do it the easy way or the hard way. Either way, it has to be done. That's the state law!"

"Bullshit, fuck you and the law!" she screamed.

"Miss, I understand your pain but I didn't make the law, I'm just following them and trying to do my job. You're making it harder to do."

"My kids are my life and you're gonna stand in my face and have the audacity to tell me dat I am makin' your punk ass job harder. Bitch, you're tryna make my life harder. Dis' is my son, I'm his protector and you're trying to take me from him." she cried.

"Ma'am with all due respect, you're right you suppose to protect your child so where was you when dis' was happening to him?" the worker asked, taking small steps backwards. When Ms. Lara looked up, she was by the door. The only thing that stopped her from knocking fire from the worker was when Junior woke up crying.

"Don't cry, baby, Mommy is here," she said, taking him into her arms and rocking him back and forth. Tears flowed freely down her face.

"What's wrong, Mommy?!"

"Nuthin', baby, go back to sleep!" she whispered, rubbing his head. "Mommy's here and I'm not going anywhere. Just go on back to sleep!"

Sad as it was, the CPS worker really hated to sunder them after what had happened to him. However, had an imminent feeling that something terrible was about to ensue so she left the room and went to get help. She returned with an officer fifteen minutes later, Ms. Lara was getting Junior dressed.

"It's very imperative dat you let go of him and hand him over to the CPS worker!" he said with a stern look.

"Mommmy, I don't wanna go. Don't make me go with her!" Junior begged.

She kissed him on the forehead. "Don't worry, baby!"

No sooner than she said that, a nurse accompanied by two more officers, rushed in to see what was causing the uproar.

"Noooooooo, yall can't do it. I won't let you muthafuckas take him!" she screamed, while clutching him tightly.

Then without warning, the nurse gave her a relaxant to put her to sleep. When she woke up, she tried to get up but was in restraint.

"Where's my son? Where's Junior? Where's my baby?!" she cried.

A nurse came running into the room.

"What's wrong, ma'am?" she asked meekly.

"I want your skinny ass to go get my son!"

"Your son is in CPS custody. We had to restrain you so you wouldn't hurt yourself or nobody else."

"Let me loose so I can go get my son!" she cried a squeaky hoarse cry and silently kept repeating, "No weapon formed against me shall prosper. God says vengeance is mine!" she screamed.

"Ma'am, I can't do dat. You caused such scene last night 'til we were afraid you were gonna hurt yourself or somebody!"

"Tell me, how far would you go to protect your child?!" she said, with tightly clenched teeth and fiery eyes. She scared the nurse so, that the woman had forgotten her initial reason for going in there.

"I can't believe you're gone, Leigha. How can somebody dat shared the womb with you do dis' to you? I really need to know. And how you just gonna leave me, girl, when I need you the most?" Neeyah said, sitting at Leigha's tombstone drinking Grey Goose and smoking a blunt. "Don't worry, I'm puttin' one in the air for you, dawg, as I speak." she cried and released smoke from her lungs. "You already know before they closed your casket, I slipped a whole pound of cush and a bottle of goose, in there for you boo. I miss you sooo. Why? Why? Why?" she asked, beating on her tombstone. "I didn't get to tell you how Flawless straight gave my ass da business. He and I had the bombiest sex ever I'm talkin' about dat niggah straight blew my back out, so he thought!" she giggled in between sniffles. "In all seriousness dis' niggah looked like he was straight packing, girl when he pulled his pants down, *I was like what do he think you're gonna do with dat?* Inwardly, you already know I was laughing my ass off. His head game had a niggah climbing da wall doe, I'm not gone even lie, bitch! I really wish you were here." she chuckled, shaking her head with tears falling non-stop. "You already know my ass talked hella shit to him, bout how I was gonna straight fuck his brains out and some mo' shit," she chuckled some more. "I was like umma fuck the shit out of you and whoop whoop."

She had to laugh to keep from crying. "I couldn't tell you when you called because dat niggah was literally in my face. You know one thing doe . . . ?" she paused briefly, "It's not about sex, I'm really feelin' him. Now whose gonna give me advise on no-good niggahs," she said, taking a long swig of the Grey Goose. "I guess you're wonderin' bout dat niggah Grievence, well he's still in da D., I haven't heard from him since he left my crib dat day, and not sure if I will ever again." she paused a moment. "The funny thing is I called him a gang of times he never answered or returned any of my calls. Anyway I'm not gonna waste no more time on him. You see, I'm out here drinking your favorite drink, niggah. Matter fact, it's your drink. Girl, you got my ass out here in a lonely-ass spooky-ass-cemetery and shit," she said, pouring some liquor on Leigh's grave. "Don't trip, umma hold shit down for you, doe, till we meet again! Dat's right bitch, umma mourn you till I join you!" she said, and then dozed off. Three hours later, she woke up to the wind whistling. After she glanced at her watch, she hopped up and headed to Leigha's Infiniti. That was now hers. "Damn, I have been knocked for a cool minute. Dat goose was on my ass!"

Leigha's mom let her go and take whatever belonged to her. When she got inside the car, she picked up her cell off the seat. It had two missed calls. One was from hospital and the other one was from Flawless. She threw

phone back on the passenger side, buckled her seat beat, and started the engine. Headed straight to the hospital. A usual 20-minute drive to there, took her 45 minutes. When she arrived, she pulled into the parking area that was located at the back of the hospital and shut off the car. Then she sighed and then opened the dashboard to put the other half of the blunt inside. Upon doing so, she came across an unopened letter addressed to Raheem from Leigha. She immediately removed the letter from the unsealed envelope it read:

Dearest Raheem:

It is very important for me to express to you how much you really mean to me. I wish I could do this in person while holding you in my arms and gazing into your eyes. However, since we are physically separated by miles of emptiness, this expression must come in the form of letters such as this. Tears flowed freely down her face.

Baby, I know it is difficult for you, she took a deep breath, paused then continued, *as it is for us to be alienated for so long. Life seems to be short and full of trials of this type that test our inner strength, and more importantly, our devotion and love for one another. After all, it is said that "True Love" is like an abyss. Endless and immeasurable and it overcomes all forms of adversity. In truth, if it is genuine, it will grow stronger with each assault upon its existence. Raheem Gerard Taylor, (I know you hate it when I call you by your whole name but it's sooo cute!) our love has been knocked around many, many times, and I am convinced that it is true because the longer I am away from you, the greater my heart is yearning to be with you again. (My auntie Lara always told me, absence makes the heart grow fonder, and she's so right) You are my air I breathe and I need you in my life bad because you're my everything, and I don't wanna pretend no more. I am your devoted all you need in a woman. I cherish any thought of you, prize any remembrance of you that rises from the depths of my mind, and live for the day when our physical separation will no longer be.*

Until dat, moment arrives, I send to you across the miles, my tender love, my warm embrace, and my most passionate kiss.

Ps. I wanna ask can you figure out the answer to this riddle (I know your probably thinking this is so middle schoolish) But here goes

I wanna see are you smarter than a fifth grader lol! . . . first comes love than comes marriage here comes Leigha with a . . .

Love Always
Leigha

"She was pregnant!" Neeyah screamed. Then she thought back on how her face was clearing up and she was gaining weight. "Dat little tramp!" she giggled, to keep from having another meltdown. "Rah Rah never knew." she repeated over and over.

ALL IS FAIR IN LOVE AND WAR

Amauri was sitting on his plush leather sofa, snorting some powder off of Passion's tooted-up ass when his Sidekick started vibrating. He glanced at it, a unknown call was displayed on the screen. Something told him not to answer it but decided against going with his instincts. It was Monie. She had gotten a three way from a three-hundred pound butch dike.

"Hey, boo!" she said in a soft tone.

"Who is dis'?"

"Dis' is yo' fiancée."

"Fiancée?! I can't recollect ever being in a relationship, let alone engaged!" he played dumb.

"So what yo' ass, got amnesia now? Dat was my sister!" she screamed. "Come to think of it, you were the one dat left the black rose, huh? What does dat symbolize?"

"What da fuck are you talkin' 'bout? I don't know you or you sister!" he retorted.

"Answer my fuckin' question, damnit! What did I pull your hoe card?" she screamed. "It means death, huh? You heartless fuck stick! How could you do dis' to me? I trusted you. I loved you with my all!" she cried realizing he had played her to the left.

"Sweetheart, love don't love nobody! In dis' world you gotta hustle or get hustled. Sounds like you fooled yo'self, ma!"

"So you're not gonna come get me. You just gone leave me in dis' hellhole to rot?!" she cried.

"Look, I'm sorry for what you're going thru, ma'am, but I don't know you!"

"What, noooo!" she screamed. "You sorry sack of shit. You meticulously orchestrated dis' whole thing. You manipulated me into doing dis'! Now I have nobody! Nobody." she screamed. "My whole family shunned me and

thinks I killed my very own sister. I have nobody." she cried, sliding down
the wall. "How, Amauri? You straight shitted on me! I will find you Amauri!"
she screamed into the phone.

"That's on you if you wanna play where's Waldo. But, look you can
save all dat shit for the birds. I suggest you listen closely to the words dat
are about to come out of my mouth on some real live shit! All is fair in love
and war. All I can say, charge dat shit to game. Fair exchange is no robbery,
boo! We're living in an everyman for himself and god for us, all world" he
said, politely.

"Amauri," she screamed.

"Ma'am,"

"I know you're just frontin', it's ok babe I forgive you. When are you
gonna come and get me?" she sobbed.

"Haaa. When pigs fly to the north pole!" he laughed and then ended the
call. After he hung up, he called T-Mobile and had his number changed.

"Seems like you've been hoodwinked, tricked, bamboozled—hell, sounds
like you didn't land on Plymouth. It landed on your ass. You know what
dat means?!" the bitch said looking down at Monie. She stared back at her
like she had utterly lost her mind. "Dat means you're my bitch now! You
belong to me," she rubbed her pussy thru her jumpsuit. "Ole good Samaritan
lookin' ass," she laughed. Monie cried like a newborn baby. She couldn't
believe that he was such a callous, calculated, bastard and thought back on
how it all began—too good to be true. Of course, he wasn't born that way;
certain things in his life made him grimy and shady. He didn't choose the
life that was laid out for him. It chose him.

"Go make a niggah sumthin' to eat or sumthin'," he whisked Passion off.

"Niggah, I don't know how to cook. You got me fucked up. How you
think my ass got so fat the Sun." she said, shaking her ass. "I be straight
eatin' fast food. Matter of fact, call up Pizza Hut ass!"

He gently pushed her towards the kitchen. "Your ass gone learn how to
cook today, a niggah burnt out on eatin' fast food and shit!"

"Alright, niggah damn. Don't get mad at me when I fuck around and burn
yo' shit!" she yelled over her shoulder. He didn't respond, instead he watched
as her ass jiggled like jelly until she turned the corner. When she went into
the kitchen, she headed over to the cabinets in hopes of finding some Top
Ramen. Instead, all she found was some empty shelves with one can of coffee.
"What a large selection!" she said, softly to herself, closing the doors back.
Then she opened the refrigerator and found some bologna and bread.

I don't suppose burnt fried bologna requires much. she said to herself grabbing it. "I can't believe dis' niggah got my ass in here cooking for him, straight got my ass all the way fucked up!" she mumbled taking the wrapper off the bologna and placing it in a pan of grease, that was enough to fry a whole chicken. Leaving it unattended, she opened the refrigerator, took the jar of mayonnaise out, and placed it on the counter. *Damn what happened to the shits you could just squeeze out* she the thought while trying her damnest to unscrew the lid. "Oh shit!" she screamed. "Damn, I know I said burnt fried bologna but, I didn't mean dat shit literally!"

She handed him the two sandwiches. "Here you go, eat up! I done straight hooked you up. Now, niggah you owe me. So pay like you weigh!" she held her hand out.

He smacked her on the ass. "That's what I'm talkin' about!"

"Ouch, niggah dat shit hurt."

"Big as your ass is, you know good and well you didn't feel dat shit!"

"Da hell you say!"

After he ate the sandwiches, he called Kadaafie. Then he gathered the huge stacks of money and put it inside his small safe located in his closet. Twenty minutes later, Kadaafie was knocking at the door. Before he opened the door, he instructed Passion to get in his bed and wait for him.

"What's good witcha, cousin?" he said, giving him dap and a manly hug.

"Ain't shit family!"

"So fill me in on what happen,"

"Well, Fam, dis is how ya' boy cleverly done it. I had ole' girl go to the door while I was stooping down by da' mahfuckin' porch, and soon as dat mark-ass niggah came to the door, *Ka Pow!*" he said, mimicking pulling a trigger. Then I went upstairs and mangled everybody in there. Having no mercy or sympathy on none. I methodically orchestrated dat shit to profession! Then I gave her dumb ass the gun, so now she has all the blood on her hands. And a niggah like me get to skate!" he boasted.

"I did see dat shit on the news while I was vacationin' in St. Thomas. Dat shit made headlines everywhere." he said recalling the news clip. "Well done!" he said, handing him the briefcase that contained two hundred racks.

"What are you watchin'?" he asked getting up to leave.

"The First 48. Dis' shit right here niggah, (saying it like kat Williams) is fuckin' crazy! Niggah be up on here confessin' and some mo' shit! I wish I would. They muthafuckin' ass can catch my black ass, red handed with my hand in da fuckin' cookie jar! I'm not confessin' to shit. Just look at dis'

stupid dumb ass niggah here, cuhz. Daaaamn, they ran Catfish over with his groceries." he tripped.

"Yea, I watched dat one episode wid the one dude who killed his whole family and went in witness protection wid them and shit, but at any rate umma gone ahead and do what it do. Time is money." he said walking toward the door and threw up his finger like peace.

"Yea niggah your days are number too. Becuz like my mama said, the same thing dat makes you laugh is the very same thing dat will make you cry,"

YOU DO YOU, AND IMMA DO ME

Swagga made an exit off the freeway, headed straight to Angie's house. He decided against sending Grievence. When he opened up the door, she was inside with a big black laced negligee on and hella candles lit, with *Bedrock by* Young Money playing relentlessly in the background.

"S-S-Swagga!" she stuttered, not expecting it be him.

He waved her off. "Bitch, don't say shit to me. I just came to get my shit, and I'm out!"

She jumped up and followed him in the other room. "But, babee, I'm sorry. I didn't mean it, babe."

"Don't touch me. Get da fuck off my dick." he said, jerking away from her. Her doorbell rang. "Aren't you gonna get dat shit?"

"It's just dat little girl lookin' for My'Destiny. Damn, can a bitch get a break from bad ass kids?" she yelled out. "Her ass already done been over here four times!" she lied.

"Angie, I know yo' ass is in there. Yo', I just spoke to your humpty dump ass not even five minutes ago!" he said, knocking on the door. "I should've known you was gone be on dat straight bullshit." he shook his head. "I can't believe dis' round spongebob lookin' ass bitch tryna hoe me?!" he threw his hands up in the air and walked away.

She froze locking eyes with Swagga. He held her gaze for a brief moment before shifting his attention to the door.

"I didn't mean to impose on nuthin'? Don't let me cock block by all means, go entertain yo' homeboy!" he flailed his arm out. "Don't you want dat niggah to make your bed rock!"

"Boo, it wasn't like dat!" she cried.

"Bitch, do you understand the words that are coming outta my mouth? I don't want yo' fat ass, neva did so miss me with dat bullshit! I don't give a hell!"

"But, boo, I love you,"

"You do what?" he scrunched up his face. "How da fuck you love me?"

"Because I do. I'm in love with you and have been for quite some time. I can't explain da shit or control it!" she screamed.

"You're in love wid me but, about to fuck some otha niggah. Get da fuck outta here wid dat hoe shit. I'll tell you what, you just do you, and umma do me!" he yelled. She pleaded with him to stay. Suddenly he snapped. Wrapping his arm around her neck. "Bitch, you got me fucked up wid one of these otha bustas you been fuckin' wid!" he screamed, as he tightened his grip around her neck, cutting off her air. She clutched at his hairy, tatted-up arm digging her nails deeply inside his skin so he could let her go. Finally, the phone rang, snapping him out of his trance. He let her go and sprinted out of the door without taking nothing. She fell down to her knees, holding her throat, gasping for air. When it dawned on her that, he didn't take his stuff, that gave her hope. The phone started ringing again.

"Hello!" she said, out of breath.

"Bitch, you on some hoe shit. How da fuck yo' bitch ass gone have a niggah come all the way the fuck over there on a humbug tip? Listen at cha all outta breath and shit must've just got finished fuckin' some otha niggah?"

"Partnah, you need to pump yo' muthafuckin' brakes while you're ahead. For one, my niggah came home early. I just got choked da fuck out, if it's any of your business, so be easy! Would you rather for me to had opened the door and he blew yo' head straight the fuck off your thin-ass body. Why you poppin' off all dat shit!"

"Bitch, you got me fucked up. I stay strapped with my joint at all times. A niggah will neva get caught slippin' I'm to fly to fall, ya dig!"

"Well, I'll keep dat in mind the next time your black ass come a knockin' when he's home!"

"Girl, yo' ass got a smart ass mouth! (pronouncing it like mouf) Why you bumpin' my dome and shit," he said calming down.

"Negro, you da one poppin' off shit, but at any rate, you still tryna break bread? Becuz dat shit you talkin' is neither here nor there!"

"Hell nall, I'm not fuckin' wid yo' ass. I might have to bring da streetsweeper out and clean dat whole area up."

"It is what it is, time is money. Hell my conversation cost money!" she said, hanging up.

As soon as Swagga got into his car, his blackberry started vibrating. It was Deuces.

"What up, my nigg?"

"Shid, nuthin' much on my way over to Ms. Mac Faye house to cop me a fish sandwich. I got one last night them shits still bomb as fuck!"

"Dat old-ass lady still be cookin' and sellin' food?!" he asked flabbergasted.

"Straight rapin' niggahs and some mo' shit!"

"A niggah mouth is waterin' right now thinkin' 'bout them banging ass-hot links she used to cook!"

"Don't trip; I'll snatch you two of them bitches up!"

"Dat's what's up, but shid what's good witcha, doe fam?"

"I was just tryna see was dat niggah, Grievence around you becuz me and his ass 'pose ta' been rollin' to da mall."

"He's not pickin' up his phone, huh?"

"No, I called the room too!"

"His ass probably somewhere wid his head stuck in somebody's pussy. You know how he do, but if I hear from him, I'll let him know, doe!"

"Aight, fam let me call you back dat's baby mama on the other end." Deuces switched lines.

"What up doe?"

"What it do, niggah?"

"Shit! What do I do you the pleasure of dis' call?" he joked.

"I was callin' to tell you your son needs some pull ups and shoes. So, can you slide me some bread?!"

"Look Danielle you put a niggah on child support, so umma tell you like dis', get whateva my kids need from them crackers becuz I ain't got shit for you. Matter of fact if dat lil niggah is 3 years old and shittin' on himself then you need your janky ass whipped."

"No niggah, you looka here you fuckin' deadbeat," she said with a little bass in her tone.

"So umma a deadbeat, huh? What about the hundred dollars I just sent your monkey ass. I don't get credit for dat?"

"Niggah a hundred dollars, what da fuck. What you want me to do? Give you father of the year for a punk ass hundred dollars dat had to be split among two kids. Your fuckin' ass is on easy fuckin' street as it is. You don't do shit and even when you was in LA you didn't even come see your kids. Then they still love your sorry behind. I do everything alone I didn't fuck myself and get myself pregnant so I'm sure and hell is not gonna take care of them alone! Every time I ask your monkey ass for sumthin' for them your only response, is get it from Uncle Sam! That's some fucked up shit you on."

"That's right bitch. Get their Christmas, school, and everything all in between from Uncle Sam. If seein' my kids mean I have to see your fat raggedy hoe ass, then I say fuck it! When my kids get big enough and decide they wanna come find daddy that's what its gonna be! And how 'bout you call me ummm . . . Never! How 'bout never, is dat long enough?" he said, ending the call. "Project Bitches!"

As soon as Swagga made it to the Trap, Stubby had one of his homeboys there that wanted to be a part of the dream team. After talking it over with him, Swagga agreed to let him join in.

"Dis' right hea' is my homeboy, Vengence."

"What up, doe?!" Vengence said, giving him dap. And then he spent twenty minutes telling him how much he wanted to eat and willing and ready to start from da bottom. Swagga half listened not to be rude. Something about the boy seemed awful familiar, but Swagga couldn't put his finger on it. He was dressed in army fatigue with some black Timbs and a hat pulled very low just about covering his eyes. Just below his eye, he had one teardrop tattooed under it. He also had his twin girls name on his neck, Mazertie and Mercedez.

"I appreciate dis' man. I need a way to feed my daughters!" he said in very deep tone.

"Daughters?"

"Yea, I got two beautiful growing, twin girls dat mean the world to me. Believe me, I've touched both games, but workin' a nine to five have your ass living from pay check to pay check. Not tryna feel it!"

"I feel you, but long as nobody gets greedy, we can all eat!"

"Now that's what up."

"What do you have up for today?"

"Shit!"

"Well, how soon can you hit the block?"

"Like yesterday!"

"That's what's up. Well, I can put you out there wid your man Stubby today."

"Fa sho. You won't regret dis'. I promise!"

"Don't make me!"

"I'm 'bout to slide over here to the party store. I'm definitely gonna need some party favors, becuz a niggah gone pull an all nighter. You want anything, my niggah?" Bread asked.

"I'm good!"

"What up doe, Bread?" an old crack head said, giving him a pound on the fist. When he turned around he noticed a young, tender girl walking up. *that's dat hot teen pussy.* he thought watching her.

"Hey, Bread!" she waved with a big Kool-Aid smile.

"How do you know me, and I don't know who you are?" he asked, with smirk.

"Say it isn't so. Damn, you make a niggah wish for younger days!" the crack head said, rubbing his chest.

"If you don't take yo' perverted smoked-out, crack head ass on, umma knock dat one tooth you do have out!" she rolled her eyes and sucked her teeth and then shifted her attention back to Bread.

"You better hurry yo' hot ass up. I didn't bring yo' ass up hea' to be socializin' and shit!" her mama yelled, from the car.

She tilted her head towards the store. "Aight, Ma, chill. Come walk in da store wid, me my mom is clearly on one!"

"You sure it's cool? I don't wanna have to karate-chop moms and shit!" he said, imitating karate.

"Boy, you silly. Where was I?!"

"You were tellin' me how you know me. You do look a little familiar." he said, staring her in the face.

"Damn, take a picture, next time it will last longer."

"Girl, you got a smart-ass mouth, but since yo' lil' ass is fine, umma let you have dat one."

"Whatever. Anyways, I'm Candy dat used to hang with your cousin Ash over on Joy Rd!"

"No, lil' Candy, from Joy Rd?!" he said, holding his hands midway in the air.

"Clearly, I'm not little no more. I'm on my grown ass woman now!" she said, making her booty clap.

"Don't be startin' shit yo' lil' ass can't finish. I knew dat I knew your face. But shid, how old are you now?" he asked, praying she wasn't a minor.

"I just turned seventeen. When last time you saw, Ash?"

"It's been a cool minute, but what's good are you tryna give me them digits or what?!"

She gave him the number while putting her things on the counter.

He pulled out a wad of money. "Don't trip, lil' mama, I got it!"

"Thanks, but no thanks," she said, reaching in purse and pulling out a wad of her own.

"I hear you, Ms. I-n-d-e-p-e-n-d-e-n-t!"

She grabbed her bags from the counter. "That's da only way I know how to be! Besides, God blesses a child dat have her own. And for da record, I start what I finish!"

When she walked out the store, the first face she saw was the smoker. "Why da fuck yo' musty ass all in my grill?"

He licked his finger and used the spit to smooth down his moustache. She shot him a look that said, *Say sumthin' and I'll fuck yo' old ass up!* So he decided against pushing the issue.

"Man, why you trying to get wid dat girl, when you know she ain't nuthin' but jail bait?!"

"Shut yo' hatin ass up, you just mad becuz she bagged yo' old ass! But, on some real shit, I'll hit dat lil' badink-a-dink like it was some badunk-a-dunk! Straight R Kellyin' her!" he said walking off.

"Tree jumper-ass niggah!" he yelled out to him.

As soon as Grievence's car made it closer, he could hear, Aston's Martin Music. It was blaring making the valet, which was a nerdy white boy, nearly jump out of his skin when he cranked up.

"Heeey!" Wet Wet said, dancing.

"That's my shit! Vibin' to the music dis' is how we do it, all night breezin' down the freeway just me and my baby in our ride just me and my boss no worries at all, heeey!" Pleasure sang, doing her dance walking low. "When I'm alone in room sometimes I stare at the walls . . ."

"I love a girl dat swallows what's on the menu," Grievence sang. "Are you guys from Miami?" he asked tryna make small talk.

"From da bottom, dat's where we reside!"

"305 babee!" Pleasure sang.

Of course, Wet Wet hopped her ass in the front. "So, Ms. Wet Wet, let's continue our convo." Nobody was paying them any attention. They were too busy singing and checking out the scenery.

"Yeah, I was sayin' my shit stay wet. I got dat gushy ushy. Some call me Aquafinna, becuz I flow like water, babee."

"You look like you got dat snapper!" he licked his lips.

"Oh trust, I got dat snapback come back. I'll have yo' ass all up in Dade County feenin' like my shit made of crack or some shit!"

"Bitch, you stupid!" Xtacy yelled, ear hustling from the backseat.

"I say put your money where your mouth is, niggah!"

"I don't even much have to boast or none of dat shit like dat dere because my shit speaks for itself. You talk to Ms. Pretty Pussy, she'll talk back!"

"Well, I think Ms. Pretty Pussy will love to meet Mr. Mandingo!"

"Mr. Mandingo . . . I like the sound of dat!"

"I know you hear me. But, I don't want you to hear me. I want you to feel me I'm tryna J. Holiday you ASAP," he said, pulling up to the hotel where they were gonna be staying the night.

BETTER IN TIME

Flawless was sitting in his leather chair tapping on his desk with his pen, wondering why Neeyah wasn't answering or returning none of his phone calls. *Adore* by Prince played softly through the company's speakers. He had been talking to her for over a month, and he was used to hearing her soft, sexy voice at least once a day. "Maybe her and dat niggah done worked their differences out seeing as though she had all these unrequited feelings for him," he thought out loud, staring out of the huge windows to the other high-rise building, surrounding his. Then his Sidekick started vibrating. He picked it up and then smiled. "What's up, stranger!"

"You, boo!"

"What's good with you, doe?"

"I'm sorry I haven't returned your phone calls, but I had hella shit going on in my life! More like a never-ending, spiraling web of chaos!"

"Well you know I care about you and—"

"There's caring and there's you know, caring?" she cut him off.

"What's your definition, Ma? I'm all ears."

"Do you really wanna get analytical about dis'?"

"Speak yo' mind and stop being so evasive and answer the question please ma'am!"

"Well, there's like kind and concerned caring, then there's like lovin' and compassionate caring!"

"All of the above I would say! But, back to subject at hand, If you would like to talk about it, I'm a good listener." he said looking around his full-scale, neatly decorated office with.

"Naw, not really, so what's good wid you?" she asked trying to change the subject.

"I've been good, thanks for asking. I don't mean to be inquisitive, but are okay? Do you need anything, lil' mama?"

"I said I'm fine, damn!" she snapped.

"Damn, a niggah was just tryna be nice to your ass, but since you got an attitude, I think you need to call me back whenever you calm down!" he said, calmly and then ended the call. She was so appalled and even after he had hung up; she was still holding the phone up to her ear like he was still on the other end. She decided to call him back and apologize, but when she did, his phone went straight to the voice mail. *Damn, I may have fucked up the one good thing I have going in my life!* she thought as she felt warm tears falling down her face. "Leigha, girl, I really need you!" she yelled out to the sky. She thought calling him would make her feel better as he always found a way to make her laugh. Now she was feeling even shitter than she was before she made the call. She got into her car with tears streaming down her face and headed home. They had to move out of the apartment because of all the memories that the home held. They had actually moved into a better neighborhood. Although, they loved their new spacious four-bedroom apartment, they didn't know or care how they were gonna pay the expensive rent, because they were both out of a job. She wasn't gonna get her check for another six months. When she got into her new bungalow-style apartment, she threw the keys on the counter and laid on the bed with her sleeping mama. Who clearly, had cried herself to sleep squeezing Junior's favorite teddy bear. She tried her best to comfort her. Before leaving her side, she kissed her and said, "God got Sonny and Junior, Ma!"

Later that night, she was laying in her queen-sized bed, thinking about everything that happened to her. And how it happened in a matter of weeks listening to *Better In Time* by Leona Lewis. A song Leigha put her on and enjoying the diaphanous breeze from the cracked window. Unable to sleep she headed down to the kitchen and walked right over to the refrigerator. Soon as she opened it, she picked up a box of hot pockets. "Naw, I better not eat no pepperoni and then lay down, my ass will have the heart burn all night." she said, sticking it back inside the freezer. "I guess I'll have some yogurt." she said, removing it from the bottom drawer of the refrigerator. Then she made her way back to her room and grabbed the remote. When she started flipping through the channels her phone started ringing. A smile slowly spread across her face when she seen it was Flawless.

"Hey, baby!" she said, ecstatically into the phone.

"If I didn't know any better, I would say you're happy to hear my sexy voice," he said, in his sexy Southern accent.

"What makes you think dat? Look baby I'm sorry." He shushed her.

"Trust me when I say I can tell dat you have a big Colgate smile on your face,"

"Yeah, what makes you think you have dat affect on me?"

"Trust me, I know you better start listenin' to me when I talk, girl."

"Girl? I'm a woman over here!" she shot back.

"Miss Lady, my B, how come you don't talk dat much?"

"It's not in my nature to be garrulous. I prefer to sit and listen to others. Besides, when you listen and talk less, then you tend to learn more! What's dat one sayin' . . . ummm," she said tryna think of it. "Ok, it's a still tongue keeps a wise head."

"Is dat right?"

"But don't take my word for it. Just try it, you'll see!"

"So, what's up wid your cousin? My homie said he haven't heard from her and when he tried calling her, the number was disconnected?" he asked. She remained mute.

"Hello? Hello?" he said into the phone.

"I'm here." she said, in a very low and dry tone.

"What's wrong, baby?" he said, sensing something was wrong. Then she decided to tell him. As the atrocious events came rushing back, it literally took her breath.

"Well, I heard talking about sumthin' makes you feel better, because having it all suppressed inside of me is driving hella insane." she sighed.

"Well, where do I start? Okay, I guess I can start by telling you that Leigha is no longer with us," she said, as big teardrops began dropping from her face.

"Oh, baby, I'm sorry. Is there anything I can do?" he asked in a concerned tone.

"Just be here for me. That's not even the half of it, she was murdered by her own twin sister, which is very horrendous. She has no idea of the pain she inflicted on us."

He shook his head. "Wow, that's some fucked-up, evil shit!"

"Wait a minute, on top of all dat, my brother killed my mama's husband of ten years for molesting my lil' brother, which is his own son. So, you see shit been hella fucked up! Some Jerry Springer type shit!" They both sat on the phone quiet. He listened as she cried silently.

"Get it out, boo, don't hold back. Let 'em flow," he said, as his eyes began to water. "Well, you know I'm here for you if you need me, don't you?"

"Yes," she whimpered.

"So, if you don't mind me asking, what is your brother's attorney sayin'? He should be getting exonerated, right?" he asked inquisitively.

"Well, right now we don't have any money to get him no lawyer. He has a public defender." she said, dryly.

"Public pretender?!" he screamed. "Don't you know they gonna try to fry his black ass! A public defender job is to get you to plead. Baby girl, don't even worry your pretty little head, I'll take care of dis'!"

"How?!"

"Don't trip, just let me do what I do! Well, I have to go handle some business, but I promise I'll call you later to check on you."

"Pinky swear?" she whined.

"Pinky swear!" he repeated, then he hung up. She felt a little better after talking to him. *Could it be I'm falling in lust? He's all dat Grievence is not!* she thought because she knew it wasn't love, being that she was still in love with Grievence. "*Or is it possible to love two men at the same time? Leigha, always said I should be with someone dat's gonna add to my life not take away, time to take her advice.*" she thought out loud while going into her mother's room. She wasn't there, which was kinda strange because her mom never went out at night.

The next day Flawless stayed true to his word, and made it happen. Since her brother had a lawyer, she felt a little at ease. However, the courts wouldn't let Junior come home.

GUESS WHO'S PREGNANT

Amauri was sitting on his patio dressed in some gym shorts. Enjoying the night air and smoking a blunt. He had just got in from playing basketball. He heard the doorbell ring.

He got up and looked out of the peephole. *Damn, dat look like Yatta ugmo ass!* he thought.

"What da fuck are you doing at my crib?" he asked, snatching the door open. "Dis' bitch done gained some courage," he turned and said as if he was talking to someone.

"I just wanted to t-t-talk to you," she stuttered. "And I don't have your number," she hung her head low.

"Bitch, I don't give a fuck. Don't ever come to my crib ever again unannounced!" he yelled.

"But, it's important!" she said, quickly glancing at him then back down to the ground.

"You got one minute. Speak yo' mind, yo'. I wanna know what's so damn important dat you felt you could just pop yo' ass da' fuck up like I fucks wid you like dat!" he said, with his arms folded against his chest. She was dressed in some dingy white shorts and a black T-shirt with some dogged-out crealed over black Rebook classics. It had been over a month and she still had the same hairstyle.

"Okay, I'll be straight to the point. I'm pregnant!" she said, looking up so she could see the reaction on his face. When she told him that, he immediately choked on the blunt he was smoking.

"Well, it's not mine. What are you telling me for?"

He knew all along there was a very strong possibility of it being his.

"Oh, it's yours all right. I haven't been with nobody else!" she said, unshakably as tears began to fall down her face. Yatta couldn't even pay a smoker to sleep with her because she smelled so bad.

"Well, you can dry them crocodile-ass tears and save all dat shit fo' them birds becuz a niggah like me, ain't feeling no sympathy for yo' dumb ass. I'll tell you what you can do, you can get da fuck off my steps and go find the unlucky-ass niggah dat got yo' mud duck-lookin' ass pregnant!" he yelled, getting ready to close the door.

"Wait!" she yelled, catching the door.

"Bitch, are you outta yo' rabbit-ass mind? I said bounce, homie!" he yelled to the top of his lungs. Causing his nosey neighbor Roselyn, to turn down her police scanner and open her blinds to see what was going on.

"Look, I know you don't want no baby, so I wanna go abort dis' bastard, but I need the money. I'm broke, and then I promise you won't have to worry about seeing my pretty little face 'round here again!"

He stood in the doorway pondering for a moment, then told her to wait outside. She grabbed a seat on the steps. He went inside and slipped on a oversized white tee and a pair of Red Monkey jeans. Before he left out the door, he stuck his feet in his wheat colored Timbs by the door.

"Fuck all dat bullshit. A niggah is 'bout ta run my ass to Walgreens and get a test. A bitch ain't gone just show up and say she pregnant and think umma give her ass some money," he said out loud putting on his blue-and-white baseball cap. "Wait right here. I'm bout to step out a second to get a test,"

"Well, can I ride?" she asked, excitedly.

"Bitch, you got me fucked-up all da way up! I don't fucks wid you like dat." he said then once he got in his truck he looked at her and shook his head and then turned and shoot her a look that said *Are you fucking serious* then he cranked up his black Escalade. It was loaded and came equipped with a pair of black 24 inch rims. *Bottoms Up* by Trey Songz was blaring when he started it.

When he was going into the store, his phone started ringing. It was his baby mama, "Long time no hear!" he said, into the phone. Whenever he was around or talking to her or his daughter, his whole demeanor changed.

"You, punk! What are you doing?"

"Shit. On my way in the store and then I'm headed back to da crib, but what's good, doe?"

"I was callin' to make sure you were still alive and kickin'! I heard your ass cruised around the world and some mo' shit. Damn, did you even bother bringin' a niggah a keychain or sumthin'?"

"You already know I got you, I just been hella busy, dat's all! So where's my princess?"

"Her bad ass is in there taking a nap. Don't you know her ass told me dat she didn't wanna live with me no more and dat she was gonna live wid you!"

"No, she didn't? Did she, chile?" he said, mocking her. "Dat's my baby girl, she can come live with her daddy!"

"Speaking of which, guess who's about to have a baby?"

"Who, chile?!" he asked, in a more or less tone going along with what she was saying instead of actually listening while looking at the EPT box in his hand.

"Amber. I'm 'bout to be an auntie!"

"Yeah, how far along is she?" he asked, dropping the box out of his hand.

"Well, she really don't know. Mama was in the kitchen frying some chicken, then she ran straight to the bathroom and started throwin' up everywhere, so I was like yo' little ass is impregnated. Sure enough, Mama went out and got an EPT, two red lines magically appeared as soon as she dipped the shit!"

"Let me call you right back!" he said in an urgency.

His mind immediately diverted back to the head-banging sex they had.

"I'm not gonna even trip," he said, walking back to his truck. When he pulled up to his townhouse, Yatta was still outside smoking a cigarette. That she had bombed off of Roselyn, waiting on his return. He threw her the test and kept pushing.

"Where am I 'pose ta' use dis' at!" she yelled out to him, looking perplexed.

"Take yo' ass round the corner [pronouncing it as *coner*] somewhere, I can give a fuck less!" he sneered, flinging his arm around in the air. With her heart ripped out of her body and as mortifying as it was, she hung her head low and did as she was told. When she found a murky area, she pulled down her dingy Faded Glory jeans and squatted down. By the time she got ready to pee, she heard him calling her name.

"Over hea'," she yelled out.

"On second thought, I think you ought to come in so I can watch yo' ass pee."

"What, you wanna make sure I don't have nobody else's pee or sumthin'?" she said, jumping to pull her jeans up.

"Damn skippy!"

Once back inside, he told her to remove her shoes. When he wasn't looking, she hurriedly took off her shoes and stuck her sock ridden with holes, into her shoes. She looked at her feet, they were all crusty and her heels had deep cracks in them.

"Hurry yo' ass up, yo'!" he yelled.

"Well, I think I need to keep my socks on the way my feet look," she said. *Damn, I knew I should've put some Vaseline on my shits!*

"What, are you gonna watch me pee too?" she asked, raising a brow.

"You just hurry yo' ass up so you can bounce!" he said, standing in the doorway with his hands folded across his chest. She wasn't expecting him to be watching her because when she was outside and she had pulled down her clothes, she had gotten a whiff of her own fish-smelling pussy, as soon as she pulled her clothes down. "My period just went off, so you might smell a little fish!"

"Bull-fuckin-shit!" he screamed, grabbing the air fresher next to the toilet. "You got my shit smelling like a dead dog and some mo' shit." he said, spraying damn near the whole can of air fresher. Her panties looked just like she had bled in them several times.

"There!" she shoved it in his hand, and pulled her panties up without even wiping. He had his shirt covering his mouth and nose as he watched her dip the test stick into the pee. Immediately, two lines appeared.

"Fuck! Fuck!" he screamed, punching the wall putting a big hole in it causing her to jump.

Better the wall than me! she thought.

"Wait here," he said, imperatively while walking toward his bedroom. Shaking his hand. When he returned, he had two racks in his hand. "Now I want you to take dis' money and abort dat baby, and here's some extra for you to stay da fuck away from me, I mean dat shit. If you ever seen me in the streets, your ass better hurry and cross dat muthafucka, understood?"

She nodded her head yes. Her eyes lit up like a Christmas tree when she saw all the big faces. The only thing on her mind was how much chronic and thizz pills she could cop. Having an abortion was the last thing on her mind. Her baby was gonna be their golden ticket outta the ghetto.

"Matter of fact, I'm gonna personally take you myself Monday morning to the first-come-first-serve clinic, so meet me here outside my complex at 7:00 am," he said, taking the money back.

Damn, she thought to herself, *I'm not trippin' doe. I just gotta formulate a plan someway somehow!*

Early Monday morning, Yatta was sitting on his steps, when he finally came strolling outta house at 7:40am.

"You early!"

"You late!" she replied, glancing at her gold-plated Gitano watch.

"A niggah had a rough night,"

"I bet!" she said, hopping up in his big boy truck. As soon as she got inside, she let the window down hoping she saw somebody from the hood.

"Uh, hmmm, ain't gonna be none of dat shit. Yo' ass ain't gonna be getting all comfortable in my shit. Matter of fact, duck yo' muthafuckin' ass down!"

She calmly did as she was told. Twenty minutes later, they arrived at the clinic. She was still trying figure out how she was gonna get outta not getting the abortion. He pulled into the nearest parking space. Amauri led the way she scampered closely behind him. He went directly to the window, gave them her name then he reached into his front pocket and pulled out a wad of money and peeled off five C-notes and handed it to her.

"Is it all right if I go back there wid her," he said, louder through the window.

"No, sir, dat won't be necessary!" The woman said, sensing that she didn't wanna get the abortion in the first place.

"I'll wait right here then," he took the receipt. The minute she said that, a light bulb went on in Yatta's head.

An hour later, she came out looking pooped holding her stomach.

"Please make sure she get plenty of rest, she's gonna need it!" The nurse told him.

"Will do! So did the abortion go smoothly?" he inquiringly, asked.

"Well I'm not at liberty to discuss dat but, Mrs. Johnson will be able to answer all your questions. If you'd excuse me I have another patient waiting for my return!"

"Excuse the fuck out of me, Miss Cranky-Bitch!" he said, turning to leave.

"Yatta, let me holla at you, dawg!" he said once they got outside.

"Can you wait 'til we get in the car?"

"That's what I wanted to tell you," he said, reaching in his other pocket, pulling out the money he initially gave her. "Here, use dis' money to call a cab or hop on the bus or sumthin' becuz dis' here is a wrap!"

Yeahhh, muthafucka, that's what you think, time to pay the piper! she said to herself taking the money. "Okay, dat's what it do. Have a nice life, boo!"

"Good riddance, deuces Beyatch!" he said, pressing the key to start his truck and peeled off.

When she saw he was outta sight, she reached in her bra and pulled out the five hundred dollars he paid for the abortion. "You shall see my pretty face again . . . Oh yes indeed!" she laughed, louder and louder.

I HEAR YOU TALKIN'

Grievence sat on the edge of the full-sized bed, dressed in a pair of hanes and socks that came all the way to his knees. While, waiting for Wet Wet to come outta the bathroom, he fired up the blunt.

"Umumm . . ." she cleared her throat, standing in the bathroom doorway. "Damn, you just gone put one in the air without yo' girl?!" she said, as she ambled towards him. When she got up on him, she playfully pushing him back on the bed and leaped on top of him. "My aren't you dressed for the occasion?" she scanned him from head to toe.

"What you tryna clown me, low key? Would you ratha me put some G-strings on?"

"Yup that'll be so sexy . . . ummm,"

"Okay, I'll put them on, but umma have to kill you afterwards. Becuz you'll never live to tell nobody."

"In dat case, you look sexy as muthafuka in them tightie whities and calf high socks." she laughed.

"Ayye, wait!" he said, holding his arm out.

"Boy, please ain't nobody gonna make drop dat do do!" she giggled.

"Whatever, niggah, since it's just do do, I guess I don't have to share."

"If you don't give me dat," she said, taking it out of his hand.

She was wearing a Chanel negligee with a long black-laced robe with some black heels embedded with fur in the center.

"You look gooder than a muthafucka!" she said, biting her bottom lip and rubbing his heavily tatted chest. "I think Ms. Pretty Pussy is ready to meet Mr. Mandingo!" she whispered, very seductively in his ear.

He smashed the blunt in the ashtray. "You ain't said nuthin',"

"Hold on a minute, doe. Umma show you how da bitches from da bottom get down," she said, getting her iPod hooked to her carry-around Bose speakers out her bag. Once connected, she strolled down to *Role Play* by Trey Songz.

He sat up. "Oh, suckey suckey now."

She started by turning around and rolling her hips, then dipped low, removing her coat. Then she bent over and made her ass clap. Then she sat in the chair and opened her legs wide as she could. He moaned and bit his lip, while she played with her pussy.

"Um bout to beat dat pussy out da frame."

"Would you like to see why they call me Wet Wet?" she asked, seductively putting her finger in and out of her pussy. While using her free hand to fondle her nipples.

He nodded his head yeah. "Well come get dis' pussy baby." she moaned louder and louder stimulating her g-spot, bringing herself to an eruption.

"Okay, I've seen enough, let's do da damn thing. I'm about to rock your dome." he said, picking her up.

"Stop talkin' and put some action behind your words. Come rock dis' shit, baby." she screamed.

"Lemme hit it from the back?" he whispered.

As soon as he stuck his dick inside her pussy he started trembling. Her pussy was so hot and wet it felt like her shit had melted the condom. He actually had to check to make sure it was still on.

"Give it to me, baby. Go deeper." she yelled. "Deeper, Ms. Pretty ain't got yo' ass speechless, do she?" she yelled, throwing it back. "Oh yesssss!" she said, squeezing her nipples.

"Do you want it fast or slow?"

"Go hard, I like to feel dat shit in the bottom of my stooomach!" she yelled, as he feverishly sped up. "Yesssssssss, babeeee!" she screamed, louder. "Like dat, Daddy."

"Everything I do, I go hard at it—you like Mr. Mandingo, don't cha!"

"Yesssss, I love it!"

"Your shit so hot and wet, damn. I think I wanna wife Ms. Pretty Pussy."

"Uh huh, niggah, I know yo' ass ain't cum befo' me!" she shot him a grimaced look.

"I can't help it. Yo' shit too good!"

"Fuck all dat shit! It ain't going down like dat, pimpin'!" she said, taking his limp dick and sticking it in her mouth. She didn't suck his dick like other females she secreted it with a whole lot of spit on it. It was so sloppy all he could hear was her slurping and she was really slurping. Then she made her way down to his balls. When she got down to them, she put them both in her mouth at the same time. He moaned louder. "Ahh, that's your spot huh?

Flip over for me." she ordered. He did as told. She opened up his cheeks as far as they would go and licked from his ball to his crack.

"Dat shit tickles." he wiggled. *Damn, I hope I don't fart. Naw her ass had better hope I don't!* he thought squeezing his as together. This was something new to him and he actually liked it. Freaky as Monie was, she never tossed his salad.

"Be still and stop cringin'. Your ass gone remember dis' bitch from da bottom for years to come." she said, licking and sucking every inch of his asshole. "Lay on your back, baby," she whispered.

"Ohhh baby. Oh shit. Get from back there," he yelled out, and wiggled his toes.

"B.I.G bring dat ass to me," she sang and then lifted his legs up in the air. He didn't know what she was about to do. For some reason he let her be in the driver seat. He wasn't at all use to being in the back seat. Suddenly, she ran her tongue from his balls down to his ass. For at least ten minutes straight, she stayed on it. "Damn, you pretty strong too, girl," he said, in between moans. She didn't respond because she was too busy freaking the shit out of him.

Five minutes later, he instructed her to lay on her back so he could hit it missionary style.

"Give me kiss baby."

"Ewwwe you nasty," he joked, as he stuck himself inside her. While he was hitting it, she took his cock out of her pussy, and rubbed it against her clit a couple of times, causing her to cum. Then he opened her legs and got in between them sideways, all he could hear was her pussy farting when he let her leg down.

"Is she talkin' loud enough yet?!"

"I can hear what she sayin', loud and clear!"

"Oooooooooh, right there, Mandino dick!" she yelled with her body shaking uncontrollably. "Yeah, I'm cummmmin'."

"Wow," he said, wiping the sweat off his forehead with the back of his hand falling back on the bed next to her.

"Don't you think we should be getting ready?"

"That's fucked up, dat bitch gone leave our ass to go fuck some niggah she only known for ten damn minutes!"

"Like that's not how it goes down in the VIP." Pleasure said, pinning her hair up.

"Not clean the fuck across country. Hell at least they reside in da' same state." Xtacy shot back.

"Get da fuck out of here with dat fuck shit!" Pleasure said.

"Her ass better come back paid!" Juicee yelled from the bathroom.

"I damn sholl hope dat niggah's brother is ass fine ass him!"

"Damn, bitch, how do you think your ass gonna squeeze Texas into Florida!" Pleasure said, looking at the small suit Xtacy had laid out.

"Fuck you, hoe! Your ass is exaggeratin' and shit. You know my ass ain't even much dat big. Melodramatic ass!"

"Huh? Yo' ass so big like the Florida sun!" they all said in unison.

"Fuck you, fuck you, and fuck you—fuck all yall hatin' hoes!" she said, pointing at them one by one.

Swagga and Vengence was chopping it up he didn't even notice the iciness of his eyes when he talked to him. Again, he was dressed in dark clothing.

"Yeah, man, I'm so glad I don't have to be fuckin' wid them hoe-ass quarter pieces. It seemed like soon as I made a quick two hundred, it was gone and I had to flip da shit! I'm so glad you let me get a slice of dis' American Pie."

"Dawg, I'm cool on the thank yous. You wanna eat as do I and da next mahfucka, so you don't have to keep thanking me." he said sipping on his Moscato.

"How da fuck yall niggahs gone be up in here poppin' bottles and shit without a niggah!" Deuces said, wriggling out of his Al Wissan he had just got from the mall. "Here dawg here's yo' food!"

"Clearly, dawg you a swagger-jacker!"

"You know how I do it! Had to snatch dis' bitch up for da quick nine hunnit. Gotta stay fly!"

"Naw dawg stop swagger jackin' and get your on swag. I can teach you how to sell dope niggah, but I can't teach you my swag!"

"I'll let you have dat one. Where you want yo' food niggah?!"

"Stick it in the microwave I'll eat dat shit in a few. I'm already knowing a niggah is about to have the munchies and some mo' shit,"

"Fasho!"

"Niggah, if yo' ass wasn't cupcakin' all night, then you could have been in on da fun, true story dawg!" Stubby said, off in the cut eating a double Quarter pounder.

"Listen at Captain Save-a-Hoe over here, if you don't shut yo' chunky ass up, you twelve sandwich-eatin mahfucka! Ole couch potato lookin' ass!" Deuces said, grabbing the bottle.

"Fuck you, niggah. I likes to eat, so umma eat. You on the otha hand can use a meal, skinny-neck mahfucka!" Stubby said, wiping the corners of his mouth.

"Yo, bitch, don't be sayin' dat when I'm hitting it from da back. I be all up in dat thang. Grindin' hard hittin' nuthin' but guts."

"Man, fuck you! You probably was in my bitch, but I got a velveteen rub from your mama last night." he said, with mayonnaise all in the corners of his mouth. Stubby and Deuces had clicked instantly.

"Yall niggahs clownin'." Swagga said, taking a grape flavored swisher from the box.

"Anybody heard from dat hoe-ass niggah Grievence?"

"He probably wid them hoes. He told me they were fine ass fuck. I can't to see them." Deuces said.

Two hours later, Grievence dropped Wet Wet off at her hotel and told her that he was gonna send a car for them. He drove back to his hotel to get ready. He spent most of the time shaving, and listening to the Trey Songz *Passion Pain and Pleasure* cd. After he was done, he went to his closet and pulled out his Bathing Ape Jeans that had a turquoise ape embellished with rhinestones on the back pockets, along with a white shirt centered with a turquoise ape. When he got dressed, he pulled his dreads back out of his face and slipped on his turquoise Gaters to match. While he was looking in the mirror, he slipped his chain on and sprayed his dreads. When he was done getting dressed, he grabbed his keys off the table and was out. By the time he pulled up at the Athenaeum Suites, everybody was already there.

"Look what da cat done finally drug in!" Swagga said.

"You know Pretty Ricky got to be the one to come in last to make his grand entrance like David Ruffins and shit!" Deuces giggled, popping a bottle of Moscato. "Oh yeah, when they walked in, I looked up expectin' to see a flag go up and some fireworks in the sky or sumthin'." he leaned over and whispered to him and then walked off. He was rocking Christian Audigier outfit with a pair of all white forces.

"Shut your Eddie Cane lookin' ass up!" Grievence yelled out to him.

Swagga was off in the cut watching the girls do their thing, when his phone started vibrating. It was one of Sal's men. When he said hello, the only thing the man said into the phone was *tre*, which was the code for death.

Swagga was wearing a Coogi outfit as usual. You would never catch him in the same thing twice. With some custom-made Coogi Forces.

"Yeah, niggah, have your fun and get your shine on. Dat will be the last piece of pussy you ever gone see." he said, watching Bread make it rain on the strippers. He was always being ostentatious.

"You got a body dat make ah niggah wanna eat dat!" Bread whispered to Xtacy's, making her blush and dance harder. "Naw, I'm just fuckin' wid ya!" he chuckled. Then he looked around expecting others to laugh. She walked off. "Did you just hear what I told dat one bitch with the buck ass teeth?" he asked, Trigga.

"Yeah, dat shit was funny as hell."

"Oh I can tell. I can see dat you laughed so hard tears started running down your face."

"Damn, niggah I laughed inwardly. I said the shit was funny. What do you want me to do? Give you the comedian of the year award or some shit? Damn!" Trigga said, motioning for Wet Wet to set down on him.

Bread walked over to Juicee. "Hey, baby," he licked his lips. "I'm like Charlie Wilson, I can do magic."

"Yeah?" she sat down on his lap. "Tell me more. How sooo," she whispered.

"First, we gone go up to my room,"

"Hummmm . . ." she bit down on her lips and moaned.

"Then umma beat the breaks off dat pussy,"

"Don't stop. I'm still waitin' on the showstoppa. The magic part." she grinded harder on his leg.

"Don't trip, sexy. I was getting to dat part. After I beat da breaks off of it, then I'm gonna make your ass disappear like it never happened." he smiled. She hopped up so fast off of his lap that she nearly sprang her ankle.

"Dis' niggah stupid as fuck," Trigga spit champagne from his mouth. "Now dat was funny as hell.

"These bitches is sweet, true story!" Stubby said, in his deep accent.

By the time the girls left, they each had at least two to three racks. They really earned it because they sucked damn near everybody dry.

"Guurrrrl, them niggah there was off da chain!" Xtacy said, counting her money. "Two thousand five hundred—not bad, not bad at all!"

"How 'bout dat niggah, Grievence twisted my ass up like a pretzel. Straight long stroking, I know I felt dat shit moving round in my stomach. Hitting nuthin' but guts. Like my shit was gone be the last piece of ass he was ever gone get!"

"Yeah, dat niggah looked like he was dipped in butter sauce!"

"Aye yo, Bread!" Swagga yelled out.

"What up doe, homie? Them girls was off da hezzzie fa sheezie!" he said, walking towards him, pulling his pants up.

"I need you to take ride wid me for a minute."

"Fa sho. Lemme go holla at my man, Trigga."

"Dat want be necessary, we'll only be a minute he won't even notice we left." Trigga was so wasted, he didn't notice him get in the car with him. Bread made the usual small talk, boasting. Swagga gave him no indication that nothing was wrong. He opened up his armrest and flipped through his CD's until he found Lil' Wayne. "Things are 'bout to change dramatically." Swagga said, pressing eject to release the cd, and then he stuck the other one in.

"I'm like Obama, I'm ready for a change!" Bread said, grinning from ear to ear. He would have never visualized in a million years that things was about to go terribly wrong.

"Dis' niggah is crazy for dis'. For free suites I'd give Paris Hilton all-nighters in about 3 years, holla at me Miley Cyrus. I don't discriminate, no not at all. I'll kit kat a midget if that ass soft I break her off. I exchange V cards with the retards and get behind the Christian like DR becuz he are." Swagga sang.

As soon as they pulled up at the Natallie place, the guard buzzed them in.

"Who shit is dis? Dis' joint is sweeet!"

"My man I want you to meet. He's my connect!" Swagga said, checking his facial expression.

He smiled like a chest cat. "Word, I'm finna meet yo' connect. Put dat on sumthin'!"

"Well if you don't believe me we can always turn around."

"I'm playin' dawg. That's the business, doe!"

"Well, I don't play I be' bout my shit, but in two minutes you guys will meet and greet!"

"Wait 'til them niggahs find out I done met the connect they gonna be hatin' and shit!" Bread said.

"Yeah, they gonna pretty green-eyed. But shid, you bringin' in all the bread!" Swagga said, walking through the gate.

Bread trailed closely behind. "You noticed dat too. Is it ok for me bring dis' black in?"

"You cool, don't trip!"

As soon as they were inside, they walked into the kitchen. One of the guards walked up behind Bread and put two to his head. It all happened so fast, til he didn't even have a chance to take his Black out of his mouth, that was still intact in between his lips when he fell over. All of a sudden, his body started jerking from shock. Then all they heard was a thud from his muscles relaxing and him shitting on himself. When he stopped shaking, the burly man put two fingers on his neck to check for a pulse.

"Swag, we'll take it from here!" Sal said, appearing from the darkness of the hallway.

He gave him a manly hug. "Okay, my man. I' preciate' it!"

As he walked toward the door, he noticed blood had splattered on his clothes. So, he hopped into his coupe and drove straight to Ann Arbor.

"Damn, where did dat hoe-ass niggah go dat fast?" Vengence said, scanning the parking lot.

I DID YOU WRONG,
YOU DID ME WRONG

Grievence sat in a traffic jam, lost in thought. One month had turned into four months. He didn't have no regrets, because he had more fun in four months than he did in a entire year. His mom was okay. He kept her with money in her pockets. She and her friend Rodney were becoming inseparable. So, she was actually enjoying her privacy. After he listened to saved messages from Neeyah, he decided to head back to Calli. When Flawless stepped off the Delta airplane, there was a car waiting for him. Neeyah had already given him directions to where she stayed. The driver took him straight there. She was in her bed knocked out when she heard *Love All Over Me* by Monica. Very loudly in her ear, nearly making her heart jump out of her gown.

"Hello," she said, sleepily.

"What's up, beautiful? I didn't mean to wake you."

"You good. Are you here, boo?"

"Yeah, my plane just touched down. Are you sure it isn't to late to come thru, because I can go to my room and come at a more decent hour!"

"Please come, I need to feel your muscular arms embracing my body. Like yesterday!"

"On my way,"

When she got up to open the door for him, she noticed that her mom wasn't in her room. Apparently, she thought Neeyah wouldn't notice she was gone. Being that it was 2:00 a.m. Just as Neeyah was about to go into a frenzy, she walked through the door.

"Neeeyah!" she jumped.

"Where you been, Ma? I was worried 'bout you."

"I couldn't sleep so I went out to clear my head."

"Oh, Maaa, we gonna get thru dis'!" Neeyah hugged her.

Ten minutes later, Flawless was buzzing in.

Four hours later, Grievence's plane touched down. He hopped in the first available cab to his mom's house. Where she and Rodney lay, knocked out. He could tell she had a rough night, because the trail of clothes from the living room to the bedroom, along with empty Corona bottles, confirmed it.

He glanced in her room and noticed they were butt naked. "Ewwwe, nasty asses. I don't even wanna know her like dat! I guess that's what my ass get for poppin' up. I stepped dead in dat shit." he shrugged, heading towards his room. Soon, as he hit his room he was surprised to see his room exactly the way he left it, dirty. He didn't bother nothing, all he did was get an outfit out his suitcase and headed for the shower. After he got dressed, he grabbed his keys to his Monte Carlo off the nightstand.

Once he was in the car, he slid in his Jaheim cd and strolled down to *Finding My Way Back*. "Damn, dis car feels hella funny."

When he drove up, he saw Neeyah kissing Flawless.

"What is a niggah doing coming from her crib at seven o'clock in the mornin'?!" he said, glancing at the clock to make sure it was indeed 7am. That's when reality hit, that he had lost her. It didn't matter that he never answered or returned none of her calls. All that mattered was he made an effort to be there at the present time. Just as he got out the car to check her, Flawless was getting into his black sedan. He threw the car in park and hopped out. "Hell naw! You not gonna hoe me, dawg!"

"Grievence?!" Neeyah screamed. "What are you doing here?"

When Flawless turned around, he was greeted with Grievence right smack in his face.

"What's good wid you and my girl, homie?" he stuck his chest out.

"Girl?" she shouted, flabbergasted. "Last time I checked you dumped my ass."

"Neeyah on some real shit you need to check yo' boy befo' I check him becuz I'm not wid dat sucka ass shit." Flawless yelled.

"Boss up, niggah. Get yo' bitch ass out of da car, homie!" Grievence sized him up with bass in his voice. Then he held up his shirt and revealed his .22. When the driver looked in the review mirror, he saw it in and peeled off.

"Dis' niggah here dipped off doing the three motion." he joked. But dat's fucked up how yo' ass gonna hoe me for a pie ass niggah!" Grievence said, pointing at the car that had disappeared in thin air.

"First of all, you left me. I cried, I begged you and now I've moved on to somebody that loves me very much and treats me like a lady. Sumthin' you don't know shit about! My mama always told me, when one door closes, another one will opens. I never understood that until now." he remained mute and listened. "But, I do wanna thank you for leaving me. Opening up new doors in my life. I'm stronger and wiser. In fact, I'm beyond wise!" she turned to walk away.

He grabbed her arm. "I'm sorry that I hurt you I got your message, and I came straight here!"

"Let go of me. I don't want your repugnant ass touching me." she said in disgust. She may as well been talking to a brick wall, because what she said went in one ear and out the other one. "Fall da' fuck back before I take off on your hoe ass!" she said with a little more bass in her voice and sticking her chest out.

"You gone take off on who, lil girl? I'll sweep yo' lil ass all through dis' gravel!" he smirked.

"Chile please! My boo is from Piru. One phone call to his homies and they'll mop yo' ass out!" she lied.

"Come here, baby." he tugged at her arm, "I was just playin', you look so cute when you're mad."

"All I wanna see is your back! That's what I'm used to seeing," she screamed with coldness and bitterness.

He could've shitted bricks. The good girl he once had was gone.

"Come and sit in the car with me, let's talk. Let's rectify dis' baby. I'm like Jaheim, I'm tryna find my way back!"

"I'll be damned!" she repulsed, snaking her neck. "Ain't no remedyin' dis' shit. What's done is done."

"I just touched down soon as I got yo' message. I came straight to you!"

"So!" she scrunched her up her face.

"So?"

"Yeah, niggah. So da fuck what! You didn't make history when you did that shit. I can give a fat baby's ass, I finally found happiness, and I'm not gonna let you fuck it up for me. Shit you ran from me like you had fire under your feet. You got da' fuck on. Now if you'll excuse me, I have to make amends with my king. I knew you wasn't shit the moment I laid eyes on you. So, like you told me, miss me with all that shit!"

"You swagger-jackin now?" he joked. "But if you really felt like that, why was you with me all that time. I taught you just about everything you

know now." he stared dead at her. She couldn't respond because she was to speechless. "Do I got your hoe card, Neeyah?"

"My mama taught me not to judge a book by it's covers and I was just tryna give your ass the benefit of the doubt." she managed to say after a brief moment of silence.

She was trying to play hard, but she knew good and well she still loved the fuck out of him, and if she was around him any longer she was gonna be all on him.

"Listen at you. I know you don't love me now. You must really hate a niggah, huh? You never talked like that."

"Actually, yes! At the same time, becuz of you I'm a stronger woman now. I deserve better and with the immense amount of knowledge, I've gained from all the shit you put me thru. I found better. I must say I'm glad dat I finally woke up after deep soul-searchin' I know you, and I would never be. I just hate it took so damn long for me to realize that!"

"I never meant to hurt you, believe me I loved you wid all my heart and still do! Boo, love is too weak to define how much you mean to me."

"Bullshit!" she shot back. "You never loved me, I loved you, niggah, wid my all. You just took the shit for granted. Baby, lemme tell you, everybody get tired! To be honest, all the love for you slowly but, surely drained out!" she lied knowing good and well she still loved him deeply." Look Grievence, the bottom line is you can talk about any and everything under the sun but I'm standin' firm and proud,"

"I bet if you give me five minutes—no, fuck that—one minute and we'll see if it's still there!"

"Look, boy, I'm on some otha shit now. I'm not 'bout to play yo' pointless-ass high school game!" she turned her back towards him.

"See becuz you know it's there!"

She turned to face him and patted her chest. "Boy, please I can assure you ain't shit in here for you! You treated me like a stray ass bitch!"

"I'm sorry," he said, trying to hug her. "You said in one of your messages that we're gonna be together forever."

"That was four months ago. Things changed."

"How, Neeyah? You left it on my voice mail a gang of times, so I know you still feel that way."

"Are you fuckin' serious? You actin' like dat shit was etched in stone. Face it, Neeyah and Grievence isn't written in da stars baby!" she wanted to give in, he looked and smelled good as usual and was wearing the same cologne that instantly made her pussy wet.

"Get the fuck off of me!" she said, tearing away from him. *Not a day past where I didn't see you in my mind, let's be together.* she wanted to say.

"I never loved anyone the way dat I love you."

"You figured that out when?" she asked, as her stance softened. He remained mute. "That line is so cliché. I just wanna know why do you feel compelled to tell me all these lies."

"I knew it all along!" he said after a brief moment of silence.

"Damn, homie it took you dat long to think of dat bullshit ass lie? Hell you're mister-on-top-of-his-game-Suave. Lies been rollin' off your tongue relentless, I mean what da fuck, Grievence."

"Damn, it's been a cool minute since you called me dat, wow. Dat really cut ah niggah deep," he patted his chest.

"Don't even get me started about that," she chuckled to maintain her composure.

"Baby, can we just sit in my car for five minutes?" he tugged at her arm. "I'm just trying to make some sense of my voice mail. What happened boo while I was away?"

She looked at him thoughtfully and said, "You got three minutes and please don't touch me," she jerked her arm away.

"Ok. Fair enough," he held his hands up in the air.

"Why you left your car running?" she asked. *Finding My Way Back*, was blaring on repeat from speakers.

"That's not important. Let's talk about the message. You was like sumthin' bad went down. So, what was it, boo?" he asked, looking over at her and noticing tears welling up in her eyes. "What happened?" he asked again lowering the volume. She sat still and mute, with tears flowing down her cheeks. Not wanting to rehash none of it.

"Talk to me, baby." he said, putting on Pleasure's song *I Did You Wrong*. "I did you wrong, you did me wrong, I'll take you back you take me back." he crooned, loudly. Putting his heart into it.

"Are you tryna insinuate sumthin'?" she asked, changing subjects then glancing out the window. *Look at dat piquant face and those huge appealing eyes* . . . she thought to herself, taking a quick glance of him.

"No, baby, just listen' to the lyrics, dis' is my joint right hea'!" he said putting it on repeat. After the second time it played, she turned it off.

"Look, there's sumthin' you need to know." she said and then paused briefly.

"Okay, where do I start?" she said, biting down on her lip.

"Let's try the beginning, boo."

Her bottom lip trembled as she felt like she was reliving the moments. "Okay. Ricky, was molesting Junior so, Sonny killed him."

"Get the fuck out of here. I knew his fat, round ass was a pedophile from the way he used to look at you. So, I take it Sonny's in jail?"

"Is that a rhetorical question? What do you think?!" she shot.

"Well, we need to get 'em a lawyer, boo."

"You're a little too late."

"What's that 'pose ta' mean?!"

"It means you're too late. Flawless handled it already." she said, with her voice quickly shifting from calm to an attitude.

"Boo, I can't even find the right word to articulate how much I love you. Me leaving you was probably by far the hardest thing I've ever had to do. I regret not being there for you. I figured that if I kept in contact with you that would've gotten in the way of what I was trying do for us. Once again I fucked up." he shook his head, really feeling like shit.

"Overrated bullshit. But, that's not even it. How 'bout Monie, my cousin that you fucked, (putting emphasis on fucked) correction, I mean that just slurped on your dick, fuckin' killed Leigha along with her niggah, Rah Rah and his two nieces." he remained mute. "What's the matter? Did I pull your hoe card? Anyways, everybody knows she didn't act alone. Definitely, fucked up by any stretch of imagination."

"Oh my goodness, boo, I had no idea. I'm sorry, how long ago did dis' happen?"

"Several weeks ago. But, had you answered any of my calls, you would've known. I guess I was outta sight so outta mind, huh?" she yelled.

"I fucked up. I really fucked up. I admit. But what can I do, boo?!" he said, grabbing and embracing her. "My back was against the wall boo, my brother needed me. I mean, what was I pose' to do, you know how janky dat hoe ass Metro is. Boo, I'm sorry, I was tryna make some money for us!" she was sick of his lies and wanted to crack him, but the Ed Hardy cologne that he was wearing, made her pussy throb for some of his good dick. In her mind, she was thinking, *take me and have your way with me.*

When he kissed her, she shrunk back. "You know I'm that competent niggah, that you need in life." he whispered in her ear. Then he turned her face toward his with his pointer finger and leaned in and then planted gentle kisses on her lips. She surrendered and kissed him back, putting her tongue all down his throat. Smitten by his deep remorse, she wanted to say, *Baby, I forgive you, let's make this work.* But, she knew deep down it wouldn't. Not then or ever. Thankfully, she had Flawless to make her realize what Leigha

had been saying all along. But, at the same time, she knew you couldn't just listen to what nobody say. You had to fall and bump your head a couple of times. That she was. She started unbuckling his belt. He kissed her harder and deeper.

"Why would I give you another chance and for what?" she screamed. "Me to turn around and find out your dickin' down some other bitch?" she calmed down. He remained mute "Anyways, you see I've moved on." she screamed, breaking away.

"No, I don't see. Please stop all the screamin', boo. I'm like right here beside you." he whispered, seductively.

"Look, you do see! And if you got a problem with my tone then you can push on now. I can give a fuck less."

"Enlighten me becuz I don't think you've moved on." he said, hurt. Ignoring her smart response

"How dare you show up and pull some shit like dis'! We've been over for a long time. You knew it; I just hate dat it took me so long to come to dat realization. For so long, I was blinded by love, but when the smoke cleared, I was left standing alone and miserable. Living in dis' idealistic world. I believed any and everything under the sun dat you told me. Those days are long gone, now I have someone that loves me. Genuinely loves me." her eyes watered. "Dat man really touches every part of me," she rubbed her body.

"I want lose you!" he grabbed her head and stuck his tongue down her throat.

"One more thing, do you remember when you told me dat you had the swine flu and we couldn't go to Vegas?" she broke away.

"Oh my goodness, Neeyah. Here we go again with the dumb shit." he threw his hands up in the air.

"Just answer the question. It's just a simple damn question,"

"Yes, boo,"

"Well how bout dis' bitch named Shari gone have the audacity to ring my phone talkin' bout she was tryin' to get in touch wid you becuz she just had your baby."

"Get da fuck out of here wid dat hoe shit. Dat bitch is MR (mild retarded) and on medication and some mo' shit. Besides, I never fucked her ole washed up ass. All the other homies have. I'm not in that line up dis' time. Ok since we got dat established, what does that have to do with Vegas?"

"It has every fuckin' thing to do with it! Ok just hold on a moment," she got and went to her car.

"Where are you going, boo? That's a figment of dat bitch's imagination. I would never stick my dick in dat fuckin' mental case. Let alone bare back," he yelled out to her.

"Just hold your fuckin' horses,"

He watched as she walked up as if nothing was wrong and got in on the passenger's side. He threw his hands up like ok.

"Ok you wanna be with me, right?"

"Right,"

"Ok. So, Grievence look into my eyes and tell me the truth. Did you fuck Shari and did you take her to Vegas?"

"Hell naw, baby. Why would I take a slut puppy nowhere besides the woods or the park bench, to bend their ass over," he stared directly in her eyes without flinching.

"Umma pretend I didn't hear dat scandalous shit. But I love the way you lie."

"Oh boy,"

"All I can say is a picture is worth a thousand words," she smacked the picture on his forehead.

"What da fuck is dis?"

"A picture of you and Shari on the bed filled with rose petals,"

Dat shady sneaky bitch snapped my picture while I was sleep, he thought to himself. "I don't know what niggah she got laid up with her ass but dat isn't me. I wish dat was us. Instead, I was home barely able to hold my head up," he lied

"Come on now. I'm sure you can reach into your ass and find sumthin' better than dat," she shook her head. "That's your scandalous ass in the flesh, boo. Here's another flick she took of you playin' the slots. But anyways last but not least, here is a flick of your beautiful baby girl. Gerrica Da'shad Phillips. Lookin' just like Ms. Maryland. Straight keepin' your namesake alive." her eyes watered she tried her damnest to choke back the tears. Grievence turned his head and stared out of the window. "How did dis' happen? When every time we fucked you made sure I had my patch on in place. In fact, you was the one who use to change my patch every week to make sure the shit was affective. Like I was tryna trap you triflin' ass or some shit. I even offered to get the shot, and you was like no becuz I don't want you gaining hella weight. Now look at dis' bitch Shari, her ass weight double's mine and you got a baby with her. No better for you."

"Whatever,"

"Huh, huh," she pushed her ear out. "What's the matter? The cat got your tongue?"

"She isn't big. Her weight is more proportioned, thou." he let slip. She could've smacked his chocolate face, red.

"Um umma act like I didn't hear dat,"

"Baby, think about it for a minute, how can I have a baby by someone I never even stuck my anaconda in. What you think I got special powers to impregnate somebody just by lookin' at them?"

"Umm humm . . . you meant a baby snake." she held up her fingers and spreaded them a couple of inches apart. "The tiny green ones." she faked coughed and cleared her throat. She was lying but wanted to make him low as she did. "Dude, I'm so serious. I love the way you lie. It sounds so natural. Just look at the picture for heaven's sake,"

"Whatever. I am not lookin' at shit. It wasn't me damnit! I can see us on Maury and her sayin' I am one thousand percent sure he fathered my child and then Maury pulls out the manila envelope and read off the results . . . In the case of Gerrick Phillips, you are not the father and then her fat ass falling to the floor shaking. But, dat bitch done sold you a dream and you can't even spend it. That's fucked up. Don't trip doe; she got a beat down comin' for scandalizin' my name like she right,"

"Just at it!" she screamed.

"Ok," he snatched it from her. When he looked at it, it was like a glow of excitement rushed through his body. Whereas, it felt like a bolt of electricity flowing through her body as she stared at him. On the outside, she tried to hold it together.

"I'm glad I'm a father lookin' ass," she chuckled, trying her damnest to choke back the tears.

"For the last time I never fucked her. So there's no way I'm the father of dis' baby. Shari ass gone come up missin' when I see her ass,"

"Grievence add it up! From February the 28th, which by the way the date we was suppose be there, to December 8th when she was born. Look at the date at the bottom of the picture," she screamed. "I fuckin' hate your sorry ass," she screamed even louder.

"Baby it's not me," he grabbed her and kissed her.

"Stop it! You just spewing out all these overrated bullshit ass lies!" she yelled, breaking away from his tight grip. "I hate you Grievence! I regret da day I ever-laid eyes on your hoeish black ass! When *Love All Over Me* started playing, she forced herself up.

"No, baby don't answer it! I love you and I never realized how much until now. I wanna marry you girl." he said and tears fell down his face.

"Honey you can dry those crocodile tears, becuz dat shit isn't workin' on me. You see real tears dat I've cried for you, fell from my heart and covered my soul. Those fake ass tears your crying or falling from your eyes are just covering your face." she said, coldly. Wanting to hug and kiss him. That was the first time he ever cried in front of a female, or anybody period for that matter.

"Wow," he wiped his face. "Let's go back to the way things were before the party." he whispered, licking in her ear. For a moment, she almost got entwined in his web of lies. He lied so well. Even thou she had the proof in her hands she was a split second away from taking him back. Then her phone continued to ring, it reminded her why they were at the current place they were in their life.

"Ooops . . . saved by the bell," she said, and pushed him off of her.

"No, don't. Send dat square ass niggah to the voice mail. Please," he begged. "What about our spot, boo? I have all the bread for it!"

"That's what's up! Now you can go play house and daddy wid dat one big bitch, becuz dat was the curtain call boo! The curtains are officially closed," her eyes watered. She was hurt beyond all recognition.

"Baby, a house divided against itself cannot stand alone."

"What? You and I are done! Dis' shit with us is a wrap. Fuck all dat shit you talkin' becuz it sounds all Greek to me. There's not a snowball chance in hell that umma fall for your blatant lies! I'm so tired of going thru the motions with you and I'm proud to say I'm done with all dis' flip floppin' shit. And you know what, Grievence," she stared dead at him.

"What, baby?"

"Your leavin' me was a blessin' in disguise and lord knows I didn't feel dat way in the beginning. And furthermore, a leopard can't change the spots on its back."

"What are you trying to say, boo? Becuz I am a changed man," he lied, because it sounded good together.

"I guess what I'm tryna say is dat you have a seed and there's no going back to shit. Nothing from nothing leaves nothing! You didn't want me when you had me so, miss me!" she yelled, hopping out of the car. "How does it feel taste to have a dose of your own medicine? But hey at least, I learned from the best," she said and slammed his door so hard it nearly fell off the hinges.

"Where am I suppose to do or go, boo?" he shook his head slowly.

"Humm, let's see . . . how I can put dis' delicately," she put her pointer finger on her temple. "You can go to hell in a hand basket!" she yelled and turned to walked away.

"Please baby, don't!" he yelled out to her. "I'll give you all of my heart. That's right it's all yours. I know you want it!" he held his chest.

"You right I do. I want it on the end of a fuckin' spear!" she turned and stuck her head inside the car window. Before he could protest, she was gone.

"I guess back to the drawin' board, huh?" he screamed out to her. She didn't stop, she just kept right on pushing. "Fuck!" he said, hitting the steering wheel with both fists. The cold part was, he didn't want her but he just couldn't take seeing her in the arms of another man. "You never miss the water till the well runs dry. On my mama, I'm fuckin' Shari's ass up,"

"Come on Neeyah . . . breath . . .," she told herself. "Come on advance not regress. I know he's fine ass shit, but he's never gonna change." she said to herself, taking slow deep breaths. "Fuck it! Dat niggah, done hurt me countless times! I guess fairy tales don't come true and picket fences only exist in wonderland. I'm sick and tired of being sick and tired." she told herself as she kept stepping. She loved him to death and seeing him made all the feelings resurface yet she found strength to push on.

KARMA IS A B-I-T-C-H

It was a cool, breezy day in mid March. Swagga grooved to *Aston Martin Music* by Rick Ross, at the Taco Bell drive through, while the sun shone on his beautiful cocoa butter skin. He was so wrapped up into the song he didn't notice the all-black box Chevy following him. *When I'm alone in my room sometimes I stare at the walls, automatic weapons on the floor but who can you call, my down bitch, one who live by the code . . . he sang and bobbed his head to the music.* "He murdered dat shit," Swagga said out loud, while pulling up to the order post.

"Look at dis' stupid, pompus lookin' ass niggah, hea?" the boy on the passenger's side said.

"Yeah, niggah get them taco, burritos, or whatever the fuck, becuz it's gone be your last meal." Vengence pulled his hat down.

"I heard dat niggah be rollin' deep," a boy named Chronic, yelled from the back.

"My dude, you need to be easy while you all up in the Kool-Aid!" Vengence shrieked.

"I'm just sayin' I know ole' boy he be on some murderous shit!"

"I ain't trippin' off none of them fools. Anybody act up I'm gonna pull out the heater and blaze the shit up, you hurd me?"

"I know them niggahs too and they ain't to be fucked with!" Chronic instigated.

"Look, homie, keep lettin' your lip pop and umma let my glock stop all yo' thoughts!" he snapped. "If yo' ass didn't know how to crack codes and shit, I'll put yo' ass out in da boonies somewhere!"

"Dang, homie, ease up. I was just jokin'. My niggah, stop being so serious all da damn time!"

Whamp! Vengence turned around, reached in the backseat and went upside his head. "Ha! Ha! Ha! Ha! Is dat jolly enough for your bitch ass?!"

263

he asked, humorlessly. He started the car. "Unfortunately, I don't have time for your dumb ass frolickin'."

Chronic grabbed his face. "Whadda you do dat for man?!" Blood flowed heavily down his face. "Your ass is fuckin' loco."

"Yall niggahs is trippin'!" his homie said.

"Fuck dis' niggah going now?!" Vengence said out loud, tuning them both out.

After three hours of following Swagga, he finally hit the expressway heading toward Ann Arbor.

"Bingo!" Vengence said pulling up to a dimly lit street. Soon as Swagga got opened his front door, the smell from the burnt chicken hit him in the nose. So, he let up the windows upstairs and cracked the patio door.

"Okay, I need yall to wait by the door while I check the area out!" he said, cutting the lights off before approaching the murky area. He was dressed in an all-black hoodie and some black sweat pants. When he crept around the side of the house, he noticed Swagga was sitting in the recliner turned in the opposite direction.

"Fatal mistake!" he said to himself as he noticed the upstairs window up. Then, as he moved a little further around the back, he saw the patio door cracked. *Dis' has to be my luckiest day ever!* he said, silently to himself as he slowly slid the door open. Wide enough for him to get through. Once securely in, the first thing he did was scanned the room. Upon doing so, he saw Swagga's gun lying on the coffee table. *Dumb ass niggah!* he thought as he crept slowly behind the recliner. Where he sat chopping it up with Deuces.

"What up, doe?" he said, putting the gun to his head.

"What da fuck!" Swagga screamed, dropping the phone and going under his shirt.

"Cuzo, you aight, hello hello!" Deuces was screaming into the phone.

"Whatcha lookin' for yo' deuce deuce, cuhz?!" Vengence screamed. Then he snatched the gun off the table, sending rippling chills down Swagga's spine. The gun belonged to Angie. She never knew that he even had it.

"Why? I fed you, niggah and dis' how you repay me? I see yo' ass couldn't bake da cake, so you gonna try to take it, huh?!"

"Interestin' choice of words, becuz if I could recall about seven years ago, dis' shit happened to me 'cept for dis' time we playin' switch!" he jerked the skully off his head.

"Bones!" he shot flabbergasted. He knew he would see Swagga again.

"You're so fuckin' smart. Karma is a bitch, isn't it? Although, Bones died when you crossed me. I bet your ass is thinkin' I should've murked your

ass when I had the chance. You're right you should've! I can't say the same thing for your hoe ass!" he screamed, pistol-whipping him. "I'm just here to get what you took from me all those years and more. You don't even wanna know how I had to bring da street sweeper out and murk da connect and his puss ass homies. They were plannin' to mangle my ass, so I had to blow their shit off first. See, fair exchange is no robbery. Oh yeah, I paid the homie Chubby, Stub—whateva da fuck his name is—to act like we were homies, but I didn't know that fat fuck from a can of paint! I'm a genius the way I devised dis' shit, huh? I should get a standing ovation. How 'bout a round of applause." he roared with laughter, as he clapped.

"Very electrifyin'. I hate to break up your elated moment you're having but, whateva niggah do what you gotta do, I'm not giving your snake ass shit. It's whateva, niggah!"

"That's how you feel, huh?!" he yelled, shooting him in his kneecap.

"Your hoe ass still ain't playin enough music to make me dance, becuz you see me," he said, pointing to himself. "I don't dance to nobody's tune but my very own, so go ahead and kill me, I done seen, and done everything anyway," he laughed, with blood flowing profusely all over his shag carpet.

"Oh, well see about that," Vengence screamed, bitting down on his lip and squeezing the trigger shooting him in the other leg. Swagga immediately fell to the ground.

"Go ahead, finish the job." he said, coughing up blood and lying on the floor shaking.

"I see your pie ass is dancin' now, muthafucka!" he screamed. "I'm gonna give you one more chance to take me to your safe!"

"Do you actually think umma take yo' bitch ass to my safe? You're the fuckin' genius so devise a way to find it and crack the code." he chuckled. "I'm only in my late twenties and I'm a self-made millionaire. You can take my shit, but your busta ass still wouldn't be shit, but a busta!" he laughed and spit out blood. Swagga knew he was in a very death-defying situation; where he knew he wasn't gonna live to tell about it. But, still wasn't gonna die a sucka.

"That's where you're wrong at, you was a millionaire. Oh, dis' is business and not personal big homie!" he said, squeezing the trigger unloading every bullet in him. He knew that Swagga wasn't gonna budge. Vengence was very disturbed young man. Nobody could even joke with him. It really fucked him up in the head when Swagga switched up on him. Once Vengence gave the ok, the other two boys came in and ransacked the place. Only to

find out there wasn't shit in there but a couple of grand Swagga didn't shit where he laid his head. The only other person that knew where his safe was located was Grievence. Which was nowhere in sight.

Deuces sat frantically on the edge of the bed trying to figure out who Bones was before the phone went dead.

"Bones! Bones, damn that name doesn't ring a bell-fuck!" he screamed, pacing back and forth. Then he got on the phone and called Grievence.

"What's up, my nigg?!"

"Niggah! Niggah! You need to get your ass back to da D. fast, dawg! I'm tellin' you," Deuces screamed.

"What's wrong, family? Where's my brother?!"

"Just get yo' black back out here, man. I can't talk over the phone, man!"

"Deuces?!" he yelled. "Don't do dis', man. Just tell me where's my brother. Where's Swagga, man?!"

"Aight, dawg, listen to me. I think someone's up at his house, and I think they may've shot him!"

"Whhhhhhhhaaaaaaat? Noooooooo. Don't tell me that shit, dawg. No, not my brother. How do you know?"

"Becuz we was choppin' it up on the phone when I heard some commotion in the background. I know I did hear him call some cat by the name of Bones, but that was it before the phone went out!"

Grievence gave Deuces the address to where Swagga lived. He headed straight to the airport and waited five intense hours for the flight to Detroit to board. Every minute that went by was very pivotal. He couldn't dare go home and face his mom.

When Deuces arrived at his house, the door was open. His worst fears was confirmed as soon as he stepped though the door. He stumbled on the most horrific crime scene. It was his cousin. His head was almost decapitated from his mangled-up body. He dropped down to his knees.

"Who did dis' to you, cuhz? You didn't deserve dis'!" he said, tearing up and scanning the scoured house. When he got up to leave, he noticed a black-and-brown skully lying near the sofa. "Dis' look awful familiar!" he picked it up. On his way out the door, he took the pair of gloves from his pocket and picked the gun up that was used to kill him. He couldn't afford to be around when the cops came because he was fresh off the papers and wasn't trying get hung for a murder charge. He headed back to the Trap, where he found Trigga drowning his sorrows with a whole bottle of Hennessey. Trigga knew Bread was gone forever and wasn't nothing he could do but mourn

him low key. Stubby was in the corner, smoking some chronic and playing Grand Theft Auto 4 on his Xbox 360.

"Fuck wrong with you? Cupcakin' ass niggah must be in love and shit listenin' to that hoe ass baby making music. Actin' all antisocial and shit!" Stubby teased.

"I'm on one right now, dawg."

"Clearly."

"Somebody killed my cousin! They shot him," Deuces yelled, busting in the door.

Three and half hours later, Grievence got off the plane. Enterprise was there waiting on him. After he handled his business with them, he hit the expressway. Pedal to the floor, straight to Ann Arbor. As soon as he reached his brother's house, he threw the car in park and got out. When he walked up to the house it was just as it was when Deuces left. Soon as he pushed the door back, he ran and fell to his cold, stiff bother's side. Tears flowed abundantly down his face. Rigor mortis had already set in. "Umma find the mark ass bustas who done dis to you, Bruh. If it's the last thing I do.

I love you, man." he grabbed his shirt and squeezed it. He couldn't even see straight. He couldn't believe that his only brother was gone and not coming back. "Man, I regret they came out with dat bitch ass law, becuz you would've still been in prison instead of here lyin' with no heat flowin' thru your veins. Why did dis' happen, man, why? Umma personally kill whoeva had sumthin' to do with dis'. On Mama!" he said, wiping the tears of anger, hurt, and confusion away. Then he called the police. When the police got there, they wanted to take him in for questioning. But, after he showed proof he had just got in town, they him let go. He went straight to Trap, smashing. Deuces was loading up his AK-47 and Swagga's .22.

"My brother is dead! My only brother is really out of the game of life forever. Deuces, man, why didn't you call the Narco's, man? He lyin' there all stiff and shit,"

"Dawg, I thought about dat shit and then I said them crackers will try and pin dat shit on me knowin' I was fresh off the papers, so I dipped off!"

"You right, man!" Grievence put on a pair of gloves.

"That's fucked up. Let's go get them hoe-ass niggahs, man. We gotta find them! Every minute we wait is crucial!" Vengence said with no remorse.

"Yeah, man, I got that niggah's beanie 'cuhz. I know my cousin didn't wear no punk ass shit like dis'!" he held it up.

Fuck! Vengence said, inwardly. He could've shitted bricks knowing how he carefully for years meticulously planned for that day. He decided to still show his face so he could keep tabs on Grievence so he could take him straight to the money. He planned it so when it was all said and done, Grievence would be the next victim, or so he thought. Grievence's mind started racing a mile a minute, then a light bulb went on his head. He decided against speaking on it. Everything was clearer. Finally, he put all the pieces to the puzzle together. Bones was his homeboy from way back when. Although Swagga didn't speak too much about it, he did remember him saying that he had robbed his homie Bones.

Upon looking closely at the beanie, he knew that it belonged to Vengence because he was the only niggah probably in the entire city of Detroit that wore that type of beanie.

"Okay, you're right. We do need to get on our shit befo' them niggahs get away!" Grievence grabbed the .22 from Deuces, and pointing it towards Vengence—"Bones!" he yelled, as four shots rang out and then he turned to Stubby. "Stubby, how did you say you knew dis' niggah, again?"

"I didn't!" he let slip out.

"Funny, becuz my brother told me you introduced him to him!"

"W-w-well." he stuttered, "I kinda didn't know him. See, he paid me ten racks to say I knew him. I figured easy money, you understand, right? I mean, I didn't think none of dis' shit was gonna go down. True story!"

"Well, that's your problem homie! You didn't think, and your need for greed is gonna be da death of you. On my brother! We gone do dis' mob style." he said, squeezing the trigger. Soon as the first shot pierce through his skin, blood splashed all over Trigga's face.

"Come on, man! The Narco's are comin'," Deuces yelled, taking the gun from him and threw it on the sofa. The only prints that was on the gun was Swagga's and Vengence. Which was both dead.

After Grievence went to Swagga's stash crib, he gave Trigga the bricks for his loyalty and told him to clean and ditch the other weapons in Lake Michigan.

"Okay, fam, we'll be in touch. Don't be surprised when one day I be like, what up, doe. I'm on my way to Calli!" he said, giving him a pound.

"You should do dat, ain't shit out here!"

"I fezell you, mayne!"

"Well, you got my number. You know my brother told me that you were a real soldier to these streets, and that's why he liked you!"

"Yeah, loyalty first. Death before dishonor. That's how I gets down! You see the tat," he pushed his sleeve. "It's all love. I live by dis' shit daily."

Two hours later, Grievence and Deuces hopped on the next plane headed to Calli. He was satisfied with the a little over a million dollars in cash. He slid Deuces two hundred racks and gave Trigga, the five bricks.

"You know, man, why you bullshittin' I met dis' one dude from Vegas dat says he killin' them out there!"

"Word?!"

"Word, niggah. The homie says that he on that pimpin' shit. Dat niggah is paid and some mo' shit. He says all you have to do is walk the strip, and the hoes will come to you like you're a magnet!"

"Sounds interestin'!"

Back in Calli, Neeyah laid on her bed. Wishing the day would come sooner when she got her money. Her phone rang, it was Flawless telling her that the lawyer said they found technicalities in her brother's case and that he was gonna be exonerated.

"I'm so happy, baby, I also owe you an apology. Honest to God, I haven't talked to him in over two and half months!"

"Don't trip, baby girl, you good!"

"It's you dat I need and want. I gave dat niggah ample times to act right. He gave me no act right, so I moved on. You make me smile, laugh, I'm so happy when I'm around you it's like I feel so safe. Your whole aura. Do you believe me?!"

"I believe you, baby. But honestly it sounds like you're tryna convince yourself."

"When am I gonna see you? Can I come to your hotel?"

"Actually, I didn't check into a hotel. I just went to the airport!"

"Airport?!" she screamed.

"Yeah, baby girl, I felt my trigger finger itching. So, to avoid all problems, I just left."

"I understand!" she said, dryly.

"I put a couple of racks in your Bank of America account. Let me call you later." he hung up the phone, changed his number, and never called her again.

"Money ova bitches," he screamed. His life was way too important.

When he hung up, she was stunned that he would just hang up her like that. But, at the same time, she was happy to have some good news about her brother. So she rushed to tell her mom, who wasn't even in her room.

"Let me get a forty!" The woman said, very fast.

"You look familiar. Don't I know you?" he asked looking at her in the face.

"Look, I didn't come here for no fuckin' reunions nor to conversate!" she snapped, handing him the money.

He handed her the crack. "Here you go. Oh, I know where I know you from now. You Sonny's mom, huh?!"

"Give me my shit, you don't know me!" she said, snatching the drugs out of his hand and dropping one. "You see what you did you little nickel-and-dimer!" she screamed, dropping to her knees. She was wearing a nightgown and a black hoodie. She scrambled around in the road. Soon as she found it she scampered away. When she got home, she found a note on her nightstand that read . . . *Don't look at where you fell, instead, look where you slipped. In other words, don't look at your mistakes instead look at what caused you to make the mistakes . . . I love you unconditionally mommy.* It was obvious that she was on drugs.

It had been a couple of days since Angie heard from Swagga. She tried calling him on his phone, but the number wasn't working. So, she went to the office to take her name off the lease. When she gave her name to the apartment manager, unbeknown to her, they called the cops. When they arrived, they took her in for questioning. After they interrogated her, she gave them Swagga's real name.

"Are you sure he did dis?"

"Yeah, I'm positive it was his dope house. Matter of fact, he told me he was gonna do it when he left my house last night!" she lied, wanting Swagga to rot in prison for the rest of his life. "If yall need me to testify, I'll gladly do it!" she continued.

"Are you sure it was last night when you seen him, ma'am?"

"Yes, sir, I can swear on a stack of Bibles it was last night becuz I had a romantic night set up for him, and he told me he had to go handle dat!"

"Which was going to kill the men, right?"

"Yes. Right, right." she agreed.

"Let me ask you, do anybody use your cell phone besides you?"

"No, never. My cell phone always stays with me. In fact, you'll never catch me without it!" she said, holding up her phone.

"So you say you were home all night waitin' on Antonio's arrival, huh?"

"That's right, I didn't leave for nuthin' at all!"

"Let me ask you another question, do you by any chance own a gun?"

"Hello? Isn't dis' the murder mitten, dirty glove city?"

"Just answer the question! Is that a yes or no ma'am?"

"Yes! But, I can assure you it's registered and locked away in my safe."

"Well, ma'am, we hate to inform you that Antonio's been dead since Tuesday, so we're gonna have to take you into custody. You are under the arrest for two murders that happened in your apartment! We found your registered gun at the crime scene! The gun may've been used in the murder of Antonio as well. That means three capital murders; you are looking at the death penalty, sweetheart!"

Her mouth hit the floor. "You guys are lying, you just want me to concoct another story!" she said, shaking uncontrollably like a leaf on a tree.

"Do you have any idea who I am?"

"Yeah, Detroit's Finest!" she said, with her voice dripping with sarcasm.

"I'm an homicide detective," he glanced around and seen it on the door.

He handed her the newspaper. "Here, ma'am, I think you should take a look at dis'!"

"What's dis'?!" she jerked it out of the officer's hand. Then low and behold, she saw on top of the *Detroit Free Press* in big bold letters: Released Just a Couple of Months Ago From a Ten-Year Bid, Kingpin Antonio "Swagga" Was Found Dead Yesterday in His Home in Ann Arbor!" she quickly tried to change her story. It was ignored. "You guys can't charge me with murder. No possible way," she screamed out.

"Who are we again? I do believe we have the authority to do whatever the hell we wanna do and you can't do anything about it," he said. Then they read her rights to her and booked her. "Now, we gave you chance after chance to tell the truth. We asked for facts, ma'am. Instead, what we get? Downright lies!" he made a fist and banged he hand down on the table. She nearly jumped out of her skin.

"Why? Why am I being arrested? I'm no murderer!" she yelled.

"Because, ma'am, your cell phone placed you at the scene last night, around the time your neighbor reported hearing gunshots." he said. Then she thought back when she was riding through trying to spy on Swagga when she got a call from her homeboy that was trying to cut something.

"Aww damn!" she cried. *How did dis' happen? Swagga is suppose to be the one alive and suffering; not me. He deserves to be rotting. And his ass skated thru life.* She thought, while walking down the long creepy hallway to the holding cell.

"Welcome, bitch. Mi casa is su casa!" someone yelled. Angie busted out crying.

"Awww, don't cry. Mama's coming for you, baby," a big burly butch dike yelled through the bars. Angie froze and looked at her and then to the door that was separating her from freedom.

"I can't do dis' she dropped down to her knees."

"Put her in here," someone yelled thru the bars. Suddenly, it was like she was in a crowded room and all she heard was tiny voices. Like thousands of them. Nobody could hear her. It was then and there, her mind had left her body. She was in the world and didn't even know it. She had gone the only other place she could go, and that was crazy. Later, tests concluded that she indeed had regressed to the mind of a preschooler.

FOUR MONTHS LATER

Grievence jumped into his brand-new two door black beamer coupe, let his top back, and headed straight to Vegas to meet Deuces. No sooner than he slid in the Young Money cd, his cell phone started vibrating.

"What's up, baby girl?!"

"Hey, you, I was just callin' to tell you that Sonny was acquitted yesterday, so he's here. My brother is home! I can finally see the light at the end of the tunnel. Thank you, Lord!" she screamed excitedly into the phone.

"That's what's up! You can see light, huh?" he said, tugging on his seat belt.

"Yep, and the good thing is, it's not a train."

"I heard that. I'm happy for you guys, so how is your mom taking the news, I mean yall ain't poppin' bottles or nuthin'?!" he asked, looking in his side mirror and making sure it was safe to switch lanes.

"Unfortunately, my mom isn't joining us, she's in rehab—"

"Rehab?!" he yelled, cutting her off.

"Yeah, she had been thru a lot the last couple of months that drove her to drugs! I never thought in a million years that she would have that monkey on her back, wow!" she said, with her voice quickly switching to a sad low tone.

"Dang, bay, I had no idea you were going thru so much!" he turned the volume down on the radio so he could give her his undivided attention.

"Don't trip, it could've been a whole lot worse." she said, having a flashback of all the signs that she had given her but she'd overlooked.

"Bay, bay, you okay!"

"I'm okay!" she said.

"You sure?"

"Yeah, I was just thinkin' back, nuthin' important, doe. I'm being selfish, how are you doing?"

"You good. Day by day is all we can take it. Maryland done lost what little mind she had left. I still can't believe my right hand is gone." he sniffed. Neeyah remained quiet while he spoke. "But shid, you know if you need me, I'm here for you!" he continued after a brief pause.

"Amen. Thanks, it means a lot to know dat and likewise!"

"Hold on a moment!" he glanced at his phone to see who was beeping in. "313 Area Code," he said to himself as the phone was reading missed call.

"Hey, don't trip, I'll call you later. I just wanted to give you the good news."

"Okay, fa sho!" he ended the call. His phone started vibrating again.

"Who dis'?!" he said, not recognizing the number.

"Hello, I tryna reach to Gerrick!"

He remained silent and was about to hang up at thought of someone knowing his government name.

"Hello." the voice on the other end called out again.

"Look, lady—"

"Listen, baby, dis' is Lisa's mom!" she cut him off. "I got your number from your mom, but umma keep dis short and to the point," she paused and fanned herself for a minute. "About two months ago, Lisa killed her boyfriend. Yesterday she was involved in an accident in jail. Just hours before she was about to be released on bail." she cried, uncontrollably.

"She's alright, isn't she?!" he yelled. "Hello!" he screamed. "She's gonna be alright isn't she?!"

"No, baby, I'm afraid to tell you my baby was killed in a riot becuz of a silly food incident."

"Nooooooooooooo!" he yelled, accidentally throwing the phone out of the window. "Why? Why? Why? Not her to lord, not Trees!" he screamed at the thought of losing the only woman he ever loved. For she touched him in a way no other woman could or begin to understand.

WHAT'S DONE IN THE DARK

"Oh shit." Yatta screamed out in pain. "Damn, I have been in dis' punk ass bed for eighteen hours straight. Go get dat nurse, bitch so she can get dis' stubborn muthafucka out."

"Calm down, boo. You'll be fine." her friend Sequoia assured her.

"Calm down my ass! Dis' shit hurt. Bitch you done had six c-sections. It's not like you feel my pain." she snapped.

On the other side of town, Amber hopped in the shower.

"Reneeeee," she screamed.

"What up doe?"

"I think my water just broke," she wobbled down the hall screaming, soak and wet.

"Oh hell! My ass can't deliver no damn baby. Hurry up and slip on your dress and let's go." she rushed. Fifteen minutes they arrived at the hospital.

"Hurry," Amber fussed and cussed.

"Them pains tearing dat ass up, huh?" Renee asked. "Do you want me to call your baby's father?"

"Funny," she smiled. *My baby's father is your baby's father, bitch*, she wanted to say. "You look a lil pudgy yourself. You sure you don't low key, got a bun in the oven?" Amber joked.

"Girl, I can assure you dis' is just fat. My big ass need to be on somebody's diet and some mo' shit!" she squeezed her stomach. "But, I just thought you wanted him here. Well, I'm about to go call Amauri to come get Kamauri's bad ass. I'll be right back."

"Nah, fuck him. I'm cool," she flailed her arms out.

"Where da hell is Amauri?" Renee wondered. After she called and left several messages on his phone. Twenty minutes later, Amber gave birth to a 8lbs, baby boy. "Oh my god he looks just like Kamauri. Wow, you must have hated my baby." Renee said, excitedly.

"Yeah, bitch if you only knew why my baby looks just like your daughter you wouldn't be all geeked and hyped." she muttered, under her breath. She hated her sister with every fiber of body. *Dis' is gone be fun watchin' your ass agonize in pain and let's see what you're gonna do when you find out dat your precious Amauri is fathered my child as well. I think umma name him Amaurese* she thought, while she mischievously smiled at her.

"Sis, what do you think about dis', only because I love my little Kamauri so much, umma name my lil stanka butt, Amaurese?"

"That's beautiful. I'm sure Kamauri would love dat!"

An hour and a half later, Amauri arrived at the hospital and went straight to the nurse's station. By the time he made it there, Yatta had also given birth to a 6lb baby boy.

"Do you know what his name is gonna be?" the nurse asked.

"Yeah. Amauri Jr." she cheesed. The nurse stared at her waiting for the last name. "My baby is da business and his dad is too. Oh did I mention he was a paid niggah?" she boasted and bragged.

"Ok. I'm waitin' on the last name. Anytime miss,"

"Oh you can just leave dat part blank. When I find it out I'll come back and add it."

"That's so sad. How do you sound? Tell me how and da hell are you gone name a baby a junior and don't even know da daddy's last name? Are you sure that's his first damn name? Excuse me if I'm a little baffled here,"

"Uh huh, I don't even pitch in your league, baby. Becuz what's sad is having six kids and six different baby daddies. And you can't pay neither one to come around and visit them demon ass kids of yours. Now that's what's sad. I know if you knew better you would do better," she shot.

"Skeezer, what you think you made history or sumthin' becuz you supposedly had dat Rico Suave niggah's baby? If so I hate to burst your bubble, becuz you didn't make history, Mary did when she had Jesus. Why you over there all smiley and tryna blast me." Sequoia shot and gathered her things to leave.

"Bitch, what da fuck you mean, supposedly? You got me fucked up. I knows who my baby daddy is unlike you. You must be jealous aren't you." she chuckled. "Hell yeah you are,"

"Please take in consideration dat you've just given birth, ma'am!" the nurse said, trying to calm them down.

"Who da fuck is you talkin' to, bitch? I'm a grown ass woman?" Yatta screamed. The nurse pushed her glasses up on her nose and stood frozen

staring at Yatta with her eyes bulging out of her head. As if she hadn't fully grasped what Yatta said.

"I'm sorry. Maybe you didn't hear me the first time. Would you like me to repeat it?" she shot, sarcastically.

"No ma'am, dat want be necessary. I understood the first time." The nurse turned to leave. Yatta stopped her. Yatta was no longer the shy Yatta, she was the confident Yatta. She had gained much courage after beating Amauri at his own game.

"Look at dis' bitch who done grew some balls overnight. But you better count your lucky stars were in a hospital."

"Looka here you skeezer, just becuz I'm laid in dis' hospital bed don't mean a fuckin' thang, becuz dis' nurse bitch can carry my baby da fuck up outta here and you can get these hands!" she said, and then shifted her attention to the nurse. "I'm sorry dat is so not in my character, it must've been the meds."

"I understand." the nurse forced a tight smile to her face.

"I'll see your punk ass when you get home and don't try to come with no shit like I just had a baby becuz I'm not gone have no sympathy on dat ass! A bitch like me don't give a damn about no stitches, staples, or whatever da fuck becuz trust and believe wherever I see you, your ass you will be leaving the scene on a gurney. I don't give a damn if it's in church, dat ass is mine," Sequoia turned to leave. "And I'm just curious to know you funky, bitch—"

"Funky?" Yatta cut her off.

"Yes, funky," she held up her hand and closed it. "I hate to be the barrier of bad news, but you do the math, Victoria Secret plus musk on top of dirt, doesn't equal fresh and clean, boo. With dat big ole tainted ass fish pussy. Dat shit smells just like it done rotten, cooked, and burned."

"Bitch, I'm Irish fresh and clean. And fuck you! You can just eat a fat dick with them big dick suckers of yours." she yelled out to her.

Just as Amauri was walking to Amber's room, which was a couple doors down he heard her say, "But yea like I was saying, his name is Amauri Jr." she held her hand up.

"Dat sound like Yatta's ass." he said, doubling back.

"Bitch," he screamed and pushed the nurse out of the way.

"Say hey to your daddy," she held the baby up.

"On second thought, umma stay and watch dis' bitch get her eyes stomped out." Sequoia smiled. "That's right no better for you bitch. And umma still tap dat ass when I see you on GP,"

"Bitch are you slow? You got me fucked up." he ran over and choked her out. She put the baby back in the bassinet just in a nick of time. Luckily, an armed guard was walking by.

"Security," she yelled when she saw him. He rushed in and handcuffed him.

"Aye yo . . . Amauri, what's your last name." she called out after she got her breath back.

"It's go suck an aids dick and die slowly, BITCH!" he said, before being escorted out of her room to an empty one right beside hers to wait for the cops arrival. He never made it to Amber's room as planned.

"I don't know where Amauri's ass is but—"

"Probably somewhere hibernatin' in somebody's pussy." Amber cut her off, as she smacked her lips and rolled her eyes.

"I'm not gonna rule dat out. But look, I wanted to tell you sumthin' that's been eating at me for quite some time. Since you're grown and have your own child makes me wanna share dis' with you even more," she took a deep breath. "I don't even know where to start but I do know I need to get you to promise me dis' forever is to stay between us."

"Listen sister, me and you us never apart . . . I cross my heart and hope to die. I would never tell nobody. What is it?" she lied.

"It's just dat I can't even find the right words to say,"

Just spit the shit out, bitch so I can have your ass in my back pocket. Becuz all dis' should I tell or should I not tell, is for the birds! she thought, looking at her. "Take your time, boo," she said. Tears started streaming down Renee's face.

"Ok, I shouldn't even be puttin' all dis' on you. You just had a baby for goodness sake."

"Stop ramblin' on and on about the shit and just spit it out already. You acting to slow. Damn, what da fuck," she muttered to herself when Renee turned her head. Her patience was wearing thinner by the second. And it was beginning to show.

"I'm sorry, you just had a baby."

Ughhh, if dis' bitch don't come out with it umma scream . . . Amber thought to herself. "Boo I'm ok, just worried about my big sister. Like I said take your time, I have all day. It's not like I got somewhere to be,"

"Ok, it started when I was around five I think, but when mommy was working night shift and daddy started bathing me. Then he started touching me and eventually it progressed to me doing other things," she said, as tears

streamed relentless down her face. "Like engaging in oral and then eventually on to sex. No one ever knew." her voice cracked as the painful words rolled off her tongue. When she looked over at Amber, she was smiling from ear to ear at the idea of her being in so much agony. Amber didn't realized she had even saw her. "Wait a minute; I think my mind is playin' tricks on me. Are you seriously smiling, doe? Because I don't see a muthafuckin' thing funny," she snapped and hurriedly wiped her eyes from her burry vision.

"I'm just shakin' my head. Dis' smile is like I'm appalled type shit. I can't believe dis', so tell me one more time so I can make sure I heard you correctly the first time," she said, because she wasn't listening to one word that was said. All she could see was her holding her stomach in pain. In her mind, she was hoping that she was diagnosed with last stage cancer or something. That way she wouldn't have to formulate a way to kill her and get away with it. All kinds of things were running through her mind. "Sorry to make you dredge dis' up. From the bottom."

"Ok baby girl, I really don't wanna go thru all the agony of starting over umma just say dis', I was raped incalculable times by our father. Slam up to I was 17 years old." she cried. This time Amber listened and it hit her like a ton of bricks. "I couldn't tell anyone because he said he would kill you and I felt it was my job to protect my younger sister,"

"I'm so sorry," Amber began to cry. This time it was sincere. "I'm so sorry; you have no idea how much. I'm sorry for it all," she cried louder. *What have I done? What have I done,* she repeated in her head. It was then she realized how much her sister really loved her. "Umma kill dat sick son of a bitch, he don't deserve to live," she snatch the IV out and tried to get out of the bed.

"No you can't," Renee stopped her. "He's on his death bed. He's getting his slowly, but surely," she whimpered.

"Come here sis," Amber welcomed her into her opened arms. "Umma help you get thru dis' I promise." she rubbed her back. "His ass is grass when I get home it's gone be like B.I.G bring dat ass to me! I'm not having no sympathy on none. He's not getting his fast enough, sick fuck! What about mom?"

"Well mom knew for quite some time and she chose to stick by her husband."

"So, you're sayin' dat bitch handed you to his ass on a platter and then shared her bed with him at night?" Amber shook her head.

"Basically. One day she came home from work early and caught him on top of me in their bed. I'll never forget how she walked in the room in

said *Sweetheart they let,* and stopped in mid sentence right there. I looked up at her with puppy dog eyes, you know like happy my mom's here and she's gone call the police type shit, while I was laying there defenseless. I was so happy becuz mom didn't say anything she closed the door. I just knew at any moment the police was gonna be there and haul his ass off to rot. He jumped his happy ass up and darted out the room behind her." Amber cried silent and listened at her. "Ok so ten minutes go by, and there was no cops banging down the door. Half hour goes by, and decide to stand in the window and wait becuz I just knew dat my mother was gonna pro—" she broke down and couldn't even finish her sentence.

"Take your time. Take your time," Amber rubbed her back.

"Ok," she inhaled and exhaled. "Where was I?"

"You were sayin' how our lovin' trifling' mother suppose to protect us."

"Oh yeah. I just knew she was gonna protect me. I just knew his ass was toast. So an hour goes by, mom comes in my room and says dat I should try to get some sleep."

"Dat bitch, she deserves to get what he gets. I had no idea."

"Yeah. Hold on get dis', I hop up after her to plead with her and then I see him hanging his head going into the bedroom. I'm like what da fuck. I think I was around 15 or 16 but after dat I ended up pregnant and I called Amauri up and had sex with him about 4 times so he would think I was pregnant by him. I even convinced myself she looked just like him and even convinced him of the very same thing. I was happy and relieve to say the least. Until dis' day I never breathe a word at all to protect you. It was you and me against the world. I couldn't leave you with them monsters so the very same thing could happen to you."

"Dat kinda stuff only supposes to happen on TV." she cried.

"I know,"

"So Kamauri isn't Amauri's? She's our father's?" she gasped, loudly. By then the cops had arrived and they were walking by when he heard her.

"Noooooooooo," he screamed. He tried to break away but he couldn't.

"Dat sounded like Amauri," they both looked at each other. Then Renee hopped up to see.

"Amauri?" she yelled out. Puzzled to see him led away in handcuffs. She saw them waiting for the elevators and she ran over to him. By the time she made it over to where they were standing, he was getting on it. When he turned around, his water-filled eyes met hers and then he just fell to his knees, as the doors was closing. He was too hurt to say anything and it was

written all over his face. Her heart shattered because she knew he had found out that her baby wasn't his. He was getting his get back and it felt like he was dying. His precious Kamauri, was his in every way accept biological. Renee too fell down to her knees and screamed out, "My baby," and then fainted. She wasn't at all talking about Kamauri. What she didn't get a chance to tell Amber was that she was around twenty-five weeks pregnant by Amauri. She figured that the proof would be in the pudding sooner, rather than later. Thirty minutes later, she went into cardiac arrest and they had to do an emergency c-section to take the baby. They couldn't get Renee back, but they were successfully able to take her beautiful baby girl. She weighed around 2 pounds and a half. It was just too much for Renee to bare. She died of a broken heart.

"Where is Renee's ass?" Amber glanced up at clock on the wall. "Her ass been gone for a cool minute," she said, pressing the button for the nurse and then a sudden onset of guilt and sadness washed over her entire body and when it did, she caught the chills.

"We'll be right in ma'am." she said, without giving her a chance to speak.

"Well damn, bitch give me a chance to tell you what I want first." she hissed and rubbed her arms. Ten minutes later, a nurse walked in.

"Are you related to the young lady dat was just in here with you less than an hour ago?"

"She's my sister, why?"

"Well I wanna first ask—"

"Where is she?" she cut her off and then she sat up and turned her feet off the side of the bed.

"Calm down ma'am, I'm just trying to figure out what led up the events that has just transpired,"

"Stop beatin' around the bush, bitch and tell me where's my sister!" Amber sneered.

"There's no easy way to say to say dis' but to come right out and say it. Your sister went into cardiac arrest and we were unable to save her. However sumthin'good did come from dis—"

"How da fuck can sumthin' good come from my sister being dead? Tell me dat!" Amber screamed and fell back on the bed. "Get out! Get out!" she screamed to the top of her lungs. Two other nurses rushed in. One sedated her and the other one told the other nurse to let her rest. Six hours later, Amber came to.

"Ok maybe I was dreaming it was all a nightmare." she tried to convince herself. "Yeah, that's what it was," she said and then looked over to the left

and seen a baby in the room with her. She didn't know whose baby it was all she knew was it wasn't her boy. "Oh lord they done switched my baby," she screamed. The same nurse ran in. "You?"

"Ma'am let me explain," Amber sobbed. Something told her to calm down and listen. She did. "Ok, as I was sayin' earlier, dis' is your sister's baby. We saved her. Dis' little sweet pea is the good that came from it. Your sister would live on thru her and your baby is getting circumcised as you okayed and I will bring him in as soon as it's complete. Again, sorry for your lost." she said and then turned and walked through the door and closed it behind her.

"Renee you better hope you're dead becuz umma kill you. I knew you were preggo's," she smiled. "How did it all come to dis'? In less than 7 hours, how?" Amber whimpered and walked over to the baby. "I promise I will love you like my very own. I cross my heart and hope to die. Just like my sister, your mom did for me. I also had a baby born today. That's right, you guys were born on the same day. His name is Renez' Lamar and your name is Renee' Lamarshia, after me and your mommy," she smiled and rubbed the incubator. She was hurt terribly and all the resentment was turned into love. For a split second, she had the sister she never had and it felt good. "Wow, I guess the power of life and death is spoken through the tongue. Grandma always said be careful what you ask for. Amauri will never know my baby is his. And as promise, bad as I want to but I will never breathe one word of what happened to her. I owe my sister dat much."

EXCERPTS FROM

"ONLY DA STRONG CAN SURVIVE"

"ONLY DA STRONG
CAN SURVIVE"

"Emily, wake up and pack your shit. Today is your lucky day!" the nasty guard, Beverly yelled into the slit in Emily's door.

"What? Wait, am I going home?" she called out.

"Let me rephrase that statement I made earlier, what I meant to say is, it's your unlucky day becuz, you're headed to PBSP (Pelican Bay State Prison) to serve the remainder of your time. 15 years baby!" she yelled, with a big smile plastered across her face.

Emily hopped up out of bed and headed to the glass wall. "That can't be right. It must be some sort of mistake."

"Oh, It's right darling. In fact, you have exactly 15 minutes to be packed and in the lobby. The van is waitin'. Believe me when I tell you he doesn't look like a happy camper."

"Fifteen minutes? Tell me how and da hell am I supposed to be packed, dressed, and out front by then?" Emily yelled.

"Ma'am that's your problem not mines. While, you're standin' here protesting you need to be packing."

"Dis shit is torture and you're enjoying every single moment of it. Aren't you?" she screamed, and banged on the glass wall. "I can see straight thru that façade of a frown you're displaying on your face. You wretched, dog shit smellin, miserable bitch! "Emily yelled out to her. Beverly turned back with a big Kool-Aid smile plastered across her face.

"Your life is my entertainment, sweetheart. You loco fuck stick!" The truth was Beverly was a miserable soul who enjoyed every moment of someone's hurt or downfall. Every time opportunity presented itself for her to inflict pain, she would and it would be blissful for her. She didn't have any family members that had any dealings with her. So, she lived in

an apartment, along with her four dogs. When she got home and stepped one foot in the door, she had to be careful not to step in feces. The place was not suitable for no humans and since she didn't have a friend or person in the world, she got off on making others suffer. The truth to the matter was, Emily was indeed going home, but Beverly wanted to make her last minutes there hell.

"Ok dat bitch done fucked with me for the last time!" Emily muttered, pulling her hair back into a ponytail. She thought back on the day when they were inside the activity room, Beverly brought her and six other patients their evening snacks. It consisted of grapes, crackers, and chocolate pudding laced with ex laxs. There were only two toilet stalls. Emily was among one of them that didn't make it to the bathroom. She remembered how Beverly walked by and literally laughed until tears were falling profusely down her face. Emily couldn't pack from thinking of all the torture Beverly put her through. Ten minutes later, Emily stood at the door waiting for them to buzz her out. Soon as the locks were released, she walked with her head high through the thick, double doors that separated the patients from the main lobby. "Where is dat miserable bitch at now?" she muttered, looking around. When she glanced out the window, she saw the van.

Beverly flashed a big smile. "There you are. You didn't think I was gonna let you leave without sayin' goodbye, did you?"

"I should've known all I had to do was follow your trail of a dog shit scent." Emily yelled out, then she glanced down the hallway and spotted the nurse coming. "*Damn, I'm runnin' outta time.*" she said to herself.

"You see sweetheart, one thing you need to remember, I love animals and hate people with a passion." Beverly started popping off at the mouth.

"Well Beverly, have you ever heard the saying about hell has no fury?" she said, in a near whisper.

For the first time, Beverly stood speechless, with a dumbfounded look on her face. Tryna wrap her head around what was just said. It was something about the way Emily enunciated the words. For some reason, her voice sent chills down her spine. Or maybe she had an imminent feeling like she was about to die. All of a sudden, Emily ran over and stuck her with a thick piece of metal wire, straight through her heart. Puncturing her aorta.

"Oh my gosh! Why did you do that Emily? Especially, since you were two point two seconds away from being a free woman!" The nurse yelled in total shock. Another guard ran up and tackled Emily. When she fell to the floor, her eyes met Beverly's.

"Ma'am do you know where you're going now?" The guard asked, with his knee embedded in her back handcuffing her.

"To hell." she replied, sarcastically.

"Well you might wish you were in the pits of fiery hell. You're headed straight to Pelican Bay!" he said, snatching her to her feet.

"Emily you were going home. Was you scared you wasn't gonna be productive in society so you had to kill an innocent human being?" the nurse asked baffled.

"Wait. Whadda you mean I was going home?" she asked. Then she immediately shifted her attention to Beverly, whom died with a smile plastered across her face. "And dat bitch isn't innocent!" she yelled stomping her with her steel toe boots.

"Yea, you were. I was bringin' your release papers." She held them up for her to see.

"She made me believe I was going to prison for 15 years. Fuck it! What's done is done, I don't have any regrets." she chuckled. "Dat bitch had it comin'," she smiled, and they took her to the back and restrained her until the authorities arrived. While she was walking to the back, at least four patients yelled out, *dead woman walkin'*. "I guess good news travels fast." she yelled over her shoulders.

"Two hundred years!" the judge screamed, hitting the gavel. Emily remained emotionless.

"What da fuck? Two hundred years. Just say you're gonna die here type shit. But, it is what it is. Again, I have no regrets." she yelled.

Three weeks later, she woke up to get in line for breakfast. "*I know dat isn't who I think it is.*" she said to herself, tapering her eyes and examing the girl that stood dead in front of her. Upon a closer look, she knew it was her in the flesh. "Oh god dis' has to be my luckiest day ever." she smiled, rubbing her hands together.